STARBREAK

ALSO BY PHOEBE NORTH

Starglass

STARBREAK

PHOEBE NORTH

SIMON & SCHUSTER BFYR

NEW YORK • LONDON • TORONTO • SYDNEY • NEW DELHI

SIMON & SCHUSTER BFYR

An imprint of Simon & Schuster Children's Publishing Division

1230 Avenue of the Americas, New York, New York 10020

SIMON & SCHUSTER BFYR is a trademark of Simon & Schuster, Inc.

For information about special discounts for bulk purchases, please contact Simon & Schuster Special Sales at 1-866-506-1949 or business@simonandschuster.com.

The Simon & Schuster Speakers Bureau can bring authors to your live event. For more information or to book an event, contact the Simon & Schuster Speakers Bureau at 1-866-248-3049 or visit our website at www.simonspeakers.com.

Book design by Lucy Ruth Cummins

Cover design by Lucy Ruth Cummins

Cover photographs copyright © 2014 by Aaron Goodman

The text for this book is set in Bembo.

Manufactured in the United States of America

2 4 6 8 10 9 7 5 3 1

Library of Congress Cataloging-in-Publication Data:

North, Phoebe.

Starbreak / Phoebe North. — First edition.

pages cm

Summary: After five hundred years, the Earth ship seventeen-year-old Terra and her companions were born and raised on arrives at Zehava, a dangerous, populated world where Terra must take the lead in establishing a new colony.

ISBN 978-1-4424-5956-4 (hardcover)

ISBN 978-1-4424-5958-8 (eBook)

[1. Science fiction. 2. Space colonies—Fiction. 3. Life on other planets.
4. Love--Fiction. 5. Friendship-—Fiction. 6. Jews—Fiction.] I. Title.

PZ7.N8153Sst 2014

[Fic]--dc23

2013011703

FIRST EDITION

For Jordan,

zeze, bashert, husband,

of course, this is for you.

I've never kept a journal before.

Never thought about it. It's not how my brain works, not really. I see colors, the ways that shadows mingle with the light. But words? I could take them or leave them, or so I always thought.

One of my ancestors kept a journal. All about how she arrived on the Asherah, *how she came to live inside the ship's dome. How she hated it there. She thought she was trapped inside the deepness of space. She could never forget it—how her freedoms had been taken from her, one by one, by the High Council.*

Her journal was passed from hand to hand to hand among the women in my family. My grandmother gave it to my mother, and eventually it found its way to me. The leather cover shines from the oils of our fingers. The pages are falling out. But it's an important reminder of where we've been before, and what we've lost.

I needed that. Without that book I never would have joined the rebellion on our ship. I never would have tried to escape either and taken off for the surface of Zehava when the riots broke out. I would have tried to force myself to be happy. I would have gone ahead and married Silvan Rafferty, a boy I didn't love. All because it's what normal girls did on our ship. They got married whether they loved their husbands or not. They didn't think about how they were trapped. We were all prisoners. Powerless, voiceless. I understood that only because centuries ago someone decided to write it all down. She told me with her words, her pen.

So when you suggested that I write my feelings down, I didn't scoff. I might not be much of a writer. I'm better with a paintbrush. After my time spent with Mara Stone, I'm better with plants, too. (Don't laugh. Please. I know you're laughing. I don't mean it like that!) But I know that maybe these words will help you understand me—not just my language but me.

And so I figured that it was worth a shot.

Now, where was I? Oh yeah, the shuttle . . .

PART ONE

THE

WILDS

1

On the night of the riots, I wasn't the only one who ran for the shuttle bay.

As I pressed across the frozen pastures, my hands balled into fists, my feet bare against the cold ground, I was joined by throngs of people. Citizens, their gazes drunk-dizzy and crazed, spilled out from the districts and the fields, clamoring for the aft lift. That day—my wedding day, the day we arrived on Zehava—was supposed to be a festive one. The citizens had been saving up their rations for weeks, stockpiling bottles of wine so they could drink from the first moment dawn cracked until the planet was stained black by the darkening night.

But the planet never went dark. Instead Zehava twinkled and glinted in the dome glass like a second sky. Lights. The northern continent was scattered with lights, clustered around the black oceans like gilt edging a page. Those lights could only mean one thing: people. There were people on *our* planet, the planet we'd journeyed five hundred years to find, the planet we'd been told would someday be our home.

Maybe they didn't believe it, those citizens who ran by me, jostling and shoving one another. Maybe they were so drunk, they'd convinced themselves it wasn't true. Zehava was theirs— their abbas had sung them songs about it; their mommas had told them about the good lives they'd live underneath the wide open sky. Maybe they thought the lights were something else, a trick of Mother Nature—phosphorescent algae or glowing rocks. Whatever the case, in their drunken fervor they'd convinced themselves that the path ahead would be easy. They'd take a shuttle down to the surface and find Zehava perfect and empty. It had been promised to them, after all.

I ran for a different reason, the pleats of my long golden gown clutched in my fists. Sure, I was just as starved as the rest of them. I wanted Zehava too; the Goldilocks planet would be our better, more perfect home. But that night? I mostly just ran for my life. When I squeezed myself into the crowded lift, the smell of sweat and wine and bloodstained wool all around me, I gave one last look back. I couldn't be certain, but I thought I saw her there. Aleksandra Wolff, leader of the Children of Abel. The captain's daughter—a woman so powerful that she'd kept her family's name for her own, defying all of the traditions of the ship. Her black braid swung behind her as she ran.

When the door shut behind me, I put my hands on my knees, panting. The air felt cold and sharp inside my lungs. I remembered the expression on Aleksandra's face—wild, hungry. I'd seen the whole thing, standing frozen in that cornfield as Aleksandra held that silver rope of hair in her hand and drew the knife across her mother's throat.

An old woman stood beside me in the lift. She touched her hand gently to my bare shoulder.

"Aren't you happy?" she cried. She was hazy with drink. "The Council, fallen! Fallen at last!"

I winced. The lift was filled with people, too many people, as it plunged into the depths of the ship. They sang and chanted, pumping their fists, but I couldn't hear their words. Instead I heard an echo— Captain Wolff's voice coming back to me, just before she made that last, strangled sound.

They won't follow you. Not after they've discovered that you killed your own mother.

Aleksandra had answered easily: *Good thing they won't find out.* But I knew, I knew—and worst of all? Aleksandra had caught me listening. On her belt she carried a knife, still hot with her mother's blood, sharp as a straight razor and twice as quick.

But I had somewhere to go. Zehava. The purple forests writhed and shifted in the corners of my memory. And I had someone waiting for me too. The boy—*my* boy—the one who'd haunted my dreams for months. He'd keep me safe from Aleksandra, and from the bodies that jostled me in their drunken fervor as they spilled from the lift. He'd be my home. My haven. My sanctuary.

He just didn't know it yet.

I stumbled from the lift into the crowded shuttle bay.

Once, the bay had been closed to all but necessary personnel—shuttle pilots and their crews, the captain, the Council. But someone had cracked the lift's control panel open. It trailed wires like a jumble of guts. When we arrived, the doors opened easily. Already the room was packed with people who elbowed one another, shouting. Most carried handcrafted weapons, table legs broken off or knives filched from their galley drawers. Someone had a shepherd's crook they'd broken down into a splintered spear. I had to duck under it as I scrambled toward the air lock entrance.

At first I just stood there staring, my bare feet flat against the rusted floor. The air lock was open. Inside waited row upon row of shuttles, gleaming beneath the dim track lighting. We'd prepared for years for disembarking. In school Rebbe Davison had taken us through the necessary drills: meeting with our muster groups, filing in one group at a time. Of course, it had only ever been for practice. I'd only ever seen snatches of the air lock before—with its precarious walkway and its long tunnels that reached out into the universe beyond—just before the air lock shut.

I heard a familiar *ding*. When I glanced back, I saw the lift doors open again. Still more people spilled out. I was frozen, my dress in my hands. But then I saw a face in the crowd in the lift. Aleksandra, her pale features drawn, stood among the new group. I wondered if they knew that she was their leader. I hadn't—it had been a secret, well kept. But now it seemed the news was spreading as quickly as a winter cold. Field-workers bowed their heads to whisper to specialists. Merchants lifted their eyes, squared their shoulders, and pressed two fingers to their hearts. They rushed toward her, flanking her on all sides. It give me time, but not much. I had to hurry as the people raised their weapons in salute. I pressed forward through the crowd, nearing the air lock door.

I'd almost reached it when I heard a familiar voice, touched with awe.

"Is that her, Deck? Is it true?"

I whipped my head up. There stood Laurel Selberlicht, her honey-brown eyes as bright as beacons. Deklan Levitt was beside her, one burly arm thrown over her shoulders. I'd known the pair my whole life; they'd been my classmates first, flirting during recess, passing notes to each other when Rebbe Davison's back was turned. Later I'd grown used to seeing them in the shadowed library, to pressing my fingers to my heart in salute when we passed each other in the dome. He was a plowman; in one season his work had transformed him from a narrow reed of a boy into a well-muscled man. But Laurel was slight, willowy. Her shoulder still bore the rank cords she'd been given by the High Council. A silver twist of thread—a special color, reserved for shuttle pilots like her.

I didn't even stop to think about it. I reached out and took her slender, cool hand in mine.

"Laurel," I said. When she lifted her eyes, they went hazy. I could smell the wine on her breath. "Laurel, come with me. I need your help."

"Sure, Terra," she said, and though there was a note of confusion in her voice, she let me pull her through the crowd. But a gruff tenor called out to us. Deklan, his unruly eyebrows low.

"Hey, where are you taking her?"

We were almost at the air lock door when I looked back. He was following us, but he wasn't alone. Two other rebels flanked him, one on either side, their expressions mirroring his concern. One, familiar—Rebbe Davison, Mordecai, our teacher, his lush black curls threaded gray. The other, a stranger, small in stature, whose shoulder bore the blue knot of a specialist.

"It's okay!" I called through the clamor, but I don't think they heard me. The trio followed us, as close as magnets, as I pulled Laurel down past the air lock entrance and into the long, dim hallway.

"What's going on, Terra?" she asked as we stopped on the narrow walkway. The air was cooler here, quieter. Few citizens had made it into the air lock. Only a pair of dark silhouettes could be seen in the distance, standing beside one of the waiting shuttles.

"You've trained as a pilot," I said, narrowing my gaze on her. "You can get us to Zehava."

"But we're not supposed to leave until we receive word back from the shuttle crew."

By now Deklan and his companions had reached us. He grabbed her to him, holding on tight—as if I were going to snatch her away. To be fair, I had already snatched her away once. If I wanted Laurel's help, it seemed I'd need to convince Deklan, too.

"She's trained all year for this, Deklan. She's a strong, capable pilot. Don't you want to see her fulfill her dreams?"

His expression shadowed with guilt. He looked down at Laurel, and I saw then the love that tethered them together. He was proud of her vocation, of all she'd done with her life, no matter how much he hid that behind gruffness and bluster.

"Of course I do," he said softly. Tucked beneath his arm, Laurel glowed. But she didn't answer me, not yet. I glanced toward the figures behind them.

Rebbe Davison lurked there, his face clouded with concern. On a night when most of the ship's population was alive with exuberant energy, he suddenly looked much older. I saw the wrinkles at the corners of his eyes, the deep frown circling his mouth.

"Rebbe Davison," I said. "You taught us our muster drills, all the procedures for disembarking when we were young. Who gave you those orders?"

He paused—behind him the sound of the crowd swelled.

"The Council," he said. "The curriculum always came from the Council."

"And what was all this for," I demanded, gesturing back toward the shuttle bay, packed with bodies, "if we're going to stay under their thumbs? They'd want us to wait, I'm sure. But that planet is our inheritance. Not this ship!"

"She's right," Laurel said. I blinked back my surprise; I hadn't expected agreement to come so quickly. Deklan held her tightly, but she squirmed away. "No, Deck. This is what I've been training for. I can *do this*. The planet is ours. Isn't it?"

Without waiting for an answer, she turned and walked away from him. There was a panel built into the wall. Her hands moved breezily over it. As she worked, I glanced back over my shoulder. The crowd was pressing closer now, threatening to spill over the precipice of the air lock. I saw a cutting figure among them, her wool-wrapped shoulders square. Aleksandra, knife in her hand, parting the crowd like they were sheep to be herded. Coming close.

But then the air lock door began to slide back into place. Her eyes widened. She shouted something, but the words were lost beneath the shouts and songs of the rebels who surrounded her. They didn't matter. *She* didn't. The door sealed shut, and we were left alone in the darkness.

Laurel turned on the heel of her leather-soled shoe to make her way briskly through the air lock. At first I hesitated beside Rebbe Davison and his friend, watching as Deklan scrambled after her.

"You're not going alone!" he cried, fixing a hand on her shoulder. She spun around, tossing her curls as she faced him.

"Then come with us."

His eyes met mine, murky with confusion, as if he couldn't believe what the rebellion had wrought: his love was ready to leap off the ship and into the void of space without him. Then he looked to the specialist and to Rebbe Davison.

"Are you going?"

At first our teacher looked wary, uncertain. But then he let his eyes slide shut. Behind us the sound of the rioting crowd could still be heard, a dozen muffled hands pounding on the air lock door again and again. When Rebbe Davison opened his eyes, they were filled with a new, razor-sharp certainty.

"Liberty on Zehava," he said, softly at first, but then again, louder. "Liberty on Zehava! Terra's right. The planet. The planet is *ours*."

There was something strange, garbled about his words. In class this kindhearted man had always spoken with confidence. Even when someone misbehaved, he'd laughed it off easily, taking every disaster in stride. Now he seemed hazy.

Drunk. They were all drunk, I realized. I'd swallowed down a full skein of wine that evening myself, but now that I was driven by a single goal, the night had taken on an uncanny clarity. I could see the rust on the grating beneath us, every rivet on every shuttle, and the cobwebs that would soon be blasted away when the ship's outer port opened. Anyone left behind in the air lock would be lost to the vacuum of space—and I wasn't about to open up the door to the shuttle bay again. So even though I heard the slur in my teacher's words, I nodded. I needed them to come with me, and fast.

"Good. Let's board, then," I said.

Rebbe Davison looked at the specialist, who considered for a

moment, mouth open. But soon he nodded too. We all turned toward the shuttles and made our way toward one at the back.

"I only have access to this one," Laurel said as we neared shuttle number twenty-eight. But the door was blocked by a pair of figures. An old man with a fringe of white hair and a bulbous nose—and a dark-haired girl, no older than ten. The man was my neighbor, Mar Schneider. He'd been a part of our clandestine library meetings too, and when he saw us, he lifted two fingers to his heart.

"She wanted to see the shuttles," he said, almost apologetically, holding the girl's hand tight. I recognized her as his granddaughter, who sat on his stoop with him sometimes to watch the traffic of the afternoon, but in that moment I couldn't remember her name. As Laurel shouldered them aside to punch in her access code, Rebbe Davison set a hand on the old man's shoulder. He spoke just a few decibels louder than necessary.

"Abraham, we're going to the planet! Would you like to join us?"

Mar Schneider lifted a hand to touch his scratchy white beard. He smacked his lips, considering. But his granddaughter didn't need time to consider. She jumped up and down on the balls of her feet.

"Yes! Yes! *Zayde*, please?"

As if it were nothing more than a request for a box of candy, he sighed. My heart was pounding. Behind me the door to the shuttle bay was pounding too—a low, steady thunder.

STARBREAK · 13

"Oh, I suppose."

One by one we climbed inside. The shuttle was small, meant to carry only a dozen people. That night we were half that. But our meager crew would have to do. As we boarded, Laurel turned toward a storage space in back.

"The flight suits are in there. Everybody suit up. And be sure to buckle up." She pulled the heavy door closed behind us. I couldn't be sure, but I thought I saw a shadow of doubt in her pale eyes. I ignored it. I needed her if I was going to reach Zehava—if I was going to find my boy, waiting for me. She added, "It might be a bumpy ride."

2

The suits were kept in hermetically sealed containers. They'd been removed only once a generation, to have their moth holes repaired by the best seamstresses on the *Asherah*. When we unfolded the garments, they resembled the threadbare quilts we all used to keep ourselves warm on cold winter nights—covered in stitches and patches, not at all like something that would keep us safe from the ravages of space.

Laurel and Deklan doled one out to each of us. I held the crinkly suit for a moment, almost not believing that this day had finally come. After seventeen years trapped on this ship, I would finally set foot on Zehava, the place we'd sung songs about in school—the place I daydreamed about as I doodled in my notebook margins. Stepping into the suit's long legs, I hiked up the pleats of my long dress. But I fumbled as I tried to pull the suit up over my waist. The dress was tightly laced from behind; I couldn't reach the stays.

"Can you help me?" I asked Laurel, feeling my cheeks heat as the men glanced over at me. She was already zipped into her suit, her springy curls still tucked under the suit's collar.

"Sure," she said. She hurried over. Together we stepped into the dark shadows near the back of the shuttle. I felt her hands make quick work of the laces. Then my breath fully filled my lungs for the first time that night.

"It's a beautiful dress," she said, leaning close. "Did you and Silvan have a chance to say your vows?"

I lifted my arms, letting Laurel raise the reams of silk over my head. It came off in a stream of gold. I didn't want to think of Silvan, not now—didn't want to consider the wounded look he'd given me when I said I wouldn't be his bride. This day was about me and the alien boy. Not about Silvan Rafferty.

"No," I whispered. My voice came out hoarse, strange. "No, we didn't."

I hefted the suit's sleeves up over my naked shoulders, then groped for the zipper. The synthetic material felt warm and clammy over my skin. When I turned, it was to see Laurel smiling sympathetically as she handed me back the bolts of golden silk.

"Good," she said. "Who'd wanna be married to a Council member, anyway?"

She left me standing there in the shadows as she took the pilot's seat. I clutched that fine, stupid dress against my belly, watching as the men sat down and strapped themselves in. Mar Schneider tightened his granddaughter's straps. His old eyes twinkled.

"I never thought I'd see it," he said. "A *planet*. Zehava. I've been dreaming about it since I was a child."

"Me too," the girl agreed cheerfully, kicking out her legs in excitement. Then she turned to look at me. I still stood in the back of the shuttle, hidden in the dark shadows. "Are *you* excited?"

I walked to the other side of the aisle, where an empty seat waited. I knew that it was crazy, this journey—and my choice of companions did little to calm my fears. A field-worker and a school teacher. An old man and a child. A specialist—who knew in *what*—and a pilot, too, but one who had never flown a shuttle before. Still, I had to hope that they'd get me to him, the boy whose skin smelled like flowers and tasted like ripe summer fruit.

"Of course I am," I said as I pulled the straps down over my shoulders. In the pilot's seat Laurel reached up, flipping a switch. There was a roar, dull at first but growing. I gazed down at the silk that I still clutched. The dress was crumpled, stained from my race through the pastures. Ruined; it was ruined.

My brother had bought me that dress, scrimping and saving every piece of gelt he could. He said it was what our father would have wanted. But our father wasn't here now. What did it matter what Abba wanted? I stuffed the dress beneath my seat, kicking at the wide skirt and petticoat until it was all out of sight.

The engine flared and our bodies were pressed back against the seats. I thought of Aleksandra, fumbling with the controls to the air lock doors. But I willed her memory away. Soon I would be free of her, of this ship, this life. The little girl looked over. Her smile was toothy, wide.

"Don't be scared," she said. But I didn't feel scared, not one bit.

I felt exhilarated.

At first the trip was rocky. I shut my eyes, imagining our little shuttle bumping and bumbling down the intake port and leaving a white-hot trail behind it. Then the noise died down; the shuttle straightened. When I opened my eyes, I saw a black sky scattered with stars in the window past Laurel's head. She moved her hands over the controls, lighting dials beneath her fingertips. I could see her face, gold and flickering in the light. Her smile was tentative, uncertain. I wasn't the only one who noticed.

"You know what you're doing, right?" Deklan asked, setting his muddy boots up on the dash. He'd taken the copilot's seat, but he didn't seem to be helping her at all. He only frowned as she hesitated over the controls.

"Of course I do," she said. "Get your feet down. This isn't your bedroom."

After a beat he did, letting them thump against the metal ground. Then he looked back over his shoulder, letting his eyebrow lift up as he turned to the men. I'd seen that look before, from Abba, from Ronen, from Silvan, too. *Crazy woman*, it meant, and it filled my belly with rage to see it. We were depending on Laurel—not just Deklan, but *all* of us. Who was he to fill her head with doubts?

But Laurel was unperturbed. She pressed a button, then sat back. She finally nodded her curly head in satisfaction.

"There. The course is set. We'll arrive in eight point six hours."

"That long?" Deklan asked.

Laurel glanced skyward. "How long did you think it would take?"

"Your intended never was one for listening in school," Rebbe Davison said. Laurel jumped a little. I think she'd forgotten that there was anyone but the two of them in the shuttle. But she smiled gratefully.

"He's not one for listening generally," she agreed. Deklan glowered at her, but after a moment his hard mouth dissolved into a smile.

"You got me, *bashert*." *Bashert*. The word made my heart lurch in my chest. Deklan had already met his heart's match. Maybe soon *I* would too. "I'll be good and let you drive. Just wake me when it's over."

He sat back in the seat, propping his arms up like he was getting ready for a nap. Laurel let out a bell of soft laughter.

"Sleep tight," she said.

As Deklan closed his eyes, I looked at the black sky filling the window. There was a streak of white light in the distance, arcing toward the planet. But I thought perhaps I dreamed it—no one else seemed to notice. The others talked, making introductions, prattling on about the lives they'd just abandoned. The small-eyed specialist was called Jachin. A biologist, he'd left behind a wife who swore her allegiance to the Council even as chaos descended on the ship. But he wasn't looking back. Instead he turned the discussion to the planet ahead. Who were the people who lived on it below? Would they welcome us?

I thought of the video I'd seen in the ship's command center just before the revolt. Only hours had passed, but it felt like a lifetime already. The men who'd held the shuttle crew hadn't been like any men I'd known in my waking life. They were too tall, too thin. Their bodies bent in ways that should have seemed unnatural to me.

But they didn't. Every night for nearly six months now, I'd dreamed of a body like that—long and cool beside me, filling my nose and mouth and mind with the scent of a thousand different flowers. In my dreams I was naked, and when I wasn't, he soon undressed me with his nimble, three-fingered hands. . . .

His eyes were black, a pair of obsidian lozenges without a shred of light inside them. The men in the transmission had black eyes, too. But their gazes didn't welcome me. In fact, the men in the transmission snarled as they forced the lost shuttle crew to parrot officious words.

Mayday, Mayday. Zehava is inhabited. I repeat, Zehava is inhabited. . . .

And yet I knew in the pit of my belly that my boy was real. He waited on that planet somewhere—the one that, just now, had only barely begun to come into view. I saw the delicate, curving lip of her oceans against the horizon, swirled with white from above. I saw the lights, winking, glinting. It was too dark to see the purple vegetation, but I knew that if I wanted to see Zehava's forests and her vines, all I had to do was shut my eyes. It had always worked before.

"Hey, lady," the little girl said. I turned to look at her.

"Mmm?"

"What do *you* think the aliens are like?" she asked.

"Alien," I thought. *What a funny word. We're the strangers. They were the ones who lived here first.*

But I only smiled at the girl. "Real nice," I told her. "They'll be so happy to see you."

It wasn't a lie, not entirely. But it was a precious, fragile hope, one that flew in the face of my sister-in-law's words. In the video Hannah had been terrified. *Send a recovery shuttle*, she'd said. But I couldn't believe it. I needed the boy, his long arms; his bright body, rank with pollen. I needed to believe that I was traveling toward something, that I was doing more than running away.

The others prattled and joked while the white noise of the engine whirred on and on. It had been a long day, too long. I'd been drunk and sober; terrified, and then calm again. Now my eyelids felt impossibly heavy. My limbs felt heavy too. Soon I found myself nodding off, tumbling toward the forest of my dreams.

It was the same as always, and yet the sight of it never failed to make me lose my breath. The lush landscape here wasn't the muddled brown and green of the dome. It was purple: deep blue flowers, craning their blossoms up through the black soil; violet vines, curling toward the sun. And stranger still, it all moved, as though the plants weren't just alive but knowing—sentient. One moment the trees would all glance up, staring into the white-gold sky. The next, they'd swivel their leaves to face me like I was a long-anticipated guest they couldn't wait to welcome home.

At first he was nothing more than a shadow, shifting listlessly in the wind and waiting for me. I saw only his shape, his narrow waist and broad shoulders. But then he started to come closer. His movements across the soft black ground were effortless. He didn't so much stroll as *glide*. Soon he stood in front of me, his body smelling sweet as summer.

I'm coming, I thought, though it was as if the words traveled through a veil of molasses. For some reason I felt unsure that they would reach him, that he would understand. Most nights we spoke with our bodies, not bothering with mouths or even thoughts. He stared up into the yellow sky.

Coming?

Yes, coming. I'll be there soon.

But his response wasn't the one I'd hoped for. Instead of enveloping me with his arms, drawing me close so I could feel safe from the intrusions of the world beyond, he hung his head. His words came swiftly, easily, like he was used to speaking this way.

No, no. You are not real. Cannot be . . .

He might as well have punched me, sinking his fist into my solar plexus and snatching away all my breath.

What do you mean? Of course I'm real. I'm right here! Just as real as you are.

No— he began, but before he could finish that thought, I reached out, grabbing his hand in mine. I pressed it to my chest, let him feel the heart that beat frantically inside.

Do you feel it? I asked. *Do you? I'm here! I'm real!*

He snatched his hand away, cradling it against his body like it was a wounded bird. I wanted to reach for him again, to make everything between us right and safe. But I couldn't. I didn't know how.

Behind us the forest was waiting for me, its branches cast back like a pair of open arms. I couldn't make things better with the boy, not now, not when we still had so far to go. So I turned around and walked into the forest, into her vines, her purple light. She enveloped me, wrapping branches around my limbs, tangling her flowers through my hair. I let her. I thought I heard his voice, soft and strangled. But I paid it no mind. What was the point? He didn't want me, not yet. But soon I would be there, standing in front of him, and he wouldn't be able to deny me.

I let myself get lost in the wild landscape of the Zehavan jungles.

I was jerked from the warm, smothering dark by turbulence.

The planet filled the entirety of the glass ahead. In the morning light, clear waters sparkled. Sprawling forests were swirled with a thousand different shades of violet, crimson red, and the bluest ultramarine you could imagine. But something was wrong. The continents seemed to jiggle beneath us like old fingers, prone to tremors.

I watched as Laurel wrestled with the controls, gripping the control stick, pulling hard.

"No, no, no!" she was saying through gritted teeth. I turned to the little girl.

"What's wrong?" I asked, but of course she didn't know. Though her legs still swam in her too big flight suit, she'd pulled them up onto the seat. She held her arms high, shielding herself from whatever was to come next. Her grandfather had slung an arm over her to protect her. I turned the other way. Rebbe Davison sat in white-knuckled silence beside Jachin.

He was my teacher, one of the smartest men on the ship. Surely *he* would tell me.

His forehead was wrinkled. But his expression wasn't like it had been during school when I tried his patience, stumbling in late day after day. Back then there had been a weary humor beneath his frown. Now there was only fear.

"She entered the wrong coordinates," he said softly, so soft at first that I almost couldn't hear it above the engine's roar. But Laurel did.

"I'm only a *talmid*!" she shouted. "I was never supposed to do this alone!"

In the seat beside her I saw Deklan reach out. He put his hand against the nape of her neck.

"Not now!" She swiped at him, smacking his hand. He shrank

back. I did too, my shoulders sinking into the bucket seat. After our long flight my armpits ached, sweaty from the straps. My legs felt somehow both numb and swollen in the flight suit's boots. But none of that mattered now. What mattered was my heart and its hard, hysterical rhythm, and the dry, shallow wheeze of my breath.

"The shuttles are meant to make a water landing." Rebbe Davison's words were murmured low. This time Laurel didn't hear them. But I don't think she was meant to. When I slid my gaze over, I saw that his gaze was firmly fixed on me. "We're supposed to land on water."

I peered through the glass in front. We were coming in over the northern continent where drifts of winter snow dappled the purple landscape white. The wide gulf of water was to the south of us and shrinking fast from view. I saw the craggy landscape change—saw gray dunes and the deep shadows beneath them.

Mountains. We were headed for the mountains. And from the way that the shuttle quavered as the peaks filled more and more of the glass, I knew we were about to crash.

3

didn't black out. In fact, everything seemed to slow down, as if the universe was trying to give me enough time to think, react, respond. I pressed my head back against the seat, clutching the armrests so hard that I thought they might break off in my fists. It felt as if all my blood were leaving my body, propelled out by the force of the fall to my extremities. The rest of me was left so cold that my teeth chattered. Or maybe they chattered from the vibrations. The whole shuttle shook as we ripped through the atmosphere. The men were talking, softly at first, a constant, urgent murmur. Then the shuttle banked sideways, and they were screaming, and the girl was screaming, and I was screaming too. Even Rebbe Davison screamed. I didn't know he had it in him, but he did—a great bellow of a bass, low and rumbling.

It's funny; I'd spent years feeling disconnected from everybody around me, alone and sad. There were nights when I stared up into the sparkling blackness of my room and wondered why I was so *wrong*. And on some nights, the worst nights, especially after Abba died, I wondered if I wouldn't be better off if I went away too. I didn't know where I would go. I just thought it would be better if I were somewhere, anywhere but in my bedroom on that ship—and there was only one way out that I had ever seen.

Now, as the metal walls of the shuttle screamed around me, as the other passengers screamed too, I realized how foolish it all was. I was too young to die. I wanted to see Zehava, and not just from behind jittering glass. I wanted to see Ronen's baby grow up. I wanted to finally fall in love. But now that was all slipping away from me, just as surely as our shuttle slipped down and down through the atmosphere, hurtling toward the frozen ground.

I didn't black out. I didn't even close my eyes. They were wide open as the window was swallowed up by white, as our limbs were lifted up, as weightless as balloons, for just a moment, a narrow moment before the shuttle slammed into Zehava.

. . .

I woke up without even remembering having fallen asleep. There was no forest, no vines, no boy. Just my aching body. I pried my eyelids painfully open, taking in the light. For a moment I wasn't sure where I was. My arms were wrapped tight around me; my chest felt squeezed. When I turned my head, my neck protested—a bolt of pain traveled down it and into my spine. I let out a small gasp, wincing.

"Terra? Are you okay?"

Rebbe Davison knelt before me. Half his face was smeared with blood, but he was whole, hopeful. I turned my head back and forth. The pain flared brightly again, then faded back.

"Yeah," I said, my voice shaking. "Yeah, I think I am."

"I'm going to unbuckle you, okay?"

He smiled again, a gentle, familiar smile. I'd been so surprised when I'd found out that he was a rebel, though I guess I shouldn't have been. Even Abba had said that Mordecai Davison was a real mensch. He seemed to be in it for the good of the people, because he truly thought it was right. Now he took his soft, kind hands and used them to unlatch my safety harness. I fell forward—when had the ground gotten so slanted?—but Rebbe Davison caught me, letting out a small laugh. I felt myself blush. I wasn't a girl anymore, one who needed her teacher to hold her up. I tried to stand straight, though my knees still shook.

"The girl," I said, scanning the interior of the crumpled shuttle. One half of it had been sliced open during the impact. Snow spilled in, and there was broken glass, and blood. "Is she all right?"

He hesitated, wavering on his feet.

"We have her outside."

I followed him, stumbling over the jagged, broken edge of the shuttle door. But almost as soon as I stepped out beneath the open sky, I staggered back. It was huge above us, golden white and endless. It stretched from one end of the world—where a tangle of black, naked branches clung to the mountainside—all the way to the other. There it disappeared beneath a sparkling field of ice. It seemed too low, too close—then I realized why. There was no glass to keep it back. Only space, wide open and free.

"Amazing, isn't it?"

I jumped. It was Jachin—the rebel who had sat beside Rebbe Davison on the shuttle. His dark hair was curly. Now he ran broad fingers through it again and again.

I stepped forward over the icy ground. Deklan was standing over Laurel, his gaze fiercely protective. Beside her sat the little girl. Their posture was the same—fetal, deflated. The girl held her hands over her face, her body shivering with tears. But they were both alive. That's what mattered.

"Where's Mar Schneider?" I asked, turning back. Rebbe Davison still stood in the mouth of the shuttle, one boot up against the broken steel. His mouth fell open. He glanced behind him to the capsule, torn open behind us like a throat. That's when I heard it—the girl let out a cry.

"Zayde!" she said.

I don't know why, but my legs snapped to action, as if they were under the command of someone else. I scrambled past Rebbe Davison, ducking inside the shuttle. I peered left, toward the cockpit, where the window glass had shattered into a thousand glinting shards. And I turned right, where the storage container had fallen open, exploding its contents across the snow-slick floor. Then I saw it, the shock of red that seeped out beneath a curved overhang of metal. I shouldn't have, but I knelt down and looked.

He was still strapped to his seat, his limbs dangling down. I saw hair. Silver wisps of hair. Then the white skull beneath them. And something else. His insides.

I'd seen bodies before—too many bodies. Momma's, waxy and still in her hospital bed. Abba's, dangling from the bedroom rafters. Benjamin Jacobi, and Captain Wolff, too. But even when I'd seen blood spill out from open throats, those deaths had been quick ones, and relatively clean. Not this. I turned and was sick in the corner. I puked until there was nothing left, until my stomach was just an empty hole.

When I was finished, I pulled myself out of the shuttle again. The light struck me dizzy after all those years spent in the dark of the dome. I collapsed in the snow beside Laurel and the girl. The child cried and cried, her face slick with tears. At first I was frozen, stunned. I'd made it to the planet, thoughtlessly pursuing my dreams, and now, because of me, an old man had died.

I looked down at the girl. She was narrow-shouldered. Young. Younger than I'd been when Momma died.

"Esther, are you okay?" I asked, at last pulling her name from my memory. Her eyes still fixed forward, she wiped her nose on the back of her flight suit sleeve.

"Ettie," she said finally. Then she honked out a cry.

"Ettie," I said, and then added, in case she'd forgotten: "I'm Terra. And I'll keep you safe."

I didn't even consider the meaning of my words before I spoke. I'd never kept *anyone* safe before. I'd always been a loner—messy Terra Fineberg, looking out for herself and no one else. But I wanted to believe that it was possible. This girl, her hair all a tangle, was alone in this strange world—helpless.

But maybe not anymore. She drew in a shuddering breath. I drew her to me, and she tucked her face in against my shoulder, letting me hold her as if we were more than strangers.

· · ·

I'm not sure how long we sat there in the snow, the winter sun bright and small overhead. Without the clock bells to toll the hour, it was impossible to tell. Might have been twenty minutes—might have been two hours. We hunkered down in silence, shivering. I guess we were all shocked from the crash. I know I couldn't make words move past my mouth.

At last Deklan pulled himself to his feet. He stared down the mountain. Between a pair of boulders was a deep cleft, wide enough for a man to pass.

"Helllooooooo!" he called. His voice came echoing back a dozen times, folded over itself. When at last it died, he turned to us. "Nobody's home."

"It's a big planet," Rebbe Davison said.

It was. Stretching thousands of kilometers out in all directions. This wasn't the ship, where there was no place to go, and anywhere you went was safe. This was Zehava, the wider world. The air was cool and biting, and there were no warm quarters waiting for us. I finally let go of Ettie's hand and stumbled to my feet.

"We need a plan," I said. "For the night at least. Otherwise we'll freeze. I know I didn't come all the way to this planet just to—" I broke off, thinking of the body smashed inside the shuttle, and how it had once been a man.

"There are supplies," Laurel said, not noticing how I tripped over my words. "We've been stocking up the shuttles for months. Shelf-stable food. Water. A tent, and sleeping sacks." She paused, as if she were afraid to go on.

"What else, Laurel?" Rebbe Davison prodded, in his placid teacher voice, the one that somehow always convinced one kid to snitch on another back when we were young. Laurel took a breath.

"Weapons," she said. "And firestarter."

"Fire?" Jachin asked. We all grew quiet again, thinking about it. On the ship open flames were forbidden. Our stoves were electric; our heaters electric too. Once a year a marshal came to make sure not a single spark would escape. We were taught from a very young age that fire was dangerous—that even the smallest flame could sear through the dome, eating all our trees, our crops, disrupting the delicate balance of breathable air. But we weren't in the dome anymore. We were on Zehava, and the afternoon was cold, and bound to grow only colder.

We started toward the shuttle.

We were lucky. Though we'd lost a dozen or so packets of dry fruit and a few sleeping rolls down the mountainside, we were able to scrounge enough to make a small hill from our provisions. Rebbe Davison asked Ettie to count them, and she seemed glad for the distraction. Sniffling, she reported that there was one tent, nine sleep sacks, forty-seven dehydrated meals wrapped up in crinkly cellophane, eight rucksacks, three lighters, a canteen of fresh water for each of us, four mess kits, twelve sonic rifles, a small ax, nineteen packs of firestarter, and a dozen helmets.

"We should have been wearing those when we crashed," Laurel said, staring down at the pile. "I can't believe I forgot. What if the air here is toxic?"

I thought of the video I'd seen in the command center. My sister-in-law, Hannah, had worn no helmet. She had a trail of blood down her face, but she breathed. I drew my own breath deep into my lungs.

"The air seems fine to me," I said. But Laurel only shook her head.

"There could be biological hazards. Diseases. And if we'd been wearing them—" She glanced back toward the shuttle, to the corner of smashed metal that we'd all avoided looking at. Deklan set his hand on her shoulder.

"It's too late for that now," he said softly. She collapsed into his arms. She didn't cry, only let him rock her silently. She was lucky that she had him—strong arms, a soft shoulder. I thought about my boy, how he'd snatched his slender fingers away from mine at the slightest touch. Looking at Deklan and Laurel, I felt more alone than I ever had before.

Soon Rebbe Davison and Ettie surfaced from under the distant clump of trees. Each one held a pile of black sticks in their arms.

"I was going to chop down a tree," Rebbe Davison said. "Like it says in the survival manuals in the library. But—" He hesitated, looking out at the silhouette of branches that shivered against the sky. When Ettie piped up, her own voice was awed despite the tears drying on her face.

"They moved! The trees moved! Like they could see us! Like they were people!"

We all stared at her. I suppose the others didn't believe it, that trees could move of their own volition. Of course, on Earth the plants turned their faces toward the sun, unfurling blossoms in the early morning light. But that was different—automatic, instinctual. And slow, slow, slow.

But I'd known for months that plants could caress you, could wrap their arms around you like you, too, were made from cellulose and wood pulp.

"There are plants on Earth," I offered when they turned to me with questioning eyes, "that move in response to stimuli. Carnivorous, mostly. Pitcher plants and flytraps—"

"Carnivorous?" Deklan asked, angling up his jaw. I hesitated. It was Jachin who answered for me.

"Flesh eating."

Deklan's eyes went wide. The corners of his mouth lifted, but I don't think he found it funny. Alarming, maybe. He wore his smile like a shield. He took the bundle of sticks from Ettie's arms.

"We'll make do," he said. He arranged them on the ground. I saw him glance back toward the fist of trees in the distance. The black clump waved at us like fingers thrust up through the crust of ice. Deklan shivered, but we all ignored it as we knelt by his side and helped him make a fire.

The flames that leaped out of the lighters were small, only tiny nubbins of orange light. But the firestarter caught the flames easily and spread them through the black twigs and sticks. First they smoldered, smoke rising, thick on the air. But soon the fire grew hypnotic, orange and dancing, blue at the base and then fading to white as it flickered into the open air. We gathered around it, warming our faces. At first Ettie hung back.

"It's *dangerous*," she said, and then she looked pointedly at Rebbe Davison. "We learned that in school."

I held out my hand to her.

"It's okay," I told her gently. "It will keep you warm. You want to be warm, right?"

She hung back a moment longer, chewing on her lip. Then, in a burst of energy, she plunged herself over the drifts and came to kneel beside me in the snow.

Rebbe Davison got us food. We boiled the packets of dried meat and dehydrated vegetables over the fire with a few splashes of our water.

"The water won't last us long," he said. "We'll have to boil snow soon and hope . . ." He trailed off. Deklan was hard-eyed. He held one of the sonic rifles over his knees. He hadn't let it go since we'd found them. Projectile weapons weren't allowed on the ship—too risky, even for the captain's guard. I guess it made him feel extra safe.

"Hope what?" he demanded. Rebbe Davison let out a small, desperate laugh.

"Hope there's nothing in their water that will kill us."

We were all quiet for a long time as we watched the water burble, as the fire beneath it burned. Rebbe Davison still held the pot out over the fire, but he used his free hand to veil his face.

"I can't believe I did this," he said at last. "I never drink. But I was drunk when I ran for the shuttle bay."

Beside him Jachin let out a snort.

"Me too."

Then Deklan and Laurel gazed at each other. In the firelight I saw her cheeks darken. He wore a wicked grin. "So were we."

Then suddenly, strangely, we were all laughing—desperate, hysterical laughter, like it was the best joke that had ever been told. All of us except Ettie, of course. She frowned deeply, staring at the grown-ups like every single one of us had two heads each.

"What's so funny?" she said, with the sort of righteous indignation that only someone under the age of ten can muster. "I don't get it!"

But no one answered her. We only breathed in deep gulps of frigid air, our laughter echoing against the mountainside.

I don't think our meager meal filled any of our bellies, but we didn't complain. There was no telling how far we'd have to stretch our rations, how long we'd have to make them last. We were used to following the leader—the Council, Captain Wolff, even Aleksandra. But we had no leader, no plan. It would have been worrying if the weight of sleep hadn't been pulling at us so heavily. The sun was barely three quarters of the way across the sky, and already we were yawning, sniffling, and blinking the sleep away.

"I can't believe I'm so tired," Deklan said. With the rifle still nestled against his belly, he pressed his face to his knees. "It can't be any later than—what? Twenty-three o'clock?"

"We don't have our pills." I thought of the little packet of pills we all ate each night, and of something Koen Maxwell had told me once. How years ago, just for kicks, just to see what it would do, he'd started palming them.

No matter what the light looked like in the dome, it was like the day inside me was getting shorter and shorter.

Jachin let out a small grunt of agreement. He lifted himself to his feet and went to fetch our tent. Laurel scrambled to help him pound in the stakes.

"Melatonin," he said as he worked to unfurl the canvas walls. "And somnescence. We're not built for Zehava's days. It's only the pills that keep our internal clocks synced to hers."

"Abba always thought—" I started, then stopped. It felt weird to talk about my father now, as I sat amid a coterie of rebels. Like I hadn't quite shed the skin of our former lives. But I guessed it didn't matter. He was a clock keeper once, after all. It had been his *job*. "My father had this theory that, given enough time exposed to the natural rotation of Zehava around its sun, we'd adapt. Our circadian rhythms would shift. But it was only a theory. No way to test it on the ship."

"Guess we'll have our chance now," Deklan Levitt said. He pulled himself upright and snatched up one of the sleeping rolls. Then he ducked inside the tent. We all craned our necks after him, staring into the dim interior. It was inviting, dry and warm. After only a moment's hesitation we followed him inside.

4

The rest of them all stripped out of their flight suits, exposing the sweat-soaked clothing beneath. But I didn't—couldn't. I wore only my underwear under the synthetic fabric. It wasn't until I was tucked inside my sleep sack that I felt okay undoing the long zipper at the front of my suit. It was strange to feel the soft fabric of the sleep sack against my bare skin. The blankets on the ship were all wool and rough-hewn linen, but these ancient synthetics had been saved by our ancestors just for landing. I pulled my suit out of the sack and left it splayed out like a second skin beside me, then snuggled down inside the covers.

Sleep came instantly. At first I was buried in the firm hold of the forest—vines lacing their way through my hair, branches looping my ankles. It was warm, safe. But wrong. I pulled forward, parting the brambles. He was waiting for me, as he always was. I guess he couldn't stay away.

I'm here now, I said. *On your planet. I'm here. I came for you.*

His back was to me, a wide violet plane that dipped gently in the middle. His shoulders were lit by the setting sun. When he glanced back at me, his eyes caught the light above. For once they didn't look flat, impenetrable. Instead they sparked and danced. Like fire—like a pair of living flames.

I can't— he said. *I don't—*

Even in my dreams I was exasperated. I threw my hands up into the air.

If you don't help me, we could die*! I came all this way just for this place, just for* you*, and now that I'm here, you tell me you "can't"?*

I was angry, my fingers cutting through the air, my jaw clenched so hard, I thought my molars might crumble in my mouth. But underneath that heat was fear, raw and real. At long last he took my frantic hands in his.

But he didn't put them on his body, like he normally would have. Nor did he press them to his wet, sweet mouth. Instead he shoved my fingers upward, toward the evening sky above. I followed the line of our intertwined fingers to the green-streaked sky.

The full dark of night hadn't come on yet. The sun was a white circle in the west. All the trees unfurled their blossoms, exposing their lewd insides to its light.

Xarki, he said, pointing fiercely. *Xarki.*

The sounds curled my tongue in new ways. Xarki. Xarki. Epsilon Eridani. Their sun. Then he moved my hand in a wide arch across the firmament, stopping at each of the three moons above. He named them.

Akku. Zella. Aire.

I glanced up. One moon was a perfect crescent; another barely a sliver high overhead. The third was full and perfect, a rose-gold circle marked by distant mountains and empty ocean beds.

Why are you telling me this? I asked. His chest was close to mine. I could smell him, fragrant, like overripe peaches and something else, something foreign, strange. He didn't answer, only pointed upward to the stars that barely twinkled to life in the evening sky.

These nine stars. The hunter in his carriage. Look for the head of his harp. It is fixed in all seasons—in autumn, in spring. And in the deep, deep cold of winter. He always stands upright as he makes his music. You will stand upright too. And then turn around. Walk away from the hunter. Stay on the rocky pathway. Avoid the forests.

The vines tangled around us, caressing our ankles, our calves. They didn't *seem* dangerous.

Why? I asked.

His eyes went dark, half-shaded. He let out one simple word: *Beasts.*

There was a shudder in the distance, like the rattle of an ancient engine, but louder, rawer. He gave his head a fearful shake and went on. *From there the path to Raza Ait lies between the shadows of Akku and Aire.*

Raza Ait?

He still held my hand up in the sky, cradled against the palm of his hand; his chest was pressed to mine. When I looked at him, I saw a fierce hunger. I felt the burn of his skin against my skin—blue, so blue, against my own pale white belly.

The city of copper. He paused, licking his lips with his bright purple tongue. *The city where I die.*

I gasped myself awake. My heart thudded so hard that at first I was afraid that the others might hear. But then, with a relieved breath of air, I realized that I was alone. Shaking—as much from the dream as the shock of the cold against my naked limbs—I rose and put on my flight suit. I could smell the ripe, rank smell of my body, but ignored it. On the ship our ancestors had been able to maintain the fiction that our society was polite, orderly. But here in the wilderness we could no longer deny the truth. We were savages.

I stumbled out of the tent, zipping it tight behind me. The others had gathered around the smoldering coals. Rebbe Davison had one arm thrown over Ettie's shoulders. He was singing "Tsen Briders" to her—that counting song about the brothers who all die off, one by one. I'd always thought it was a ghastly song, even when we all sang it together in school. Ettie didn't seem to like it either. She squirmed beside him.

I trampled over the hard-packed snow. We were still deep in night, even if our bodies didn't know it yet. The only sign of the sun—*Xarki?* I asked myself—was in the delicate blue wash at the eastern edge of the sky. Soon, in a few hours maybe, dawn would come. But for now it was all wild, unbridled night.

I gazed up at the sky. The stars were different here from now they'd been on the *Asherah*. There they burned steadily, as if someone had punched perfect circles in black paper. Here on Zehava, with the thick atmosphere between us, they twinkled. As soon as I fixed my gaze on one, it winked out, before again blazing to life.

At least the moons stayed in place when you looked at them. There were three—one crescent, one that was hardly any more than a narrow slip of light, and a third, so full that it resembled swollen, blushing fruit.

Akku. Zella. Aire, I thought, and felt my stomach clench. He'd tried to tell me something, something important. But I hadn't quite understood the importance of moons, scattered across the sky, and the stars between them. *Akku, Zella . . .*

This sky wasn't like ours. On the ship the stars above were always shifting, from night to night as we coasted through empty space. There was a new sky every evening; new stars, too. Once, we'd learned in school, sailors had navigated according to the stars above. But ours were inconstant. And we had no moons.

My hands dropped to my side, suddenly as cold as ice. My gaze searched the sky. There were so many stars—hundreds of them, glinting and gleaming, some in straight lines, some in shimmering clumps. But then I saw it. A white star at the apex of the sky, one that burned just a little brighter than the rest. The head of the hunter's harp. Abstract, sure, but I could see it. The hunter, the hunter in his carriage, holding a harp in his hands. I spun around, realization dawning on me.

"Terra!" Deklan called, his voice teasing. I'd forgotten that he was like that—the sort of boy born to be an older brother. "You'll catch flies standing around like that!"

I heard Jachin let out a mumble: "Haven't seen any flies. Haven't seen any insects at all. . . ."

But I ignored them. Overhead was Aire, so full it might burst,

and Akku, the sharp-edged crescent. The mountain dipped between them, forming a moonlit path toward the ice fields in the distance. When I let out a white, joyful breath into the cold air, I heard Rebbe Davison's song putter to a stop.

"Terra?" he asked. "Are you all right?"

I laughed. Choking, giddy laughter, laughter so hard that my chest ached. I lowered my gaze and turned back toward my companions, all gathered around the dying coals.

"I know where we have to go," I said.

"What do you mean you had a dream?"

They'd gathered around me, Rebbe Davison and Ettie, Jachin and Laurel. But Deklan hung back, hugging his rifle to his chest like it was his intended, not the skinny girl who stood just a few meters away. His dark eyes were hard with disbelief, and they pressed me for answers I knew I didn't have.

"I don't know how to explain it," I said. "I *know* it sounds ridiculous. But *that* star"—I pointed up, to the head of the hunter's harp—"is a pole star. We can navigate by it."

"Navigate to where?"

I squinted through the darkness at Deklan, the words dying on my tongue. I knew that if I said "Raza Ait," then he'd never believe me, never believe that there was a city waiting for us at the bottom of the mountain where a strange, blue-skinned boy waited for *me*.

"Civilization!" I said, throwing my hands into the air. "You saw those lights. Thousands of them, all along the coasts. It can mean only one thing: people." My eyes darted toward Rebbe Davison. He'd been the one to teach us about cities, years and years ago. It had always sounded like some sort of perverse dream—villages that grew and stretched until they could swallow up our enormous ship entirely. It was hard for me to believe too, so I wasn't surprised when Deklan shook his head.

"Aw," he said, "you're delusional."

"Deck!" called Laurel, but Deklan hefted the gun up onto his shoulder and headed back toward the fire. After a moment she followed him, but not without hesitation. I saw her bite down on her full lower lip, like she was considering something—turning the idea of it over in her mind. But what good were ideas? Soon we'd either freeze or starve. If I were going to make it to the boy, I needed to do something. I needed to take action. I buried my face in my hands, letting out an unhappy groan.

I felt a tug at my sleeve. It was Ettie. She pulled my fingers down.

"I believe you, Terra," she said. Her expression was earnest, heartfelt—her dark eyebrows knitted up and hopeful. But it helped, more than I thought it would. I smiled weakly.

"What do you propose?" Jachin asked at last. The man had spoken

little since the crash. Though he'd helped us with our inventory, his words then had been perfunctory. Officious. Yet now his expression was hopeful. "I asked HaShem to save us, but I didn't think an answer would come so soon."

"HaShem?" I asked. Jachin's cheeks went pink. Rebbe Davison answered for him.

"Mar Levi here is a believer. That's why he joined the Children of Abel."

"My family passed our religion down like an inheritance. No matter what the Council said, I've never stopped believing."

I examined the man's features. Small, close set. But intelligent. It was hard for me to believe that a specialist—a biologist—believed in God. The only other person I'd ever known who believed in God was Rachel, my best friend. And look where it had gotten her. She'd been trapped in the clock tower when the riots broke out. And now, who knew?

"Someone *died*." I said at last. My skepticism was obvious—it trickled out like water down the surface of a frozen rock. But Jachin didn't waver. He didn't even flinch.

"But *we* lived. And now your dreams have told you where to go. That's miraculous, isn't it?"

I let out a long sigh. I didn't believe in miracles. There was an answer here—I just had to find it. But I suspected it wouldn't come until I found my boy, so I changed the subject.

"We'll walk south." I turned back to where the mountain pass sloped down beneath the light of two moons. "That way. Toward the largest cluster of lights. That's our best chance to find people to help us. We should spend a few hours preparing our supplies, then take off by the first light of dawn."

"It's a crazy plan," Deklan called from the fire pit's edge. "Following some dream!"

"Do you have something better in mind?" Jachin snarled back. Deklan clutched his gun against his chest, apparently shamed. No matter our differences in philosophy, I was glad to have the specialist with me. He didn't merely believe in some unfathomable spirit. He believed in me, too. If we were going to make it to Raza Ait, I'd need that faith.

"Good," Jachin said, and just like that it was decided. "South, then. By dawn's first light."

In the gray light we gathered our supplies, stuffing each knapsack to the brim with as much food as we could carry, making sure the rifles were in good working order and fully charged. We watched as Deklan propped one up onto his shoulder, flicked the safety back, and shot into the mountains. The noise seemed to ripple on the air. We all flinched; Ettie let out a squeal that was lost under the sound of the shot.

"They work," Deklan said, holding the hot barrel in both hands. Rebbe Davison gave a nod and began to dole the weapons out, his mouth a grim line. I took one, feeling the awkward weight. It had a switch on it, from two hundred fifty to a thousand sones.

"Can this kill someone?" Jachin asked. Deklan glanced uncertainly at Rebbe Davison.

"If you calibrate it correctly," our teacher said, "yes."

I thought of the boy's warning, a single word that suggested danger lurking in the forests beyond. *Beasts*. But we hadn't seen any animals yet, not even a single, buzzing insect, as Jachin had pointed out. And I felt perhaps foolishly certain that my boy's people wouldn't hurt me. I kept the gauge on the lowest setting. Enough to stun but not enough to kill.

We ate a breakfast of hard jerky and dehydrated noodles sprinkled with something salty from a silver packet. Overhead the stars were fading; we knew that it was finally time to go. We each hefted our bag up onto our back, surveying the remnants of our first Zehavan home. But then our eyes each struck the same place: the shuttle, silver in the sunlight despite the way that crash had warped her hull. The blood that had spilled over the snow was dry now, as brown as mud. But we all knew better.

"That's my *zayde*," Ettie said, her eyes growing wide and watery. It was as if the realization surprised her. I remembered what that was like—the moments of normalcy right after Momma's death, cut through by loneliness and guilt. She added, "We can't just leave him here! We can't!"

She was right; of course she was. But out of the corner of my eye, I saw Rebbe Davison wince.

"We can't bury him either," he said. "The ground's too hard."

We stared at the shuttle for a long time. Mar Schneider had been my neighbor. When I was young, he'd visited Momma, sharing stories of his childhood with her. It was boring, but I never minded. He always brought over ribbon candy for me and Ronen to share.

"We'll burn the body," I said at last. "Set it on fire. Make sure he's safe from . . . whatever's out here."

"Burn him?" Jachin said. "But we're supposed to return him to the earth."

When we all regarded Jachin, questions on our brows, Rebbe Davison piped up in agreement.

"He's right. It's in the ship's contracts. It specified that bodies will be buried, not burned. Within twenty-four hours. It was all very specific. . . ."

I wasn't sure what to say. But Deklan butted in, waving his hand. "Old laws. I never signed that contract anyway, did you?"

Jachin glanced at all of us, pleading. But no one answered.

"Okay, okay," Jachin said at last, but he didn't sound happy about it. He sighed, long and low, and hung his head. "Let's do it."

Deklan was the one who cut Mar Schneider down, hacking at the straps with his razor-sharp survival knife. But I was there with Rebbe Davison to catch the body. We wrapped his old, stiff limbs in one of the extra sleeping sacks. I made myself look at his gray skin and the meaty flesh that spilled out of it. I told myself that it was only a body, not a person. And this was no time to be afraid. The day was coming in fast; before we knew it, it would be night. So the three of us carried the body out, and set it down over the already spent coals.

We lined the fire pit with black-barked twigs and all the firestarter we'd been unable to fit inside our packs. In the gray light of morning, I could see how haggard we all were: dirty, tangle-haired. Bags shadowed all of our eyes. Maybe we'd always looked like that—maybe the light on the ship had been too dim to show our true faces. Or maybe this grave, simple work had transformed us into new creatures, half dead ourselves.

Deklan volunteered to be the one to light it. I was glad to have him there—he was brave and bold in ways I wasn't. The rest of us stood back, tucked into the shadow of the mountain. On muscular legs he scrambled forward, a lighter in his hand. For a moment we couldn't see him; he was lost behind an outcropping of rock. I held Ettie against me, my arms draped over her shoulders. Soon I felt Laurel's hand bumble out and reach for mine. She squeezed tight as we all waited. In this distance there was a *click* then a gentle *whoosh*.

"Did it light?" Rebbe Davison asked as Deklan appeared again. But he didn't have to answer. We all saw the flames roar up into the frigid air. We all waited, watching as they leaped, orange and feral, past the mountain's rocky edge. Finally I heard Jachin let out a mumble of words.

"We should say something," he was saying. "Someone should say something."

"Captain Wolff always led us in saying that kaddish." We all turned to look at Laurel. Her cheeks flamed as brightly as the fire in the distance. "What?" she asked.

Deklan gave his head a hard shake. "We're rebels," he said. "We can't say the kaddish."

I felt my temper flash, white and wild, at that. "Just because we're rebels doesn't mean we have to throw *all* our traditions away. What's the harm?"

None of them said anything. They were all staring down at the ground, or out, bleak and empty, toward the fire.

"On our hallowed ship, or on Zehava," I said, enunciating each word with great care. At the name of the planet, I saw their faces soften, all of them. "May there come abundant peace, grace, loving kindness, compassion . . ."

Ettie was the first one who joined me.

"Long life," she said, her voice cracking as she spoke, "refuge . . ."

And then Laurel and Jachin lent their voices as well.

"Healing, redemption, forgiveness . . ."

By the time we'd reached the end of it, they'd all joined in. Even Deklan.

"And salvation for those in the heavens and on Earth."

I still held Ettie against me. I felt her rib cage quake.

"Shh," I said, squeezing her. "Shh, it's okay."

Everyone was quiet for a long time. Then, at last, we turned away from the pyre and its black column of smoke and toward the narrow pass that cut through the mountain below.

5

We trampled down the mountainside in silence. The cliff faces were black and dripped with ice so thick, it looked like icing on a cake. Soon we found a chasm in the mountainside, a deep split in the rock almost as wide as a body. One at a time we launched ourselves across. Deklan caught Ettie as she leaped. For a moment she wavered within the cage of his arms. But then she righted herself, blushing.

"Thanks," she said shyly, then darted her hand out to take up mine.

It was strange how quickly she took to me. I'd never been good with children, though it often felt like they were everywhere in the claustrophobic space of the ship. Maybe she liked me because I'd known her grandfather—or maybe it was because of what we shared. Ettie was different from the rowdy boys and girls who roamed the school yard. Her dark eyes were huge, pensively taking in the world around us. She'd lost so much—one moment, standing in her grandfather's shadow, the next, marooned on a planet, alone with a pack of strange adults. I saw in her a well of secret strength. She pushed her long hair behind her ear, tucking it out of the way of the wind so she could better see the world around her. Then, as we reached an apex, she stopped, shielding her eyes with her gloved hand.

"Terra!" she called. "Terra, look!"

I came to stand beside her, where the wind whipped in our faces, so cold that it seared my skin. The forests spread out for hundreds of kilometers beneath us, a white path a shining line between one set of dark branches and the other. Most of the trees were firmly rooted, though their limbs seemed to stretch and waver in the air, just like Ettie and Rebbe Davison had described. But not all of them. As our companions made their way toward the path's mouth below, we saw purple vines shrink back from nearby branches, flinching from the sound of their footfalls. The vines' movement was rapid—almost frantic. Ettie and I watched as the whole sea of purple constricted, fading into the distance as the vines unraveled themselves from the trees and retreated into the forest.

"What are they doing?" Ettie asked me.

"I'm not sure," I answered, scrambling down after the others. When we'd made it down the sloping cliff side, I ran toward Jachin, though the sound of Ettie's footsteps soon joined mine. "Jachin! Jachin!" I yelled.

He turned to me, eyebrows lifted.

"Hmm?" he asked, hefting his pack up high. I gestured toward the forest beside us, darker now that the vines had made their retreat.

"What do you make of this, biologist?"

"You're the botanist," he said, though there was something odd about his tone. False. "Haven't observed much relevant to my own work, myself. No sign of birds, or insects. No scat, so no small animals."

"Maybe that's it," I said as I peered into the dark, dense woods. I didn't want to tell him what the boy had said—that there *were* animals here, and not only that. There were dangerous, deadly *beasts*. The thought was too frightening to bear. "If there aren't any birds or insects, then there are no pollinators, right? Other than the wind. Maybe that explains the plants' extreme motility. In order to pollinate they have to move *themselves* closer together."

I was used to talking like this, spouting off theories to Mara and

having her confirm or deny them for me. But Jachin wasn't my teacher; he was a stranger. And a mostly very serious one, at that.

"I don't know, Terra," he said in a low voice. He waited for the others to walk past us, smiling tersely at Ettie as she jogged on ahead. Then he turned to me. "I don't want to scare the child."

"Scare her how?"

"All this talk about carnivorous trees is bad enough. And so soon after her grandfather's death! My son is her age. Full of bluster, but still screams at night for his abba sometimes."

"What happened to him?" I asked. It was hard to imagine this man, responsible and serious, leaving his children behind.

"The night of the riots I told my wife I was a Child of Abel." Out of the corner of my eye, I saw him swallow hard, as though it hurt to push the words past his lips. "She kicked me out. Told me to stay away from them. So I did."

I felt my stomach clench. Jachin's children had an abba, one who cared for them, who wanted to see them live and grow in a world where they could flourish. And yet still they were alone. Like I'd once been. Like Ettie was now too.

At ten I'd still needed my momma. My father, too. I'd been terrified by the ghosts my brother said haunted the engine rooms at night, never mind the real, unseen dangers that lurked in the ship's darkness. Now Ettie faced monsters stranger than any I'd ever glimpsed in nightmares. *Beasts*. All because I'd been in too much of a hurry to leave her on the *Asherah*. Queasy, I turned my gaze to Jachin.

"Tell me about the dangers," I murmured, and though my voice was low, it was fierce, too. I *needed* to keep Ettie safe. He hesitated, surprised by the force of my words. Then he pointed to a ragged line that cut across a row of nearby trees, two meters up from where they were rooted in the black Zehavan earth.

"I study predators on the ship," he said. "Which ones are necessary for pest control, which ones are safe. Those marks. They look like the markings of felines. They'll rake their claws on trees to sharpen them and spread their scent."

"Felines." I smiled, thinking of the tomcat who still waited for me in my brother's quarters on the ship. "So I was wrong. Maybe there are house cats here—"

"Terra!" Jachin said, his voice suddenly as sharp as broken glass. "I don't mean tabby cats. There are other felines, ones we've never seen fit to awaken. Panthers and mountain lions and tigers. Do you have a cat?"

"Yes," I said. "Pepper. He's—"

"Think of Pepper. Think of the way he acts when he smells a mouse, or when another tom walks by the window. Now imagine that he weighs, oh, say, three hundred fifty kilograms."

I swallowed hard, thinking of the way Pepper sometimes dug his claws into me when I stroked his stomach wrong—kicking out his back feet, leaving long marks raking my forearms.

"Maybe the plants don't move for pollination," I said. "Or not only that. In the greenhouses we had a touch-me-not. *Mimosa pudica.* Mara showed me how if you let your fingers grace its leaves, it shrinks back, hiding. From animals who might *eat* it."

I was doing it again. Rambling, musing aloud. But this time Jachin only nodded his head in agreement.

"There might not be pollinators here," he said. "But I suspect there are predators."

We didn't tell the others about the dangers that lurked in the forests. Instead I kept my head down, watching my boots strike the earth as we made our way over the frozen ground. I was underdressed in my flight suit—the cold cut straight through, numbing my calves and thighs. But the rhythm of the walk kept me going, a straight line south toward the city.

Toward my boy.

We stopped near midday, when Epsilon Eridani was high in the sky. We'd reached an open plain coated with dense grass, gone blue from frost and trampled flat. I wondered if the others noticed as they set down their packs and squatted over the cold ground to eat, but apparently their attentions were elsewhere—Deklan trying to beg an extra handful of freeze-dried fruit off Laurel; Rebbe Davison arguing with Jachin about the place of religion in our colony to come. I was alone in my reflections, staring out into the forest with wary eyes. Or so I thought.

Because halfway through our meal I heard a shout. A child's voice, distant, punctuated with laughter.

"Hey! Hey, look!"

Ettie. I whipped my head around, searching for her. I found her at the edge of the clearing, her hair a dark veil down her back.

Stay on the rocky pathway, the boy had said. *Avoid the forests.* But there she was, holding one hand out and open toward the darkness beyond. The others only watched at first, but I scrambled to my feet and raced toward her. When I reached the place where the grass grew spare and knotted with roots, I grabbed her by the shoulder and spun her skinny body around.

"What are you doing?"

She broke herself from my grip and staggered back. Her expression was pleasantly puzzled, not angry or upset.

"I wanted to see the forest. Look!"

She extended one hand again. I started to reach out to stop her, but by then the others had come to see what was the matter. I tamped down my fear until it was nothing but a slender lick of flame. And watched.

There was a vine that had tangled its way around the nearest black-barked tree. The vines' leaves were a deep violet lined with veins the color of heliotrope, and they flickered as the plant began to unfurl its tendrils. How did it know that Ettie stood there, arm outstretched, her brave smile showing crooked teeth? It didn't have eyes or ears. I reached back in my mind, trying to recall what Mara had taught me about sensory systems in plants. Meanwhile the coiling vine slithered down the nearest branch, reaching and stretching, until its leaves graced Ettie's smooth, small hand.

"Ettie!" I cried. There was a chorus of murmurs from the others. Her impish grin grew wider and wider as the vine climbed her arm, knotting through her unbound hair. The movement was slow, strange—but beautiful. Like something from a dream.

"See, Terra?" she said, smiling faintly. "It's okay!"

Beside me Rebbe Davison let out a chuckle. "The curiosity of a child," he said. But Ettie wasn't the only one who was curious. Deklan took a heavy step forward, reaching out his hand.

"I guess you were wrong about the carnivorous plants," he said, looking pointedly at me. But instead of climbing *his* palm, the vine shrank back. By the time he'd turned back to Ettie, it was already gone—retreating rapidly into the darkness of the forest.

"That's strange," he said. Laurel leaned forward, pressing a kiss to his cheek.

"It's because you smell bad."

"Hey!"

Laughing, the pair made their way back toward our supplies. After a moment Ettie and Rebbe Davison followed. Not Jachin, though. He hung back, standing beside me, his hands on his hips.

"It could be instinctual," I offered. "Responses to stimuli."

But Jachin gave his head a shake. "A different response to the child's touch than to Deklan's? That implies a degree of judgment not typically seen in plants."

I stared at him. "And what would it mean in an animal?"

"That it's afraid," he said. "HaShem help us, afraid of *what*?"

We walked, and walked. As the afternoon wore on, clouds began to crowd the sky. They seemed to skate across the golden expanse above, tinting everything gray. It was so different from the way that dark descended on our ship—evenly and predictably—that at first I didn't even notice the wisps of smoke in the distance.

"What's that, Terra?" Ettie asked, tugging on the sleeve of my flight suit. I stopped, cupping my hands over my eyes. The smoke was dark and thick, a column that stretched into the clear sky.

"Fire, it looks like."

"Does fire just *happen* like that?" Deklan asked.

I pursed my lips uncertainly. "Wildfires. Mara told me about them.

But it's too cold here. And the fire's just in one spot. It hasn't spread."

"Like our campfire," Rebbe Davison said. We all squinted into the distance.

"Should we walk out toward it?" Laurel asked. I was surprised to find that she'd turned toward me. I lifted my shoulders. I wasn't sure what to say—wasn't used to even being asked *anything*. But Deklan cut in before I could answer.

"We're trying to find civilization, right?" he asked. I had to admit, it sounded good when he spoke. Like he was strong and sure, like he could keep us safe. "A campfire means people."

"But it means leaving the path," I protested. And not only that— we'd have to head east into the forest, rather than south, away from Eps Eridani as it sank behind the mountains. Away from the city, too. I felt panic rise in my throat. "I don't think we should. My dream—"

"Aw," Deklan said. He pawed at the back of his neck, looking sympathetically down at me. He was so tall and broad-shouldered. He must have felt invincible, even out here in the elements. I wondered what it was like to feel so strong and certain. "I know you had a dream, Terra. But if we're trying to get out of the wilderness, it seems to me like finding *someone* is our best bet. Dream or no dream."

His smile was wide and charming. I wanted to believe him, but I couldn't. It flew in the face of everything that I knew was true. My boy. His words.

"I suspect there are animals in the forest," Jachin finally declared. At that, they all started. Even Ettie. She snatched up my hand, and then pressed her face against my upper arm, hiding.

"Animals?" she said. "Alien animals?"

Jachin watched the girl as she peered out from behind me. His knitted eyebrows and thin mouth offered no comfort.

"Alien animals," he agreed.

Her moon eyes were huge. "What if they're not *nice*? What if they're *monsters*?"

Jachin gazed at me, pressing his mouth into a line. When neither of us spoke, Laurel did instead.

"We have weapons. We'll be okay." She clutched her rifle to her chest. When no one answered her, she looked to Deklan. "Right, Deck?"

Her intended hefted his gun high onto his shoulder. He'd entertain no more protests, not from us. "That's right. Come on. We can't just keep wandering around the wilderness forever. Our rations won't last half that long."

Jachin and Rebbe Davison shared a look. At last, reluctantly, Rebbe Davison nodded.

"Maybe he's right—"

"Of course I am," Deklan said. "Let's go."

With that, he turned and walked into the forest, Laurel hot on his heels. After a moment Rebbe Davison followed. And Jachin, too, after giving his head a slow, fearful shake.

"I hope this isn't a mistake," he said as he disappeared between the shifting black-bodied trees.

I hesitated, Ettie's clammy hand still tucked into mine.

"Terra, I'm scared," she said in a whisper. Her eyes were tightly closed, as if she could ward off any dangers she couldn't see.

The truth was, I was afraid too. Halfway to terrified, in fact. The boy had given us a path, and here we were straying from it—heading deeper and deeper into the undergrowth. I knew I had to follow; I'd never make it to the city alone. I wasn't strong enough or knowledge-able enough. I needed the others, as much as I hated to admit it. And that only frightened me more.

Still, I didn't want to scare Ettie.

"We'll be okay," I said, giving her hand a gentle tug. "I promise."

But as we headed into the forest, I wasn't sure it was a promise I could keep.

But we didn't find beasts in the forest. Not at all. Nor aliens like the boy, their bodies bending in the wind like reeds. What we found was even stranger: human voices, speaking Asheran, our native tongue. The low murmurs rose up from the forest behind a patch of shifting, snow-dotted trees.

"Her shuttle crashed northwest of here."

"We'll break camp after dinner and head that way."

"People!" Ettie cried. She began to run ahead, her dark hair tossing against her shoulders. Calling her name, Rebbe Davison took off after her. The others followed. But I just stood there, frozen on the path, the gun clutched in one fist and my pack a saggy lump low on my back. My hands were slick with sweat against the metal barrel of the rifle. My heart beat hard. One of the voices was strange, new. But one spoke with familiar clarity. It was a woman's voice, strong, commanding, without a hint of doubt. It was a voice that hadn't cracked even when she'd struck her mother down.

Aleksandra Wolff. Aleksandra Wolff was *here* on Zehava. I cast my head back, as if the golden evening sky could offer me escape. It couldn't, of course, though the trees reached their naked branches out like arms to embrace me. It was like they wanted to bolster me, keep me safe. Maybe I could have fled deeper into the forest. But the boy had said that there were animals there, animals that could harm me. Would they bring me greater harm than the people who sat in the grove ahead? My mind was spinning wildly; I couldn't pin it down. I was still gaping up at the sky when Laurel appeared at the mouth of the clearing. The grin across her mouth was wide and toothy, like all her worries had been washed away.

"Terra!" she called. "Aleksandra Wolff is here! She's going to save us!"

I stared at Laurel, at the gleeful smile that tugged at the corners of her mouth. Of course. Laurel was a rebel—Aleksandra, the leader of the rebels. It was only natural that she'd be glad to see her. Not terrified that Aleksandra's long, narrow blade would soon find itself buried in her belly.

"Terra?"

There was nothing else to do, nowhere else to go. I took staggered steps toward Laurel. As I walked, I held my gun against my chest, hoping that it would hide the way that my hands shook, and the way that I was unable to keep them still.

6

hey'd set up their camp on the edge of a bubbling stream, where their shuttle sat, bobbing and bright, in the water. It looked like it had been a smooth landing. Aleksandra was unscathed, and not a scratch could be seen on either of her two guards, who were dressed, head to toe, in flight gear. They'd built a fire, a wide tower of freshly chopped logs that smoldered as they burned, unlike the fists of brittle detritus we'd gathered for our own fire the night before. I winced to think of it—one of those still-living trees struck down like it was nothing. But I suppose to the guard who had felled it, it *was* nothing. What did he care that the trees stretched and reached as if their branches were human arms? It was all the same to him. Now the guards' motions were efficient, robotic as they doled out dinnertime rations.

I stood at the mouth of the camp, unable to make my feet move. There was Aleksandra, knelt down beside the fire. Her helmet sat on the log beside her; her long, black braid snaked out to one side. She didn't hold a knife, not anymore. Now she wore a gun in her belt, and while I had one too, I felt sure that she'd be better at using it than I was.

She hadn't noticed me, not yet. *Maybe,* I thought, *if I just stay real still, she won't.*

"I can't believe she's here."

I turned toward the familiar voice. Rebbe Davison leaned in close, holding his bowl of rehydrated stew against his chest.

"We were in the same clutch, you know," he said. "In school we passed notes back and forth, like you and Rachel Federman used to. After we found out about the Children of Abel, it was like a fire lit inside her. She wrote so passionately about our cause."

"Our notes were always about boys," I said dully. I was hardly listening to him. My eyes were fixed firmly on Aleksandra as she flicked her braid back over her shoulder to keep it away from the fire.

"Ours were about rebellion," Rebbe Davison said. "She decided she didn't just want to fight for our liberty. She wanted to lead the cavalry. That was always our plan. I'd be the brains behind the outfit, and Aleksandra—she'd be the brawn. After all those years of wrestling with her mother for control, she should be up there on that ship. Not *here*. I was drunk when I left, but Aleksandra . . . I don't know why she came."

For me, I thought. *She came for me.*

At long last she lifted her brown eyes up. They shone like a pair of moons. When she saw me, she smiled hungrily. I felt the blood drain from my hands. I dropped my rifle; the metal clattered over the frozen ground. Rebbe Davison looked sharply at me. They all did, pausing over their meals to watch me tremble where I stood. She'd been there when they'd struck down Ben Jacobi. Then she'd been the one to draw the knife across her mother's neck. I was surely next. When Aleksandra rose from the log, I thought I might wilt right there in the middle of the forest.

I waited for her to take up her own rifle, cocking the safety back and pressing its barrel to my head. But she didn't. Instead she only bent over, taking my gun in her free hand and passing it back to me.

"Terra Fineberg," she said, a smile cold on her lips. "I think you dropped this."

Then she turned to Rebbe Davison. Her finely plucked eyebrows were arched, as if he'd just told her the funniest joke in the world.

"Mordecai," she said. "My old friend. Come, break bread with me. We have a lot to talk about."

I sat as far away from Aleksandra as I could, pressed on a log between her pair of guards. The others ate and ate—without any care for the supplies that might one day dwindle down to nothing. But I'd lost my appetite. Sitting beside Rebbe Davison, she looked so clean, so composed. Her hands made swift motions through the air as she spoke. The others were all enraptured. Laurel gazed up at her as Aleksandra described the rebel victory. Deklan wore a proud smirk. Even Ettie listened, one ear tilted up as Aleksandra told her story.

"Once it was clear I had unseated the Council," Aleksandra was saying, "I knew we could no longer hesitate. We had listened to their lies about the probe results for too long. It was time to see the planet for myself, to assess the situation for *my* people."

Her smile didn't falter one bit as she wove her words into a bright fabric. So urgent was their journey, she said, that they'd taken off that very night. She didn't mention chasing me down through the fields and pastures, or riding the lift in hot pursuit of me. She didn't mention that she'd been the one to kill her mother—even as Captain Wolff begged her for mercy—or that she'd followed me here to make sure *I* died too.

"But, Alex," Rebbe Davison said, massaging his fingers over his worried brow, "what about the Asherati? They need you—need a leader. Without your mother to lead them—"

Her words came, too fast, too fierce. By the firelight I could see the emotion that flamed beneath her cool visage. "My mother was a traitor to all of us. Though I mourn the loss of her in the riots, you will *never* speak of her to me again. Do you understand, Mordecai?"

I sucked in a breath. In our musty library meetings it had been common for the rebels to speak ill of Captain Wolff. They called her a cow, pinning all the ship's woes on her. But I knew better. She'd done her best for our people, even when her best wasn't good enough— sending out probe after probe to Zehava in the hopes that the planet would support us and be our home. Each probe had been lost, but it hadn't been her fault. She'd been shocked when she'd discovered the truth of the missing probes; she hadn't been hiding them from us at all. I remembered her face, gnarled and scarred, and the story Rebbe Davison used to tell about her. How she saved a boy from a thresher when she was young, the first of many noble acts she'd undertaken for us.

Rebbe Davison swallowed hard. "Of course, Alex," he said, still clinging to her childhood name. I wondered what it would take for Alex to die for him—for her to become Aleksandra. "I just can't help but wonder what's going on up there on the ship."

"No need to wonder. I have this."

She reached for something on her flight suit belt, a square of rusted metal with jutting antennae. Fiddling with the controls, she flipped a switch. A burst of static came back.

"This is Wolff," she said into the mouthpiece. "Give me an update on the ship's status."

There was a long gasp of white noise—so long that I thought they'd never answer. But then I heard a garbled voice.

"Rafferty continues to make his threats, but the coward still hasn't moved to action."

"Rafferty?" I said. I thought of Mazdin, the doctor who had killed my mother. I thought of his sweat-slick face on the night the *Asherah* reached Zehava. I'd done that to him—poured poison in his wine. But I'd hardly thought about him since. I was too busy running, too busy working to stay alive.

Aleksandra stared pointedly at me. She still held the radio up in one hand, letting the static stream out. "He means Silvan," she said. "Your intended."

She'd wanted me to murder Silvan, to get him out of the way so that she'd be free to lead. But I'd been a bad rebel. Disobedient.

Aleksandra shut off the device.

"It's funny," she said, though her tone suggested that it wasn't *really* funny at all, "how much of this could have been avoided had you followed your orders."

I remembered that night. Feeling the weight of the poison in my coat pocket after Mazdin had told me about killing my mother. He'd said that we were weak, helpless—no threat to him. I'd been desperate to prove him wrong.

"Alex, we have the ship," Rebbe Davison said. "What more do you want?"

His voice sounded hoarse, fearful. Aleksandra clipped the radio to his belt. She studied his face—his thinning hair, the wrinkles that formed parentheses at the edges of his mouth. And then her own mouth softened.

"Nothing, Mordecai." Her lips spread into a wide grin. It was a politician's smile—charming, trustworthy. "I'm as happy as a clam."

He hesitated—nodded. But as he turned away, her eyes caught mine. Her expression? Went as cold as ice.

"We'll go east," Aleksandra said as the fire began to fade. By then the sun had pressed deep into the mountain ridge. Two of the three moons were rising. Akku and Aire. I saw how we'd strayed from the path in our quest to find the source of the fire, drifting farther and farther into the woods. But how could I come out and tell her we were going the wrong way when all eyes were on her, shining with admiration? The words caught at the base of my throat.

But Rebbe Davison spoke for me. "What's east?"

There was an intensity in his question that was new; it made me sit straighter on the log. Aleksandra sat forward too, her eyes as dark as the smoke that whispered around us. Suddenly she stood, grabbing a slender twig on a nearby branch. The twig undulated in the open air until she snapped it off and it was still. Dead. She pressed the narrow end into the crust of snow and began to draw a jagged line with it.

"This is the coastline," she said as the others scrambled to gather around her. I stayed where I sat, glimpsing her rough diagram from between their shoulders. "Before we departed for the planet, my mother received a transmission from the shuttle crew. It originated from here, near the largest array of lights. They said that the inhabitants are hostile. At least one crew member was injured."

Hannah, my brother Ronen's wife. Council-born daughter. Cartographer. The last time I'd glimpsed her pretty features, they'd been streaked with blood. She'd sounded so *afraid*. I clenched my hands between my knees, wondering if the cold that bit through my flight suit gloves came from the chilly evening or from within.

"The next closest light cluster is here," Aleksandra said, jabbing the stick higher along the coastline. "East of our current location. I'm hoping that the inhabitants there will be amenable to negotiations if the others aren't."

"Negotiations," Rebbe Davison echoed faintly. He glanced eastward as if he could see the city straight through hundreds of kilometers of forest and mountain. "What makes you think they'll be willing to talk to us? We're strangers to them. We're nothing."

Aleksandra stood tall. She thrust the stick into the embers. We all watched as the flames leaped up, enveloping it. "You remember what we learned in school, Mordecai," she said, a smile curling her lips. But it was a fond smile, teasing, without malice. "The planet Earth was fractured. Many cities. Many cultures. Even on the *Asherah*, we've had factions. The Children of Abel on one hand. The Council on the other."

"Diversity," Rebbe Davison said. "You're right. It's unlikely that we'd find a monoculture here. But even so, that doesn't mean that we'll even be able to speak to them—"

"Maybe we won't," Aleksandra agreed, tucking a hand inside the open flap of her flight suit. On a knife's hilt, I realized. She carried the ceremonial blade of a guardsman with her even now, so far away from the culture of our ship. But she'd carried it not only for ceremony but also for the death it could bring. "There's a chance that any alien life forms we encounter might be hostile. But the eastward settlement is closer, and smaller. We need to be patient, and we need to be on guard. If we're going to conquer these lands—"

"Conquer these lands!" The words spilled out before I could stop them. I firmed my jaw, gazing into the blue-tongued flames even as Aleksandra turned her attention toward me.

"Yes, Terra?" she said. This time her smile had teeth.

"They're not our enemies," I said fiercely. I thought back to the boy, to the way his arms enveloped me like vines on a wall. I felt so *safe* inside them. But Aleksandra didn't know that. She only let out a short, dry laugh.

"You saw the transmission," she said. "Care to tell the others what you saw?"

"The aliens," I said, weaker now, as she found my cracks and fixed her fingers into them. "Their bodies move like grass in the wind. Their eyes are black. A night without moons or stars."

"Tell them about Hannah," Aleksandra prodded. I drew in a breath, held it. Finally I drew my gaze down to my knees.

"She was bleeding. She asked us to come save her."

"They sound real friendly," Deklan said, letting out a skeptical grunt. He turned away from me and toward Aleksandra, who was ready, even as the night deepened around us, with her plan.

I felt my stomach sink as she spoke. We'd leave with the morning's first light, tracking Epsilon Eridani as it rose through the sky. I remembered the way the boy's voice sounded in my head as he urged me south. Fearful. Passionate. But none of them knew anything about *that*. Instead they only saw the sharp, certain movements of Aleksandra's hands and heard the ferocity of her warning. Hostile. The aliens were hostile. Her followers all held their rifles to their chests, not just her guards but Rebbe Davison, and Deklan, and Jachin, and Laurel, too.

Only Ettie stayed apart from the rest, sitting beside me on a log, watching as the embers died. For a long time she didn't speak. Her hair was a dark net over her eyes. But at last she slipped her hand in next to my hand.

"I don't like this plan," she said. "What if there are *monsters*?"

"I'll keep you safe from them," I said. I'd brought Ettie here, after all. I wasn't going to let *anything* happen to her.

"With your gun?"

The weapon still rested across my knees. Ettie reached out and touched the barrel gently, as if the metal might spring to life at any moment.

"With my hands and fists and teeth if I have to," I said. I put an arm around her and held her close. Her body shook next to mine. I realized she was weeping then, but I wasn't surprised. It had been a long day—for all of us. I knew I should have said something, offering apologies for her grandfather's death or comforting words. But I'd never been any good at that. Everything I could offer seemed awkward, wrong. My words withered before I could speak them

"Now I think it's time we get some rest," Aleksandra said, speaking too loudly, I think, to mean only the group gathered around her. She meant the rest of us, too—Ettie and me especially. "It'll be a long hike tomorrow before we can reach the city."

Ettie rose, still sniffling. To my surprise she turned to look back at me.

"Thank you, Terra," she said. I gave an uncertain nod. It seemed like I'd done so little—shared a hug, a few comforting words. But maybe, just maybe, my being there had been enough.

The rest of them worked together, driving their tent stakes into the hard, half-frozen ground. But I only watched. My eyes were wide, taking in the darkness. I needed to go to the city, where I would be safe, where the boy waited for me. I needed to stand up to Aleksandra, to prove to her that I was someone worth listening to. And if that didn't work, I needed to strike out on my own. But I *couldn't*. I watched as Rebbe Davison held a stake and Ettie swung the mallet, grinning proudly as the tears dried on her face. She was here only because of me. They all were, and I knew it. My guilt was an invisible thread tying us together. We were bound even as they all crawled inside the tent and disappeared into the darkness, leaving me alone there with Aleksandra Wolff.

"When I said it was time for bed," she said, standing over the fire, her shadow long and dancing against the writhing foliage, "I meant you, too."

I still held my gun across my knees—the metal was cold, as heavy as dead flesh. Useless. What did I know of guns?

"We shouldn't go east," I said. I couldn't bear to look her in the eyes, only stared down at that stupid gun. "There are animals in the forests. If we head south, there's a path. We can walk to Raza Ait—"

"Terra," she said. She didn't sound sneering, or vicious. Just tired, like she'd lost all patience for me. "Shut up."

So I did.

"I don't know what you thought you were doing when you took that shuttle," she said. "A sixteen-year-old girl, head screwed on backward! You can't even follow the simplest of orders, and you thought you could negotiate with the natives?"

I hadn't thought that, actually. In my mind the path ahead had been simple: I'd find the boy, fall into his arms, and the world around us would fall away. But now, with Aleksandra standing over me, I could see how naive I had been. There was a whole ship up there, crumbling into chaos. And a whole world down here, dangerous and new. I winced but didn't answer.

"I came down here to stop you from ruining our chances of settlement. Now you might be useful," she said, speaking cautiously. "My mother said that Mara Stone was pleased with your progress in your vocation. But unless it's about plants, I don't want to hear a single word from you. You're only a botanist—a *talmid* at that. You're no diplomat. Do you hear me?"

Her small brown eyes bored into me. She wanted an answer, so numbly I nodded.

"I remember my mother talking about Alyana Fineberg," she said, letting out a low sigh. "Common-born, but she always wanted to be a leader. Thought she could rise up the ranks through the Children of Abel, march us into glory. We all know how that ended."

I'd never wanted to be a leader. In that moment I wanted nothing more than to be left alone. But Aleksandra took my silence for a protest. She spat on the ground, hard.

"Remember who's in charge," she said. I wasn't about to forget it as I watched the dark shadow of her back disappear behind the flimsy fabric walls of the tent. My throat was dry. I clutched my rifle. There was no way I was going to follow her in there, lay my head down in a sleep sack only a few meters from her plotting, murderous hands.

I pulled the synthetic blankets out of my pack, then wadded up the bag beneath my head. Still dressed in my sweat-drenched flight suit, I squeezed my eyes shut. I was sure that I wouldn't sleep that night, out in the open, the wind frigid and biting against my cheeks.

But from almost the moment my eyes closed, I was plunged into the world of turbulent dreams.

We sat in a patch of thorny brambles only a few meters apart. But it might as well have been kilometers. I clutched my arms around my naked body, shielding myself.

Come, he said, reaching a willowy arm out to me. I wanted to grasp his hand in mine, to furl my body around his, as tight as a fiddlehead. But I couldn't. East. We were going east. Aleksandra had decided.

And yet he said it again. *Come!* If those black eyes reflected anything, it was the heat of his desire. But I couldn't figure out how to bridge the gap between us. The ground was frozen, hard and slick. And netted with thorns.

Over the past two days—during our shuttle journey and our sojourn in the Zehavan wilderness—I'd kept one goal in mind: reaching him. And no wonder. Through hard month after hard month, he'd been my respite. His hands, preternaturally long, had graced my white belly. His mouth, soft and wet, had pressed against my throat. I hadn't understood the passions that lurked beneath my flesh, but I knew that he made me happy. If there was one certainty, it had been that.

Now I hesitated. Maybe I'd made a mistake in coming to the planet. Maybe I was only a foolish girl, as Aleksandra said, sixteen and with a head stuffed full of dreams. After all, I'd been stupid enough to think myself in love before, but I'd been wrong about that. I remembered standing in front of Koen Maxwell, whom I'd hoped I would marry, waiting for him to make a move. I'd been starved for his kisses, for the steady pressure of his hard hands against my skin. And then, when Silvan came along?

I'd been so glad to lay my body down in the soggy leaves, to let him press his hands over my belly, my hips, my thighs. It didn't matter what the Children of Abel wanted. It didn't matter that there were times when I hated Silvan, despising those pretty lips and the words that tumbled from them. All that mattered was feeling: his body on top of mine, his fingers and tongue and lips and palms, the way his slender hips jutted out, and the fine fur over his belly. How was this any different? I'd endangered all of them—killed Mar Schneider too—just so that I could feel loved.

The boy reached for me. I saw his arms stretch out, long and blue. I felt his desire, how he wanted to fold me into his body. I knew that it would be better than what I'd shared with Silvan. Safer. Purer.

But I couldn't. For sixteen years I'd convinced myself that everything I did was noble—right. When the truth was, I had no idea what "right" even meant. All I'd ever understood was desire. Anger. Emotions that I carried with me even now. For sixteen years I'd lived like a loaded gun.

I can't, I told him as he laced spindly fingers through my hair. *I can't. I can't.*

His fingers froze at the nape of my neck. They were so cold. Sometimes I wondered if blood even ran beneath the surface of his jewel-toned skin. Maybe it didn't. Maybe he had no heart, no mind. Maybe he didn't exist.

He drew away from me, hugging his bandy legs to his body.

Come? he asked. Then he pointed out toward the sky above.

In that moment I couldn't be sure if I were asleep or awake. The moons overhead were real, I knew that much. Akku shone down on me, the color of a just-ripe fruit. But Aire was far, far west. Who knew how long it had been since our group had last walked the path between them?

No. I can't. Aleksandra is leading us east—

But the beasts! The beasts! He waved his fingers wildly, gesturing at something in the darkness, something I couldn't quite see.

But I heard it. Something halfway between a click and a shudder, so loud that the trees all around us recoiled, tucking their branches under, hiding themselves away. The frozen ground beneath me shivered. I turned toward the boy. His bottomless eyes gaped back at me. He snatched up my hands, gripping them tight.

Promise me you won't go any deeper. Promise me! I can't lose you, too.

Too? I asked, but he didn't answer. In the distance the shudder grew louder, and louder still—huge clouds of snow rising up in the distance. Fear rattled through him like an oncoming storm.

I promise! I promise! I said, just as the snow and ice swallowed up us both.

1

The sensation of falling wrenched me from my sleep. In my ears that animal racket echoed. But when I sat up, the forest around me was quiet, the sky the color of pale gold in the morning light. Strange, here, how there were no birds. It made everything seem lonely, half dead. Still shivering from the dream's aftershock, I rose. My body felt stiff, aching at a thousand points where it had touched the ice-cold ground straight through my flight suit.

"Good morning," Laurel called to me from across the cold,

ash-spent logs. She swiftly rolled up our tent. Ettie, at her side, seemed to be doing more to impede her progress than to help. But Laurel didn't seem to mind much. Under Aleksandra's command, I guessed, Laurel had found new purpose. She tied the tent straps tightly around the bundle, then slipped it into her pack.

"Morning," I grunted back. Who knows how long they'd all been up, milling around me, conversing, listening to me whimper in my sleep? I'd always done it. My brother, Ronen, used to tease me for the things I said. But if I'd said anything embarrassing, none of them gave any sign. They continued to drink their coffee substitute out of enamel cups as they broke down our camp.

"You're finally awake, then?" Aleksandra called as she came down over a nearby ridge. She was flanked on either side by a guard. The radio on her belt still spluttered static. I wondered who she'd been talking to up there. I wondered how everyone was. I felt a sudden stab in my chest, sweet and cutting. I'd left so many people up there on the *Asherah*: my best friend, Rachel; Koen; Van; my brother, Ronen; and his newborn daughter. Even Mara Stone.

"Is everyone okay?" I asked, my eyes lingering on the radio. She flashed her hand down over it, gripping it tight.

"*Now* you care? They'd be safer if you'd disposed of certain difficulties."

From beneath her fingers I heard muffled words: "Silvan Rafferty

has sent out a message to the Council-born: join him in the captain's stateroom to be safe from the violence of the dome. What should we tell the people, Giveret Wolff?"

I saw Aleksandra's thumb bend as she depressed a button. The voice was silenced. But still I'd heard it. Violence in the dome. I thought of Rachel, waifish, gentle, dressed in silk and lace. Concerned with boys and clothes and little else. What defenses would *she* have against violence?

"We're heading east," Aleksandra said. "All of us. Understand?"

I still heard that echo, deep inside me, that animal clatter that had reverberated in my dream. I heard my own voice, too, timid and frantic, promising the boy that I wouldn't take a single step deeper into these woods.

But then I looked at the others. Ettie was busy plaiting her long, tangled hair against her shoulder. Laurel had leaned her mouth against Deklan's ear to whisper a secret. Jachin stood at the corner of the camp with Rebbe Davison, talking about the path that lay ahead. The crash had bound us all together. If I led them south, and was wrong about sanctuary waiting for us there? If one of them got hurt, or worse? I could never forgive myself.

"I understand," I said to Aleksandra, hiking my pack up high onto my shoulders. "I'll be right behind you."

She nodded her head crisply, then commanded her guards through the forest.

. . .

The trees grew thick all around, towering up meters and meters above. And yet they still shifted their branches curiously, peering down at us. Aleksandra's guards walked up in front, their steps cautious as they peered into the forest beyond. They'd finally removed their helmets, but only that. The globes of glass clattered at the hips of their flight suits. One was an older man, haggard and gray-faced. The other was hardly any older than I was, a soft gold beard curling out past the neck of his suit. When he spoke, it was timidly. But we all followed him in a scattered line. Even me. Even as every cell in my body objected.

South. South. We need to go south. I swallowed hard, forcing the thought away. Aleksandra was in charge now, whether I liked it or not. She knew how to take care of us—how to lead.

She walked by herself, rifle in one hand, the radio clutched in the other. Every few minutes the radio would let out a gasp of white noise. She'd speak into it, and then the voice on the other end would give its report.

"Rafferty attempting to mobilize forces."

"Council rations low."

"Nineteen bodies found in the lower level."

"Rafferty's control limited to the bow."

When I'd last seen my family, they'd been up in the bow with the Council, all gathered there for my wedding. Ronen, dressed in his best drab suit, had looked sweet and dopey—even hopeful. I wondered if he was still up there, or if he'd been pushed out into the dome by the wave of rebellion. Funny, I thought, how little I knew of him. We'd never even discussed politics. I had no idea how he felt about the rebels' plans.

I'd been so eager to act that I'd never even bothered listening.

But my ears were sharp now. Past the thick trees ahead, buzzing through the tangled undergrowth, I heard a sound, low and steady, familiar. At first I told myself that it was nothing. After all, not even Aleksandra's guards seemed to hear it. They just stalked on ahead, oblivious to everything but their rifles and the commands that Aleksandra gave them.

But then the sound grew, and grew. It reminded me of bamboo shoots striking one another—or maybe bones. A hollow, empty sound.

"You guys," I called, softly at first. If they didn't hear that insectile gnawing, of course they didn't hear me, either. So I shouted again, louder this time. "Hey, do you hear that?"

Deklan glanced over his shoulder, the corner of his mouth lifted. For the first time I noticed the dimple in his cheek, and the proud, unruly hairs of his dark eyebrows.

"Don't worry so much," he said easily, swinging Laurel's hand in his.

I fumbled for a response. But I never got to answer. Because at that moment a beast came trouncing through the woods, trampling whole trees beneath its feet. It reared back, brandishing its massive horns, and then jabbed one straight through Deklan's chest.

His scream rose up and died as his body was flung across the forest. The creature was easily four, five times the height of a man, covered in hard yellow skin, as gnarled as old scar tissue. When the guards lifted up their guns, I knew it would do no good. And I was right. The sonic blasts succeeded only at making *us* shield our ears. Even though the nearby branches shifted, flinching back, the weapon seemed to do nothing to the stampeding creature. Soon the beast ran over the handsome young guard, smashing his lean body to pieces.

Ettie screamed as she knelt down on the forest floor, clenching her fists over her head. I acted on instinct, dashing across the clearing toward her. My fingers flashed out, grabbing hers. We had to duck a fury of thick legs and dash away from the tail that twitched wildly through the air, but we made it. Over the rattles I heard heavy, ragged tears. Laurel stood nearby, blood splattered on her clothing, tears streaming down her face.

"I—was—holding—his—hand!" she sobbed, each word punctuated by a wheeze. Ettie flung her arms at Laurel, hugging hard. But this was no time for comfort. I peered over the rocks. One guard had been crushed by the beast; the other cowered behind Aleksandra

as if he expected she would save him. There was blood everywhere, spilled over the gray old snow and the bare trees and especially over Aleksandra Wolff's white face.

She stood about ten meters back, her posture tense as an alley cat that was ready to strike. At the other end of the clearing, the beast reared and kicked, digging its horn into the remaining guard's body. I had to look away from the stream of blood, but Aleksandra wasn't scared. I saw her lift up her rifle. She aimed it carefully and gave the trigger a tight pull.

The sonic boom sounded. But the creature didn't care. If anything, it only seemed annoyed now, rearing back on four legs as it prepared to strike. I saw Aleksandra hesitate, staring up at the massive beast over her rifle's sight. She coiled low, preparing to run—but only tripped on a nearby root instead. The beast put thundering feet down against the permafrost and started to charge.

I had a thought: *Aleksandra is going to die.* And even though that meant that I'd probably die too, I couldn't help but feel a spark of relief at the idea.

But then I heard another sound, not the animalistic growling of the beast but strains of music wafting up through the winter air. How strange to hear music here, in such a savage space. Notes intermingled, weaving together like beautiful threads shimmering and opalescent in the midmorning light. It was haunting. No, hypnotic. I found my breath slowing, my heart slowing too. The beast also heard it. Massive front feet fell gently against the ground. It turned back, searching over one hulking shoulder for the source of those sweet, twisting notes.

Aleksandra didn't fire another shot. She didn't even lift her rifle to aim it again. Instead she took a few stumbling steps toward the sound. I stood up from behind the rock where I was crouched too, listening. Every note was bittersweet. It seemed to cut right to the heart of me, spelling out some part of myself that had, up until now, been unreadable. I suppose the others felt the same way. Together we took slow, careful steps over the frozen ground. The beast didn't rear up. It didn't seem to even see us. It just walked closer and closer to the music, and we followed.

That's when a vehicle streaked through the forest, tracing the path of the trees that had been felled by the beast. It had no wheels—no wings, either, from what I could see. Instead it was draped with long bolts of multicolored fabric, which hung down like the tail feathers of some tropical bird. In a glass capsule on top, three passengers could be seen, three bright faces with pitch-black eyes.

Their skin was the color of the inside of a pomegranate. Bipedal, smaller than us, with faint red hair covering their arms and heads. One held a stringed instrument against his chest, his fingers almost invisible as they tripped over it. Soothing, strange music streamed out of a speaker on the vehicle's side. We stumbled closer as they landed their craft in the clearing's center, as the vehicle's gleaming glass top lifted away. The musician kept playing, his song flitting like water over stone. But the other two aliens climbed out, hefting spikes of metal in their three-fingered hands. They approached the beast and felled it with a single blue burst of light, moving with perfect, measured efficiency. They reminded me of my cat, Pepper, hunting mice. Their focus was so tightly narrowed on the beast that they missed the people who stood, frozen, before them.

But as the creature collapsed, cracking snow and branches beneath its heavy body, we came closer. In the craft, the musician played on and on. I raised my hands to my cheeks. I was crying—and not for the loss of the guards or Deklan, who lay splayed out and bleeding on the forest floor as vines enveloped his broken body. I cried because for the first time, I felt sure that someone *knew* me. This music proved it—it told my story, lacing my story's notes through the chilly air.

But then something happened. The musician paused, and Laurel jostled me as she stepped forward, and the spell was broken. The music now sounded tinny; half the notes were out of key. I stopped where I stood, the wind making my flight suit crinkle, my hands dead weights at my sides. But my eye caught on something. A dark shock of hair, streaming in the wind.

It was Ettie. She stood before one of the creatures, facing him earnestly. He was busy slaughtering the beast, exposing organs, yellow and fatty. The air stank of tallow and flesh. And yet despite the stench, Ettie let out a sweet laugh.

"The music!" she said. "It's *my* music, isn't it?"

In a flash the alien's focus shifted. He darted black eyes up to her. His face was strange. His mouth was too broad and full of teeth, and, above he had only a flat gap of wine-red flesh where his nose should have been. The long slits that traced the edge of his jaw widened. He glanced over his shoulder at his companion, letting out a stream of strange words.

"Ezaz xoslex aum dazzix vhesesazhi osiz tauoso?"

His companion grunted. *"Dadix aum eddi tauoso."*

"Please," Ettie said, "tell me more about my song!"

The creature looked at her, not quite understanding her words or her intentions. He gripped Ettie by the shoulder, lifting up his metal stick. He was no taller than she was, but I knew it would be nothing for that flash of false lightning to come again, striking her down. I tightened my fists. I had to *do* something, to prove we were more than animals for slaughter.

I glanced desperately up into the golden sky. It was too early for the stars—too early for the moons, Akku or Zella or Aire. But the sun still shone, a steady bright light in the sky. Epsilon Eridani. Eps Eridani, we called it on the ship. But that wasn't their name for it. I knew because I'd dreamed it, because the boy had whispered it into my ear even as I'd slept.

"Xarki! Xarki!" I screamed, pointing up at a sun that shone like a polished coin in the sky.

The music finally stopped.

"Xarki! Xarki!" I screamed, gesturing wildly. "The sun! That's what you call it, right? And the moons? Akku, Zella, Aire?"

My voice cracked, was wild and raw. Everyone had turned toward me now, even Ettie, who looked like she'd just woken up from a pleasant but mildly puzzling dream. The creature who stood before her lowered his silver spike, holding it limply. He gazed toward his closest companion.

"Ahatho raizaz!"

"Raizaz eddi ahatho, taurax zhiesesik!" The creature in the vehicle bared his teeth. A disagreement, perhaps? We all stood there in helpless confusion as they growled at one another, blood soaking through all of our clothes.

"Tauoso vhesesazhi taurax," the musician said. There was a hint of resignation in his wheezy voice. He reached out over the lip of his vehicle and grabbed Aleksandra by the crook of her arm. But now that the spell was broken, she resisted, twisting and struggling in his grasp.

"What are you doing?" she snarled. "Where are you taking us?"

The creature lifted her effortlessly into the vehicle. Soon the others were rounded up too, herded into the craft's wide cab. The dismay and fear was clear on their faces. But I walked willingly toward the creatures, my head held high. I knew that if we were ever going to reach the city—if we were going to escape Zehava's wilderness and the creatures that roamed her forests—then we'd need their help. As I went to scramble into the vehicle, one of the creatures gripped his weapon tight.

"*Ososhum es!*" he snapped. I stared at him, my gaze even, trying to ignore the frantic way my heart seemed to fill up my mouth.

"Raza Ait," I replied. "We need to go to Raza Ait. City of Copper. Do you understand? Raza Ait."

The creature's wide mouth split open, showing teeth, too many teeth—hundreds of them, as sharp as needles, as hungry as wolves. He took his weapon's tip, nudging it against my ribs.

"Hyuuuu-mon?" he asked darkly, in a tone that chilled me to the bone. I sat down in the craft beside Ettie and prepared for take-off.

"Yes, human," I said simply as the vehicle's glass lid lowered over us.

8

The craft moved far faster than our legs could have possibly carried us, streaming first only a few meters from the ground and then higher and higher still as we sped southward. Below, the trees became sparser; the forests became frozen plains, uninhabited save for an occasional slow-moving beast. But I think I was the only one who saw the beasts, the only one who couldn't help but glimpse down through the glass and watch the scenery change. The rest of them—Aleksandra, Laurel, Rebbe Davison, Jachin, and Ettie—

all sat silently, their clothes and faces splattered with two shades of blood—human and beast both. They looked like they'd had the air wrung out of them. Now they were nothing more than stone.

"I can't believe it killed him," Laurel said at last, but faintly. Her voice was almost swallowed up by the wind. Before I could respond, Aleksandra gave a hiss.

"Get a hold of yourself. Do you think I had time to mourn when I learned my mother died?"

I glanced away from the shifting landscape, from the blue lakes and white mountaintops that glittered below, and over to where Aleksandra sat with her chin angled up. It was a strange fiction, the idea that she had *learned* that her mother had died, rather than drawing the blade across her mother's pale skin herself.

"Of course not," Aleksandra said, answering the question when Laurel didn't. "I knew there was still work to be done. More important things that I needed to attend to."

She met my gaze, her dark eyes boring into me. Hate. They were filled with hate. I'd saved *all* of their lives, and yet she watched me now with gritted teeth and poison on her tongue. It didn't make any sense to me—she was the captain's daughter, the leader of a great rebellion, a killer. And I was nothing more than a sloppy, selfish girl.

But maybe I wasn't. Maybe I had something she wanted. I knew things about Zehava that no one else did: words, geography. Thanks to the boy, I could communicate with the strange creatures that populated our new home. Aleksandra glared and glared. I forced my eyes down into my lap, where my hands were clutched so tightly that my fingers had started to go numb.

"What work do I have left to do?" Laurel said. "I crashed the shuttle, and now Deck . . ." Her words became strangled, then died. Out of the corner of my eye, I saw Rebbe Davison reach an arm out. He tucked Laurel's shoulders under it, pulling her close.

"You'll be okay," he said softly. "You'll be okay."

But Aleksandra didn't say anything, and I didn't either. I still felt her eyes burning into me, as steady as starlight, as the craft streamed through the air.

The creatures were like my boy, but then again they weren't. Separate races, maybe. Or closely related species. I counted their differences. He was tall and as thin as a reed; they were smaller and squatter. His eyes were far-spaced and lozenge-shaped in his bald head; their flesh was lightly furred, and they had close-set eyes. His teeth were small behind thick lips. Their mouths seemed to hold dozens of fangs.

They spoke among themselves as we traveled. They seemed to be arguing, baring their teeth between their words. Jachin watched them with peculiar intensity. I wondered what his biologist's mind made of them, of their smooth, efficient movements and their three-fingered hands. As I studied them—their small bodies, draped in loose fabric, as fragrant as flowers under the feeble winter sun—I heard Mara Stone's voice in the back of my head, listing the impossibilities. She would have said that it was unlikely that we'd find a humanoid species here. One that was bipedal, one that used language as we did, one that hunted and used technology and argued in a manner hardly any different from man. It was some kind of stroke of luck, insane and unlikely.

There's no such thing as luck, came the memory of Mara's voice. If she were here, what could I have possibly said in response? Chance then, as slim as a splinter. But the proof was right there in front of us. There were people on Zehava. Sentient people. Humanoids, at that.

"They don't breathe," Jachin said suddenly. I turned toward the creatures, who bickered over the craft's controls. Beside him Rebbe Davison snapped his head up.

"What? How is that possible?"

"Their chests don't move, not even when they speak. Their respiratory systems must be completely different from ours. Who knows how they vocalize?"

He was right. As they argued, their bodies were strangely still, the fabric that wrapped their torsos not stirring a single millimeter. I suppressed a shudder. Less like us than I thought, then. That would comfort Mara, if she ever had the chance to meet these creatures. She'd never been one to believe in miracles.

"They might respire passively," I suggested. "Through pores in their skin, or stoma. Like . . ."

I trailed off, remembering the vines that had fled from Deklan's touch—the vines that had reached out to envelop him when his body had collapsed on the forest floor.

"Like what?" Rebbe Davison pressed. I shook my head. It seemed too absurd to contemplate. But then my eyes caught the craft's pilot as he curved his body back, reaching for a hunk of meat from the cabin. It bent too far, wrong. Like there weren't any bones inside.

"Like plants," I said faintly. "Like plants."

Chuckles arose from the others, weak laughter. Even Laurel, in her tears, cracked a dim smile. Not Ettie, though. She set her little fists on her hips, jutting out her lower lip.

"It's not funny!" she said, then spared a proud glance to me. I gave her a grateful nod.

But inside I was cringing. *Plants?* The idea wasn't even miraculous. It was absurd.

Soon plains melted away into marshy bogs crowded by ice floes. At first the craft's shadow was the only thing that could be seen moving across the gray, dappled ground. But then hulking shapes joined it. Beasts—hundreds of them—moving in a herd through the swamp. They kept their young at the center of the pack, but even they were as a big as a shuttle craft. Beneath their massive feet they left a stretch of flattened mud wherever they went.

"Megafauna," Jachin said, gazing over the craft's edge. "Destructive, at that. Their caloric needs would be huge, as would their methane output. It might explain the lack of genetic diversity."

I looked at our captors, packed into the front of the craft with their rotting spoils. The driver was moving his spindly fingers over a console built into the craft's dash. This time they didn't park the vehicle or disembark to hunt. They only noted the presence of the herd, recorded it, then sped rapidly through the sky.

"They're not the top of the food chain, though," Rebbe Davison said. Jachin nodded in agreement. Then his expression shifted, darkening.

"HaShem help us," Jachin said. "Imagine if we'd continued east. What if we'd encountered a herd? We'd be mincemeat."

No one said anything. The sound of the motor was high and whistling. At last I forced a smile—but a jangly one, full of nerves.

"It's funny you're religious," I said. "Mara always told me that religion and science were incompatible."

Jachin frowned at the notion.

"My parents gave me my faith," he said. "When the Council assigned me my vocation, I worried it meant I would have to abandon those beliefs. But the more I learned about evolution, the more

it became clear to me. How would such a complex system develop without the help of God's hand? Sometimes I think that we wonder about the afterlife, about a higher power, because it helps us endure. No other Terran animal has such an awareness of his own mortality. And none has been as resilient as us either."

"But we haven't had God on the ship," Rebbe Davison said. I could tell from his expression that this was an old argument, one they'd rehashed many times before. "And we've gotten along fine."

"We've *lived*," Jachin replied. "But have we *thrived*?"

Had I? I stared down at my hands. There was blood caked under the nails. The truth was, I'd never worried before about living well. I'd been too busy just barely surviving.

"Hey," Ettie shouted, drawing me out of myself as she pointed out toward the horizon. "What's that?"

We all turned, staring out past the craft's copper walls. The swamps had faded, and the beasts with them. In their place was a sprawling complex of white stone and green copper, hundreds of kilometers across. It spiraled out from the crowded center like a web growing wider and wider as it had expanded. Like our ship, the main hub was capped by bubbled glass. But this glass was ancient, fractured by a thousand tiny cracks. Brassy metal and sandstone structures towered up inside it, each one trying to touch the ceiling overhead. And a blood-colored jungle seemed to glow inside the city's walls.

Raza Ait. I had named it in my mind without even realizing it. It was the first city we'd ever seen, many times the length of our ship and far more surprising. We watched it grow longer beneath us as the metal capsule came in close.

I spoke softly, speaking aloud without thinking. "The copper city."

But the sight of it didn't fill me with relief. Because in my head all I could hear was the echo of the boy's voice, pitiful and lonely; all I could see was the wounded look in his eyes as he'd drawn his hands away. *The city where I die,* he'd said. I found myself crossing my fingers in my lap, hoping against hope that it wouldn't be true.

Hoping that my boy was a survivor too.

The city was gated with bars of towering copper filigree, dozens of meters high. Through the gaps we could see the shadows of buildings, though we couldn't touch them, not yet. Especially not after the hunters tied our hands in front of us with lengths of synthetic rope.

At the gates we were met by a retinue of aliens. Their clothes were finer than the others, though they, too, carried long metallic prods at their sides. As the gates swung open, groaning on hinges gone green, the aliens examined us with black, lively eyes. In whistling tones they conversed with one another. Then they lifted our arms, smelled our hair, bared their teeth. I watched as Aleksandra pulled away from one of them, growling, as though their touch seared her skin. But I stayed as still and calm as I could. For one thing I didn't want to scare Ettie, who stood just a small way up ahead, her bound hands twisting in their shackle. For another, I thought if I watched carefully, then perhaps I'd see my boy—if not among our fur-faced escorts, then definitely among the city's wider inhabitants.

The atmosphere inside the city walls was different. It was as warm and fragrant as summer here, the air as sweet as fruit left to rot on the *Asherah's* damp ground. On the ship such a smell would have only attracted houseflies. Here there were no insects. But there were people. Thousands of them. They loitered by the mouths of buildings and underneath the thick canopy of the interior forest. It seemed that they'd gathered for our arrival, and they craned their necks as we passed among them. Many of them were furred, small in stature. They seemed bold—dashing down the thoroughfares to catch a glimpse, grabbing for us as we walked by.

But they weren't alone. There were other creatures, smooth-skinned, their bodies shining like rubies in the afternoon sunlight. They wore gowns stitched from bolts of smooth, metallic fabric, but even from beneath the lengths of cloth, I could smell them, summer-sweet as they perspired. They kept to the edges of the streets, and though their gazes were no less curious, they seemed somehow afraid of us. Most clutched the nearby hands of their companions—long, three-fingered hands—and, owlishly, watched.

They stood three or four heads taller than the aliens who guided us through the streets; one or two heads taller than any of us. And as we passed, they twisted their spines, gazing down curiously. Their bodies coiled and crept like vines. It reminded me of something.

It reminded me of the boy.

He was here, he had to be. I whipped my head about, searching. But if he was tucked somewhere among all these bright, shining people, then I didn't find him. Only teeth and eyes and fingers greeted me, probing, cold. I stumbled at the sight, but then one of the creatures pressed his weapon against my spine, pushing me forward. I walked on.

Up ahead Ettie cried. I heard Rebbe Davison trying to comfort her, repeating over and over again that everything would be all right soon. But I didn't feel so certain. It was so crowded here—in the pavilion up ahead were hundreds of aliens, lazing beneath the dripping vines. And they all *watched* us, their toothy mouths open, murmuring "Hyuuu-man, hyuu-man" as we passed. No wonder Ettie was upset.

"I'm scared! I'm scared!" she panted, and her progress stopped dead. She wouldn't go any farther. The others from the *Asherah* turned back to look at her, but pressed by prods and alien hands, they all walked on. I felt my heart squeeze hard in my chest. Rushing ahead, I crouched down so that our gazes met. Her eyes were the color of mahogany, flecked with amber bits. And they were full of tears.

"Ettie," I said, my voice serious. I didn't want to lie to her. That's what the grown-ups had always done to me, telling me that my mother would be fine, that my family would be fine. They'd said that we just had to keep our chins up and live on and everything would be okay. But I'd been smart enough to hear their lies even then—even though people thought I was nothing more than a stupid little girl. Ettie was smarter than that now. "It's scary, isn't it? This place. So much bigger than the *Asherah*."

She reached her small, dirty hands up, cradling them over mine as she gave her head a fierce nod. "I don't like the way they look at me," she said, and let out another hiccup of tears.

"No," I said. Behind me a creature pressed his prod to my back. His mouth was open wide. There were probably four dozen teeth in there as, sharp as needles, all lined up in front of his bright purple tongue. "I don't either."

"Ettie!"

It was Aleksandra. Her hair was coming undone, stubborn black hairs worming out of the braid. She seemed to have lost all of her patience, all of her poise. Just another difference between her and her mother, I guess. Captain Wolff could keep up appearances, but Aleksandra's emotions were much closer to the surface of her pretty white face.

Ettie turned, staring fearfully at Aleksandra.

"What?"

"Pull yourself together. You're not a baby."

Her words might as well have been a slap, for the way that Ettie winced at them. In the distance I saw Rebbe Davison give his head a dismayed shake. My own brow furrowed. But Ettie didn't see that through her sheen of tears. She wiped her eyes against her shoulder. Her chin trembled. But soon it stilled.

"I'm sorry, Giveret Wolff," she nearly whispered. She trudged forward, her hair a black net over her eyes.

I gaped at Aleksandra. The edge of her lip ticked up at me.

"It's up to me to see that our people stay strong. Even the young ones."

But when I looked at Ettie, I wasn't certain that Aleksandra's words had helped one bit. Her small shoulders were hunched; her head hung down as if she couldn't bear to face the city that surrounded us. And what about the people Aleksandra had left behind—hundreds of them, packed like sardines into the tin can of our ship? How was she helping *them*?

But then I felt something cold against my back. A weapon's blunted end. I glanced behind me. There was an alien, snarling, showing every single tooth.

"I'm going! I'm going!" I said, and continued the long march into the heart of the city.

• • •

The dome overhead seemed to amplify the sunlight; it burned strong
enough that soon my body swam with sweat inside my flight suit.
The others didn't look much better off: Aleksandra's hair was pasted
to her neck. Perspiration rolled down Jachin's face in a steady stream.
Though Rebbe Davison's hands were bound, every few minutes he
still managed to wipe his palms against his flight suit trousers. And
Laurel?

Well, I couldn't blame the heat for her condition. She sniffled hard
again and again, trying to suck back the tears. But it didn't do any
good. By the time we reached the western edge of the city, where the
ground dipped into an overshadowed park, she'd slicked the entire
front of her flight suit. But she didn't seem to care, and if she did, I'm
not sure she could have stopped anyway—no matter what Aleksandra
said.

The aliens led us through the jostling crowds, past towering buildings that stretched like arms overhead, and through groves crowded
with fragrant fruit trees. Finally we reached a fenced area, where copper links were interlaced with sheets of synthetic fabric. It was a tent,
an enormous tent, with a hole at the center of the roof and smoke
streaming out. An alien stood guard at the gate; he nodded to our
captors.

"*Xadse zhosoui, xadse zalum zhieselekh,*" their leader said, and gave

Aleksandra Wolff's binding ties a fervent shake. Her eyes were wide, inflamed at the violence of his touch. But the guard only appraised us carefully.

"*Ezli aum aze zasum,*" he replied. Then he entered something into a keypad at the door and stepped aside to let us pass.

They didn't come with us. They just pushed us inside and left. Metal against metal rang out like a bell.

We struggled to right ourselves. Lifting myself from the dusty ground, I appraised the situation. Under a white canopy yellow light danced and flickered. Meager lean-tos had been constructed, all around the same central point—a fire circle, not unlike the one we'd built at our own camp only days before. But this one had weeks' worth of ash ringing the stones.

It smelled different here from how it did out in the city. There the atmosphere smelled saccharine-sweet, filled with pollen and the promise of summer to come. Here the air was as pungent as vinegar, as feral as animal musk. This smell wasn't alien, not at all. It was the unmistakable smell of human body odor. I held my arm up to my mouth, hoping to block the scent.

The old shuttle crew crawled out of their tents on their hands and knees, scrambling to their feet to greet us. They seemed perplexed— as if they'd thought they might live and die in this city without ever seeing another human face. They were haggard, their faces gaunt, their hair frizzed back in thick ponytails that had begun to turn to dreadlocks. Some of them still wore flight suits, stained beneath the armpits, the once-white fabric gone murky and brown. The others were dressed in the worn, holey cotton they'd donned the day they'd left the ship. They drew close, removing the bindings from our hands.

I took in the gathered travelers. They were all there, all nine of them. And though I almost didn't recognize her at first, soon my gaze caught sight of a familiar face. Dirty, her black curls lank and dust-grayed against her shoulders. But unmistakable. Hannah. My sister-in-law.

"Terra?" she shouted, laughing. She pushed past the others to reach me, then buried me within a bear hug. I staggered back, but soon was lost within her arms. It didn't matter to me how bad she smelled, or how dirty her clothes were, or, how much she'd missed of what had transpired on the ship—the dingy council rank cord was still sewn to the shoulder of her uniform. It mattered that she was familiar, that she was safe. Living and breathing right next to me, her heart beating beside mine.

I heard Aleksandra let out a snort, as though the sight of our embrace disgusted her, or worse. But by then the others had drifted away—gone to embrace the shuttle crew, the fellows who we'd thought we'd lost. This time Aleksandra was left standing alone, her curled lip her only companion.

9

annah held me at arm's length, appraising my condition. I examined her as well. There was a scar on her forehead, where blood, caked with hair, had been allowed to congeal. But she was alive and otherwise whole—in better condition than the other flight crew members. One had an arm in a cast, the skin all swollen and yellow beneath the bandages, the fingers uselessly limp. Another was missing the entire front row of his teeth. But that was old news to her; Hannah was used to their injuries.

She brushed *my* hair aside, gave a sniffling smile, and said, "Terra, what happened to you?"

I grinned through my shock and exhaustion. "We crashed in the wilderness. Out in the mountains up north."

She glanced back over her shoulder to Aleksandra. "The Council let you go? Didn't they get our message? We can't settle here."

I gazed back too. Aleksandra shifted, smirking.

"The Council doesn't rule us anymore," she declared proudly. At her word, the rest of the flight crew turned to stare. She touched two fingers to her heart. "My mother, may her spirit rest, was murdered. I rule the ship now, with the Children of Abel at my side."

Murmurs of dismay and confusion rose up from the crew. Hannah took me by either shoulder, her expression frantic. I'd forgotten, in my relief at seeing her, who she really was. Daughter of two Council members. Gold thread was knotted through that rank cord.

"My parents," Hannah said, her words coming out in a rush, "are they okay? And Ronen? Alyana?" Her voice choked on the name of her daughter, the peanut of a baby girl she'd left behind.

"I—" I said, then hesitated. I'd left Ronen in the ship's bow with the other Council members. I'd run away from them, fleeing toward the dome. At the time I'd thought I could help. Save Captain Wolff, maybe, from her daughter's hands. But what had I forgotten in my hurry? People—people I loved—that I'd left behind. I hung my head.

But not Aleksandra. She simply gripped the radio in hand and spoke right over the others.

"My men and women report that the Council-loyal have holed themselves up in the ship's bow where the life support systems are housed," she said. "They're following that brat Silvan Rafferty. He's yet to make his move, but we have reason to believe that he's planning retaliatory attacks against those who have refused to join him."

She paused. Her tone went icy. "Of course, if that happens, my men will have no choice but to neutralize any threats. Still eager to join your parents, Hannah? Be a good Council girl?"

Hannah's hands dropped down.

"No," she said quickly. "Of—of course not."

Aleksandra turned to the closest shuttle crew member, the man whose arm was all swollen and green.

"Show me the perimeter," she demanded. "We need to start planning our escape."

With his good hand he rubbed his ratty beard. "Yes, ma'am," he said at last, and led Aleksandra toward the back of the camp. Hannah turned to me. She tucked her hand under my elbow, pulling me to the circle of charred logs and spent ash.

"What's happened up there?" she asked as she pulled me down to the hard ground beside her. I didn't know what to say at first as the others began to gather around us. I turned pleading eyes to Rebbe Davison, but he only bowed his head.

"Tell her," he said.

So I did. Not everything, of course. I didn't tell her about the poison—didn't mention that night in the Raffertys' quarters, clouding that bottle with powdered foxglove. I didn't yet tell her about the blood on my hands.

But it was easy—surprisingly easy—to talk about the Children of Abel. I told Hannah about the meetings in that musty library, about the librarian and how he'd once passed messages among us all. I told her about the journal that had been shared between the women of my family, all those hand-marked pages about the first rebels and how they'd resisted the Council every chance they could. And I told her about the riots. The people had flooded the dome, jubilant, drunk, their chants and shouts echoing under the ceiling of glass. They took the granaries. The fields. The shuttle bays. As I spoke, Hannah held her hands between her knees, giving her head a few forceful shakes.

"No, no," she said softly. "They couldn't. They couldn't. Didn't you get our message?"

I remembered the grainy video I'd watched with Silvan in the command center. The air around us had seemed alive, electric as I'd listened to Hannah's words. But mostly my attention had been on the men in the background, with their translucent skin and endless black eyes.

"We did, but it was too late. The riots had already started."

Silence stretched out, the only sound the wind stirring the camp's white walls. I leaned forward, watching Hannah intently. "What happened down here? What happened to you?"

I touched my hand to her hairline, to the brown scab that split her forehead.

"It was awful," Hannah said at last. She nudged at the hard earth with the toe of her boot. "Do you know what the locals call their world? Aur Evez. 'The crowded land.' The cities are packed, and the wilderness is filled with *monsters*, Terra. There's no room for us here, and even if there were, the Ahadizhi—"

"Who?" asked Jachin, sitting forward on his log. Hannah pressed her lips into a wistful smile.

"The furry ones, with all the teeth. They're carnivores. Hunters. They see us as no different from the animals outside. When we first reached the city after landing, we were hopeful. They ignored us initially. But then something changed. They attacked us. I thought we would be torn apart."

"If it weren't for the Xollu, we'd be dead. The tall ones? Travel in pairs? They're scientists. Scholars. They saved us so that they could study us. But they still don't understand."

"Understand what?" Rebbe Davison prodded. Hannah only

stared at him. Finally one of the crew members, a young man with dirt-darkened curls, answered for her.

"Animals," he said. "They don't understand animals. They're not like us. It took us days to figure it out. The tall ones, the Xollu, they don't eat at all. They seem to survive off water and sunbeams. They don't even need to breathe. Even the Ahadizhi move like branches in the wind. They're plants. That's our theory, at least. The only thing that would explain it."

We all went silent, staring into the fire. It fit with everything I'd noticed about the planet, the way that the vines tripped through the forests, the way that the hunters had moved, lithe and flexible but not breathing a single breath. And yet it was ridiculous. Completely ridiculous.

"Plants?" said Rebbe Davison. "It can't be. It just can't."

I thought of the boy, of his smooth, tender hands. Of his body, pressed beside mine, cool and fragrant. It seemed right. But it also sounded absurd. What would Mara Stone have to say about this?

"Good thing we brought a botanist," Jachin said. His lips lifted wryly. It was *supposed* to be a joke.

But nobody laughed. Not even me.

When the sun began to fade through the tent's walls, Hannah rose from the ground and took my hand in hers.

"Come with me!" she said. "All of you."

The others scrambled to their feet, dusting off their dingy clothes. But Aleksandra didn't like to be told what to do. She stayed where she was at the edge of the fire, scowling into it.

"Why?" she asked.

Hannah led us across the compound to where the tents shivered in the warm wind. Her smile was thin, a little ruthless. She wasn't like the rebels, who fell into line so easily at the sight of their fearless leader. In fact she hardly seemed to have any tolerance for Aleksandra at all.

"Dinnertime," was all she said.

With that, the gate clanged open. A gang of Ahadizhi came in, hefting a garishly painted cart behind them. They hummed as they worked, throwing down slabs of green, fatty meat. Though the sound was tuneless, meandering, I still had to fight the urge to drift close again. Even Aleksandra stood, watching them, a hungry intensity in her eyes.

But they ignored her, pushed the cart away, and left without so much as a growl.

The crew set upon the food like a pack of wild animals. Dipping their arms into the green puddles of blood, they sorted out the meat that was too slimy, too fetid, too old. Then they began to build a fire to cook it all down.

"When we first got here," Hannah said, spearing a chunk of meat on a spit, "they didn't seem to understand that we needed to eat at all. Then they started giving us food, but we had no way to cook it. We were sick, all of us, for days. I thought we'd die. Until their translator came in and suggested fire."

"Translator?" I asked. Hannah didn't seem to hear the eagerness in my voice. She only gave a small nod, hefting the meat over the smoking coals.

"He's a Xollu, but he's not like the rest of them. Honestly, we thought they all were nothing more than savages at first. Shouting at us and shoving us around. But then one afternoon he walked in. He held his hands up high, like this"—she lifted up her free palm to show me what she meant—"and he said, as clear as day, 'Hel-lo.' I think he'd been listening to us for ages."

"He's the one who told you," I said, watching the flame char our dinner, wrapping it up in blue and orange and black, "all about the Ahadizhi and all of that? And the name of the planet? Aur Evez?"

"Yeah," she said. She drew the spit out of the fire, tearing at the burning meat. Once I'd admired Hannah for her poise; she'd been the mannered daughter of two Council members, after all. Now so much of that had fallen way. She was only a person now, dirty, half-starved. She offered me a sliver of meat. I took it, chewed. "He's almost nice to talk to. All of the Xollu seem curious—you'll see, later. But he's the only one who has a handle on Asheran. He's friendly. Even if he's, you know, different."

I *didn't* know. Still chewing, I shook my head. Hannah watched me, considering.

"They call him a *lousk*. The others, I mean. At first we thought it was his name."

"But it's not?"

"No." Her lips pursed. "I'm not sure what it means. 'Outcast,' maybe. There's something sad about him. Don't take this the wrong way, but he almost reminds me of you. He seems to carry his sadness with him, like his heart has been shattered to bits."

My heart was in my throat, pounding out a panicked beat. I thought of the boy, and his arms around me, and his fingers cold against my burning skin. I thought of the way I felt when I was dreaming, so happy that I was afraid the forests around me would be burned away by the force of my joy.

"What do you mean, 'you'll see, later'?" I asked, eager to change the subject before she heard the labored, frantic movements of my heart. Hannah shrugged her thin shoulders and tore off another strip of meat.

"They come every morning," she said, "drag us away in groups to study us. I hate it. It makes me feel like an animal in a cage. We need to get out of here, Terra. They'll never see us as *people*, only as lab specimens." She wiped her mouth on the back of her sleeve and looked toward Aleksandra, who still stood over the fire, staring down into it as it burned.

"You know, I never liked her," she said, cocking her thumb back, "but I'm glad she's going to get us out of here."

I bit down on my lip so hard that I tasted blood.

That night Ettie, Laurel, and I all piled into Hannah's tent. It was so much warmer there than it was in the world outside the city gates. We stripped off our flight suits; Hannah handed me a dirt-stiff undershirt and a pair of shorts she'd worn on the day of the crash, to cover up my bare limbs. Even that was almost too much as we laid out our sleeping rolls and tucked ourselves in for the night. It was funny, to watch Hannah put a protective arm around Ettie. I guess she'd missed being a mother, all that nurturing gone to pot as she waited for rescue on the planet. Ettie seemed to be growing used to the treatment too—the grown-ups holding her, comforting her, protecting her from the savage world beyond. Which was how it should be, I thought. If we were going to survive here, we'd have to learn to be a true community, not just a collection of families with only gossip holding us together.

Together they tumbled toward sleep almost immediately. But not me, and not Laurel. She'd hardly spoken since the beast had struck

Deklan down. Now her eyes were like two shining stones in the darkness. They gleamed like glass, polished, sharp. After a moment, both of us tucked down inside our sleep sacks, she began to cry, letting out tiny gasps of breath.

"Laurel," I whispered. I reached a hand out, offering it to her. She stared ahead. At last she put her clammy hand in mine.

"I can't believe that he's gone, Terra. We were always friends. For as long as I can remember."

I remembered too. The pair of them, holding hands in school, walking together, laughing and joking, long before the rest of us had discovered what boys were for. His friends had been cruel ones, jeering, teasing. But I'd never heard him say a truly unkind word to Laurel.

"You loved him," I said.

"Of course I did." Her answer was quick—almost defensive, as if the suggestion otherwise offended her. And then the heat dripped away from her words, and she was crying again, worse this time. "Of course I did."

I did the only thing I could. I held her. We'd never been friends, not really. Before that day in the library, I knew almost nothing about her life outside of school. But we were the same now, the two of us. Not only because we'd been through so much together—the rebellion and the riots, the crash and our long journey south—but because we'd both lost people we'd cared about. It was like a scar that we both wore, a secret sigil that made us different from everyone else.

As I clutched Laurel to me, rubbing her heaving shoulders, I thought of Hannah's words about the translator. She'd said he was like me—that he carried his broken heart with him wherever he went. I wondered if he'd lost someone too.

"Terra?" Laurel asked, her voice coming, shaky and weak, through tears. She pulled away from me, leaving a soggy gap in her wake.

"Yeah?" I whispered back.

"I don't know how I'm going to do this. How I'm going to live on without him."

I let out a long, low sigh. As I pressed my head against the cold ground, I thought back to Abba. Since his death I'd learned a lot about survival. About living on—the very thing that he'd never been able to do. What would I have told him if I could have?

"At first it will be hard. Almost impossible. You'll wake up and feel like Deklan's been pulled from you and all that's left is his silhouette inside your body. It will be with you all the time. Every breath you take will be a reminder that he's not here and breathing anymore. People will try to tell you things to make you feel better, but it will only make it worse. 'It's so sad,' they'll say, and you won't be able to tell if they miss him because of *him* or because their grief will make them look noble. Sometimes it will feel like they're trying to steal *your* grief, your story.

"But you'll keep breathing, and you'll keep living. And one day you'll be sitting down at breakfast or talking to a friend and you'll stop. The blood will drain from your fingertips, and you'll go so pale, because you'll realize that it's been hours since you last thought about him. Maybe even days. His loss will always be with you. You won't forget. But time will move on and it'll get easier, and easier until one day it's just something that's always been there. A part of you, but not all of you. Not anymore."

She didn't say anything. A warm breeze stirred the cotton walls. I looked up at the dark shadows in the corners of the tent.

"It'll surprise you," I said at last. "You'll be changed by his death, sure. When something like this happens, it blows your world apart. But in a way, when you patch your world back together, it'll be stronger than it was. *You* will be stronger than you were. I promise, Laurel. Really. You'll be okay."

There was another hiccuped breath. At last, in a small, sad voice, she said, "Thanks, Terra."

She turned her back toward me, and I, too, turned away.

I didn't know if what I said helped her. I hoped it did, as she stumbled toward sleep that night. What I did know was that my own heart was heavy, my mind leaden with doubt as I pulled the covers over my head and retreated into the dark.

• • •

He waited for me in our usual place, in the leaves and vines that formed a bed in the warm black earth. Maybe I should have gone to him with questions. Maybe I should have asked him where he slept in the city that night, what sort of person he was, if he really was a *plant*. But, as always, my heart was impetuous. It wanted what it wanted. It didn't want to think things through, didn't want to ask questions or talk.

I wanted him. His mouth, his hands. As soon as I saw him, broad in shoulder, narrow in waist, and familiar, utterly familiar, I pulled him down against me. I felt the cool caress of his skin and the relief it offered. I *wanted* him. I made that clear.

His response was laughter, or something like it. He didn't tumble away, but he did look at me. His black-eyed gaze was steady; each eye held the very same promise—deep, and even, and true.

I'm here. I'm here, I said, hardly able to keep my excitement in. Looking in those lozenge-shaped eyes, I had the strangest sense of import. My ancestors had fled a dying planet. They'd traveled five hundred years. They'd lived and died all so I could be here with *him*, us tumbling our bodies in a bed of violet leaves. It made me giddy to think about it. I let loose peals of laughter too. Or something like it.

His fingers wrapped around my wrist like a vine. He watched me for a long time, smiling at first. But then that smile faded; his wide lips pressed together, hiding his rows of tiny teeth. That's when I felt it for the first time—the pain inside him. Worse than *anything* that I'd ever known. Worse, I think, than what Laurel felt that night. Worse than even the pain that had driven my father to fritter his life away. It made me want to cut myself open, to spill my guts out on the open ground. It made me feel halfway crazy. It was a desperate and ugly sensation; I found myself scrambling to get away. Not because I thought it was his *fault*. Of course not. Only because it hurt too much to stay there, his body aching on top of me.

I sat up in the soggy leaves, staring at him. He made himself small, drawing his knees to his chest.

I wanted to ask him questions. I wanted to demand answers—who did that to you, made you broken and jagged, strange? But this wasn't a night for questions. It was a night for touching, a night for feeling. I wrapped my arms around him. And even though he was stiff against me, cold to my touch, I ran my warm fingers over his shoulders, his arms. I touched him—his long fingers in triplicate, the smooth palm that had no life line at all. I knew I couldn't heal the fissure in him. The pain was too cutting, too ancient, too true. But I could try. I figured it could never hurt to try.

I'm here, I said again, rocking him against my body. His posture finally softened. He touched a hand to my face, feeling my eyelashes flutter against his hand. *I'm here. I'm here.*

10

orning was bright and muggy. I woke to sweaty limbs, a parched throat, and a strange, sad sensation deep in my belly—but I couldn't name it, couldn't quite pin it down. I put on my flight boots, pulled myself out of the tent, and went to the fire, where the others were already gathered. They talked in low tones, turning skittish glances left and right as if they were waiting for something. What, I couldn't be sure.

Laurel sat stooped over a log, eating a fist of burned meat. Her face was still puffy from the night spent crying, but it was no longer slick with tears. She glanced up at me and gave a weak smile. I wriggled my fingers back, then went to the stack of supplies the shuttle crew had stacked up just past the fire pit, hoping to find even a small ration of fresh water.

They'd lined the jugs up all in a row. Half were from the shuttles— the tempered polyglass that had been crafted by our ancestors and filled by a fleet of old women in preparation for our journey. The other half were of a foreign design. Their shapes reminded me of the curling flasks Mara Stone used in her research. Their bottoms were sturdy, but the necks looped and twisted. Each was corked with a plug of bright green wax. Some had been punctured, drained. But I found one still three quarters full. I jammed my thumb into the seal, break- ing it—and leaving a ring of dirt around the glass lip. I didn't even care. I held the mouth to my mouth, and drank and drank. It might have been alien water, but it was clean. Cold. Healing.

I was standing there, my head cast back, a bottle shaped like a swollen gourd pressed to my lips and the water dripping down my chin, when the gate at the front of the camp gave a great shudder. I turned, my stringy hair catching on my still-dripping mouth. It was through the blond veil of hair that I saw a line of Ahadizhi filter in. I understood then why the others had seemed so apprehensive. The Ahadizhi grabbed on to them with three-fingered arms, prodding them with their weapons. The whole camp was filled with flashes of light, sparks. Ettie let out a cry. It seemed to rise up over the cacophony of electricity. I dropped the bottle against the hard-packed dirt and went running, grabbing her by either shoulder before one of the Ahadizhi could do the same.

"Go hide," I told her, pushing her toward the tents. She scrambled forward, her hair a dark streak behind her. I watched her tuck herself into one of the rear tents and zip up the flap behind her. When I turned back, it was to a new sight.

The Xollu. They walked two abreast, skirting the edges of the camp. Their eyes were black holes bored into their smooth-skinned faces. But there was a flash of curiosity there too. They seemed to be appraising us, looking us up and down like we were animals being judged fit for slaughter.

The Xollu didn't take everyone. One by one they appraised us, touching their smooth fingers to our chins. I saw them give Jachin's scraggly beard a tug before they shoved him off with the other stubble-cheeked men. Standing shoulder to shoulder with Laurel and Hannah and Aleksandra, I watched as the Ahadizhi dragged the men forward and through the open gates. That's when I spotted him. The translator. He stood at the gate's edge, speaking in low tones to a Xollu pair beside him.

He was tall and lean. Though his shoulders were broad beneath his tunic, his waist was narrow. He was a Xollu, most definitely, in body and eye and tooth. But his flesh was a deeper shade than the rest of them. Indigo. That had been the name of my favorite pencil in the set my momma had given me years and years before. He matched it perfectly, whereas the others were mulberry and carmine and poppy. He alone was bright, bright blue.

I knew that color, knew how it would look over the pale slick of my belly. From a dozen meters away I knew how his body smelled, and even tasted. It was so strange to see him standing there, lips lifted to reveal a row of tiny needle teeth. The others were afraid, but not him. He put his hand on Rebbe Davison's shoulder, stopping him. He said something I couldn't hear, and Rebbe Davison responded meekly, tapping his hand against his own chest.

I needed to stop the translator, needed to get him to draw those night-dark eyes to mine. There had to be words that would turn his head toward me, that would compel him to bridge the gap between our bodies—meters and meters, entirely too many. I groped for syllables, sounds, reaching back through dreams. My lips found the name almost without thinking. Vadix. Vadix. I whispered it twice, tasting it.

Was that his name? He'd never told me, but somehow I knew. And now, having realized it, I couldn't hold the knowledge in any longer. Maybe I should have plotted, waiting for the perfect moment to take him aside and whisper it into his earslits. But what if that chance never came? I had to stop him—and fast, before the moment passed.

"Vadix! Vadix!" I called. "It's me, Terra! Vadix!"

I know he heard me—the long slits along the side of his face opened at the sound of my voice. But he was the last one to lift his head. When he did, his black eyes were less like glass and more like stone. Hard and solid, letting none of the day's weak light through. What did he see when he glanced up? A dirty girl, dressed in someone else's stained undershirt, waving her fingers through the open air? A fool? An animal?

Whatever he saw, it didn't matter. He put his three-fingered hand on Rebbe Davison's shoulder and pushed him through the open gate. Then he turned his back on me. He walked out of our camp without a single glance back. I called his name out one final time, but the syllables died on the muggy air.

In the awkward silence that followed, the Ahadizhi led the rest of the men out. The Xollu trailed after, their expressions grave as they clutched at one another. The gate slammed, and I fell down on one of the fire pit logs, my posture slumped, my shoulders sagging.

But the others didn't drift away. In fact, both Hannah and Aleksandra stood over me, looking equally perplexed. Maybe Aleksandra wanted to threaten me, to question my gall. But Hannah spoke first. There was weak laughter on her voice, but a question, too.

"Terra," she said, "I don't understand. How did you know his name? I never told you . . ."

Aleksandra stared at her, expression stony. Then she stomped off on her boot heels. I watched her go before I turned to Hannah again, lifting up my dirty hands.

"I don't know, Hannah," I said, because it was true. "I have no idea."

One night, when the path ahead was bleak, I sat with Rachel in the guest room of Ronen's home. The room was the same as always—same floral bedspread; same painting, done by some long-dead bubbe of ours, pinned up on the wall. But Rachel had changed. I'd changed too.

Once we'd talked only of boys, of jobs, of what the names of our children might be. We'd traded these dreams the way other children might trade marbles or jacks. We wove our futures together like an embroidered bracelet. But the path ahead was uncertain on that night, so Rachel's thoughts had turned inward. As was always the case back then, she talked about her religion, her newfound faith. Her hands moved quickly through the air. She gave me advice based on her readings, offered me stories that weren't often told on our ship. When I sat back on my heels, chewing my lip, she put her dark hand on mine.

"You don't believe, do you?"

I didn't. I wanted to be filled with the same passion and assuredness that she was, to feel my heart swell, safe and warm, in my chest. But it didn't. I remained closed to the possibility. When I thought about life after death, the only thought I had was for the ground's cold embrace. When I thought of a higher power watching over me, I felt only uneasy, not bolstered like Rachel did. No, I didn't believe. I shook my head and said so.

"It must be so sad for you," she said, dropping her chin to her chest, "living a life without miracles. All alone in the world."

I didn't know what to say. At the time, I didn't say anything—just sat up straight and changed the subject.

But I've thought a lot of those words in the year since. Turned them over and over in my mind, examining them. Because the truth is, Rachel was wrong. My life was hard, even then. And sure, I was lonely sometimes. Still am, on days when the winter feels endless, on the days when the storms are whiteout thick and the light feeble.

And yet I'm never, ever alone.

I've thought back on Rachel's words and decided that the very fact of my being—the very fact of yours—is miracle enough for me. Of all the people who could have been hatched on that ship, all the genetic combinations that could have ever come to pass, mine was hardly likely. My ancestors could have just as easily perished on Earth, or on the journey over. I could have died in the shuttle crash, or on the long trek to Raza Ait. Dead, like Deklan Levitt, a beast horn through my chest.

And you? Well, we know how unlikely you were. Yet there you are, and here I am. We found each other, even though the odds were stacked against us. I'm here writing you this journal, these words.

It might not mean much to you. I know that, like Rachel, you have religion. I know there are times when you care for me despite and not because of my lack of belief.

But I thought it might be good to tell you, at least, that because of you, I believe in miracles. The miracle of our meeting, however unlikely it might have been. Because of you, I have faith—faith that I am loved.

Back then, though? Back then I wasn't so certain. When the path ahead was dark, and we were so, so new . . .

PART TWO

THE BOY

11

We waited. The afternoon wore on with no sign of the men. We waited more. I could feel the sweat ring my armpits and stream in little rivers down my back. I sat beside Hannah by the fire pit's edge, watching the coals shimmer, watching Ettie gather rocks and sticks from the outskirts of the camp and toss them in. Someone should have scolded her, telling her not to feed the meager flames. But no one did. We were all too spent.

Except for Aleksandra. She stood at the far end of the ring of stones, shouting into her radio.

"What do you mean, he has the life support systems? You were supposed to *stop* this from *happening!*" Her voice was filled with strange accents. I snapped my head up. Despite the heat of the day, my hands had gone cold.

"What's Silvan done now?" I asked. But she furrowed her brow and turned her shoulder away.

"Don't you worry about Silvan," she said. "You had your chance to take care of him."

In her hand the radio spat static and white noise. A garbled voice came stuttering from the speaker. "He's threatening . . . Wishes to return to Earth . . ."

Beside me Hannah let out a low cough of laughter.

"Return to Earth. That's an idea if I ever heard one. Our ancestors fled for a reason."

I watched as Ettie flung another handful of packed dirt into the fire. The flames billowed, loosing sweet white smoke on the air. I thought of all the things we'd learned of Earth in school—how after the asteroid hit, the planet was plunged into an endless winter, the sky as black as night even in the middle of the afternoon. Crops would have died. Animals, too. Our planet had betrayed us. There was no way we could return to it now.

"I never thought it would come down to this," Hannah said. "Choosing between a dead planet and a hostile one."

Hostile. It certainly seemed true. Zehava's frozen wilderness, with its strange living trees and bloodthirsty beasts, offered little sanctuary for my people. But still I wanted to believe that there was some hope left. Even if the aliens were strange, they were people, weren't they? Speaking. Thinking. There had to be some way to reach them. I thought of the look on the boy's face as I called his name. He didn't seem angry. He seemed *afraid.*

At last the gates were thrown open. I jumped at the rush of sound— alien, not human. Reedy, buzzing voices let out incomprehensible shouts. The Asherati men were jostled and pushed by Ahadizhi, but they themselves were strangely silent as they streamed into the quarantine camp. Ettie raced toward Rebbe Davison. Her little fingers grabbed at the thick ropes that bound his wrists, twisting and pulling until he was free. The Xollu at the back of the crowd watched this development, their heads cocked to the side as if they were jotting down mental notes. I didn't have to search the line of alien visitors to know that my boy wasn't among them. My heart was too still; my breath too calm. I rose from the log and went to help the other crewmen free of their bindings.

"Thank you," said the shuttle pilot, a middle-aged man by the name of Aben Hirsch. He rubbed his rope-worn wrists where the skin had turned pink beneath his thick arm hair.

"What did they do to you?" I whispered. He flashed a small, unsteady smile.

"No worse than Doctor Rafferty's checkups. But their bedside manner leaves something to be desired."

Doctor Rafferty. My own hands fell against my thighs, limp and helpless. As the aliens left the camp, the gate slamming behind them, I found Aleksandra Wolff. She watched me, her delicate lips curled. Then she shoved a lock of hair behind her ear and lifted the radio to her mouth.

"Tell them we'll be returning soon," she said, speaking into it. "Tell them that we don't want any funny business until I'm back on the ship."

More static. At last a cough of words: "Aye, ma'am."

Aleksandra clipped her radio back onto her belt. She turned toward those of us who had gathered there, the men rubbing their wrists, the women squinting into the sun.

"My operatives have received word that Rafferty wants to return to Earth."

There was a murmur of dismay. Rebbe Davison's mouth fell open. "That's impossible. We don't have any fuel. And Earth is dead. The asteroid—"

"Fuel isn't an issue," Aleksandra said, looking away from her old friend. There was something cloistered, almost shamed about her expression. Her narrow mouth tightened as she glanced down at the dusty ground.

"Alex," Rebbe Davison said sternly. He was using his teacher voice, the one that compelled you to obey even if you should know better. "What are you talking about?"

"It was a fail-safe," she said, in the voice of a chastened little girl. "A secret. They couldn't tell the citizens, my mother said. Not unless we wanted to be diverted from our journey."

She lifted her head. Her voice hardened again, growing as chilly as the day outside the city's walls. "A fail-safe, in case we arrived and the planet was uninhabitable. Or worse. In case it wasn't there at all. Over the generations our captains told the people that we had impulse fuel enough for one trip, but that was a lie. We had enough for two. We could take off again if we needed. Take off for another planet. Take off for Earth."

"You *lied* to me?" Rebbe Davison asked. He stood not far from Aleksandra, shaking his head over and over again. "You *lied*?"

"Not me," Aleksandra said. "It was the Council. It was Mother. I knew only because I overheard her telling that boy—"

"What boy?" Rebbe Davison prodded. Aleksandra's lips tightened.

"Rafferty! Her new captain. Who else?"

"We can't return to Earth," Laurel said in a strange, dull voice. She'd been sapped of all passion, all energy. I wondered if this was one development too many for her. "It's dead. We can't—"

"Of course we can't," Aleksandra agreed. "And we can't reach an accord with the natives, either. Which is why we need to break out of this camp, return to the ship, and settle on the southern continent. There are no cities there. It's uninhabited. Which means it's as good as ours."

But the shuttle crew wasn't so easily swayed.

"What if it's uninhabited for a reason?" Aben asked. "How do we know we can settle there?"

"It doesn't matter. We'll be safe in the dome. It's what it was designed for. Not for crazy, blind journeys back to a ruined planet."

The dome. I thought of the honeycombed glass ceiling, the fields, so familiar, that now lay fallow in the winter cold. My heart hardened against the possibility. I couldn't return there—not to fly off to Earth, and not to land beneath the Zehavan skies, either. I knew every blade of the *Asherah*'s grass, every single crack in the cobblestone. It was less a home to me now and more a prison. No matter how crowded, no matter how full of bloodthirsty hunters, even the walled, foreign city of Raza Ait was better than returning to the ship.

Hostile was better than dead. New was better than old. Rebbe Davison seemed to think so too.

"We overthrew the Council so that we could be rid of the dome, Alex. You can't really be suggesting—"

"We need to make do. This is our lot, Mordy." His child's nickname dripped from her lips with disdain. "Do you have a better idea?"

Rebbe Davison didn't answer. He only wrung his hands, hesitating. So I answered. I spun to face Aleksandra.

"What if I do?" I asked, and then winced—my words surprising even me.

"*You?*" she asked. Her lips lifted, revealing pale gums. I firmed my chin.

"Yes, me. Who saved us when we were attacked by beasts?"

"I would have taken care of that if you—"

"But you didn't. I know things, Aleksandra. Things about the planet that no one else knows."

"That doesn't matter," Aleksandra said. She looked at the others, her dark eyes narrowed into slivers. "The dome is the only place where we'll be safe."

"That's not true! In my dreams . . ." I began, but my words puttered off. Suddenly I wasn't certain what had made me so bold. I wanted to be strong—because my boy was here in the city, all fragrant flesh and smoldering eyes; because of the way that Ettie looked to me, desperate and afraid as she stood at the edge of the cluster of adults. But I didn't feel it. Aleksandra's hot gaze hadn't left me for a second.

"Dreams, Terra." Laurel said at long last. Her eyes were filled to the brim with an apology. I knew, then, that she'd lost too much to ever put her faith in someone like me. "They were only dreams. And they didn't stop Deklan from dying, did they? They didn't help one bit."

It wasn't fair. I'd tried to lead them *away* from the beasts—to keep them on the path to the city, to keep them safe. But that didn't matter to Laurel. All that mattered was Deklan, gone. She would have thrown me into the fire if it would get him back. I lowered my eyes, unable to escape everyone's stares.

Aleksandra set her hands on her hips, and then let out a long, withering sigh. She turned away from me as her voice rang out through the muggy air.

"I think our best option is brute force. Tomorrow morning we launch a counterattack on the aliens. We rush through the city and return to my shuttle."

"Alex," I heard Rebbe Davison say. He was shaking his head, his eyes as big as a pair of saucers. "That's absurd. We'll never make it through the city—"

"It's our best chance," she said flatly. "Our only chance."

I heard mumbles of agreement, assent. I knew then that it was useless. She'd captured their hearts long ago; now she held them too tightly in her thrall for someone like me to shake them free. So I didn't raise any objections.

But that didn't mean I wasn't afraid as I stomped off toward the fire. Her plan wasn't only dangerous for us—for my sister-in-law, for Rebbe Davison, for Laurel, and for Ettie. It might be dangerous for the translator, too. If Aleksandra had her way, he'd be tossed to the side like just another felled tree. The boy. My last, best hope.

I needed to save him. I needed to save us all.

"Vadix."

Sitting in the tent alone, the light filtered in all yellow and white, I let myself say his name. Not for the first time, but for the first time intentionally. I pushed it out into the air like it was an amethyst sliver of truth, one that I had somehow missed for the first sixteen years of my life, one that I was only now awakening to.

"Vadix." I stretched out the vowels, let the consonants buzz and then stop short on the tip of my tongue. "Vadix. Vadix."

I couldn't remember him speaking it. Not even in my dreams, as he wrapped his body around mine and drew his lips down the soft flesh of my neck. And yet still, I knew. He was Vadix, and he was real, and he was *mine*. How long had I lived in denial? Once I had told myself that they were only crazy, embarrassing dreams. Everyone had dreams, right? Rachel used to tell me about hers—she and Silvan, back in the alleyways behind her father's store. Koen, too, had fallen victim to dreams that shamed him. Hot dreams, he'd said. Wild dreams.

I turned over on my stinking blankets. It was time I admitted the truth to myself. My dreams were nothing like Rachel's dreams.

And they weren't like Koen's, either. Both Koen and Rachel might have dreamed of boys, of kisses, of frantic flesh pressed to flesh. But their dreams had never invaded the waking world with such color or force. They never dreamed of constellations and then, only after, found those stars shining overhead. They never dreamed of boys who then walked into their lives, speaking foreign languages, their alien bodies fragrant as summer flowers. I really *was* different from the other Asherati. I was freakish. Weird.

Aleksandra knew it. She'd seen that difference in me and sneered. But maybe my difference wasn't only a weakness. Maybe it could be a strength, too. After all, it had gotten us down from that mountain. And it had stopped the Ahadizhi from slaughtering us. I knew things. Things that Aleksandra didn't. Things that she could never, ever know.

His body. His mouth. His name.

"Vadix."

As I rose on shaking legs and pulled myself from the condensation-dusted tent, I saw Rebbe Davison break away from the others. He stood over me, staring into the fire—far enough away that it might have been coincidence or happenstance. When he spoke, it was out of the corner of his mouth.

"This is dreck, all of it. She's going to get us killed."

I watched her as she stood among them, proudly orating. Their

eyes were wide at the prospect of freedom; smiles lifted their lips.

"Look at her," I said. "She's their leader. She was born for it. They'd follow her off a cliff."

"Someone else could lead."

His words spilled out into the humid air with all the levity of lead. I turned to look up at him, though his gaze was still fixed forward into the fire.

"What? Me?"

"Yes, you. You were right—you know things about this planet that no one else does. I don't understand it, but I know how powerful you are. Necessary."

I snorted. "Necessary? I'm not even a real botanist yet."

"With the right people behind you," Rebbe Davison said, his voice dipping down low, "you could be whatever you want."

When I didn't answer, Rebbe Davison bent over and tossed another log onto the fire. As the flames crackled and billowed, hiding us from the others, he flashed his gaze to me.

"Just think about it," he said, then rushed off to rejoin the others.

I did. Me, a leader. I imagined myself dressed in wool, my shoulders squared, my hair combed straight. It was absurd. There had been days when I'd wanted to belong, to be swept up in the tide of the Children of Abel, to feel loved, supported, safe. But I'd never wanted power. I'd never even considered it.

But he was right. My connection to the translator was a sort of power—a gift, unasked for, unearned.

Vadix. Vadix, I said to myself, the name just as much a question as an invocation.

Funny thing. In my head, I could have sworn I heard another voice come echoing back. Not the murmured, familiar sound of my own inner voice. But a strong tenor with a hint of music somewhere behind it.

Terra?

My eyes went wide. I stared into the flames, and waited.

Soon the Ahadizhi arrived again, brandishing their silver-handled prods. This time they grabbed the women. But we went willingly. Even Aleksandra rose from where she'd been crouched down for more than an hour, flicking her thick braid over her shoulder and lifting her chin up high as she stood. It was all part of her plan—comply for now so that the Asherati attack could catch the aliens off guard. Only Ettie hung back, hiding behind Rebbe Davison. Hannah bent low, putting her hands on her thighs.

"They won't hurt you, Ettie," she said, though her own owlish expression had some fear behind it. "They just want to study you."

Ettie turned to me.

"Aren't you frightened?" she asked. But I was too busy scanning

the scattered group of Xollu who had gathered around the gate. I didn't see him there, not at first, but I *felt* him, a steady pull that began somewhere deep in my belly and then tugged upward, through my throat and solar plexus before drawing me out.

"No," I said at last, as an Ahadizhi spun a length of rope around and around my wrists. One word ran through my mind. *Vadix. Vadix.*

Finally I found him—a flash of blue skin at the back of the crowd. I ambled forward, ignoring the sparking prods that stood in my way.

Vadix, I thought, hard. And just like that he lifted his black eyes up. I studied his features, forcing myself to look at him—really look—for the first time.

His body seemed as strange and boneless as the rest of them, moving with unnatural flexibility and grace. But there was something handsome about him too. He was tall and skinny, richly dressed in opalescent robes. The pleats and folds formed an oil slick of green, and they rippled with purple thread. The lips that murmured orders to the others—*"Zhesedi ate!"*—were thick and full. But serious. There wasn't even the slightest hint of a smile behind them. When he flashed his teeth, it was only for a moment, and then away again, gone. Hannah was right. He carried his sadness with him. I could see it in the firm line of his jaw, in his studied movements. I imagined I saw it even in the endless depths of his eyes.

Soon I stood in front of him.

"Vadix," I said, the words floating, strong and clear, between us, "I need to talk to you."

He tried to look away again, tried to deny it—deny me, deny us. I couldn't let him. It was either this or go back to the ship's dome. And I couldn't do that—my body objected to the very idea.

His fingers were moving as he spoke, but I caught his arm, holding one wrist in the cup of my bound hands. His deep blue skin was cold and smooth. There was none of the fine fur of my own skin, no wrinkles, no warmth of veins beneath. But there was something else. A jolt, raw and live. I hadn't known fire before I'd come to Zehava, but I knew electricity—the danger of exposed wires in the damp dome, the blue-white light of a single spark.

I startled back. He did too, his lozenge-shaped eyes gone huge and wild. My heart was frantic, thrumming in my chest as one of the Ahadizhi butted me with his prod and pushed me through the open gates.

But I heard Vadix call out to the Ahadizhi grunt, his strong tenor voice lifting a smile to my lips.

"*Tatoum dauosoum daidd esedezhi dheseolo ut daosoez xaizu. Dauosoum zadix dheseolo, voze eseouu, aum daosoez zhiahaoloe!*" He added, in Asheran, words that could be only for me, "Bring her to me."

12

The building they took us to might have been a hospital, but it was nothing like the three-storied square of old brick we knew on the ship. The outside was a narrow tower of green metal that reached up and up toward the sparkling cupola, and it was dotted with a hundred gleaming windows of every possible hue. Between the round panels of glass, violet vines craned upward, coating the sills with their curling fingers. The building branched toward the top into separate compartments, looking as much like a tree as it did any inorganic structure. But we wouldn't see the topmost towers—and we wouldn't glimpse the city below through colored glass.

Instead they took us into a basement. After the searing light of the afternoon, it was strange to step into a shadowed interior space again. The halls were painted white, and they sweat with copper-tinted condensation, leaving green streaks on the curved walls, and our mouths full of the taste of metal.

The Ahadizhi led us down the corridor. Most of the women were silent. Laurel kept her head low, her curls shadowing her face. Hannah just set her jaw, like she was used to every insult the aliens could possibly offer. Ettie cried silently. But if Aleksandra was afraid, she refused to show it. In fact, she wasted no time in finding me. We walked shoulder to shoulder like old friends. But of course we both knew better.

"I don't know what you're plotting," she murmured, "but whatever it is, it won't work."

At first her words did nothing to deter me. I walked with my shoulders squared. Then she leaned her arm into mine. From anyone else it would have been a fond, friendly gesture. But she pushed, hard.

My heart pounded wildly as I tried to grab the cool, slick metal of the wall. But before I could answer her, an Ahadizhi nudged me with his stick, whistling a command.

"Dhahare elez!"

I staggered to my feet, groping at the sloping wall with my bound hands. As I hurried to catch up, I shouted out to her.

"I'm not plotting anything!"

"I saw you and Mordecai chatting," she called back. "Remember who you are, Terra. A petty lackey, prone to fits of rage. We both know what you did to Mar Rafferty. Don't think I've forgotten."

I stopped where I stood, my mouth hanging open. I needed to say something, to strike her back, proving that I could be cunning and dangerous too.

"I saw what happened in that field!" I called, but Aleksandra only flicked her braid over her shoulder with her bound hands and kept walking.

"I don't know what you're talking about," was all she said.

But of course she did. I'd seen it, in that frost-covered cornfield, watched as red blood sank into the brown earth. Aleksandra was a killer. I was sure of that. And now she seemed intent on leading the rest of us toward destruction too. She glowered as the Ahadizhi separated us, shoving her into a cell. But there was nothing she could do, not yet.

As I sat in my own narrow compartment, I smoothed out my hair with one hand, sat straight and tried to look like someone who hadn't spent the last several days unwashed. Aleksandra's words had only galvanized my anger and my fear into something hard, hot—useful. I would convince Vadix to help us. He *would* be swayed to our side. Unlike Aleksandra, I knew that without the help of the aliens, all hope would be lost. Not just for me, though my stomach clenched to think that I might have a long road ahead alone. But all of us—Hannah and Laurel, Rebbe Davison and Ettie, too.

I shifted on the crinkly paper that covered the table, clutching my hands in my lap. My knuckles were veined with blue and yellow lines beneath the shadow of days of dirt. They weren't very strong hands. I could think of only one day they'd served me well—the day I shook that poison into Mazdin Rafferty's drink. But even that had been a tempestuous act. Nothing like that cool, calculated plot of Aleksandra's, when she drew her mother into that field and slit her pale throat. How many years had she waited for that moment? How had she found that strength, that patience? It seemed to be eluding her now, as she snarled and hissed accusations. But it wasn't as if my own heart were steady. It beat wildly, a series of staccato bursts. I drew in a breath and held it there. I needed to be calm, sane, if I was going to get the translator on my side.

The door slid open. There was Vadix. His mouth formed a silent line. Beneath the bright light, his skin was as translucent as a jewel. His lips, slightly wet, parted. But he didn't speak.

"Vadix," I said, testing his name against my tongue again. He flinched; it was a surprisingly human reaction.

"How do you know this name?" he asked. His voice was high and clear—it made it that much easier to hear his offense.

"I don't know," I said helplessly, lifting up my hands and dropping them against the paper. "You tell me—"

"Terra."

He said my name. *My* name, two syllables so ripe they dripped juice down onto the metal ground below. It was almost enough to shake my resolve away, to make my hands dart out, lace his fingers in mine, and draw him close to me. But not quite. My hands were still in my lap, and he stayed frozen near the door of the little room. Not breathing at all.

"This cannot be," he said at last. "You are an animal. You are made out of *meat*."

Despite the gravity of the situation, I wanted to laugh at that. The absurdity pulled at my stomach, drawing all the air from it. But he seemed so *serious*. To him it was no laughing matter. His narrow earslits widened as he waited for my response.

"They say you're a *plant*," I said. "Do you know how strange that is? A talking plant?"

He shook his head. It was a very human thing to do. Maybe it was something he'd picked up from watching the shuttle crew over these last few weeks. From watching us.

"There are no thinking animals here. When the Guardians found your people, they did not believe it. They thought them dinner."

"But not you?"

"The Xollu do not partake of flesh."

My cheeks began to heat. It wasn't until I pushed a tangle of hair back behind my burning ear that I realized he was talking about *diet* and not sex. In the wake of my embarrassment, I wasn't sure what to say.

"Why have you brought us here?" I demanded at last. The words tumbled out, as sharp as an accusation. I winced at the sound of my own voice, but Vadix didn't.

"To study you. There is a Xollu pair, scientists. Ardex and Aile. They wish to see if there are any chemical differences between the human sexes, as there are among Xollu. The other females will have their bodies scanned today. Aile believes that despite your beastly nature, some females may have ethylene receptors—"

"We're not lab rats," I said, but my words sounded dull—passionless. I knew that we would do the same if we were in their position. Shove them into cells, study them. Slice their skin down to slivers and hold them under a microscope, as I'd done to so many other plants, so many times before. Maybe we were more alike than I cared to admit.

Vadix's lips lifted, showing a thin line of teeth.

"No. You are not. We are only trying to understand you. Your nature. The Ahadizhi, they have not believed that animals are capable of language, of logical thought."

"No?" I asked. "But they've heard us. They should know by now that we're not just animals."

"Does the hunter believe that sounds a beast makes constitute more than growls and grunts? Of course not. But perhaps if we listened, we would find the beast believed differently."

"You're a philosopher?"

"No. I study the meaning behind words. Foreign words—foreign languages. Yours, for instance."

"Translator," I said, angling my chin up. "Linguist. That's what Hannah said."

Vadix nodded. "I study for many years in Aisak Ait. South of here, where the summer is longer. I learn to listen. But—"

He reached a long finger up, touching his earslit. I watched him, wondering at the strange precision of the gesture.

"But what?" I asked.

"I understand more than I should. In the days after the first probe landed in Raza Ait, I was called to translate the glyphs atop it. It was easy, too easy. And then your shuttle crew arrived. I was summoned too. The words that spill from my lips? Too swift. I should not be able to speak to you so simply now."

I fell silent. The dreams—it had to be the dreams. They'd scattered knowledge through my mind too, images I should have never seen, words I shouldn't have understood. But here we were.

"Vadix—" I began, but, waving a three-fingered hand through the air, he cut me off.

"No matter. The senate has grown weary of these experiments. You will not find yourself this 'lab rat' soon. They have asked me to call your ship's botanist to the surface. She will speak to us, negotiate your people's place on our world, if they might have any."

"Wait," I said. My tongue felt suddenly heavy. "What?"

"Your ship's botanist. I have spoken to her myself, a 'Mara Stone.' She speaks to plants, does she not?"

I brought my hands up over my mouth, smothering my shock. "Mara Stone?" I asked, through a web of fingers. "Vadix, she's no diplomat."

"She is not?" He stood with his broad shoulders squared, his wide mouth firm. I saw then that he was stubborn—proud. He was the type of boy who didn't like to be told he was wrong.

"No," I said carefully. "She *studies* plants. Where we're from, plants don't talk."

A pause, a long one. Hurt and confusion bruised his full mouth. "No?"

"No. Mara Stone is my teacher, and she—well, she's not even very good at talking to *people*."

"She is a scholar, then? A scientist? Surely it will be fine."

I thought of my haughty little teacher, the diminutive woman with the crooked nose who liked to taunt and tease. And I cringed at the memory. But before I could warn Vadix, the door behind him shivered open, revealing a stern-faced Xollu.

"Sale xaullek esedh, dora zhiosouek."

"Ehed sale!" he shouted back. *"Vaulix aum xaullek razi."*

The door closed. He turned back to me.

"What did she say?" I asked

"She said that the sproutling—a girl, I believe you call it? Her scans were quite unusual. High concentrations of phytodistress receptors. It is quite unusual, unlike anything they have seen in man."

"Phytodistress receptors? Like plants use to communicate damage?"

The way his mouth opened was almost like a smile. It did something to me, for all that his lips were too wide and too full of far too many teeth. My belly and rib cage swelled with warmth. Yet he began to turn toward the door. "Yes. You understand. I should go translate for them before—"

"Wait!"

I reached out, setting my hand on his slender wrist. We both flinched at the spark that flew between us, but this time neither of us drew away.

"Vadix," I said, my voice low. Passionate. "You asked them to bring me to you because I knew your name. I shouldn't know your name.

I shouldn't know anything about you. And you shouldn't know anything about me, either."

For a moment the light that flashed at the back of his coal eyes was gentle. I felt certain he would bend his head down, press his lips to mine. My heart was beating very fast. But then he pulled his smooth wrist out from my fingers' grasp.

"Phytodistress receptors. The sproutling has them. You are young, are you not? Perhaps it is nothing special."

He spoke in a rush, like he was trying to convince himself. Trying to convince me. But he was wrong. I'd never met anyone who had dreams like mine—dreams of a crowded jungle, filled with vines, where flesh touched flesh across hundreds of kilometers. It *was* special. It had to be. I shook my head.

"Please, Vadix. If I mean anything to you, let me speak to the senate with Mara Stone. My people are in danger. *I'm* in danger. If you don't help us, I don't know *what* we'll do."

He stood there, his long, flexible limbs stiff. At last he answered.

"They say that a Xollu is even hungrier than an Ahadizhi," he said. "Not for meat. For knowledge."

"You want to know the truth as badly as I do," I said in a low voice. "The truth about me, and you, and our dreams."

He didn't deny it. But he didn't agree, either.

"I must go," he said instead, and turning on his slender feet, he rushed out the door, and left me sitting there, on the crinkling paper, alone.

When they brought us back to the quarantine camp, the Ahadizhi had already delivered the day's ration of meat. The shuttle crew worked in silence, sorting out the good from the bad, the rancid from the fresh. As they worked, Aleksandra sat on the edge of the fire pit and continued to detail her plan. From what I could hear, it involved fashioning weapons from the sticks they'd given us to roast our food, rushing the Ahadizhi when they returned the next morning to take the men, and fighting our way out of Raza Ait.

I thought of the world beyond. The crowded city, filled with sharp-toothed hunters and delicate scholars, who would watch, fascinated and birdlike, as the Asherati were torn to pieces. It was dangerous, crazy, but aside from Rebbe Davison, their eyes were all bright—even Ettie's—as Aleksandra gathered up the roasting sticks and set them to work sharpening the ends into points.

I sat alone, turning my meeting with Vadix over and over again in my mind. Under normal circumstances I wouldn't have expected this strange boy to listen to my pleas. But these circumstances weren't normal. I *knew* him. Nothing else could explain the electricity of his touch, or the way he'd looked at me, his head angled down, his soft mouth open. Maybe he would listen to me. Maybe . . .

"What did he do to you?"

The log beneath me suddenly bent with the weight of another body. Laurel. Her expression was flat as she stared into the fire.

"What do you mean?" I asked.

She sighed, and pushed her dingy curls away from her face. "We all heard you talking to the translator. Heard him asking for you."

I winced at the memory. Waving my arms at him, shouting, shoving to the front of the crowd. In my urgency I'd forgotten that there were others watching. Of course, my eager shouts hadn't inspired confidence in Laurel. They'd been the childish cries of a girl, calling out for her boyfriend as he walked across the dome.

"Nothing," I said, ignoring how my cheeks had begun to heat. "We just talked."

"Oh," Laurel said. Then, after a moment, she let out a small, humorless laugh. "I thought maybe he . . . I thought he *touched* you. You've been so quiet."

"Touched" me? I turned my head sharply, staring at Laurel. She'd been quiet too since we'd returned from the hospital. We all had—all except for Aleksandra.

"Laurel?" I asked, reaching out and grabbing her by the arm. She flinched away from my hand, bending her fingers into a tight fist. "What did they do to *you*?"

"Nothing!" she said, a high blush crawling over her cheeks, making her freckles nearly invisible. "It wasn't like *that*. They just examined us, and put us in this tube. Scanned us. But I can't stand being around them after what happened to Deklan. And it's not even just that. There's something about them. It makes my skin crawl. The way they move. It's just not human, just not right. Sitting there in that little room, I just got more and more nauseated. And the smell of them . . ."

I thought of the summer-sweet scent of Vadix as he stood beside me. An unconscious smile lifted my lips. But then I noticed her watching me, and I hardened my mouth into a frown.

"What's wrong with their smell?"

"It's just not *human*!"

Laurel was right; they weren't human beings, not at all. The people I had known all had the same odor—musky, like the recycled gray water on the ship. With our water rations and our hard work, few Asherati smelled like roses. Momma's hands had been dusted by the odor of yeast and flour; Abba's clothes had been perfumed by the cedar boards in the clock tower where he'd worked. Field-workers smelled like fresh-turned dirt. Granary workers like dust and corn silk. But I'd grown used to the smell of flowers. Their pollen stained my lab coats yellow, and the mossy scent of the greenhouses stuck to my trousers and hair. Vadix's scent was like that, only amplified tenfold. Sweet, pungent, rich.

"It's not," I finally agreed. "Because they're not like us. And if we're going to live here among them, then we have to get used to it."

"Among them," she said, and shook her head. "But Aleksandra says that we can't. She says that we need to get back to the ship and land the dome. She says it doesn't matter what *they* want."

I glanced over at Aleksandra, at the way she brandished one of the hand-wrought spears and jabbed the air with it. Her body seemed so lithe, strong despite the trials of the past several days. If anyone could push their way out of the city, Aleksandra probably could.

But it wasn't going to work, I felt sure of that. It was too dangerous—would be too bloody.

"It's a terrible plan," I said, turning back to Laurel and dropping my voice down low. "The city is full of aliens. You'll die, Laurel."

She watched me impassively, her mouth a faint line.

"We have weapons," she said at last.

"Sticks! They have knives and prods and who knows what else."

There was a long stretch of silence. We watched the other adults pick up their spears and skewer the air. Their movements were far less graceful than Aleksandra's but just as forceful.

"It's our only way out of this place," Laurel said at last. She lifted herself up from the log, then gestured overhead—to the white canopy, the city's cupola, and to space, far, far beyond. "I just want to go home, Terra. There's nothing for me here. Not without Deck."

I didn't know what to say. I looked at her, swallowing hard to chase away the lump in my throat. I'd never convince her, not me, not after all that had happened. And besides, she didn't even give me a chance. She only shook her head, once, twice, then went to join the others.

I didn't stick around to watch her pick up a spear. Instead I rose, and ducked inside my tent. Squeezing my eyes closed, I willed the whole world—Laurel, Aleksandra, the city, all of it—away.

13

He waited for me in the forest. Or maybe I waited for him. It wasn't clear how the physics of this place worked. Sometimes I felt like the paths were familiar, an extension of the domed forests of my childhood but grown wild in the corners of my mind. Sometimes the paths felt new and strange and foreign—as foreign as his body, foreign as *him*. But there he was, at the center of them, and there I was, and we both hurried down the overcrowded paths toward each other, our bare feet slapping against the flattened soil as we drew near.

But we stopped just short of touching. We watched each other, cautious, uncertain. Now that we'd seen each other in the flesh, how could we ever go back to that raw state where we tumbled together and I kissed him until I couldn't tell where my mouth ended and his body began? When I'd believed him to be imaginary, it had been easy to draw him into my arms. But now that he was Vadix . . .

Is Mara Stone here yet? I asked. His lips parted. He wet them again—a nervous tic. I was beginning to see so many, like how he touched his hand to his chest when he spoke, covering a wound that was buried deep under his translucent skin.

The botanist, he said. *No, she has not arrived. But her shuttle should touch the planet shortly.*

Good, I said. And then, silence. I wasn't sure what to say.

You are not supposed to be here, he said at last, *in the dreamforests.*

Familiar vines dripped across the treetops and crept over the path, enveloping our ankles and toes. They didn't seem to mind my presence here.

No? I asked. He shook his head: no.

It is the purview of the Xollu alone. Not even Ahadizhi come here. Our Guardians say they dream only of the hunt. Their dream lands are killing fields.

And what are your dream lands?

Vadix was serious at first, but then a shade of a smile lit the corner of his mouth. He held out a hand. A nearby tree stretched down, settling a fruit inside his palm. He picked it, and held it in his palm, caressing the fuzz that covered its tender flesh.

Fertile grounds. This is where we walk with our mates even when we cannot be with them in the flesh. Over short nights and long winters. Our scripture says the god and goddess made this place for us. It is where our souls live before we sprout, and where we return when we die. This is why, when we close our eyes at night, we feel ourselves returning to familiar lands. Because we are. Dreamforests. Ahar Taiza.

I held out my own hand. A nearby tree wrapped a branch around it, encircling my wrist like a bracelet. *Our dreams aren't like this,* I said. *The things we see and learn and do in them aren't real. I don't understand how this works.*

Vadix dropped the fruit. Where it settled in the rich black earth, a dozen seedlings sprouted and grew, all while we watched.

How does your dreaming work? he asked.

I don't know, I said. I felt myself blush at my own ignorance. *Electricity and synapses, I guess.*

For us, it is the same. Electricity and synapses. One guesses. He smiled then, the toothiest of possible grins. A joke. He'd told a joke. But he didn't give me time to get over the shock of the strange sight of sunshine in his endlessly dark eyes. *When the Xollu still clung to caves, we had no words. We spoke with our minds. Chemical connections, hormonal.*

But we are limited. We speak only to our mates. From the first moment we are sprouted, we walk together, aware of another's thoughts as we are our own. This is why we walk the dreamforests. First as sprouts, going hand in hand. Friends. Doing all things together, until we are grown. Living and breathing and mating and thinking. Electricity and synapses. Chemical. Eternal. Shared.

Vadix told me all of this, standing before me, blue and bare. He wasn't like the other Xollu, nor the plants that swirled around us. The fruit that moldered on the forest floor was ruby red. The vines that wrapped my arm? Red too. But he was blue. Different.

You're alone, I said. And just like that, the smile was gone, vanished as if it had never really been there at all.

Yes, he said. *I am alone. And you are not supposed to be here.*

Just like that, the forests were gone, and I was pulled into the ocean of blackest sleep.

I woke to raucous shouts, the sound of rough voices lifting up through the muggy air. Pulling myself from my sleeping roll, I parted the dingy flap to step into the bright light of day. Before the fire, silhouetted against the camp's white walls, Aleksandra's small army of recruits practiced. I stood watching as they thrust their spears into the air over and over again. Even Ettie, who made clumsy movements with a weapon ill-balanced for her small body, jabbed that whittled-down stick and let out a shout: "Yah!"

But Aleksandra wasn't among them. She leaned her weight on her spear, listening as Rebbe Davison screamed until his ears turned red.

"She's only a child! You will *not* endanger her!"

The captain's daughter remained calm in the face of his anger. "We can't leave her here, Mordecai."

"She doesn't know what she's doing!"

Aleksandra walked toward Ettie, setting a hand on the child's small shoulder. "We all deserve a chance to protect ourselves."

Rebbe Davison let out a sound of frustration, throwing both hands into their air. Stomping hard, he came toward me, and collapsed on a log in front of the fire. I sat beside him.

"Don't you need to train?" I asked.

"I don't fight unless I have to," he said. Then he added, with a wince: "Aleksandra never had to be here. She should have been up there on that ship. All those years, watching and waiting. Just because we rushed down to the surface didn't mean she needed to follow. And now she's going to get a little girl killed just to get back to it. Maybe we'll all die. It makes no difference to her."

I didn't know what to say. There was no sign of Vadix yet, and none of Mara Stone. I had no assurance that the translator would do as I asked, and if he didn't, I'd be as vulnerable to Aleksandra's decisions as anyone else.

Maybe more, I thought, watching as she thrust the spear through the air.

"Did you think about what I said?" asked Mordecai, casting his gaze sidelong at me. He didn't look at me, not directly. His words were merely a low murmur. "I'll support you if you want to take up the mantle."

"Why me?" I whispered swiftly in response. "Why not you?"

My teacher let out a low laugh. "I decided a long time ago that I'm a scholar, not a leader."

"And you want *me* to lead?" I asked, dry laughter seeping into my own voice. "Of course I want to get us out of here safely. I want to find a way for us to settle here too. But I'm no leader, Rebbe Davison. I'm clumsy, awkward. I'm always late. Can hardly keep a secret. I mean, look at Aleksandra. She was born to lead."

We watched her pause in her thrusts to show Ettie the proper way to hold her spear. The way she gripped it suggested deftness that went beyond competency. I wondered, for a moment, how many men and women Aleksandra had taught to kill. She'd been a leader for the guard once, after all. But my old teacher only let out a snort of laughter.

"She does look like she knows what she's doing, doesn't she? That's always been her trick. Her mother's, too. Don't show any fears or doubts and the people will follow. You could learn that too, Terra. I've known you since you were a toddler. You're bright. You learn easily. But more important, you're a good person. I know dozens of rebels. But none I trust more to put the peoples' needs first."

I looked down at the toes of my flight boots. They were scuffed from our long journey, my feet inside blistered and dirty. Rebbe Davison didn't know what I had done, the violence I'd wrought on that night in the Rafferty's quarters. I was a vengeful killer, blood on my hands. No better than Aleksandra, certainly. And probably much worse.

"I don't think so," I began. "I'm not like her, not in the ways that matter."

As if to underscore that point, Aleksandra spun toward us, thrusting her spear through the air. There was a flash of brown, a high-pitched whistle, and then an echoing thud. The spear missed us, but narrowly, or perhaps it had fallen precisely where she intended. It jutted out of the log between our hips, swaying between us from the force of impact.

When we finally turned our wide eyes forward, it was to the sight of Aleksandra walking square-shouldered toward us. Behind her the others paused in their lesson. They couldn't hide the shock that left their mouths open and gaping.

"Aren't you two going to join us?" she asked, false sweetness lacing her voice. But I knew better. Aleksandra wasn't sweet. She was anything but. For a moment I tasted my heart in my mouth; I worried she might walk straight through the fire to reach us. But she only stopped at the circle's edge, resting her boot against one of the taller stones.

"I think I'm going to sit this one out," Rebbe Davison said, holding up both hands. Funny, I'd never noticed before how my teacher's palms were calloused, knotty with scars. I'd known him all these years, but I knew so little about his life.

"We're in this together, Mordecai." She didn't even bother looking me in the eye. This wasn't about me; it was about her and her old friend. But Rebbe Davison only shrugged.

"I wasn't—" he began, but his words were cut short. The camp gates swung open, and there stood Vadix, broad shouldered and swaying in the wake of those metal links.

"Damn!" Aleksandra said. She had no spear now, no weapon to flash at him. She looked toward to her newly gathered army, but they all hesitated, every single one, clutching their spears to their chests. Finally, with a cry of impatience, Aleksandra's hand reached into the open flap of her flight suit. I saw a glint of light catch on metal. Her knife. The Ahadizhi must have missed it when they frisked us at the city's gates, wrenching our guns from our hands.

"No!" I cried, rushing to my feet. "He's here to help! Stop her!"

My steps forward were clumsy, slow—too slow.

But Rebbe Davison was faster.

Out of the corner of my eye, I saw him pull the spear from the log's damp wood. He didn't *throw* it at Aleksandra. He was too unschooled for that. But he ran toward her and took a mighty swing, striking her square in the back.

There was a great burst of dust as she fell forward. She didn't cry out. None of us did. There was only silence as her knife went spinning on the ground and landed at Vadix's feet.

"You!" Aleksandra roared as she pulled her body up. Rebbe Davison was frozen, the spear still pointed toward her. Weaponless now, Aleksandra wasn't going to test him. But that didn't mean she couldn't wound him, not at all. "You idiot! You do what *she* says?"

"He hasn't harmed you." Rebbe Davison spoke through gritted teeth. The translator only stood frozen, as calm as still water, at the camp's open gate. "There's no need to strike him down in cold blood."

"Cold blood," Aleksandra said. She wiped the back of her hand against her mouth, where a trickle of red had appeared. "I'll tell you about cold blood. That girl?"

My hands went icy; my eyes went wide. I'd carried the burden of Mazdin Rafferty's death with me across the Zehavan wilderness, but I'd never spoken of it aloud. Did the rebels already know what I'd done, or had Aleksandra kept her knowledge to herself? What would my teacher think of the news? Laurel? Ettie?

What would Vadix? He still stood in the open gate, watching Aleksandra with keen eyes.

"*She* murdered Doctor Rafferty. In *cold blood*. Poisoned him. For nothing so petty as revenge. And she's the one whose command you follow? Good luck with that."

Aleksandra's feet hit the ground hard as she walked. It was the only sound as silence stretched on and on and on.

"Terra," Rebbe Davison said, his voice going soft as he lowered his spear. "Is it true?"

He knew now what I really was. They all did. His plans for my leadership melted away right before his eyes—in a wash of poison and wine.

But before I could answer, a familiar figure stepped out behind Vadix. Diminutive, hook-nosed. Her lab coat was clean, well-scrubbed, white among all this dingy, mud-stained fabric. Mara Stone. She bent over and picked up Aleksandra's knife. Tucked it into her belt.

"Hello, *Talmid*," she said. She tilted her head toward the gate. "Come along. I've been asked to speak to the senate, and I believe I need your help."

My eyes flashed to Rebbe Davison.

"Please, stop them from doing anything rash. I'll be back soon. I'll fix this," I said. He didn't answer. I could only hope against hope that he still found me worthy of regard—someone worth listening to after all he'd learned. Holding my head high, I turned away from him, and went to meet Mara.

14

It was the first time I traveled through the city as a guest, not a prisoner, but I didn't feel like one. As we were escorted to the train by an Ahadizhi guard, I trailed behind Mara and Vadix, looking down at the toes of my flight boots. They were conversing in polite, officious tones—as if I hadn't just been revealed to be a murderer.

Of course, it was nothing to Mara. She'd known Momma, and Mazdin Rafferty, too—she'd been the one to supply me with poison, after all, that pretty purple foxglove she'd ground down into a powder with her own gloved hands, a deadly concoction meant to kill the doctor's son. She knew the rage in my heart, how deeply I'd been scarred by the loss of my mother. And she knew that Mazdin was the one who had done it to me. So perhaps she could be excused for proceeding at a brisk pace beside Vadix, taking in the wonders of the sprawling alien city that was laid out before us like an overgrown summer garden.

But Vadix hardly knew me. He hadn't known Momma. Hadn't known Mazdin Rafferty, either. And unlike the Ahadizhi who jostled us as we passed through the city's thoroughfares, he'd never even known the taste of flesh—much less brought about another creature's demise. I knew this instinctively, saw it in the cool, serious set of his lips. Though I'd known his passions to flame brightly as we slept, I knew that at his core he had no taste for killing. That was for other creatures: the Ahadizhi, the beasts in the wilds beyond.

And me.

We made our way through underpasses and over cobbled bridges—the roads looping according to some logic that I couldn't quite grasp—and I glimpsed Xollu pairs hugging the buildings wherever we went. They reminded me a bit of climbing ivy, desperately clinging to each other, afraid, or perhaps simply unable to venture out on their own. Their eyes were huge at the sight of Mara and me—animals, and gravely threatening to them, our bodies musky and fragrant, and our bellies hungry for flesh like theirs. But despite their fear, they carried no prods; unlike the Ahadizhi, there were no twin-bladed daggers strapped to their ropey belts. They were helpless, defenseless. Not predators; prey.

Yet the line of Vadix's broad shoulders was square. Unafraid. What made him so bold? What let him walk alone, unique among his people?

What made him dream of me at night—of a bloodthirsty animal, a killer?

As we drifted up a narrow stairwell, that question weighed heavily on my mind. We were nothing alike, not in biology, not in nature. He led us to a train platform that dripped with vegetation. The lacy moss had more in common with him than I did. A single copper rail furled out in either direction. As if to confirm how little he thought of me, Vadix turned away from us, tracing the line of the single hanging train track. I bit the inside of my cheek. Mara noticed; her gray eyes sparked.

"Cat got your tongue?"

"No," I said. Then, studying the frown that had etched itself into Mara's wrinkled face, I shrugged. "Yes. I don't know."

She flashed an arthritic hand through the air. "Oh," she intoned, "don't worry about what that hellion said about you. She might have held their hearts up *there* for a moment"—she gestured toward the

glass ceiling, to where the ship waited somewhere above—"but they've been scrambling like children in her absence. Why, a hundred of them have reaffirmed their loyalty to that Council-fat brat of yours."

"Who?" I asked.

"Silvan Rafferty, of course. Or did you change your intentions before you jacked one of the Council's shuttles?"

"Yes," I said, my eyes traveling the broad plane of Vadix's back. I could have sworn his earslits opened as he listened in on our conversation. But maybe I was mistaken. Maybe it was nothing. "We . . . I decided against marrying him."

"Just using him for his body's pleasures, then? Not my style, girl, though I guess he *is* handsome enough."

Now I was sure of it—Vadix was listening in, his delicate chin angled toward the sound of our voices, his earslits open wide. But Mara didn't notice. She only jabbed her elbow into my ribs, then prattled on.

"The point remains—Giveret Wolff has risked too much in leaving the ship. I wouldn't be surprised if Rafferty goes through with his plan and takes off for Earth again."

"It's ridiculous," I mumbled hazily, though my eyes were still on Vadix. Watching. Listening. "Earth is dead."

The train arrived then, streaming up on its rail, as silent as a whisper. The copper cars shone like chips of gelt in the sunlight.

We waited as the reams of Ahadizhi boarded—then a steady trickle of Xollu, walking skittishly on their narrow feet. At last we stepped inside. Vadix grabbed a metal vine that hung from the ceiling, then indicated an empty bench of seats against the wall. Mara and I pressed into them, our shoulders touching. It wasn't until the door slid shut behind us that she replied.

"It will be a thousand years since the asteroid's strike by the time we return," she said. "Chances are, the effects will still be widespread. But Rafferty isn't looking to science anymore. I believe he's been exploring notions of faith."

Faith? Silvan? I didn't know what to say to that. I clutched my hands between my knees and stared down at them as the train pulled away from the station.

The journey was brief. The world outside was a stream of copper and violet and white. Vadix stood above us, his body swaying as the train car streamed along its rail. His gaze, of course, was fathomless, incomprehensible, as always. But I couldn't ignore the way my knees just graced the green curtains of his embroidered robes. I wondered if he could feel the heat of my body from below. The only thing I felt was the familiar pull, urging me to reach up, to wrap my fingers around his and to feel the metal handle, cool, beneath both of our palms. But I didn't, couldn't. We were too different—strangers.

Vadix was silent, but that wasn't the case for the Ahadizhi who packed our train car. They couldn't keep their eyes off us; they licked their lips, bared their teeth, regarded us like a meal fit for supper. And they spoke, in low, whistling tones. One word, repeated over and over again, like a song:

"Hu-man. Hyuu-man. Hu-man."

The news of the crashed shuttles must have traveled quickly through the city. I should have expected that—up in the ship, where the walls towered around us, where we were trapped like flies under glass, news traveled quickly too. Maybe in some respects we were more like these aliens than we were different.

"Human. Huuu-man."

But as the train bucked and lurched, another word joined the first. A single syllable, a long whisper of sound. The Ahadizhi voices grew brighter, clearer. Undeniable. The way they looked at Vadix was undeniable too.

"*Lousk,*" they said. "*Lousk.* Hu-man. *Lousk.*"

"What does that mean?" Mara demanded, nose wrinkling in offense. Mara didn't like whispers or secrets—everything about her could be plainly read on her face. Vadix stared at her, carefully considering. But before he could answer, the train pulled to a stop, and the door shivered open. He inclined his head toward the bright space outside. I couldn't be sure, but I think I saw a wisp of relief there. He didn't have to answer her.

"Come," he said, "we have reached the Grand Senate."

He walked outside without another word. Our Ahadizhi guard waited for us to rise, her prod held between both hands. Mara shrugged her narrow shoulders and pulled herself to her feet.

But before I could follow her, our guard put a bright hand against my arm.

"*Lousk. Lousk,*" she said, and then added a single, improbable word of Asheran: "Alone."

I stared at her. She only gave me a smile, too wide and toothy for me to bear. I nodded uncertainly back, and then hustled out the open train car door.

In school we'd learned about the great buildings that had been lost when we left the Earth. The Flavian Amphitheater and the Pyramids of Giza; the Dome of the Rock and the Western Wall. But the images in our textbook had been small, drawn by some ancestor who had never seen the building firsthand. Maybe the Sydney Opera House had looked more imposing in person, but I could never get a sense of its scale on paper. All those fanning, curved walls meant nothing to me. The sight of them left my heart cold.

That wasn't the case with the Grand Senate of Aur Evez.

It was located in the center of the city, where the cupola was highest overhead. A stone pavilion spilled out of it like water over the brim of a cup. Under the feet of hundreds of aliens, the marble tiles sparkled in the growing daylight. The majesty of it didn't hit you all at once; in fact, at first I didn't even notice it. I thought it was a wall, or yet another housing structure up ahead. But then I saw the strange shape of the shadows cast by the structure's heights—rippling on the ground beneath our feet—and gazed upward. And my breath was stolen from my chest.

The structure resembled a blossom—wide and round. Each level bloomed out from the one beneath it. Triangular windows peeked out of its walls, lending them a delicate translucency. The lowest level was open, revealing a shadowed space below. The warm air of day drifted in and out just as easily as the city's inhabitants did. The Ahad-izhi chattered and clicked laughter as they walked, hardly sparing a look at us.

But there were more Xollu here than I'd seen almost anywhere else in the city. Finely garbed in robes of every imaginable shade, they took stately steps, stopping now and then to speak to their mates. A few glanced curiously at Vadix. He only let out a whir of words in response.

"Vhahari vori!"

At first I wondered why his usually clear tenor had gone so gruff, and why he stepped even more quickly across the marble, rushing through the towering gates. But then I saw how the other Xollu glanced away as soon as he'd passed, speaking to each other behind their long fingers. I'd seen those looks before. Not here but on the ship, after Abba died. Everyone had felt so sorry for me that they almost couldn't help it, pursing their lips, knitting up their brows. Apparently, the other Xollu felt sorry for Vadix, too. Their black eyes were full of pity. I could hear their whispered words on the wind.

Lousk. Lousk.

We stepped into the cool, shadowed space of the central hall. The marble changed to tile—a mosaic. There was the dark mouth of a cave, and before it, a pair of figures. They had come to greet a whole pack of Ahadizhi who spilled out from the purple forests in the distance.

"What is this?" Mara Stone asked, gesturing to the image beneath our toes. It seemed as though Vadix was worn thin, distracted. He touched his gaze to her, then looked away.

"It is the dawn of our people. We rise from caves and are discovered by the Ahadizhi. Together we build Raza Ait."

"Ah!" Mara said. A smile lit her lips. "A Romulus and Remus story."

"Rom-yu-less?" Vadix spoke the name carefully. Mara seemed relieved. I think she was glad to be able to instruct him. It was a familiar role for her; she wasn't used to standing passively, to listening. But I cringed as she prattled on, her hands clamped proudly behind her back.

"Two brothers who founded one of Earth's greatest cities. They were raised by a she-wolf. They argued over where they should build the city, and one of them died in the squabble."

"Died?" The frown grew deeper and deeper on Vadix's lips. This was the wrong story to tell. Hadn't I warned him that Mara was no diplomat? "Our cities were built to *keep* us from dying."

"Yes, well," Mara Stone said, unaffected by the offense that shone on his teeth. He leaned forward, bending his body toward her.

"Your people are often barbarous, are they not? Brandishing knives and sticks. Striking their own crèchemates down. They cannot be trusted to cool their tempers."

He spoke to her, but I could tell that his words were meant for me. I'd killed—felled Mazdin in cold blood. Could I be trusted? I wanted to tell him that I could, but the words froze in my chest. Mara didn't even seem to notice the laser intensity of his eyes as they narrowed upon me.

"Of course they can!" she snapped. "Now, don't we have a meeting to attend?"

Vadix leaned back, watching as Mara fiddled with the lapels of her coat. His lips lifted wryly.

"Indeed we do," he agreed, then started off toward the twisting central staircase.

15

"Aulsix aum elix tauziz!"

"Yes, my apologies. Senator Saida feels that it would be inappropriate to discuss the proliferation of Terran food animals on our planet before we have agreed to permit you to settle on Aur Evez."

"We can adapt to a vegetarian diet, of course. But ideally we're omnivores. And we've carried our flocks all this way. You can't expect us to slaughter them after five hundred years of travel?"

"Taot?"

"Saoso elix zhosozazhi, saudd thosolo."

"Aikri thosoloezhi, aikri sore zhosozazhi. Tatoum, Senator Sadex agrees that this is a delicate subject to raise, particularly in the presence of our esteemed Xollu senators. Perhaps we might turn the subject back to your likely environmental impact on this world."

In the senate antechamber at the top of the Grand Senate building of Raza Ait, I sat with my head in my hands. Bringing Mara here was a mistake, just like I'd told Vadix it would be. But there was nothing I could do about it now except gaze out the glass wall beside me, down into the massive amphitheater that formed the main senate room below. I could see the junior senators coming and going in their silver robes, looking harried and distracted. But those seated among us were senior politicians, garbed in lengths of copper and gold. Little emotion showed on their alien faces; the "human problem," as Vadix had called it as we sat down around the table, was one they hoped to resolve quickly, with little fuss.

Mara Stone, however, had other ideas.

"Your esteemed Xollu senators! Well, I'm sorry if their sensibilities are offended by the diversity of our diets. I know they're plants, but they *must* consume something besides sunbeams and vapors."

"You'd think that," I murmured. Mara turned sharply toward me.

"What did you say, *Talmid?*"

I shrank back in my chair. I was no diplomat. I was hardly even a scientist. But Mara had no patience for my doubts. She slammed the heel of her hand against the table.

"Spit it out! You've been here for days. Surely you've learned *something*. You're not so dense."

"The Ahadizhi are carnivorous," I said softly. "But the Xollu don't eat anything."

"That's absurd," she said. She swung her gaze to look at Vadix. Nostrils flaring, she took in the sight of him—his height, the ease with which he moved. "Motile plants would have to have astronomical energy requirements."

"You would know more about astronomy than we," Vadix said coolly. "But it's true. We may eat, but we rarely do. Instead we sleep."

"Sleep?"

One by one the pairs bowed their heads.

"All the long winter," he said. "Our bodies wrapped around our mates, we sleep. It is only our alliance with the Ahadizhi that protects us from the claws and teeth of beasts over the winter's depths."

"Winter?" I asked. "But it's winter now, isn't it?"

Mara waved her hand at me, not even deigning to meet my eyes. "We haven't seen anything yet, girl. I'm sure by the time deep winter sets in, this city will be buried. Am I right?"

Vadix gazed down at his long fingers, clutched over the stone table. "*Tatoum*. Yes, this is correct."

"Won't be long now, will it?"

"Three passes of the moons before we sleep."

"That's, what, five weeks? Six? But what I don't understand," Mara began, leaning forward in her seat; she pointed a crooked finger at all the Ahadizhi who sat idle at the far end of the table, "is what *you* get out of this deal. You're clearly intelligent. Don't pretend like you don't understand me. I know you do."

One of them flashed Mara a view of his mouth, full of a thousand tiny blades.

"*Tatoum,*" he agreed. She gave a nod.

"So what is it? Are you slaves? Do *they* call all the shots?" She jerked her thumb toward Vadix. For the first time his countenance faltered.

"No, no!" he protested. But the Ahadizhi gave a slow blink and smiled. He reminded me of a feline when he spoke, purring, complacent—but with hidden claws.

"No slaves," he said, his tongue hissing against his many teeth. "Partners."

Mara turned to Vadix. "Explain," she said. Then she added, smiling: "*Taot?*"

Vadix pressed his lips together in a frustrated line. It bothered him, I think, to have Mara pick up even the smallest pieces of his language. He didn't want his place at the table superseded, not the slightest bit.

"Partners," Vadix said, then hastily added: "In the service of the hunt, they have developed their arts. They had words first. Music and poetry. Art and writing. Their minds are not like ours. They are hidebound, well-planted in the land where they sprout. But we are curious. We study. We scheme. We are scientists. Scholars. Political strategists. They are hunters, builders, artists, musicians."

I thought of Rebbe Davison, of what he'd told me about his plans with Aleksandra back when we'd first stumbled across her out in the wild. She was supposed to become the brawn behind the rebellion—Mordecai Davison, the brains. Apparently the aliens of Aur Evez had opted for a similar setup. Vadix went on.

"In exchange for their protection, we build them cities. And they fill them with music and color, and care for us during our long winter's nap."

"And it's worked for you, hasn't it?" Mara asked. She sat back in her chair, apparently satisfied by his explanation. "Almost too well. These streets are crowded."

The corner of Vadix's mouth twitched. It was as if Mara had stumbled into an old, old argument. But she didn't seem to notice his reaction. She lifted a cutting hand, then let it fall.

"Well? Too crowded for us, isn't it?"

Vadix dragged his gaze away. Touching his chest, he turned to the senators.

"Vala xezlu aum aizzu zhososezhi zaizikk aiosoa?"

The senators erupted into conversations. Even the Ahadizhi joined in—gesturing wildly with their stubby fingers, leaping to their feet and brandishing the double-edged daggers they kept hidden beneath their robes. Mara glanced at me, her eyebrows lifted mildly. But I didn't look back at her.

My gaze was on Vadix. He was watching them all, his expression as still as the *Asherah*'s reservoirs and nearly as dark. He didn't seem to be stirred by their arguments. The ruddy-skinned Xollu pairs clutched their hands together and drew close to each other, frightened by the sudden explosion of sound. The Ahadizhi hissed and muttered angry words. But Vadix only sat square in his chair, calm and silent. At last, without a single word, he rose from his seat. He stood tall, tucking his hands inside his robes, and regarded the senators who had gathered there.

"Vhesesa auriz," he said, his voice as smooth as velvet. But when their argument continued, an impassioned jumble, he repeated himself. His shout echoed against the glass walls of the antechamber. *"Vhesesa auriz!"*

I sat forward in the hard stone seat, gripping the armrests. They were decorated with gemstones and filigree, delicate carvings that bit into the palms of my hands. I held on tight to them. Because as Vadix surveyed the senators gathered there, I had the sudden, sinking feeling that it was all slipping away.

"We did not ask for you," he said. I felt the air go out of the room as he turned toward me. He stared at me. No, he stared *into* me, uncovering parts of me that I'd been sure were buried deep. "We did not invite you here as our honored guests. You are simply driftwood, cluttering our shore. And now you rise up, elbowing us aside. You want us to make room for you? You come, full of weapons and ambitions, stirring the passions of our Guardians, demanding acreage for your cattle and sheep. You think we have space for them? We hardly have space for ourselves. We did not ask for you. Animals. Killers. We do not want you here. We do not want *you*."

His earslits narrowed. He would hear no argument, accept no reply. Every single word he spoke sliced into me, as quickly as a hand-hewn spear, just as surely as any knife. He didn't want me. Bloodthirsty. A murderer. I felt my heart break in my chest.

But not Mara. It was nothing to her. She sat back, flashing her hand. "What of the southern continent, then? We haven't seen any sign of a city there."

Vadix leaned his hands against the table, but I could hardly hear him as he spoke. "It is wild. Untamed. The Ahadizhi there are not our allies; we do not speak their tongue. And without them the beasts will destroy your settlement. This is without a doubt."

"We have a dome."

"Do you think your ancient glass will protect you? In winter our

Guardians patrol thrice daily. With prod and song and double-bladed dagger. And still some of them are lost to us at the claws of the beasts, may the god and goddess grant them many seedlings. The southern beasts would tear you apart, swallow your weak flesh whole." I watched him—watched the jagged line of his teeth.

The grimace was strange. So unfamiliar. I'd known the many moods of that mouth—joyful and teasing, hesitant and gentle, loving and lusty and coy. But I'd never known him to look so *hateful*. It wasn't right. *This* wasn't right. I felt something swell within me. Not the familiar flare of anger, that hot spark that led me to do dangerous, murderous things. Something else, shining and true.

As he and Mara argued, I lifted myself to my feet. My hands were cold, numb. But my mind wasn't. In my determination everything had gone bright and clear—especially Vadix's expression. His lips hung open. I felt his fear, hanging over the heads of all these senators and dignitaries. He didn't want me to speak. But I had no choice. Otherwise our fate would fall back on Aleksandra. On violence. On certain death.

"No," I said firmly. He looked at me, and Mara looked at me, and all the senators swiveled their heads to look at me too. A dozen black eyes took me in. I tried to keep my voice even. I didn't want my emotion to spill over, revealing me as delicate and sensitive. Weak. I had spent too much of my life like that, soft-bellied and afraid. "It's not right. *This* isn't right. We need your help. You can't turn us away!"

"What do you know of 'right'?" Vadix scoffed. He finally pulled his long hand from his sleeve—and pointed a spindly finger right at me. "You are not like us! Dangerous aliens, with untamed, murderous hearts."

I stared at him, at the anger that flared wildly across his face. But no matter the heat of his words, I knew the tender boy that was hidden deep inside. He already knew my heart. He'd clutched it to his body. He'd accepted me before he ever knew me, found me worthy, whole. Good.

"Oh, Vadix," I said, my own voice softening. "You *know* that's not true."

This time I didn't have to touch him to let him feel the electricity that tied us together. Words alone were sufficient. He snatched back his hand as if he'd been shocked.

"Lies," he hissed. But they were all looking at us, the Xollu and Ahadizhi and Mara Stone, too. The Xollu sat forward in their seats. The Ahadizhi exchanged puzzled glances before looking back at me. And Mara's mouth was creased by frown lines.

"Terra," she said, her voice surprisingly gentle. "What are you talking about?"

Up until that moment Vadix had been fearless—strong despite his willowy frame and slender limbs. But in that moment he looked like the slightest wind might blow him over. For the first time his eyes had taken on the same fearful cast as the rest of the Xollu's.

"Vadix knows," I said, my voice hoarse. "He knows why he has to help us. He knows why he has to help *me*."

One of the Xollu senators sat forward in her chair. She inclined her head to Vadix, speaking gently.

"*Vadix lousk, aiosoez daullu aum auru thahari voraz daze?*"

"*Shesezi daiosoez,*" he said. In Asheran he added, "No. No, she is wrong."

"Terra," Mara said again, more sharply this time. Her patience was wearing thin. But suddenly I was the most patient creature in the world. He knew who I was. He could deny it all he wanted, but we both knew the truth.

"I dream about him," I said. "Every night, for months and months. Before I ever knew him, he was there. I don't know how it happened, or why. If it has something to do with the chemicals in my brain, or magic. But I know that together we walk through the dreamforests. The . . ." I reached for the words. They were there, at the back of my mind, buried deep in my subconscious. "The Ahar Taiza. Together. Vadix and me."

A collective gasp rose up from the Xollu senators. One of them fixed his red hand against the sleeve of Vadix's robes.

"*Vadix lousk,*" he began, "*auru thahari voraz daze?*"

Vadix didn't answer.

"I know we're not supposed to take off into space again," I said. Part of me wanted to plead with him, to throw myself at his feet and tug on his long robes. But I wouldn't let myself. He knew me. He knew what I was to him. I needed to trust in that. "And I know we're not supposed to land the dome in the south. Not without you, Vadix. Not without the two of us together. We're supposed to be a team. We're supposed to *help* each other."

I felt something shift, changing inside him. I can't tell you how. Outwardly he was the same, immobile as a statue. But he was gathering up his courage like a heavy cloak, wrapping it around himself. Keeping himself safe.

"No!" he said. "Lies!"

He opened his eyes up wide. They were black as space and twice as endless as he spun on his heel, his robes a whirl of color and light around him, and rushed from the room.

For a long time we were all silent, watching the door that hung open at the back of the antechamber. Finally Mara reached up her hand to me.

"Oh, *Talmid*," she said. I could see in the sad turn of her mouth what she thought of all of this. To her I was nothing more than a girl—a silly girl with a crush.

But I wasn't. I knew better, and so did he. I pulled away from her.

"Vadix!" I called. I almost tipped over the heavy stone chair as I rushed for the door. "Vadix!"

Mara called out for me to stop. After a moment a dozen alien voices joined hers. But I didn't listen. I rushed through the door and down the wide stairwell, shouting after him as I pressed through the crowds.

16

Traveling alone, the city was a whole new beast.

At first I chased Vadix, watching for the blue smear of light among the jumbled crowd of red. He led me across the wide pavilion and past the train station, down a twisting underpass and through a grove of shifting trees. Then he turned down an alleyway. I went after him, but ran smack into a Xollu pair. They flinched from my body's touch, pulling back their hands as if I were diseased.

"Sorry! Sorry!" I breathed. Sniffing, they moved past me. But when they did, I realized that I had lost him. The pathway up ahead was packed full of bodies. Ahadizhi streamed in and out of the storefronts along the alley's lowest level, stopping to watch me with inquisitive eyes. I shrugged off their grabby fingers, shouldering past them. Surely he had to be *somewhere* up ahead. So I trudged forward.

The smell of meat was thick in the midday sun. The shop counters were piled high with it. There were insects here, the first I'd seen on the planet—hairy, and as big as both fists, swarming heavily on the wind. They were held back from every shop door by a translucent skin of netting, but they clouded the path ahead. I heard the pound of footfalls. A group of diminutive Ahadizhi scampered past. Their furred skin was blue, the color of a burst berry. Children, I realized. They were children. They let out clicking laughter as they gamboled past.

I watched them go, tracing the bruisey blue of their bodies as they disappeared into the crowd. Was Vadix a child, then? He didn't look like one. He stood just as tall as the others, and his countenance suggested experience. He'd lived, seen things—perhaps too much. I knew there was a story hidden beneath his sad, full lips. As I scrambled forward, sweat streaming down my face, I wondered what it was that made him different from the rest of them. Other than the fact that he was alone. Other than the fact that he was mine.

I gazed forward, searching the pathway for any sign of him. But no luck. Up ahead the road dipped and twisted, finally arching over a burbling stream. I hurried across the wide stone bridge, pausing halfway to take stock. Underneath, Ahadizhi piloted painted craft. I watched as they pulled up eel traps, filled with yellow, slithering creatures. There was shouting, clucks of laughter, the music of splashing water. Light danced and jiggled against the hulls of their boats. I reached up, touching the back of my neck. Beneath my fingers I could feel my skin burning—like I had a fever. But I didn't *feel* ill. I pulled myself to the far end of the bridge, and continued on my way.

I'm not sure when my journey changed, when the road ahead became as muddied as river dirt. I walked over bridge after bridge after bridge, crossing the canals as they looped and knotted through Raza Ait. The sun overhead was relentless, amplified by the sparkling cupola overhead. I'd never known anything like it. On the ship the artificial sunlight was never so bright as to make my eyes water or to leave my throat parched. But the city's inhabitants didn't seem to mind. I saw young Ahadizhi splayed out against the hot cobblestone, soaking up the light. Even stately Xollu pairs paused in their walking, unlacing the tops of their robes to bare their red shoulders to the sun.

Meanwhile I stopped by the water's edge to splash water over my face.

Cool and sparkling, it trickled down my dirty neck, leaving pale rivers in its wake. The water tasted like metal and earth. Sharp, familiar flavors, not so different from the waters of home, but somehow cleaner. I wanted to dive in, to strip off my clothing and wash away the weeks of dirt and sweat and blood. But I couldn't. I had to find Vadix. He was here somewhere. He *had* to be.

I turned and looked over my shoulder, half expecting to see him there behind me. But an Ahadizhi woman stood there instead. She pushed a cart ahead of her on rickety wheels. The painted vehicle was piled high with scrolls of paper. I ambled forward. Lozenge eyes opened wide at the sight of me; her mouth fell open, showing teeth. So many teeth. Wiping my damp hands against my shorts, I picked out a scroll and slowly unrolled it. Paint had been spilled against the reedy canvas in great, dripping splotches. The pigments were lovely, one color layered over the next. A sunset. It showed a sunset. A white-yellow circle stood stark amid all that blue and green and violet.

"Xarki," I said, my hand barely gracing the bright shape. "You're very talented."

"Tatoum," she agreed. She put her hand over mine, helping me to unroll the scroll to its full length. She was standing close to me— maybe too close. Her body smelled so sweet in the sunlight, wilder than Vadix's, and more fragrant.

The bottom of the scroll had been only lightly washed with paint. There was the pale blue of snow and a distant red line of trees. I could practically see them moving against the skyline, writhing, shifting. I drew my gaze downward. There at the bottom was a green splotch of color, heavily shadowed with black.

I held the painting at arm's length. The Ahadizhi woman's hand still touched my own. But my fingers slowly went cold under hers. A body. It was a body. One of Zehava's great beasts, torn to pieces, its guts splayed out across the frozen winter fields.

The Ahadizhi woman didn't seem threatening as her fingers dug gently into my arm. But even in my addled state, I remembered the pitcher plant. Mara had taught me all about the tubular flowers, which drew insects close with their sweet scent before drowning them in their nectar. They didn't *look* dangerous. They were green and red, their bells narrow. Delicate. But in truth they were deadly.

I dropped the scroll back down into the cart. Slowly, carefully, I backed away. It wasn't until she tried to close her hand on mine again, squeezing my fingers tight, that I snatched them back and broke out into a run. Without looking back, I raced across the next bridge and away.

I could *feel* myself cooking, the skin of my bare arms and face growing pink in the sun. As I headed toward the city's outskirts, I kept trying to clamp my hands down over my neck, shielding it from the hot light of day. Xarki. Miserably I glanced up. Even as I squinted into the amplified sunlight, my face ached. It was too much. I didn't know how all these scattered Ahadizhi could stand it. They lingered in the doorways half naked, chatting and laughing and looking at me. Then again, they were plants, and I wasn't. I was an animal, one of the only living mammals under the glass ceiling of Raza Ait. I didn't belong here, and looking at the Anadizhi, with their toothy mouths, I didn't know how I hadn't seen it before.

Their bodies moved in nightmarish ways, wavering and bending as they reached out to point at me.

"Hu-mahn, hu-maahhn," they whispered to one another. Their arms were too long, their bodies too thin. They reminded me of snakes who slithered over cobblestone. No, that wasn't right. They reminded me of vines, winding themselves up and up toward any light source. Ferns or flowers, they'd never been frightening to me before. But now, wrung out by the sun, my mouth as dry as sandpaper, I saw the hunger there. Images flashed before me. Flytraps snapping shut on butterflies. Sundews curling their tentacles tight around black-bodied flies. No wonder Laurel had been so afraid of the people of Aur Evez.

I collapsed in a shadowed doorway, tucking my face into the crook of my arm. For the first time in ages, I felt my solitude. It had been easy to chase away since I'd crashed on the planet. There had been survival to contend with, and then Aleksandra. . . . I hadn't had time to mull over my lot.

And I'd had Vadix. Even if he'd been merely a dream, he'd been *there*, his kisses working to cure my loneliness. But he was gone now, who knew where, or why. No, that wasn't true. I'd stood right there as Aleksandra had told him the truth about me. I was murderous, a killer. No better than her, and certainly no better than the Ahadizhi who drew close to me now, examining me with curious eyes.

I'd collapsed on the precipice of an Ahadizhi home—a squat, circular building whose stone walls were pressed with multicolored glass. The door behind me had been left open; the space inside was blue-dark and cavernous. There was only one beam of light inside, subtle, muted. It landed at the center of the entryway, filled with dust motes that swirled a lazy dance.

And there was music. Someone was singing a sweet, gentle refrain, slow notes that lingered for just a touch too long. I'd heard this song before, but it didn't matter. It was my song—*mine*. It wove the story of a girl whose mother had been lost to her, a girl whose father had left her just when she needed him most. It was the song of a girl who had lain awake in her bed at night, staring up at the endless dark, wondering when the strange dreams of an unseen love would leave her, when the boys in school would finally look her way, when she'd finally feel real and fully formed—grown-up. It was all carried in the aching notes that reached out that open doorway, wrapping their slender arms around me. I rose, leaning forward so that I could better peek inside that cool, inviting space.

A sharp scent hit me, putrid and slimy. But there was that music. It wore me down until I was tender, until my heart felt raw in my chest. I stepped forward along the stone floor. The fall of my flight boots was as quiet as rustling paper, drowned out beneath the sound of that voice. It told me about my mother, her limbs all tangled up with Benjamin Jacobi's—the dead librarian, her lover. It told me about the hope in his eyes the last time we ever spoke, the day I got my vocation. Like he was examining me for any sign, however small, of *her*.

Inside the house the air was chilly. There was a long counter, illuminated by a pair of horn-shaped lights. They swayed from their chains, casting sinister shadows on the floor. Beneath them were sides of meat hacked up into pieces; the spaces between the limbs were slick with green blood. In front of the counter sat an Ahadizhi man. He sang as he worked his double-bladed cleaver into them, slicing massive limbs into smaller and smaller portions.

But that song, that song—it told me about what was supposed to have been my wedding night, when I'd answered that final, lingering question. I could have married Silvan Rafferty, could have given him my heart even if I would have never cherished his. I could have been normal, in a way. But I hadn't done it. And I wasn't normal. I stepped closer. I wanted to wrap that music around me, pull it tight like a blanket.

Terra.

My head snapped up. Vadix. His voice, unmistakable. Tender and worried. Worried for *me*. I answered him without speaking, from a place deep inside me where there were no words. His voice came back at me again, stronger this time.

Terra, leave this place. It is not safe for you.

But I had nowhere left to go! No one understood me. No one but this singer, who despite his work—up to the elbows in blood, two glinting blades in hand—began to turn his head back toward me, hoping to get another look.

Terra, I understand you.

I felt something then: a jolt. Electric, sure, but there was a story in the current. Love, warmth. Separation. And then something else, a cleft that had torn his good senses away from him. Now there was only an ache, tender and throbbing. A curious sensation, like an itch, but worse. The desire to pull his skin away, to make his body weep. I stumbled backward through the front door, out into the blinding light of day again. There were footsteps insite the round house, calm, even. And a face. Smiling, but far from benevolent.

Terra, Vadix said. His words, in my head. How was it even possible? But I'd learned the possibility of many improbable things over the past few days. Him. Me. This city. Our dreams. *Terra, run.*

The Ahadizhi man reached out for me, but I jerked my hand away, gave my body a twist, and ran.

· · ·

As I raced through the streets of Raza Ait, something changed. My body still dripped sweat like a faucet; my mind was still hazy from the heat. And yet the image of the roads before me split. I could see the cobblestone, the bridges, but a second image joined them. Memories. Vadix had walked these paths recently, heading from the quarantine camp to his own house. He'd seen the Ahadizhi turn toward him. Back then the word on their lips hadn't been "human." It had been smaller, simpler—and more cutting, too.

Lousk.

He'd turned a corner, and so did I. He'd let his body drift down a wide staircase, so I clutched the railing in hand and descended. Beneath the overpasses a whole wild forest grew. To the aliens it was nothing more than a park—dotted with purple leaves, full of flowers that glowed like lanterns. Vadix knew this place well; it was one of the only notes of joy in his thin, meager life. To me it was dazzling, full of color and movement and the sweet scent of new growth. I wanted to stop, to sit on one of the stone benches and watch fresh water drip down the face of a massive fountain. But I didn't settle into the soft, cool dirt. I still had a ways to go yet: through the fruit grove up ahead.

The ground between the shivering trees was soft and black. The air was chilly, more fragrant than any I'd yet breathed on Zehava. I took a deep breath, held it in my lungs.

Vadix likes it here, I thought. *It reminds him of the place where he's meant to be.*

I shook the thought from my head. It made no sense. It wasn't mine to have. And yet I still marched on and on through the cool forest, toward the enclave of abandoned houses through the break in the trees. Because of his presence, strong and steady in my mind, I knew that those houses were some of the oldest in the city. First came the senate, then the funerary fields, then the winter caves. Then these small abodes, made from hand out of alabaster earth and glass. They'd housed the first Ahadizhi, before they sprouted child after child and outgrew the round walls. The hunters had abandoned the houses like old, ill-fitting clothes when they headed for the new buildings above. Now most of the hollow lumps of clay were dark. Their doors hung open on their hinges with only blackness shining out into the afternoon. But I knew that there would be one that was still well kept, inhabited. It was the oldest, the largest. It had belonged to the first Ahadizhi senator. For the time it had been a grand accommodation. Shaped like a nautilus, the house had a thousand shards of colored glass pressed into her walls—a thousand tiny windows into the life inside. As I drew near, my steps slowed. There was a light on somewhere, and it made the flints of green and blue and gold gleam.

I stood in the shadow of the house, breathing hard. I had come through the wild alien city, half baked by the sun and utterly lost.

And I had found it—the multifaceted jewel in all this darkness. The house. *His* house. I wanted to cry at the sight of it, but I was too tired, too spent. Instead I just stood, my mouth open. I was dirty and tired. My flight boot had worn a blister in my heel. But I was alive. Whole. And here.

The door clicked open. There was Vadix, his dark skin looking almost black in this dim light. He'd taken off his outer robes. Now he wore only a pair of trousers whose lengths were embroidered with sparkling threads. Decorative flowers trailed along the lengths of his limbs like roses on a trellis. His body shone, freshly washed, still damp from the shower. But his chest was not the smooth blue plane I'd seen in dreams. He was covered with dozens of pale scars, every one the exact width of his own fingers. I saw a flash in my mind's eye: Vadix, alone at night, using his bare hands to rend his skin open again and again and again.

Maybe I should have had a speech prepared. In the stories Rebbe Davison read us when we were young, there was always a speech. The young shepherd comes for the princess and tells his story. *It may be that I am bewitched, or dreaming, for my adventure passes all belief.* But I had no pretty words. I only pulled my tired body up the wide front steps, hung my head, and said:

"I came. You told me where to go, and I came. Here I am."

Vadix's response sounded choked, almost painful, like he didn't want to force the words past the bounds of his scar-strewn torso. "You were in danger. I couldn't bear to lose you. I will not survive such a loss again."

I still avoided his eyes. It felt like something strange might happen if I met them, something beyond my control.

"You told me you didn't want me," I said. "You *told* me—"

"I was afraid. This has never happened. These bonds exist only for Xollu. Not Ahadizhi, much less a beast."

I flinched at the word; he let out a thrum of sound. A sigh, or something like it.

"I do not understand your nature, Terra. It is as foreign to me as the nature of the Ahadizhi. They hunt too, but they are not all bad. They taste flesh. Have strange passions. But they are kind. Clever. Passionate. You are these things too. I am assured. Do not ask me why."

His mouth quivered. I wanted to press my lips to his, to still them. But I didn't, not yet. Did aliens even know how to kiss?

"All those dreams, for all those months," I said, my chest fluttering. "At first I thought they were dreams like the other girls had. About boys, you know? But then I realized they were *different*. I felt—I felt like a freak, Vadix. Wrong."

"Perhaps it is wrong."

"It doesn't *feel* wrong," I blurted. And then my eyes met his. I could have clamped my hands over my mouth, taking my words back, holding them in. But I didn't want to. Instead I watched him. He pressed his fearful lips together and was still for a long moment. Then he smiled. A slow, warm smile.

"No," he agreed. "It does not feel wrong. It does not feel wrong at all."

His words were small and simple, just as plain as any others. But they were all I needed. My heart open, my eyes open, too, I reached out for him.

He caught me. Our bodies touched. For the first time in the flesh, I felt right. Happy. Whole.

17

Sometimes it seems to me that there are two types of love. The first starts small—like a drop of pigment against a wrinkled page. At first it looks like nothing but a smudge of color, stark against white. But then you add to it: a laugh, a conversation, the way that he kisses you. One brushstroke after another. Like art it fills the paper slowly until the image is undeniable. On the ship most marriages worked out like that. As we grew older, we hoped for friendships that would slowly flower into something else—by then too world-weary to expect the passionate embraces that had been promised to us in stories and in dreams.

And that was the other love, the sort we whispered of in the school yard, bright as sex and twice as dangerous. A love that caught fire like a match in the darkness, ready to burn oxygen, our lungs, our lives. *Bashert, bashert,* we whispered, half afraid we would find it was some-day true. Because it was a risk, wasn't it? To love hot and ask questions later. We wanted it, but we didn't want it. By the time I'd found Vadix, I was sixteen—old enough, really, to know better.

But sometimes you need a forest fire to clear the ground for new growth. Mara had taught me that long ago—a lesson she'd hoped I'd use on our new planet, though I don't imagine that she ever meant it *this* way. Vadix and I stumbled back toward his bedroom, heading straight for the round bed at the center. He peeled my clothes off as we went, leaving one dirty layer after another in a pile on the floor. His hands were long, familiar. I found in them a thousand tender mercies. They graced bare skin, caressed my rib cage and my belly. Electricity arced and flickered between us. How could I have ever doubted my own worth? Because no matter what Abba had said— and Aleksandra, and Mazdin Rafferty, and so many others—*he* found me worthy, urging me to love and love and never leave.

I kissed every uncountable scar. There were so many of them that soon I was dizzy, desperate for air. He laced fingers through the matted locks of my hair, drew me closer and closer still. I thought of the vines curling around one another in the forest, desperate to make their parts meet. I empathized. Why couldn't we just have one body, one mind? It seemed to me a grave injustice that we had been born separate, different, that we had wasted so much time so far away from each other. That afternoon and into the deep golden evening, I endeavored to correct that. We would be one. Whole. Formidable. A new sort of creature.

The forest burned, but anyone who tells you that nothing is left in its wake has never felt what I've felt, has never seen the green promise of new growth turning up its head toward the sun—all in a darkened world of char and ash.

A funny thing happened that night, as we tumbled together and apart and together again. Our thoughts mingled, becoming one. I couldn't tell you where I ended and he began. I wasn't even sure whether we slept, tussling in the dreamforests, or whether we were awake, breathing, my heart pounding against his still chest. Mostly we spoke without speaking, without even words.

Love? I would ask, the question merely a flash of color in the dawning darkness, and his answer came back surely and swiftly: *Love.* Vines blossoming in the forest, furling out in wild curlicues, color, and color, and life.

It was a crazy thing to ask—a crazy answer, too. We hardly knew each other. And the future was uncertain. There was no room for us here. No room, even, for me. In a rare moment of respite that night, I turned my face up, peeling back the covers. The ceiling overhead was made of glass, so clear it might as well have been transparent. We were near the heart of the city, not far from the senate where our day had begun. If we went any deeper, we'd be underground—heading toward the funerary fields and the caves where the Xollu slept their long winters away. I knew this but didn't know it. I knew it because it was his life, his truth. But staring up at the leaves that crowded the edges of the glass, and the stars that twinkled far, far above, past the translucent cupola, I wondered what all of these things meant. The truth was, I wasn't used to being *happy*, and certainly not for long. The sadness began drifting back almost as quickly as we'd chased it away.

The strange, familiar solitude washed over me. I pointed up at a star that was silver and still in the sky above. It looked familiar, and then I realized the difference. The other stars twinkled, filtered through the atmosphere. This star shone steadily, like the stars through the ship's glass once had.

"What's that?" I asked. Vadix turned to me, a plush round pillow wedged between his arm and face. He pressed his face into it, blinking slowly, smiling.

"This is your ship. What is her name?"

"Asherah."

"Hmm," he said. *"Ash-er-rahhh."* He drew out the syllables, lux-uriating in their foreign sound. But then his expression changed, weighted by his sadness. If there was one thing I was to learn about Vadix that night, it was that he wasn't used to being happy either.

"I used to know not what name to curse. That star, burning steadily above. When it appeared weeks ago, our people flung out wild theories. It was a bad portent. It was a sign from the god and the goddess. It was a satellite, come to steal our technologies, sent by sinister . . ." A pause. His smile returned, wide, showing all those minuscule teeth. "Aliens."

"I'm not an alien," I said. I reached out, cupping my hand against his smooth cheek. *"You're* an alien."

"You are alien to this planet."

"But not to you." I drew close, pressing my lips against his. I think it surprised him, the warmth and wetness of my open mouth. But after a moment his cool body softened, leaning in. Our first kiss, gentle, tender—and as long as the night.

His round bed was the perfect size and shape for two long bodies. But I kept myself snuggled close to him. His half of the mattress was bowed beneath his weight—he'd spent too many nights in it alone. I let my fingers trace the scars over his shoulders. Some were old, deep, and faded into his skin. But some were white, new, raw. For the hundredth time that night, I pressed my lips to one, tasting sweet sap. I wished I still believed that kisses could heal like I had when I was a child. But I knew better now. No kisses would heal this.

I wanted to ask, but I couldn't make the words come to my lips. So I spoke without speaking, the way we had in dreams.

You did this to yourself, didn't you? I asked. I felt him shift so he could see me better. He was surprised, I think, to hear my voice so clear in his mind, but also pleased. This speech was as natural to him as breathing was to me.

I am a lousk, he said, as if that explained it. I drew myself up, putting my hand flat against his chest. It seemed so strange against his skin, so solid.

I don't know what that means.

"Every spring seedlings sprout from their parents' bodies," he said, slipping into real speech as easily as one slipped into a new set of clothes. "Thousands of them. The funerary fields are full of light and joy. From our first conscious moments we are paired. Those who are alone wither and die. They are the first *lousk*. But most survive, thrive in our crèches. Never lonely. Never wanting companionship. Best friends. At night we walk in the dreamforests together, where we are one body and thought and mind."

"*Bashert,*" I said. "Mate."

Vadix nodded, the motion small and quick, his eyes still fixed fast on me.

"Zeze," he said. "That is our word for it. God and goddess willing, we live long, happy lives. Working. Mating. Praying. Learning. Until our *zeze* dies. Then we are a *lousk."*

"Widower," I said. "That's what we call it. Abba—my father—he was alone after my mother died. A widower."

His hand was utterly still on top of mine.

"Velsa," he said at last. "Her name was Velsa. We were always different from the rest. Brave. Ambitious. We did not like how crowded our cities had become. We wished to settle the southern lands, to build a city there. But no northern Ahadizhi would stray that far from their sprouting fields to join us, and no Xollu has ever shared words with the Ahadizhi in the south. We knew we needed to broker peace if they were to be our Guardians, to keep us safe in the long winters when we sleep and the animals roam."

"You wanted to make a new city. For you and her."

I saw it in his mind's eye: nights spent whispering to each other though they lay a thousand kilometers apart. They would build their own empire, new and beautiful. Because they were young and brave. They would settle new ground, something that the Xollu hadn't done for centuries.

"Yes. We were foolish, proud. I would be the translator, speaking

the tongue of the southern Ahadizhi. She would learn diplomacy. I went to school in the south, in Aisak Ait. And she stayed here. They all said we were crazy, to live our young lives apart like *lousku.*"

He sat up, draping his arms around his knees. I wanted to touch him, to wrap my arms around him again and draw him close. But I knew better. It hurt too much. He was still too raw. "Velsa—Velsa died. There were riots when your people sent their first probe. The Xollu were afraid—the Ahadizhi determined to protect us from the danger. I did not see this. I was far, far away."

I closed my eyes, remembering the days between the departure of the first probe and the news that the results had been lost. They'd been long, lonely days—and even darker nights. Until I saw him for the first time in the black of evening, drifting through my dreams. He must have lost her then, in the days before he was mine.

I could almost see it. The dust in the air. The crush of bodies. Velsa, on her way to her towering university in the south of the city. She and her friends had traced their favorite river, hoping to see the long painted boats whose multicolored flags flickered in the wind. But the pier was crowded and then there was a shout. Someone had found a strange machine in the water, with wide metal wings and eyes that blinked like beacons. It was covered in text, words no one could read.

But as the Ahadizhi dock workers began to pull the panels of the machine back, they smelled flesh on the air. Strange, alien odors in every fingerprint that had been left on the metal hull. They bared their teeth—gripped their weapons. Double-bladed knives gleamed in the sunlight. The crowd pushed forward, closer to the scent of danger. Velsa found herself swept up in the tide of bodies.

If I pushed harder, deeper, I would find the truth myself, feel the pain of the dagger's thrust and the rush of sweet sap down the front of her robe. But I knew it would hurt him to have those memories turned over again like dirt for a fresh planting. So I drew back.

I'm sorry, I said silently, but I regretted that thought almost instantly. I'd heard those words said at Momma's funeral and at Abba's, and at least a hundred times in the dark days since. Once, I'd rolled my eyes, cracking awkward jokes and laughing. *Why?* I always said. *It's not your fault.* I knew that my condolences were meager, nothing compared to the grief he felt. His sadness dragged me down too, like a boat that had sprung a leak and sank into the ocean. I was sorry, so sorry, and it wasn't nearly enough.

When he spoke, it was as if every word came with great effort. "We never mated. I was fallow until tonight. There would have been no children. But on the day she died, I understood something I never had before then. How a *lousk* is not merely a rare shadow, fleeing to the funerary fields. He is possessed. He will tear his flesh with his fingers, cast his body down to the soil. I should have done this dozens of days ago. My dead, fallow body has wanted it—to be with her, to be together."

He wants to kill himself, I realized. Now it was my turn to harden beside him. My hands dropped down into the sheets. I watched him sitting there, his shoulders hunched up and still.

"It is the only thing left for a *lousk* to do," he said. As if it were nothing, as if it were natural. I suppose for him it was. "But I saw something in the darkness. A face. The pale muzzle of an animal, with a mane of tangled gold. She wandered the dreamforests. I asked her for her name, but she did not answer me. Night after night I dream of her. She touched me, and I felt—"

"Whole," I said, finishing his sentence for him.

"I was remiss," he said, "In my duty to Velsa. I should have rushed home, laying my body down on top of hers. We should have been one. But I was curious. And then the senate came to me. There were glyphs on the machine, and recordings embedded in it. They knew I was gifted in foreign tongues. They asked me to translate. I did. It was easy—too easy. I studied many years in Aisak Ait, but never had a language slipped so freely from my lips. I knew things I shouldn't have. Soon your shuttle crew stumbled through the gates of Raza Ait. There was violence again, fear at these foreign beasts. The senate asks me to speak to these animals. You, who have brought Velsa's death. Broker a peace. They say I am the only one who can. I decide I will help them. Then I will be with Velsa, as I should. But I met you."

I drew in a slow breath, pulling my legs up to my chest. Our bodies were so different—his legs so much longer and leaner than my own. But somehow I managed to sit in a perfect mirror of him, my arms hugging my knees, my shoulders high.

"I didn't expect you either," I said. "But I've been dreaming about you for months and months."

"Me too, since the night Velsa left me," he admitted. "An animal girl, with a wild swirl of hair. Wrong, I thought it was wrong. I thought I was a freak."

I smiled despite the heavy weight of the night. For all those months he'd felt just as strange and broken as I had. He let his violet tongue wet his full lips and went on.

"Then, after, every night since, without fail. There you are. Animal girl, hair the color of morning. I think, maybe this is what happens to *lousku*. They go mad. But here with you, I do not feel mad. I feel— what is the word?"

I reached out, wrapping my fingers around his.

Sane?

Yes, this, he agreed. He drew my hand against his chest. I could feel the laughter there, weak but growing. *Not all sane. But a little sane.*

I wanted to tell him that I felt that way too. Better when I was beside him. Less crazy. Less wrong. But I didn't have to say it. As he pressed his lips to mine, a thousand blossoms turned their faces toward the light inside my mind.

• • •

Will you still do it?

The night had passed its darkest hour. Now the sky was turning dull gray at the corners. Soon the light would go green, then gold again, and the night would be over. There were so many stones still left unturned, so much about him I still didn't know. I wanted more than a night. I was selfish. I wanted a lifetime.

"Taot?"

Vadix had tucked an arm over his head and gone still, utterly still. Without breath or heartbeat his sleep seemed as deep as death. It wasn't until he jerked himself awake and turned toward me, black eyes shining, that I was at all reassured.

Will you still do it? Will you still go to the funerary fields?

I felt his cool body stiffen beside me. Though his long legs still touched mine, it felt like he was halfway across the galaxy. He spoke aloud, lonely words.

"It is my *nature*, Terra. This is how new life is made for my people. We live all our days together, sleep our winters away with our bodies tangled around the same stem. And then we return to the dreamforests, hand in hand."

I felt my stomach clench. What crashed through me like white-licked waves wasn't jealousy, though there might have been some shade of that. Mostly what I felt was the stormy churning of my own desperate loneliness. I'd traveled so far, over hundreds of kilometers of cold, frozen ground. All on account of him, on account of the promise his body offered. My dreams had told me I wouldn't be alone anymore, that I would be safe. My dreams told me that this strange boy could love me like I needed.

"Here," he said, mistaking my silence for something else—a sullen protest maybe. He lifted a spindly arm, wrapping it around my shoulder and drawing me close. "I will show you."

I pressed my head against his unbreathing chest. At first there was nothing, only the gray light all around us, the stars fading overhead, my breath. But then I felt his mind nudge mine open. I felt a jolt of heat, saw a vomitous flash of color. This should have been a perfect moment, as sweet as those high spring afternoons when the scent of clover was all around and Rachel had laced dandelion chains through my hair. It wasn't. His mind was jumbled, as fractured as broken ice. I could see the fissure at the bottom of it, and it was shaped like a shadow of her—Velsa.

He wanted to tear his skin apart. This urge to join her, to end himself, wasn't about me. It was a compulsion, like hunger or thirst, only worse. It formed the very core of his being. And if he dug deep enough, he'd finally uncover it.

Lousk.

I wanted to draw away, to fold my body in on itself and hold myself tight. But I couldn't bring myself to move. After everything I'd been through, I was going to lose him. Like I'd once lost Momma. Like I'd lost Abba, too.

Abba. That's when I realized that Vadix could see my thoughts and memories just as well as I could see his. He could hear the creaking in the rafters, the splintered rope groaning under the weight of my father's body. He could see the strange, distorted image of his face—like someone had taken out all the pins that held it together, that made my father vital and strong and *real.* If you'd asked Abba, he probably would have told you that he died years before, when his wife lay down with another man, and then was lost to him.

Without Alyana, he always said, way back in the days when my parents were young and we were happy, *I'm nobody.*

In a way Abba had been a *lousk* too.

Vadix fixed a narrow finger beneath my chin, angling my face up to meet his. "This pains you. This loss. Your father."

"Of course it does," I said, and sniffled. My face was suddenly covered in inexplicable tears. I hadn't expected to cry tonight—but then, I hadn't expected to find myself in his bed either. "Maybe it shouldn't. He didn't—he didn't treat me well. Called me names. I think he was mad at Momma for leaving him and me and my brother. Or maybe he saw her in me, in the way I looked at boys and was always late to everything and always in my head. Maybe. I don't know. I just know

I needed him to be someone else, someone who could take care of me."

"Maybe he wasn't able to be anyone but himself for you," Vadix said, his words plucked out carefully. I wondered if he was really talking about Abba at all. "Maybe he did try his best."

"Maybe. It wasn't enough."

He set his head back on his pillow, staring up at the sky above. I watched him draw his tongue over his lips to wet them. When he spoke, his words were still tentative. Nervous. "I do feel a connection to you. Just as I once did with Velsa. The wild child, the animal girl of my dreams. I do not lie about this. One cannot deny one's *zeze*. Now that I have met you, I wouldn't be able to now even if I tried."

I didn't doubt it. Why else would he have welcomed me into his home, his bed—even the dark corners of his mind? But I wasn't sure what to say, if there were any words that could make the situation between us better.

"I will do my best not to cause you harm," he said at last, the words thudding resolutely onto the sheets beside us. "I do not wish to hurt you. I will see that your people are safe and well cared for before I—"

He broke off there, but he didn't need to finish his sentence, not really. We both knew how this ended. I'd seen it before, with Abba— that stupid, hopeful look as he settled his life in his last days, arranging to have me married off. Abba had meant to see to it that I was safe, too. But safety was never what I wanted, not really.

What could I say? Vadix held me tight against his fragrant body, the strength of his grip undeniable. He'd said it himself. He didn't want to hurt me. He was trying his best. Wasn't that enough?

Of course it wasn't, but it was no good telling him that. I buried my face in his cool flesh and murmured my consent. He drew me close. It wasn't all of what I wanted; it wasn't half of it. But in that long night, our first, it would have to do.

18

ay had already begun to blot out the stars, but the silver light of the *Asherah* still burned above. I kept my eye on her as I lay sleepless in his bed, my hands folded over my stomach. Even here I couldn't escape her shadow. Up there, within her walls, I had killed a man, shaking clouded powder into dark wine. I had seen other deaths, too. Abba, his body a heavy weight that bowed the rafters. Mar Jacobi, his blood spilled out on the engine room floor. And Momma, years and years before. The first loss. Sometimes I felt as if everything else in my life spiraled out from that.

As I pulled myself from his bed, the cool morning air met my naked body. I tugged free the sheet, draping it over my shoulders. The fabric was soft, more luxurious than any I'd ever known on the ship. The smooth weave reminded me of his skin. I gazed wistfully at him, curled into a ball at the center of the mattress, his long body surprisingly small in the nest of blankets. Because I was awake, his dreams were long and black. Peaceful. So I let him sleep.

The night before, we'd hurried toward the bed in a fevered rush. I hadn't had time to explore his home. Now I went from room to room feeling like an interloper in the small, private life he'd made. His accommodations were sparse. There was no art on the walls; the floors were bare, either white stone or white sand that had been packed flat and then smoothed down. But in truth the house needed no decoration. The light of the dawn poured through the decorative glass, dappling everything red and blue and green. Each room was curved—sloping walls, rounded counters, bubbled ceilings that showed daylight and trees and the city's veil far beyond. I found what appeared to be a bathroom, a narrow slip of space at the center of the home covered in dark mosaic tiles. There was a waist-high bench with a narrow hole in the top that seemed untouched. Some sort of toilet or waste receptacle, I supposed. Meant for the original inhabitants, not a Xollu who subsisted on "sunbeams and vapors." But I wasn't like them; I hopped onto it, did my business.

Then I wandered out and toward the kitchen. It was a bright space, even in this early hour, with a glass ceiling overhead and a counter that shone with opalescent tile. But the plants that sat all around—in hanging baskets from the ceiling, in long planters along the floor—raised few complaints. They only turned over their leaves, exposing themselves to the sun. There was no icebox, no stove. But there was a shower stall in the corner, behind a door of frosted glass. I opened it, considering. A long spigot hung down with a green copper chain beside it. It had been days since I'd washed. Too many. I dropped the sheet down at the center of the floor and stepped inside, pulling the frosted glass door closed behind me.

I gave the chain a tentative pull. On the ship, pipes rattled and clanged, so caked with generations of lime that the pressure was never more than a splutter. But here the water was instant, the force strong. It didn't taste mossy or stale like the ship's water. In fact, it tasted like nothing at all as it rained down my face in rivers. I watched the dirt roll off me in sludgy streams and tried to count how long it had been since I'd last bathed. Five days, or six? I remembered scrubbing my skin with a honey wash on my wedding night, but it felt like a lifetime ago already, not the better portion of a single week.

As I scrubbed my hair, the scent of fire that had been trapped in my unwashed tresses blossomed, and then faded. When the water at long last washed clear, I stepped from the shower stall. Through the cloud of steam I ambled—until my hand bumped the counter, and found a pile of fresh cloth folded there. It was a bolt of silver fabric—one of Vadix's robes, and a pair of matching trousers, too. I put them on. They were too big, billowing around my curves. But they were comfortable and clean, a world apart from the dirty cotton I'd left littering his bedroom floor.

You are awake.

Vadix's voice in my mind startled me. I turned, glimpsing him in the doorway. He'd pulled on those loose green pants again. But as he strolled into the kitchen, I found myself frowning. Perhaps it was just the light—sparkling, gold and strong—but the skin over his flat belly looked different. It was darker now than it had been, nearly the color of the inside of a pomegranate. I watched him closely as he went to one of the two counter spigots and filled up a round glass bowl. No, it wasn't the light. His arms and face were still the same mellow blue, but his belly and chest were now dark, an almost ruby red.

"What happened?" I asked. When he only stared back, I pointed at his midsection. He glanced down. His lips parted. He clicked laughter too.

"You happened," he said. "I am no longer fallow."

"Oh!" I replied. I felt my cheeks burn, suddenly furiously hot. He put down his cup and came to stand beside me.

"What's this?" he asked, angling my face up to his. "Are you fertile now too?"

It was all so ridiculous. This conversation, this morning. I wrinkled my nose at him.

"No, no," I said, suddenly embarrassed. "I'm only blushing. Thank you for the clothes."

I pulled away, doing a quick spin across his kitchen floor. Silver fabric rippled after me. He watched, smiling.

"You look less like an animal than before."

"Is that meant to be a compliment?"

"It's meant to be—"

A high-pitched chirrup interrupted Vadix's words. He tilted his head to the side, glimpsing a panel set into the far wall that had just gone light.

"Excusing me," he said, holding up one long finger. As he strolled across the floor, I leaned my weight against the countertop. His hands made quick work across the screen. Meanwhile I picked up his bowl. It didn't look like ordinary water. The bottom was slicked with oil, shining greasy golden.

"*Taot?*" he demanded. Out of the corner of my eye, I glimpsed the face of an Ahadizhi woman. She let out a loose stream of words.

"*Zeza dhosoou zozax aum dhesedi deosoaz. Zhieserak dosoe! Dosoe terix zhieserak, zozax thosouu—*"

"Arum azax aum dasa dhosoou rausiz zeza?"

As they spoke, their voices hit strange, passionate heights. I leaned against the counter, peering past Vadix's naked shoulders and toward the screen. A pair of Xollu could be seen in the background, stern-eyed and serious. I wondered what had happened that had so offended them. Maybe it was because of me and my flight through the city after Vadix. In my rashness I could have spread disease or discord through Raza Ait. We were meant to stay safe and secure in our quarantine camp, instead of rushing out to mingle with the city's inhabitants. I swallowed hard, gazing down into the bowl. My throat was suddenly dry, tight. I pointed one pinkie finger and dipped it into the bowl, then plunged it into my mouth. Whatever it was that Vadix had been drinking, it was terribly sour, with a sweetness that I couldn't taste until after I swallowed.

"Terra!"

Before I knew it, the screen was off and Vadix stood beside me again. Stern-eyed, he plucked the bowl from out my hands and placed it on the counter.

"How do you know this sweetwater will not poison you?" he asked. He sounded angry—honest to goodness angry. I gave my shoulders a shrug.

"I don't know. I thought—"

Vadix closed his eyes, pressing long fingers to his forehead. I saw him standing there, his reddened belly stormy, his expression pinched.

"Something's wrong," I said, watching as his earslits fluttered. That old fear, familiar from my years of living with Abba, was back again. I'd done something terrible, and now the hammer would fall. He was going to yell at me, call me names—but he didn't. He only dropped his hand and let his head hang down.

"The Ahadizhi have called for humanity's expulsion from Zehava."

"What?" I demanded. I couldn't return to that dank, dark ship, live out my days with no hope ahead. I needed to be here. With him. My stomach clenched with fear. "Is it my fault? My outburst in the senate antechamber. I didn't mean to harm negotiations. I thought—"

He took my shaking hands in his long, smooth hands. I felt his mind nudge mine, cool and calm.

No, he said, speaking the words without speaking. *It is not your fault. I promise.*

My breathing once again returned to normal. But in the wake of my fear and worry, I still felt a tenderness inside. I would have to leave him, sooner than I'd thought. I drew close to him, pressing my face against his bare chest.

"What happened?" I asked as he slid his arms around me, holding me tight.

"The quarantine camp," he said. "That woman. That Aleksandra.

After her attack on me, I ordered more guards to watch over them, to gather their weapons away. But she was ready this time. She attacked them. Your people broke through the walls with spears and stones. Two Xollu pairs were lost to the fields—may the god and goddess honor them with many seedlings."

"Oy *gevalt*," I said, pulling away from him. I don't know if he understood the meaning of my words, but from the way that he thinned his lips, I think he caught my drift.

"I am to bring you to the senate chamber, where the terms of your expulsion will be discussed."

He held my hands in his, gently rubbing his smooth finger pads over my knuckles. I held on tight. In truth I wanted nothing more than to turn away from this room, so full with the light of day, and bury myself in his covers again. In his bedroom we could kiss and touch and ignore the world beyond. No one would be able to reach us. We would be strong together, hidden.

But I knew it was just a stupid, childish dream. I had to face the future—the blinding morning, and the darkness overhead.

"I don't *want* to go," I whispered. His smile was wistful, full of understanding.

I know, he said. And then again, out loud, punctuating the thought. "I know."

• • •

Another crowded train. This time we both stood, our hands hanging from the same metal vine. Maybe I imagined it, but I think the Ahadizhi watched us even more closely now. Certainly when they called out to us—"*Lousk, lousk,* huu-maaan"—their hissed words had grown fierce. And no wonder. My people had once again brought violence to this city.

Vadix kept his shoulder pressed against mine. We must have looked like a strange couple, a human girl and a Xollu widower, dressed in Xollu robes. But in mind we were one and the same. I could feel his tempestuous thoughts, how they pulled his body in too many directions at once. There was the constant, ever present desire to flee this world for the silence of the funerary fields below, but now that was joined by something new. Now, if he had to live, he wanted me beside him to chase away the dark. Of course I wanted that too. Wanted it more than anything else. As the train paused at a station, I put my warm hand over his. He smiled at me—a thin, distracted smile.

What are you thinking? I asked wordlessly. I think it surprised him how quickly I'd taken to speaking this way, but I didn't want the others to listen in. They were strangers; their mouths were full of a thousand glinting teeth.

I am thinking of what will happen to your people when you return.

I considered it, unconsciously angling my face up toward the train car's copper ceiling, searching for the silver blot of light in the sky high above. I'd left in the middle of the riots, but already so many stores had been looted, so many windows turned to glinting dust. The place I'd fled hadn't been so much like a city as a ruin.

I don't know. We might try to settle without your help.

Vadix's mouth pulled down in disgust.

Impossible! The southern beasts are massive and bloodthirsty, not to mention the Ahadizhi there. What hubris, to believe you can do what generations of Xollu have never managed.

I didn't want to mention Vadix's own hubris, that once he'd believed he could do the same. He'd already paid for his pride, after all.

Well, there's always Silvan's plan. Rumor has it, he wants to launch us back toward our home planet. Earth.

He leaned forward, his robes mingling with mine as the train car streamed along.

This is a possibility?

I wanted to laugh, but it wasn't really funny.

No.

Why?

I stared out the bubbled glass, thinking about it. Beyond, purple trees streamed by, shifting in the wind. No matter how fallow Raza Ait became in winter—no matter how many meters of snow piled up all around the walls of the city—this was a vital, living place, one where the seasons turned and life, new life, poked its head out beneath the detritus of what had come before.

We left because our planet died. It's funny. I have this book written by one of my ancestors, and she talks all about how polluted and overcrowded the cities were there. But we didn't kill our planet. It was chance. Hit by an asteroid. We left because we would have died if we stayed. I don't know why Silvan thinks we can go back there now. It's crazy.

Vadix watched me, his gaze piercing even in the train car's colorful light.

So you have options. But all of them bad.

I didn't know what to say. I only nodded. In our silence the train car stopped, and the doors shivered open. Gently he took my hand in his and led me toward the senate building, where my people, and my future, waited.

19

We weren't allowed to hear the deliberations about our fate. Vadix led me instead to the senate antechamber, where just the day before, Mara had tried to argue for our settlement. Now the room seemed to me to be little more than a holding cell, packed full of restrained Asherati. As Vadix and I approached the open door, he gave my hand a squeeze—then was cleaved from me, gone, and without a word of farewell. I tumbled through the doorway. Tired faces lifted tired eyes. Their wrists were bound by rope and dripped with blood. Only Mara Stone walked freely, watching the proceedings through plate glass. She was the one to greet me.

"Talmid," she said. "Nice of you to join us."

I gazed at the others, crowded around the table, watched over by Ahadizhi guards who brandished prods. Hannah was hunched at the table, her face drained of all color. Rebbe Davison sat beside her, watching over Ettie. The child's face was stained, with blood, or dirt, I couldn't tell which. And she avoided my eyes, robbing me of any answer. My stomach twisted at the sight of her. I'd failed her—failed all of them.

Some of them had been injured. One of Jachin's ears was marked with a black burn; Aben Hirsch's already injured arm now hung at an odd angle. He clutched it to his body, rocking in pain. But they were alive at least—mostly unharmed. Except . . . My gaze roamed around the table, searching, counting. Someone was missing. Not Aleksandra. She sat back in her seat like a queen surveying her kingdom. But someone . . .

Laurel.

"Where is she?" I asked, stumbling forward. Two of the guards drew near. They didn't restrain me, but one let his prod spark—a warning. I stopped several meters from the table.

Are you all right? came Vadix's thoughts, but I could tell that he was distracted down there in the senate room, waving his hands, try-ing to cut in. They didn't want to listen to him; he wasn't one of

them. They'd only ever wanted him to translate, not to speak for himself. I sent a comforting flood of feeling back to him, false though it was. In truth my mind was frantic, swarmed with miserable, buzzing thoughts. Laurel. She hadn't been a friend, not quite. But she'd grown up beside me, become a woman, an ally. What had happened to her?

"Laurel!" I said, her name bursting desperately from my lips. "Where *is* she?"

One by one they all turned to look at Aleksandra. But she only stared back at me, her expression as hard as the winter's frozen soil. When her silence stretched on, I heard Rebbe Davison lift his voice.

"She's dead, Terra," he said. Somehow I'd known this was coming. She'd been holding so thinly on to the life ahead. But it didn't make the news any easier. I let out a cry, clamping my palm over my mouth. Beside me one of the guards startled—and pressed the prod into my back. But he didn't shock me. He just let Rebbe Davison mumble on. "She was the first one to attack. I think she wanted to make up for Deklan. Strike them down. Strike back. That look in her eyes—so fierce. I'd never seen her like that before. The rest of them rushed the door. I went to help her, but it was too late. Her body . . . flailing. Those damned weapons."

The rest of them all lowered their gazes, pressing fingers to their hearts. Not Aleksandra. She just stared at me, waiting for me to speak, to strike out—to strike *her.*

But the guard's prod was still pressed between my shoulder blades. I needed to be strong, steady, like I never had been before. I angled my chin up.

"You did this. She was following *you*, and now she's dead."

Aleksandra's lower lip jutted out. There was no sadness in her gaze, no regret. Only pride.

"She gave her life for us."

"It didn't have to happen," I whispered. My voice was calm, but I wasn't able to keep my shoulders from quaking.

"If there's to be liberty, there will have to be sacrifice. Laurel understood that."

"Sacrifice! How has her death helped us? What good has it done?"

Aleksandra didn't have an answer for that. She responded to my question with another question.

"Do you think you're better than me—that you haven't harmed a single soul? That you're still sweet, helpless Terra? We all know better. We all know what you've done."

I felt my anger harden to a lump inside me. It no longer mattered what I'd done or what Aleksandra had done—what mattered was our *future*, our colony, crumbling before our eyes.

"And I know what you've done!" I roared. It was as though I were possessed—as if Captain Wolff were beside me, whispering into my ear. *Tell them. Tell them.* I had kept Aleksandra's secret all this time, and for what? So I opened my mouth and said it. "You killed her. Your own mother. In that field you took your knife—"

"I did no such thing," Aleksandra replied, her tone firm and proud. But that was before she turned to look at the rest of them, at the way Jachin had buried his face in his hands, whispering prayers into his palms; the way that Hannah's mouth fell open in dismay. The way that Rebbe Davison slumped down in his seat, looking as though all his strength had been sapped right out of him.

"Mordecai," she said sadly, the wound uncovered for all to see. But my teacher only stared at her, no apology in his gaze. Only exhaustion. Hurt. Betrayal.

He'd been a young man on our first day of school—barely twenty years old. We'd been five, all giggles and jokes, Silvan and Rachel, Koen, Laurel, Deklan, and me. Now he was so much older. He'd lost so much. Now he'd lost his best friend too.

"We told you to keep your hands clean. We talked about this, Alex."

"Mordy, you *know* what she was like." Aleksandra sounded so small in that moment, but it didn't matter to Rebbe Davison.

"Is that what you'll tell the people? That Mama was mean to you, so you had to cut her down? Do you think that will convince them?"

"I don't—" she began, but before she could say another useless word, Mara Stone interrupted her.

"Something is happening."

Mara's breath fogged the glass in front of her. From the table the Asherati all glanced up. But they were bound, watched. I was the only one able to break away—finally moving the prod from the center of my spine. I ignored Aleksandra. And I ignored the tears that still dried on my face, so I could gaze down at the senate chamber and the chaos below.

Rows and rows of senators, Ahadizhi and Xollu both—resplendent in their colorful robes. Even through the thick glass, I could hear the pound of their voices. They all spoke over one another. Nobody seemed to listen to anybody else.

Until someone streamed down the steps, his green robes flying after him. Vadix. They all turned to see him, the boy whose limbs and neck still showed blue beneath the hems of his robes, no matter how red his belly had been made by our night together. Vadix, the *lousk*. He was shouting.

Zhiesero sauziz! Zhiesero sauziz! I couldn't hear his words, but I felt how raw his tongue was in the recesses of my mind. I put a hand against the cool glass, pressing forward, looking down at him. Silence echoed around him; then the voices rose up again. He glanced up toward us, his black eyes finding me behind the sheen of glass.

What were you saying? I asked as he trudged up the stairs, clutching the pleats of his robes in his long hands.

I was asking for mercy, he replied. *You are not invaders. You are refugees. I told them that.*

I winced, almost afraid to ask about their response. But I had to. This was our future we were talking about—unraveling right before my eyes.

And?

But Vadix had been doing this for longer than I had—speaking silently, without words and across great distances. He was better at it than me. And he knew how to turn away. No answer came back. Only silence. I looked away from the glass to Mara, and shook my head.

She reached out her small, work-worn hand and rested it against my shoulder.

"Be strong, *Talmid.* We'll find a way."

But I couldn't see how. I looked over to Rebbe Davison, to Hannah, to little Ettie. To the shuttle crew, or what was left of them. They all seemed weak, exhausted.

The door burst open, and in walked Vadix. His lips were drawn in a straight line, faint in his dark face. I could see the bustle of senators behind him, crowding the wide stairwell with their arguments and their demands. But he stood alone before us. He tucked his hands— hands that I had held, kissed, touched—into the arms of his robes.

"The senate has made their decision," he intoned. There was

something odd about his voice—distant. Broken. "You have brought violence to the great city of Raza Ait. Violence to your people, and to ours. In accordance with the wishes of the Grand Senate of the twelve cities, and upon the consensus of the Ahadizhi and Xollu people, you shall depart from the surface of Aur Evez at once. Return to your ship, and let your people know you are not welcome here."

I felt my gut squeeze. I couldn't leave, not when I had finally found him.

Vadix! I cried out in my mind. But he didn't respond. His dark gaze swept over the rest of them. My compatriots, who were chilly in their silence.

"You will be escorted to the pier at the south end of the city," he said, "where Mara Stone's shuttle craft awaits your arrival. You shall depart at once, all but one of you."

We all turned toward him, froze. For a moment my heart was filled with childish hopes. Perhaps I'd be permitted to stay here, tucked within the arms of my *bashert*. But Vadix's expression remained grave. Chilly.

"All except the leader among you. Come forward."

The Asherati exchanged glances—fearful, confused. But not Aleksandra. She only held her head firm as she stepped toward him. Vadix held out a long, three-fingered hand.

"You," he said in a grave voice without warmth or light. "Are you the leader of these people?"

Aleksandra didn't smile, not quite. But the way her lip curled was certainly proud. "Yes," she said, squaring her shoulders. "I'm their leader."

He glanced at the two closest guards.

"Ekku zheserazhi, ekku sesez vheseri."

They moved fast, flanking her, pressing their weapons into the small of her back. She jumped back, struggled. But my lover's face went blank—his expression, extraordinarily cold.

"It is the decision of the Grand Senate that you pose too great a threat to the people of Aur Evez to be permitted the liberty of life."

Her skin went waxy, pale as a moon. "What?" she began, then craned her neck, glancing behind her. She called out, "Mordy! Mordecai!"

But Rebbe Davison wouldn't look at her. He opened his arms, welcoming Ettie into them. The child pressed her face to his chest, hiding from what was about to transpire. Rebbe Davison rocked her, whispering words of comfort. But he did nothing to comfort Aleksandra. She cried out, an animal sound. Vadix flinched. I could still feel the turmoil deep down inside him. He didn't want to give the command. But he had to. The senate had decided.

"May the god and goddess grant you many seedlings. Hunters, have your meat. *Zhosora aivaz.*"

There was a great crack of sound, and the antechamber filled up with blue, blinding light. I heard a thud. Aleksandra, falling to the floor. She stared up at the ceiling, dead and empty. Beside me Mara Stone let out a breath of sound.

My chest was tight. I could hardly breathe as Mara stooped over and closed Aleksandra's eyes. Soon Vadix was beside me. I felt his hand at my elbow, the pressure firm but insistent.

"Come," he said, his voice husky with emotion. "I shall walk with you to the pier."

"Vadix," I said, and the name echoed in my mind. *Vadix.*

But he was still closed to me, to my words and thoughts and heart. He gave my arm a tug, not even daring to look me in the eye.

"We must go now," he said, pulling me out of the room as the others were jostled to follow by Ahadizhi prods. "If we wish to say good-bye."

The pier was on the city's outskirts, past the warmth of the towering wall that contained Raza Ait. As we walked down the crowded thoroughfare, I winced at the cold air that cut through the robes I'd borrowed from Vadix. The sky overhead was full of heavy-bottomed clouds. And the sea in the distance churned, brackish and peaked with white. It stretched on and on until it disappeared against the horizon a curved, far-off place. It seemed this world was infinite, never ending. I wondered what was beyond my grasp, felt a knot in my throat at the thought that I'd never see *any* of it.

The others were flanked on all sides by guards, but they didn't seem to notice. They trudged ahead with drawn expressions, with shadows under their eyes like bruises left in the wake of so much death—Aleksandra's guards, Deklan, Laurel, now Aleksandra, too. I hadn't participated in the bloodbath down at the quarantine camp; I hadn't earned bound hands. But that didn't mean I walked alone.

Vadix was beside me, his body shielding me from a southward wind. He kept one long hand draped across my back—but his mind might as well have been lost out there in the middle of the sea. It was distant, cold, and cloistered. Had I kissed those lips, pressed my body against his? It felt almost like a dream as we shouldered through the crowds to the end of the pier, where Mara Stone's shuttle craft bobbed against the waves.

The others were pushed and jostled until they relented—then they slipped inside the dark recess of the shuttle. But I hesitated at the door. We were surrounded by guards, by fishermen, by people and voices going about their day. My companions still peered out at me, expectant, waiting within the confines of the shuttle. But it didn't matter. I couldn't leave, not yet, not after all we'd shared.

We can't end it this way, I said, stepping close to him. He turned his face away from me, scanning the horizon.

"Snow," he said aloud. I turned too. The air around us seemed alive, sparked with tiny flakes. They drifted and swirled all around us, catching in updrafts, dotting the stone walk of the pier before disappearing—like they'd never been there at all. I felt them hit my cheeks, my sunburned arms, like a thousand tiny kisses. I saw them dot Vadix, too. He flinched at the cold. "Only a few more moons until winter, and then the Xollu of the city sleep."

"Will you be among them?" I asked, my voice breaking out, fresh and raw. He didn't look at me, not yet. "It's over for you now, isn't it? We're leaving. You did your job."

Silence. Snow dotted my eyelashes, tangled in my hair. When I stretched out my mind to touch his, only frigid cold came back. The lump in my throat was huge; the one in my heart, even harder. I began to gather up my strength. I should have known better than to hang my hopes on him, to act like he was someone I could depend on.

I took the first step toward the shuttle, my robes brushing his. But his hand darted out and gripped mine.

"How can you say this?" he demanded. I twisted my body, looking back at him. At his endless, endless eyes, reflecting the falling snow like stars. "I made you a promise. Safe. I will see that you're safe. Do you think I will break it?"

When I didn't answer, he cradled my fingers against his body. Clutched so closely, it was almost as if they moved of their own accord—wriggling beneath the line of his sleek, heavy robes until they rested against his chest, red and bruisey. No warmth, as usual. No beating heart. But I felt the familiar sparking thrill of our connection. His mind opened to mine, and he saw what I had seen. My memories.

The riots. Men lifting fists. Women brandishing stones and sticks and kitchen knives. Windows exploding to pieces, and the pasture herds, once docile, widening their eyes at the sight. He saw me running through the dome, garbed in that harvest-gold dress, now long lost to the wilds. He saw me stumble through the cornfields, my breath and fear and urgency all a fury of white on the air. He felt the scratchy stalks, as dry as paper, as I drew them apart and stared down the row and watched Aleksandra Wolff fell her mother like an animal who had outlived her usefulness. I leaned in, letting my hair veil my face as he showed me what I already knew: the *Asherah*, falling to pieces, without me.

"The ship is not a safe place for you," he murmured, wrapping his soft arms around my shoulders. "Or for your people."

"We have nowhere left to go," I whimpered. I saw the chaos over and over again, how the angry mob flooded the shuttle bay, desperately reaching for the freedom of the world beyond.

"I will find a place for you," he said. "I will not rest until that day dawns when you are safe."

It was enormous, what he was promising. Even now I could feel the urgency in the pit of his belly—the desperation that crawled over every centimeter of flesh. His body wanted to go, go, go and be with Velsa. But that didn't matter. His *mind*, his spirit, the very essence of him was still mine, steady and unwavering beside me despite the force of the wind. He gazed down at me, his lips softening. Reaching up, I cupped a hand behind his slender neck and drew close.

Vadix gathered me into his long, cool arms. My heart beat furiously in the tangle of embroidered robes. I could feel the sea beneath us, the snow all around. I felt *him*. My bright, strange boy.

I knew by now that his people didn't kiss one another. They were all hands, pollen, skin blossoming red. But he knew what a kiss meant, how it felt to open your mouth to someone else's mouth, to taste their tongue, their breath. To be open and vulnerable, all liquid and heat. He pressed his lips to mine. My body seemed to melt into his. But somehow we were strong together. His arms wrapped around me, I didn't feel the gazes of the Ahadizhi who watched—didn't hear the shouts of the dock workers or the murmurs of the guards with their prods. They didn't matter. We were one. If it had been summer, all the flowers of the world would have turned their faces toward our light. But outside the city's walls it was the first gasp of winter, and snow had come, dusting my hair and his bare head. At first I thought his voice was my voice inside his mind. That's how tangled up we were, how similar we had grown.

I will speak to the senate, he said, and then out loud he added, "This is not good-bye."

I gave his fingers a squeeze. Behind him an Ahadizhi guard let out a grunt.

"*Ahadhu Esh!*"

"You must go," Vadix said. Then he smiled wistfully. "We offend them. They do not understand."

"They don't have to," I returned, my mouth still raw from the force of his kiss. I stood up on tiptoes and pressed my lips to his cheek one final time, breathing in the summer-sweet scent of him. It was intoxicating. It smelled like *hope.*

Then I ran for the shuttle, not looking back even once as I slammed the steel door closed behind me.

20

As I ducked into the shuttle craft, all eyes were on me. Even Mara Stone, garbed now in a heavy flight suit and helmet, had a gaze that seemed to burn straight through her visor's artificial glass. After pulling the heavy door shut, and spinning the handle closed, I turned back to face their prying eyes.

"What?" I asked. From a seat beside the wall, where she sat with one arm crooked over Ettie, my sister-in-law leaned forward in her seat. Hannah's voice was muffled as she spoke, thanks to her thick helmet, but her words were undeniable.

"You. And the translator."

I squared my shoulders. If there had been any doubt about the connection between Vadix and me before, then our kiss had made it crystal clear. But I had no reason to be ashamed. I walked to the back of the shuttle, where the flight suits waited in their box. I hated to garb my body again in the synthetic fabric—but at least I still wore Vadix's soft robes against my skin. They enveloped me, as strong as any embrace, as I stepped into the suit and fumbled for a zipper. I saw a flash. Laurel's soft, pale hands, helping me out of that impossible dress on the last flight I'd taken. Now a stranger was our pilot, an old man who had waited all this time for Mara Stone's return. I swallowed the lump down, and zipped the suit up tight.

"He's going to help us," I said, bending over to fish for a flight helmet. I spoke easily, like it was nothing—like it was normal to kiss an alien boy. "Speak to the senate on our behalf, see if they might not be convinced to reconsider."

"Why?" came Jachin's voice, hard and chilly. "Why would he care if we're to return to Earth or not? What's in it for him?"

I clutched the helmet, staring at my reflection in the glass. My face was a blurry, pale blot in the visor. But the shadows of my eyes were huge—my mouth small. I was grotesque. Strange. And alone. Outwardly you could see no sign of Vadix, though I felt him even now. He walked down the pier, his head held high despite the ice-and-dagger sting of the snow-swirled air. Determined. Resolute.

"He's a kind person," I said softly. I stood and found an empty seat in the row in front of Mara. They were all quiet, their helmets turned expectantly toward me. They wanted answers, but I didn't know how to give them. Not yet. "He wants to help."

"You mean he wants to help *you*," Jachin said. Beside him I saw Rebbe Davison raise and let fall a hand.

"What's wrong with that? Does it matter whether his motivations are pure if he wants to help us?"

At this they all erupted—their voices rising up even over the sound of the warming engine. At last, out of the corner of my eye, I saw Mara Stone unbuckle herself, stand. She pushed a button on her helmet. The visor slid back, revealing her haggard face. And yet when she spoke, she spoke with force.

"Quiet!" she bellowed. Their arguments tripped, stuttered, and finally spluttered to a stop beneath the engine's roar. They turned their visor glass toward her as they waited for the botanist to speak. "Do you know who else was concerned with the romantic lives of their people? So worried about who bedded whom, about the foolish hearts of the Asherati and how they might be led astray? The Council, that's who! No better than the lot of them. Is this to be the new guard, same as the old? Disgusting!"

I peered curiously up at Mara, though she didn't meet my gaze. Who had she been once, when she was young? I knew she'd put off marriage until the Council made one for her. I knew she'd put off children, too. But had she ever loved someone? Maybe it had been a strange, forbidden love. Like Koen and Van's. Like mine.

I expected someone to object. Through the blurred glass of her helmet, Hannah stared at me across the aisle. But even she didn't dare to speak. Mara settled in again, pulling her straps down over her shoulders.

"She's right," Rebbe Davison said. He was speaking slowly, carefully. "Aleksandra was afraid of Terra's connection to the translator, but she shouldn't have been. Without that, we'd have nothing. We might as well do what Rafferty says, pack up for Earth and leave with our tails between our legs. But the translator's powerful. He has connections with the senate. That makes Terra powerful too."

Jachin whipped his head up. "What are you suggesting, Mordecai?"

My teacher lifted the glass of his helmet back. As his gaze went to me, he drew in a breath, holding it for a long time.

"We're without a leader now. I have no desire to take up Aleksandra's mantle. But if we don't throw our support behind someone, a usurper is bound to take her place. I'd like Terra to step up instead."

For a long time no one answered. There was only the roar of the warming engine. Then Hannah began to laugh, dry, skeptical laughter. But no one joined her.

"How do you feel about this, *Talmid*?" Mara asked. I turned to her, expecting to read judgment in her eyes. It had taken her so long to support the rebellion. She thought that we were outsiders both, not joiners. But her expression was patient, intent. I realized she would accept whatever answer I gave. Maybe leadership was different in her eyes. Maybe she thought I could effect change better by standing with my people—not against them.

How did I feel about it? I sat back in my seat, gripping the armrests with both hands. Once, the idea would have seemed laughable. I'd never wanted power; mostly I'd just wanted to be left alone. But it seemed that was no longer an option. I looked out across the shuttle's rows, caught Ettie's gaze, held it. She'd come here because of me. Now it was up to me to see that she was cared for, safe. Still, my heart was weighted by my doubts.

"I killed someone," I said softly. "Mazdin Rafferty. You all know that. I'm no better than Aleksandra."

"Sometimes leaders have to make difficult choices," Rebbe Davison said. "Aleksandra's mistake wasn't killing her mother. Not only that. It was that she never dealt with the consequences that were waiting for her up there on that ship."

I closed my eyes. I could hear my pulse in my ears, feel the overwhelming fear that tightened my throat. But then I heard a voice, warm and soft inside my mind.

I believe in you. You can do this. You are strong—stronger than they know.

"I'll do it," I said, my voice still hoarse as I opened my eyes. "Yes. I'll do it."

Rebbe Davison smiled at me. Mara, leaning forward in her seat, gave my shoulder a clap. The others might have regarded me doubtfully, but I ignored them. Mara and Rebbe Davison believed in me. Vadix, too. That meant the world.

"Well, then, *Talmid*," Mara Stone said, "give the order."

I glanced forward doubtfully, uncertain at first. But then I saw Jachin lift his lips in a bemused smile. He gestured toward the shuttle pilot, the one who waited with his hand on the ignition.

"Pilot!" I said uncertainly, and they all smiled at that. "Prepare for takeoff. It's time to go home."

He made a noise of agreement, but it was gobbled up by the engine's roar. Searing. Deafening. It was almost enough to wash away my shock, the idea that now, thanks to Vadix, I'd be in a place to engineer a future for the Asherati.

But not quite.

• • •

Hours passed, and hours more. Soon I was plunged into the land of dreams again, my mind lost in those now familiar forests. But this dream was strange, different from the rest—more like the nightmares I'd known as a girl than the comforting landscape to which I'd grown accustomed. In my dream the winter's storms had begun, blotting out the cupola and all her light. The whole world seemed cavernous and blue. Silent. Half dead.

Vadix and I walked through Raza Ait together arm in arm, examining the familiar scenery and how it had been transformed. It looked like a ruin. Everything was hollow, empty, the wind whistling through the towering structures like a mouth playing a thousand reedy pipes. The copper walls, once coated in shifting branches, were now buried beneath desiccated vines. Thanks to winter's invasion, the forest had gone to rot. There was a sharp smell on the air—oxygen, moisture, decomposing leaves. I walked forward, fascinated by the way the snow cover muffled our voices and our footsteps. Or my footsteps at least; as we walked, Vadix's pace grew slower and slower still.

Soon he crouched down against the freezing cobblestone.

Go on without me, he said. *The winter has begun.*

He drew his knees to his chest, pressing his face between his legs. I watched as the fabric of his robes began to split and tear. Tiny roots were shooting out of his flesh, tethering him to the frozen earth.

Soon his skin took on a translucent cast as a net of leaves cocooned his body. I knelt down beside him, frantically clearing those leaves away. Sap covered my wrists. The cold numbed my palms. But I couldn't fight off the progress of the season. His body grew hard, still. I watched as he was lost to me, lost to the winter.

Then I heard something—a savage howl. I glanced up toward the snow-covered glass; looked left, then right, to the city's high walls. A beast was coming, but from where? I had no weapons—no prod, no double-bladed knife. I hardly knew how to fight, much less hunt. How could I ever protect Vadix from the oncoming storm? I wrapped my arms around his body, my shoulders tense and high. The howling went on and on and on.

I wrenched myself awake. But even there, in the dark confusion of the shuttle, the howls didn't stop. Crying. Someone was crying. Wild, whooping tears. Clutching the armrests, I leaned forward. My heart was still wild in my chest, but I told it to be quiet. Vadix was fine. It had only been a dream, a nightmare. These cries were human; they came from no beast.

I pushed the button on my helmet. The visor snapped up. In the dim space of the shuttle, I found Ettie. Her visor was up too. In her helmet she sobbed uncontrollably, her hair plastered to her face. Hannah did her best to console her, rocking her back and forth. But it was no use.

"Would you pipe that child down?" Mara groused. Hannah gave her head a rapid shake.

"I'm *trying!*" she said. She examined her—the girl's face had gone glossy with tears. "*Pupik*, what's wrong?"

"We can't go back!" Ettie howled, a cry so fierce, it made my eardrums shake. "We can't!"

"We have to, honey," Hannah said, her smile gentle but uncertain. "We have no choice."

"But the boy!" she cried. My mouth was suddenly very, very dry. "He's waiting for me!"

"What boy?"

"The one in my dreams! He's waiting for me! We can't leave, Hannah! We can't!"

She collapsed in my sister-in-law's arms. Hannah stroked Ettie's narrow shoulder blades with the flat of her palm. Then she looked up at me.

"How is this possible?" she asked. "You and the translator—and now the child, too?"

I remembered what Vadix had said about the scans, about Ettie. Phytodistress systems, ethylene receptors. But that didn't matter, not right now. What mattered was Ettie, crying. Terrified of all that she'd left behind.

"Ettie," I said evenly. In Hannah's arms Ettie stilled. But she didn't draw up her head. "Esther, look at me."

At last she did, pushing her wild hair from her tear-sticky eyes with one hand, snuffling.

"Ettie, I promise you that we'll find him. Just because we're going back to the ship now doesn't mean this is the end. You have your whole life ahead of you—and his, too. Do you understand?"

Ettie sucked in a breath. "Do you promise, Terra?"

I didn't feel certain. I'd never been a leader before—never been good at keeping my own dreams safe, much less anyone else's. But I had to believe it was true. Not just for Ettie, or the people up there on the ship. But for me, and Vadix, too.

"I promise," I said, firmly, fiercely. Ettie only nodded. She drew her legs up to her, hugging her arms around them. Hannah gaped at me, doubt and confusion clear in her eyes. But I ignored it, ignored her. I leaned back in my seat, closed my eyes, and waited for the shuttle to take us home.

Winter, 1 Year, 1 Month After Landing

Life wasn't easy for me back then.

Don't get me wrong. It's not exactly a picnic now. We all know that,
given the option, I never would have chosen this work. But I guess I
never expected I'd have a choice. When I was a kid, I hoped so bad
that the Council would leave me alone to do my art. But when they
told me I was going to be a botanist, I let myself become resigned to
that fate. It was what happened on our ship. People became plowmen,
or carpenters, or librarians because the vocational counselors told them
it was best. After all, they'd given us tests, conducted interviews, person-
ality profiles, had private chats with our parents and teachers. Aptitude
was what mattered. Passion never, ever figured into it.

I watch how life has changed, how now my people do the work
that's necessary and not just the work that someone else says they do
best. It's still not exactly a matter of choice—it's merely what we need
to do if we're going to survive here. Just last week the western wall collapsed under snow cover. I was the one who made the announcement:
we would all put down our daily labor so that we could attend to the
damages. There was quite a bit of grumbling. Some of our people even
tried to shirk their duties. But I stood my ground, and within two
days the avalanche had been cleared. The cupola still has a crack—we
won't be able to repair that until summer—but you wouldn't even

know where it was if you didn't already know where to look.

It's times like these that I wish you were here with me. At first I wanted your support. How could I possibly do my job without you there bolstering me, believing in me? How could I ever tend to every single need of our precious community? Every time I had to speak to the citizens, my hands shook—my voice caught in my throat. I was a wreck. I suspect they all saw it; that's probably why I had to work so hard to convince them. I wouldn't be an easy sell either, if I were a grown man or woman and some seventeen-year-old girl were telling me what to do.

But lately I miss you for another reason. I miss you because I suspect you would be proud of me, of how I've learned to clutch my hands behind my back to keep them steady, and how to angle my chin up, speaking clearly and with strength even when I feel anything but strong. I've changed in these last few months. It's not just that I'm taller, that I've grown muscular from the afternoon hunt. It's that I'm braver than I ever thought I would be.

Because there were times in my life when I thought I was very, very weak. Back when Momma died, and then Abba . . . back when Koen Maxwell broke my heart, and then I broke Silvan Rafferty's. But I think I was never quite so afraid as the day we returned to the ship. I thought it might be the ending. I didn't realize that it was the start of everything—like a seed, just sprouted, ready to grow into the mightiest of trees.

PART THREE

THE SHIP

21

The air lock was empty upon our return. There were no crowds waiting for us, no family to greet us with open arms. Only dim lights that flickered on and off as we walked down the empty corridor. I hadn't exactly expected a parade or banners to welcome us home, but some sign of life would have been a comfort. The air lock's walls were as dark as a coffin. The path outside the craft was long and echoing. We shed our flight suits and made our way down the hallway, but cautiously. Mara Stone led the way.

"We need to be careful," she said, bringing her hard voice down to a whisper. "There's been violence since the riots. The Council hasn't been able to contain it. Students roam the streets like packs of dogs, refusing to be tamed."

I heard a whimper cut through the silence. Ettie reached up and grabbed Rebbe Davison's hand. He touched the crown of her head.

"It's all right," he said, but from the look on his face, I could tell that he didn't feel certain. So I squared my shoulders, standing tall.

"Have the shuttles been pillaged?" I asked. Mara gave her head a shake.

"I don't believe the rebels realized what they contain. They were still fully stocked when I left two days ago," she whispered.

"We'll gather the sonic rifles from the shuttles. One for each of us. When we return to the districts, I want you to gather what remains of the guard and bring them down here to secure the rest of the weapons. We need to arm ourselves."

"Arm ourselves," Hannah said. Her voice was sharp, mired in confusion. She hadn't seen the riots—didn't know about the passions that lurked beneath the breast of every Asherati. "Is that really necessary? Silvan Rafferty's a good Council boy. He wouldn't harm us."

Mara went to fetch our weapons, her steps brisk and officious against the narrow walkway.

"I taught Silvan myself," Rebbe Davison told my sister-in-law, still clutching Ettie's hand tight. "Since he was a boy, he's been proud.

Entitled, like many Council children. I hope you're right, Hannah. I hope he won't hurt us. But better safe than sorry."

My brother's wife hugged her arms around herself. She'd been a Council child herself once, dutifully following the Council's laws. She'd never expected their safe, steady rule to be upended, and certainly not with such force.

Mara returned. She handed us one rifle each, all except for Ettie. She only clung to Rebbe Davison, her eyes owlish. She was too young for guns still—too young to face a shuttle crash or days out in the wilderness or the attack of a wild beast or the attempted escape from an alien city too. But she hadn't had any choice. I held out my hand to her, wriggling my fingers.

"I'll bring you home, Ettie."

Her eyes widened. She flung herself at me, squeezing my fingers so tight, I thought they might fall off.

"I still wanna go back," she whispered. My smile wavered. I thought of Vadix—down there in the city, hustling toward the towering senate building, his robes streaming after him. I wished I were standing beside him, preparing to fight my own battle. Instead of up here, fighting the Council. Again.

"I do too," I said, prying my fingers away just long enough to flip the rifle's safety off. "But we have business to see to. I need to go speak to Silvan, before he does something rash."

But Rebbe Davison stepped forward, putting a hand on my rifle. He glanced toward the light of the main bay, feeble against all this darkness.

"Not yet. We should take tonight to sleep," he said. "To be with our families. They must have been worried about us." He paused, his gaze growing distant. "And I'll want to break the news to Aleksandra's family before I speak to her other advisers."

Rebbe Davison winced, and I quickly realized why. Children. Aleksandra must have had a husband and children—a son and a daughter. I'd never imagined her as a wife, or a mother. But of course she must have been both. Like every Asherati woman, she would have had little choice in the matter.

"Do what you must," I said, gazing down at his big, calloused hand still wrapped around my gun's barrel. "But hurry. I need to see Silvan before—"

"Terra, these things take time," Rebbe Davison cut in. "We need to see to it that the people are behind us first. We'll call a meeting. Tomorrow night. Not in the library—the Council might be expecting that. The school. Nineteen o'clock."

I gripped the gun, tight, pulling it away from his scarred hands. "A meeting. What good will a meeting do?"

"You can't just march in there," he said. "It could be dangerous. We need to wait. Plan. Aleksandra—"

"Aleksandra is *dead*," I hissed, as the others all turned away in the face of my words. I saw Jachin lift two fingers to his breast. Saluting his leader—even in death.

"I've been doing this longer than you," Rebbe Davison said. His voice had gone chilly, stern. I clutched my gun against my breast, holding the cold metal tight. But then I exhaled, relenting.

"Fine." I paused as the lights flickered above. "But you don't know Silvan like I do, Rebbe."

The corner of his mouth ticked up. "I know. But I know our people better than anyone else. Anyone left alive, at least."

I gave my head a slow shake. "I hope you're right," I said.

At first we stuck together as we roamed through the streets, taking in the broken glass and the windows boarded up with rotting, reclaimed wood. Solar lights flickered, making the whole street jitter and shake like an ember dying in a fire pit. It wasn't just that the world of the *Asherah* seemed meager after the splendor of Raza Ait; our society had, in fact, been crushed by the riots. Once, the lift would have opened to the bustling commerce district, where the perfume of food and wine, where the sight of fine silks and sturdy wools, would have greeted us. We would have heard the music of the barter, the clamor of a sale. Now there was only the smell of dust and the low, constant whistle of the wind—circulating from starboard to aft over and over again, stirring the bare winter branches, rattling the shutters that hung loose on their hinges.

The faint glow of light in the dome meant that it had to be near midday—close to the thirteenth hour, when, once, children and workers would have all tumbled toward the districts for lunch. Now there were only a few timid eyes that peeked out from behind the curtains of nearby stores, then hastily hid again when we turned toward them.

"Where do you live?" I asked Ettie.

"Starboard. Ninth Street, between the vegetable garden and the—" But before she could finish, Hannah pushed by us, her boot heels hitting the cobblestone hard.

"I need to get to the bow," she said in a low, nervous voice. "Find Ronen and Alyana."

But Mara Stone called out to her. "Not so fast, Giveret Fineberg."

Hannah stopped on the path, her eyes flitting left and right as she did.

"What is it, Mara?" she asked impatiently. I think my sister-in-law was done with rebels—done with us. Ready to rejoin her family, her people.

"I stopped by your quarters after the riots. Thought after she made her escape from her nuptials, I might have found my *talmid* there."

Hannah clutched the gun tight. I could read the questions in her eyes: Was Ronen all right? Had he survived the attacks? "And?"

"He's waiting for you, both of you, in that dark little galley of yours. Suspect you'll find him there, not with the Council folk."

"He—" Hannah began, her features twisting. "He *waited* for me? But it's dangerous! He should have been keeping Alya safe in the bow, not waiting for *me*!"

Mara gave a snort. "Best take that up with your husband, then."

And with that, the botanist rested her gun on her shoulder and took off for the port districts. We watched her go, white lab coat disappearing in the early twilight.

"I can't believe he'd do something so *stupid*," Hannah said softly, shaking her head in Mara Stone's wake.

"Ronen? Really? You can't?" I asked, and couldn't help but lift my lips in a wicked grin. Hannah glanced sharply at me at first. But then the smallest smile lit up her mouth too. She reached out and took Ettie's free hand in hers.

"Come on, girls," she said, glancing down the litter-clogged streets. Once, the cobblestone had been swept clean every night. Wood and metal and glass would have all been recycled, food thrown into the composters, not a single scrap wasted. Now boxes spilled out of the broken shop windows. What food hadn't been pillaged had been left to rot. "Let's get home before ..."

She trailed off. The lights overhead flickered and blinked. There was laughter in the distance, eerie and echoing. We glanced at one another, eyebrows raised fearfully. Then, without another word, we hustled off.

As we walked through the starboard district, silent save for the beatings of our hearts, we passed Rachel Federman's house. Once, it had been the prettiest on its block, her mother's garden full of blossoming flowers, their front windows bright with embroidered curtains. Now the flowers were trampled, the curtains gone. In fact, the front door hung open, showing a gap of black space inside. I asked Hannah and Ettie to wait on the curb, and I headed up the front stoop.

Be cautious, a voice in my head warned. Not my voice. How strange to think he watched me even now, in this solitary moment, as the hairs on my scalp all stood up. But to be fair, if I closed my eyes, I saw him, too. He sat in the senate antechamber, arguing with a senator, pounding his long fingers down against the stone table over and over again.

"Rachel?" I called, pushing the door open. "Mar Federman? Giveret Federman? Hello?"

I peeked in, but in the murky daylight, all I saw were fine vases, smashed, and the walls, once covered in paintings and hangings, now stripped bare. I rushed back down the stairs, shaking my head to Hannah and Ettie.

"No one," I said. "There's no one there."

Hannah's answer came perhaps too quickly. I saw her give Ettie's arm a tug as she hustled her down the street. "I'm sure she's *fine*, Terra," she said, looking pointedly toward Ettie. She didn't want me to scare the girl. Fair enough—but Ettie had seen much scarier in the past seven days than an empty house full of pottery shards.

"I'm sure she is too," I said quickly. Ettie shook her head. That's when I knew the little girl didn't believe it. I felt the possibility settle over me like winter's first frost. What if something *had* happened to Rachel? I'd last seen her on her wedding day, just before she was to marry Koen Maxwell. Had their marriage been sealed? Had they made it out of the clock tower alive? I winced, trying to push the thought away.

"I'm sure she's fine," I said again, but this time the words were meant for me and no one else.

Ettie's home, at least, was in better shape. Though the flower beds had been turned over for winter, a faint light still glowed in the front windows. This time it was my turn to wait on the curb while Hannah led Ettie up the stairwell. They knocked together, waited. At last the door opened a slender crack. It was an old woman—too old to be Ettie's mother.

"*Bubbeleh!*" she cried, and scooped the girl up into her arms as though she were little more than a toddler. Hazy eyes pressed into Hannah.

"Where *was* she?" she asked, faint accusation ringing. But Ettie pulled back from her grandmother's grip, her toes touching the concrete step again.

"I was on Aur Evez, *Bubbe.*"

"Aur Evez?"

"Zehava," I said quickly. "Mar Schneider took her on one of the shuttles." I braced myself, drawing in a breath. I'd never been the bearer of bad news before—and definitely nothing like this. But somehow Ettie's grandmother knew without my saying. She drew a wrinkled hand to her mouth.

"Oh, Abraham," she said, her eyes welling with tears. Her hand fell against her thigh and she let loose a ragged laugh. "He always said he was going to live to see that damned planet. Oh, I hope you're happy, *bashert.*"

I didn't know what to say, but then I didn't have to say a word. Ettie answered for me.

"Don't be sad, *Bubbe.* Please don't be sad. We said the kaddish for him and *everything.*"

Giveret Schneider smoothed down her granddaughter's hair. "I'll do my best, *Bubbeleh.*"

"Besides," Ettie said, "soon you'll be able to say good-bye to him yourself. Terra says we're going back there, so I can find my boy."

"Your . . . your boy?"

"My *bashert*. The one I keep dreaming about. Hey." Ettie glanced over her grandmother's shoulder, into the warm light of the galley beyond. "Where're Tateh and Mama?"

Ettie's grandmother let out a long sigh. She glanced up at us—silent, grown-up conversation traveling through the artificial wind.

"We have a lot to talk about," she told Ettie, leading her inside and closing the door behind her.

"Poor kid," I said as we hustled down the empty street toward my brother Ronen's house. I'd once been where Ettie was—small and scared and confused, no parents to guide me. And my dreams had offered no escape, only mounting darkness and confusion. Even if they gave temporary respite—me hidden away in the dreamforests, his body's love soothing the parts of me that were wounded and raw—I'd wake up every morning and be all alone again in the universe. But Hannah didn't understand. Of course, she'd never been there herself. As we walked, our heels striking the cobblestone sharply, she narrowed her gaze on me.

"Yeah," she said. "Poor kid, and poor Terra, and that poor alien she ran off with." She reached out, touching the silver folds of my Xollu robe. "Do you intend to tell me what happened down there?"

I stopped, standing in the yellow light cast down from a nearby streetlamp. It was so *dark*, despite the early hour. Hannah gazed expectantly at me.

She will not understand, Vadix warned. But this was Hannah—sweet, tender Hannah, my brother's true love. She used to try to talk to me, to give me the advice I'd missed because my own mother had died. I had to try.

"You said it yourself," I began, choosing each word carefully. "We're the same, Vadix and me. We carry our sadness with us, and—"

"A crush, Terra? He's not *human*."

"It doesn't matter if he's human or not," I said. "He's *like me*. More like me than anyone I've ever met on this ship!"

I indicated the solar lights, flickering overhead, the rattling tree branches, the concrete fronts of every identical town house.

"I wasn't going to find anyone here. Look at me. You know it's true."

She did. Hannah stared and stared, her mouth firm.

"But Koen, and Silvan—"

"Just distractions," I said, giving my head a sad shake. "We were never meant to be together. Not really."

I gazed at my sister-in-law, standing there in her rank, dirty clothes. And then I saw the flash of a memory: Hannah on her wedding night, her slender body swathed in gold silk. Her olive skin had been clean.

There were flowers in her hair. But most of all I remembered how she seemed to glow, her eyes and teeth and laughter radiating love as she bound herself to my brother.

"I was only twelve when you and Ronen got married," I said. "Momma had just died, and Abba treated me like I was invisible. But for all my self-pity, all of my doubts, there's one thing I never questioned. You were meant to be with Ronen. No matter how much I hate him sometimes—my stupid brother, the same one who used to pull my hair and pinch me and call me names—it was obvious when you looked at him that you had the same heart, the same soul. And I couldn't help but think, 'Oh, how lucky he is.'"

Hannah rolled her jaw. I could see that she was fighting off a smile as she glanced back to the road beyond—where her husband and her daughter waited.

"But Ronen and I grew up together. You've only just met the alien."

"That's okay," I said, calmly at first. "We have time. Assuming Silvan doesn't do something rash. Assuming I can get us back to that planet."

Hannah pressed her lips together. I saw then that she didn't *want* to return. She wanted to stay here, where it was familiar—even if it was no longer safe. I didn't know what to say to change her mind, so I said nothing.

"We should go," she said. "Ronen and Alyana are waiting for me."

I looked at her and pressed my lips together too. Together we headed down the empty street.

The tiny front plot of my brother's home was all trampled, and it sparkled with broken glass like a whole new sky. There was paint on the front door, red letters that seemed to have dribbled and dripped onto the stoop like blood.

TRAITOR, it said, the word jagged as the breath that I heard Hannah suck in as we stood on her front walk. And then a second hand had added, in smaller, squarer script. *COUNCIL SCUM.*

She was stunned, frozen in the middle of the slate pathway. I let out a sigh and pushed past her, then rapped my knuckles against the old, familiar slab of cedar wood.

I heard everything go quiet in the house—footsteps paused, hesitant, on the precipice. So I knocked again, harder this time.

"Damn it, Ronen, let us in!"

The door swung open. My brother stood there, his tiny daughter slumped and sleeping in his arms.

"Terra?" he said, his face lighting up brightly. And then he looked past me, to where his wife still stood in the middle of the walk, surrounded by her annihilated flower beds. Hannah began to cry, and the baby woke, hiccuping tears, but it didn't matter. Ronen rushed past me and down the steps.

I would have felt odd, ill-fitting, at the sight of their perfect family reunion if I hadn't had my own old friend waiting for me just past the open door. There was a small, furry shadow there. The cat arched his back, letting out a curious meow.

"Pepper!" I cried. I moved past the doorway, feeling almost like my body floated several feet off the ground. I swept my cat up into my arms and buried my face in the warm fur between his shoulder blades. He smelled the same as he always did, like old fish and dust bunnies and dead mice. But I didn't care. I clutched his purring body against me, pressing kisses between his ears.

"I'm glad to see you too, Sister," my brother said, watching me over his wife's shoulders. But I didn't care. I snuggled Pepper to me, laughing through tears.

Because if my cat had survived these long, strange days without me—survived the riots, survived the tumult of my whole world falling apart—it meant there was room for light in all this darkness.

It meant there was room for hope.

22

n the time that we'd been gone, my brother had lain low, hiding amid the cobwebs and the unwashed clothes that now littered his quarters, hoping that the violence outside would soon pass. His home had a musty, human smell, of diapers and crusty food and slept-in sheets. Even with my face pressed to Pepper's fur as I snuggled him at the galley table, I could smell it—rank and musky.

But Hannah didn't mind. She bounced Alyana on her knee,

gurgling to the baby about how much she'd missed her. My brother watched, blushing.

"I knew you'd be back," he said. "I just knew it. Your parents—"

And then he broke off, pressed his lips together, and leaned back in his seat. He was pensive, like his mouth held secrets inside it.

"Are they all right?" Hannah asked, her baby's fat fingers still wrapped around her own.

"They're fine." He paused, waiting a beat. "They've left for the ship's bow with the Council. They wanted us to join them, Alya and me. But I told them I had to wait for you, to make sure you knew where to find us when you returned."

Hannah gazed at him, her lips gently parting.

"Oh, Ronen," she said, and the way she said it made my heart lurch in my chest. She was so relieved to be returned to him. Her old face and voice and manners had all begun to come creeping back in his presence, like she was once more being woken to life. "I can't believe you waited."

"Of course I did. I kept thinking about what might happen if you were lost to us on the planet. I kept wondering what I would tell Alya about you when she was grown. How her mama just slipped away to Zehava's surface and . . . disappeared." My brother's voice grew choked, as if it hurt him to say those words. "And how we just left her there, as if she were an old toy forgotten in someone else's quarters."

Hannah's face shimmered in the dim light of my brother's quarters. But she didn't get a chance to respond to him, to tell him he was a fool for waiting—and that she was touched by his foolishness too. Because a knock sounded then at Ronen's front door, a little jittery rattle, so quick that at first I thought it was nothing but the wind. Then again, louder this time. We all turned and stared.

"Might be those kids again," he said. "Since the riots, they've been roaming the streets like hooligans, knocking things over, throwing eggs. Probably best not to ans—"

A third rattle cut him off. My brother still remained seated, and his wife, too. So I rose and put Pepper on the floor. The cat looped my legs over and over again as I made my way over.

"Be careful, Terra," Ronen warned. And I was. I opened the door just a sliver, peeking through the crack.

A smooth face. A slender neck. Lovely dark skin the color of a chestnut shell that disappeared into the collar of her fine wool coat. *Rachel!*

I threw the door open, and my arms around her. She hugged me back, her face pressed against the silver fabric of my robes.

"Terra, Terra, Terra!" she cried, laughing. "I thought I'd lost you! I thought you were gone. When I heard about the shuttle, I came as fast as I could."

I gave a fierce shake of my head. I thought of the open door of her parents' home, and all the broken shards of china scattered inside. I remembered the fears that had risen up inside me: Rachel, dead and gone like Ettie's parents. A fate too dark for me to even imagine. I'm sure she'd thought the same, imagining my body dashed to pieces on Zehava—she'd seen a future stretch out ahead of her where she was alone, and I was gone.

"No," I said, and forced a laugh back too. "I'm here. I'm here."

I took her by the hand and led her inside.

We went up into the empty bedroom on Ronen's second floor, the room where I'd stayed in the days before the riots broke out. It looked the same as it always had—like a guest room. My single box of belongings sat in the corner gathering dust. The blankets on the bed were scratchy spares that had been inherited from Hannah's parents, pulled taut across the mattress in the time since I'd been gone. But Rachel hardly seemed to notice the sparse accommodations. She now moved with a measured serenity, her delicate jaw held high. As usual she was dressed stylishly, but her clothes were darker and more conservatively cut than they once would have been. She wore a long black skirt, one that touched the threadbare rug as she walked, and a black turtleneck too. I watched her settle on the floor, her legs tucked beneath her body. She folded the pleats under her. Then she glanced brightly up at me.

"You've changed!" she said. I stopped dead in the middle of the tiny bedroom, one hand clutched against my chest. It was true, of course. I had. And nothing announced those changes so well as my lover's clothes, wrapped tight around my body with a long cloth belt.

"Have I?" I said, sitting too. I could feel the blush over my cheeks, but I ignored it. Maybe it was coy of me, but it was old hat, this pat-ter—the secret of boys, and Rachel, prying them out of me.

"You look so grown-up. What happened to you down there?"

"Oh, not much—" I began, but before I could go on, Rachel squinted at me.

"Have you lost weight? And that robe is like nothing I've ever seen."

She reached out and touched the sleeve, her hand lingering on the fabric. I smiled. Rachel could never resist talking clothes—it was almost as important to her as boys.

"It's not silk. Or cotton. What is it?"

Recyclable synthetics. Plant based, the voice in my head intoned. I gently tugged the sleeve away, ignoring Rachel's question.

"It doesn't matter. Tell me, how have you been? Your parents and brother? I've been worried about you, Raych. Stuck up here." The last I'd seen her, she'd been about to go marry Koen Maxwell. Dressed in gold, flowers in her hair. Beautiful. Delicate. I hadn't just been worried—I'd been *afraid* for her. "I wish I could have taken you and Koen with me."

Her expression went dark, pinched. "We didn't marry," she said quickly. "I haven't seen him since the day of the riots. One moment we're about to be wed, the next he's running down the clock tower stairs with Van Hofstadter and his wife. Don't look at me like that, Terra. It was a blessing, really. We never should have gotten engaged."

I chased away the frown that had begun to tighten the corners of my mouth. "I didn't want you to get hurt."

"I know. You warned me. But everything's worked out now."

It was Rachel's turn to let her lips coyly lift. I sat back, examining her. The long, dark clothing—good for moving unnoticed through the hostile space of our ship's dome—was punctuated by a single flash of color. It was so *expected* on our ship that at first I hadn't noticed it. A knot of thread on her shoulder, merchant red, declaring her rank.

And a gold cord woven into it, declaring her loyalty to the Council.

"You've been staying up in the ship's bow," I said, speaking carefully. A realization dawned on me, crystal clear and as bright as morning. Rachel had been loved once, more fiercely and firmly than I ever had been before Vadix. By Silvan Rafferty—the boy who let her down, then turned his attentions to me. What had transpired in the week that I'd been gone?

Her dark skin grew darker. She lowered her gaze, picking up the hem of her skirt and tugging at a loose thread.

"After the riots I heard that Silvan's dad was sick, and that you were gone. I went to see Silvan. I thought I might offer him a prayer. I wanted to comfort him. And—and it was like no time had passed at all."

Staring at her, I found that hard to believe. Back when she and Silvan had tossed and tumbled in the back pathways in the atrium, she'd been soft and giggly. A girl, really. And now she was grown; she sat tall, with her shoulders squared and her spine straight. Though that old, familiar smile still played on her painted lips, some dark flame danced behind them. Secrets. No, *wisdom*.

Maybe that meant Silvan had changed too. Maybe he had grown up, transforming from the sullen, proud boy he'd once been into someone with the empathy to lead. I hoped so, at least. I took Rachel's hands in mine.

"I'm so, so happy for you, Raych," I said. Her fingers were stiff in mine, unmoving.

"Are you?" she asked. "I thought you might be mad. I know that Silvan cared for you. I know the two of you—"

Her words choked off. She was unable to complete her sentence, but she didn't have to. I knew where her mind went, to that night when Silvan and I had kissed in the street, our bodies so close that not a single gasp of air could slip between us. Hip to hip, chest to chest. His breath. My breasts.

"It wasn't like that," I said quickly, drawing my hands away. Then I clutched my arms against my body, unsure of what else there was left to say. Because it *had* been like that, hadn't it? I felt a pressure in my mind, a flood of warmth. Vadix. Letting out a slow stream of breath, I added: "It's over, anyway. You don't have anything to worry about."

The frown between her eyebrows was deep as she considered me. Finally she saw the truth—the love that glowed over my sunburned flesh. "Terra, did you . . . have you *met* someone?"

Inside my mind there was that same familiar sensation of flowers bursting to life, scattering their pollen on the wind. I didn't answer Rachel. But I didn't have to. It was as plain as day on my face. I'd fallen in love.

"Who was it? I know a few men slipped away on that shuttle with you. One of Aleksandra's guards? Not—not Rebbe Davison?"

I wrinkled my nose. "No. You know he's married!"

"Then . . ."

My smile wavered as I tried to find the words. Maybe I'd spend the rest of my life trying to explain it—how I'd gone to Zehava and met my *bashert* in Raza Ait. How my heart's twin was an alien boy who slept the winters away and whose skin changed color in response to my touch. In the dim light of my brother's guest room, my friend lifted an eyebrow, and waited for my answer.

"His name is Vadix," I began. "I—I don't know if he has a last name. He's a Xollu. They're— It's difficult to explain. They've lived on Zehava for thousands of years. He's a translator for the Grand Senate. He's important to them." I paused. Waited a beat. "He's important to *me*."

The smile hadn't returned to her lips, not yet. In the room's canned air she felt very far away.

"An alien. You've fallen in love with an alien."

Once her words would have shamed me, but they didn't, not now. No matter how much shock dripped from each one, I wouldn't let it poison what I knew was pure and right and good. Vadix, his arms around me. Vadix, promising to keep me safe.

"Yes," I said softly.

In a flash Rachel lifted herself to her feet. She walked over to the dresser, staring at the painting that hung on the wall there. A covered bridge—the one on the dome's lowest level. Once I'd sat on that bridge with Koen and talked about my dreams. Dreams of Vadix, months and months before I'd ever known his name, before I'd ever even been sure he was real. She stared at those brushstrokes as if she could will them to change.

"Silvan and I," she said in a strong, clear voice, "have talked a lot about the kind of world we want to build for our people. The Council did a lot of things we don't agree with. Getting in the way of marriages, for instance. So long as his father and Captain Wolff and the rest of them were all in power, our love could never be. It's not right. I believe that so long as a husband honors his wife, and provides for her—and as long as she's dutiful and sweet to him, well then, what does it matter if he's the captain and she's a merchant girl? It shouldn't!"

I could tell from the way that her smile grew, and then faded—from the way that she jutted out her jaw, steeling herself for my response— that Rachel was warming up to something, some argument that she held dear.

"But then Silvan asked me about marriages between two men, like Koen and Van. Or even two women. He asked me to look in the Torah, to find out what it had to say. He's only just learning, but he wants to understand the world, like I do—what our rituals mean, and how we can do them better."

My mouth was dry as I watched her. I'd never seen her like this before—so passionate, so certain. She wasn't even thinking about how her words might hurt me. She hadn't even considered it.

"I found stories. Sodom and Gomorrah. Two cities, visited by God's messengers. They were in search of good, honest men. But the men of the city were wicked, and wanted to lie down with them. To *schtup* them. God destroyed them for their depravity." She gazed at me pointedly, like I was meant to read the meaning between the lines. She wasn't only calling Koen and Van depraved. In Rachel's eyes I, too, had wicked desires.

"I'm not depraved!"

My answer came, quick and frantic, but Rachel hardly heard it. She just kept talking.

"You'll find someone else. We have years and years—our whole lives. Silvan doesn't want to force people to marry. He wants them to *choose*. You'll find someone. Maybe not Silvan or Koen, but—"

"No," I said swiftly, cutting her off. "There's no one else. It's Vadix or it's nobody."

I hadn't realized it was true until I said it, how already my image of the future was getting all tangled up with him. But it was. And no matter how hard Rachel tried, she wouldn't be able to cut those threads. They were made out of steel.

"But you'll have plenty of time to get over him," she said. Before I could answer, she added: "The whole trip back to Earth!"

"Earth?" I couldn't help but scowl at the word. "It's a fool's quest! Destroyed, Rachel, and we all know it."

"But we were spared!" she said. And that's when I knew that the idea—the whole crazy lot of it—began and ended with Rachel. "It's happened before, don't you see? In ancient times God sent the floods to the Earth to cleanse it. But he had a man named Noah build a boat to save his family. And then later we were slaves in the deserts of Earth, but he saved us then, too—just like the people of the *Asherah* were spared the asteroid's wrath. We're special, Terra. Chosen. And God gave us a home once. On Earth. 'I swore to your ancestors that I would give them this land, and now it falls to you to inherit it.'"

Her chest quivered as she spoke. I'd never seen her like this before. I'd seen her happy, and I'd seen her sad. I'd seen tears trickle down Rachel's pretty face, and I'd seen her collapse into hysterical laughter. But I'd never heard her speak with such gravity. Her words sank into me like a rock dropped from a great height into silver water.

"It's called Israel. Israel. And it's out there somewhere. Silvan asked the Council scientists. They say that there's a chance the Earth might be inhabitable by the time we return. There's a chance it wasn't destroyed at all! Can you imagine it? Coming home one thousand years after our ancestors left?"

I leaned over, hugging myself. "No, I can't imagine it," I said. And I couldn't. Earth was dead. I'd read all about it in my schoolbooks, and in the journal I'd inherited through my mother's line. Near the end days, there were riots there, too. Bombs. The religious waited in their enclaves for their gods to save them. I guess Rachel was no different, placing her trust in forces she could not see. She had faith. But my ancestor hadn't been like that, and neither was I. Maybe it was genetic. Maybe I was too cynical, too hard. Whatever the reason, Rachel's words didn't comfort me. They only made my stomach clench.

"A chance," I said. "You'd hang your children's future on a chance."

I bit down on my lip, peeling away the sun-scorched skin. Rachel reached out. She put her dark hand on mine.

"You don't believe, do you?"

"No," I said swiftly as I tasted blood. "No, I don't."

"It must be so sad for you, living a life without miracles. All alone in the world."

I *wasn't* alone. I had Vadix. But to Rachel his love didn't count. It was too twisted, too *depraved*. When I only stared off into the dark corners of Ronen's guest bedroom, she drew her hand back and forced a laugh.

"Look at us," she said. "Fighting like old times."

It was ridiculous. We'd hardly ever fought when we were young. No, the fights came later—with boys and secrets and adulthood, with choices that mattered. But I made myself smile at her. It was no use holding on to a life that had already passed me by.

"It's not why I came, anyway," she said, a wistful smile gracing her mouth. "I heard you were here, and I wanted to ask you to join us."

"Me?" I went cold. I had so much to worry about already—the Asherati, and the senate and their decree, and Vadix far, far below. The last thing I needed was to worry about hurting Rachel's feelings.

"I can't return to Earth, Raych. I've been waiting my entire life to settle Zehava. We—we had a contract," I said weakly, reaching for any

strand I could grasp. "We were peaceful and compliant. In exchange the Council has to give us Zehava."

"We can't live on a planet that isn't *ours*," she said. I heard a curious echo in her voice. Smug. Self-assured. Silvan. "Liberty on Zehava— isn't that what the rebels wanted? Well, it's not going to happen. We land there, and we'll be beholden to those *creatures*. We'll be slaves. Is that what you want?"

"It wouldn't be like that. The Xollu and the Ahadizhi—"

"The what?"

"The aliens. They've worked together for centuries—"

Millennia, Vadix gently corrected. But by then Rachel had turned away from me. I set my lips into a scowl.

"I didn't come here to debate politics," she said, her voice trembling. "You need to come to the bow. I don't want anything to happen to you. Silvan doesn't either."

I thought of the poison—the look on Silvan's father's face on what was to be our wedding day. Sweat had trailed over his face in rivers, pasting his silver-scattered hair down against his head.

"If Silvan only knew—" I began, but shut up quick when Rachel turned back to face me.

"Just think about it," she said, silencing me. She held out her hands one final time. I lifted mine, took hers. She said, "Tomorrow. Come tomorrow. Please, think about it. For me?"

Automatically my pinkie finger found hers. Wrapped itself around it. Squeezed tight. It would be the last time we'd ever do that, Rachel and me. I didn't know it then, but I had my suspicions. I think she did too.

So I lied when I answered. It may not have been the truth, but it was a kindness. For my friend. For everything we had once shared.

"Okay, Raych," I said, and forced a smile. "I'll think about it. Promise."

I stayed up late that night bent over my sketchbook, Pepper asleep across my ankles. My mind swirled around and around and around. Mazdin. Rachel. Earth—somewhere out there, dead as a ruin. No matter how deeply Rachel believed, I didn't. Couldn't. The science had been laid out too plainly for me in schoolbooks and in my lessons with Mara Stone. Again and again I'd been told of Earth's destruction. The asteroid strike. The long, long winter. All her forests and trees, withering in the empty dark.

You are a skeptic?

All through dinner with Hannah and Ronen—meager rations six days expired, stretched thin between the three of us—Vadix had been quiet. He'd been occupied somewhere else, busy down on the planet below. In the hazy corners of my mind, I saw him standing outside the senate, speaking to whoever would listen. A *lousk,* standing alone in the senate pavilion, begging the gold-robed senators to consider his pleas. He probably looked like a madman. Maybe he was. But now, as my pencils made quick work across the page, I was glad to hear the gentle pressure of his voice in my mind.

I suppose. Are you? I answered.

In his big round bed in Raza Ait, he turned over, letting the light of three moons spill over his bare shoulders. He was quiet as he formulated his response.

I have always believed in the union of the god and the goddess. He led us out of the caves where we cowered away from the wrath of the winter and the savagery of the beasts. She spoke to the Ahadizhi for us at a time when few of us could speak. It is the foundation of our society, our world. I am a believer, yes.

If I closed my eyes, I could almost feel his assurance that there was a larger plan. It had sustained him during the many moons of separation from Velsa, and then later, on those interminable nights after her death. As he'd picked open his skin and watched it weep, he'd whispered prayers to the empty air:

Zaide airex ososh, airka theselizhi—
orrax aum airex velaz.
Saillu zhiosouum, saillu sauosoez ososh.
Zaide aille osooezhi ososh ut sauosoez orrax.
Zaide airex ososh, airka theselizhi, aum sauosoez zhiosouum.

I paused in my drawing, considering the sounds of the syllables. They were quiet, gentle, the sound of whispers among reeds. *What does it mean, Vadix?* I asked. I think he was surprised that I heard this memory, buried as deep as it was inside of him. But he knew that he was safe with me in the darkness of our minds. He translated swiftly, without any trouble.

In this hour of winterdark, we cry like the newly sprouted—
god and goddess, hear us.
We have walked together, and now we walk apart.
Give me strength to walk alone like you, my god, toward spring's first light.
Give me the goddess's voice, a song to sustain me, even as I sing without her.

I opened my eyes again, groping through my sheets for another pencil. I didn't want to think about his solitude—how it was hard for him, even now, to lie in bed alone. But the steady, familiar rhythm of my pencil against paper soothed me. I layered red atop blue, a drop of blood in a stormy sea.

I wish I could believe like that. It must be comforting.

Under the glass ceiling a slow smile lifted his lips.

It is. But surely you must believe in something, Terra, if not in gods?

I picked up the black pencil, sketching in a pair of eyes. His eyes, filled with unimaginable secrets. Then I drew the soft line of his mouth.

I think . . . , I began, the words coming slowly. *I think I believe that a new day will come tomorrow, like it has every day before it. Sometimes I hated it, you know? How time kept slipping away from me, taking me one day further from Momma, and Abba, too. And every day was just like the last one. The walls here felt like they were closing in on me sometimes. But then I remembered why those walls were here. Why I am here. My ancestors left our planet because they had hope for the future. They weren't on this ship because they wanted to live here. They were on this ship so that someday I could live somewhere else. Someplace better.*

I paused, looking down at the page. In my sketch Vadix stared back at me, his expression grave and uncertain. It had been easy to draw him, even if his body was thousands of kilometers below. I would never, ever forget.

I think that's why I can't abide by Rachel's plan to return to Earth. If nothing else, I've always believed in the promise of Zehava. I still do, I think. Not because of you, or me, or us. But because of Momma and Abba and all the people before them. Everything they sacrificed. I have to hold on to that—on to hope for a new day tomorrow, and the day after.

I don't think he knew what to say to that. So he simply said nothing, his mind tightly curled around mine—like we were two bodies in a bed, embracing each other. With a sigh I glanced down at the page. I wished he could be there with me, in flesh and not just in spirit.

I think he wanted to be with me, too—or to be closer at least, sitting beside me in bed, talking with words as well as thoughts. I felt him peeking through my eyes. It was a curious sensation, one that sent a shiver through me. He drew back, but it was too late. He'd already seen.

You made my image. You are an artist.

Even alone in my room I felt myself blush. *I don't know if I'd say that. It's just something that I enjoy doing. It's not—it's not my job or anything.*

His thoughts were deliberate. *It does not matter. You are talented. Like an Ahadizhi. Such images could hypnotize even the wildest animal.*

My blush only deepened. I pushed a lock of hair behind my ear. *Oh, Vadix,* I replied. *You're teasing me.*

Perhaps, he said gently. *Perhaps.*

Mara told me once that old maps of Earth bore the images of dragons near the margins in those foreign countries where the cartographers had never dared to travel. On that workday, long past, I'd been wondering aloud about Zehava's continents, her seas, and Mara said that all of that was nothing more than dragons we'd someday uncover—shapes that science couldn't even imagine, not yet, not when the ship was so far out.

Uncovering dragons. That night, as we lay in our separate beds, I recalled the phrase. It seemed to be an apt name for what we were doing, peeling back layers of ourselves to expose foreign shapes, new lands, and strange continents. I felt like a cartographer as I sketched him inside my notebook. I drew his long limbs, his curves, and the bright contrast of his hand against my hip. I committed him to memory so that I would never, ever forget.

As if I ever could.

Of course we tumbled together that night, our bodies becoming one and whole in the depths of the dreamforests. Maybe it was frivolous of me to ignore the path ahead in favor of his body, his fingers, and the wet sweetness of his mouth. But I couldn't help but lose myself in the violet space inside my mind. The days ahead were uncertain. There were so many problems. Silvan. Rachel. The senate below. Perhaps I should have been drawing plans, plotting strategy. Perhaps I was avoiding my troubles in favor of flesh, sweet and warm and good.

But deep in my belly I knew that this was nothing like my nights with Silvan. Back then lust was for forgetting all the pain and darkness of the future, and the stark, bone-deep solitude of the present. But now?

In the recesses of our mind, inside the wild jungles of our shared sleep, his body healed mine. It bolstered me, made me whole. It was less a distraction and more a salve—and I knew I'd need my strength in the coming days.

In the darkness of the night, I woke in sweaty sheets, curling my body up like a crescent moon. Akku, or maybe Aire. I wasn't sure which.

23

woke early the next morning, rising swiftly in the impenetrable dark. Pepper mewled from his spot on the end of the bed. I buried my face in his dust-soft fur, snuggling him for just a moment before I made my way down the hall and toward the head. After days unwashed on Zehava, I don't think I'd ever gladly forgo a shower again. Not even this one, with its rattling pipes and thin, brown stream of water. Funny how I'd never noticed before the way the ship's water tasted. Dingy. Not quite clean. But I'd never known any better, and now I did. I soaped up my body quickly, rinsed quickly too. The lights flickered overhead, but I ignored it.

What will you do today? Vadix asked as I pulled on my clothes. It felt odd to wear my tired old linen pants and holey sweater again, but I thought it best to avoid the strange Xollu garb if I was going to be out today—among my people.

I'm going to go speak to Van Hofstadter. Spread the word about the meeting tonight.

But what about Silvan?

I remembered Silvan. Rumple-haired. Proud. I bit the inside of my cheek and tried to ignore how my stomach flip-flopped at his memory. I couldn't trust him, not entirely—but there was nothing I could do about that, either.

Rebbe Davison said it can wait. We need to gather the Asherati. We need to plan.

All right, Vadix said, but I could hear the doubt that seeped from his mind to mine. I groped through the darkness for my boots, and swiftly changed the subject.

Do you *have a plan today?*

Yes, yes, he said hastily. *I shall continue to petition the senators to let me speak before them on your behalf. But they are wary of your people and the strain you all would place on our cities. And I have combed the records dating back six centuries. It is quite unheard of that they might change their minds after making such a decree.*

Unheard of. I stomped my feet down into my boots, one at a time, then tugged the laces tight.

They need to lift the banishment. Without that we have no chance.

I am aware, Vadix said, his voice wry in my head. *I am trying. I fear that I am unable to advocate forcefully enough for your people. I will defend you until my body returns to soil, but—*

Don't you want me to be safe? You said it yourself!

Of course I do! But . . . His thoughts petered out. I hissed out a slow breath of air, letting my head hang down. There was no use getting angry—not at him. He was only trying to help. Besides, I needed to be even-headed on that chilly morning. Strong.

Thank you, I said, sending a wave of warmth across the kilometers of space. *For all you've done so far.* I pulled my left bootlaces into a bow and streamed down the stairs. I wasn't sure if anyone on this ship went to work anymore, but if they did, I intended to catch Van Hofstadter before he left for the library. There was no time to linger. I put on my coat.

But as I drew the front flap across my body and slipped the buttons into place, I heard footsteps on the stairwell.

"Terra?" A sleep-drowsed voice called out. I turned. My brother stood on the steps, wearing my father's bathrobe, looking down at me.

I wasn't sure what to say. I lifted my chin, staring back. "Yeah?"

"It's not even six yet. Where are you *going*?"

My hand rested on the doorknob. It was true; on any other day I would have slept in—finding solace in dreams well into the late morning. But how could I ever explain that to my brother? He came down another step, his wide feet bare against the metal.

"Out," was all I said.

"Well," he replied, giving his lips a sleepy smack, "don't be gone too long. Hannah and I are going to the ship's bow today to join her parents. We'd like you to come with us."

"You want to return to Earth?"

Was it just the light, or did Ronen go a shade paler at the suggestion?

"No," he said. "But I don't think the rebels have a better plan."

My coat still half buttoned, I marched back across the galley. I stood at the foot of the stairs, looking up at my brother. He was unshaven, a thick beard coming in over his chin. His eyes had sleepy circles beneath them—too many nights up late, tending to my young niece alone. When I'd moved in, it was to help him shoulder the burden of parenthood. To become the sort of family we'd never been for each other. But I'd run off, failing him in that.

"Wait, Ronen," I said, my voice a whisper. It wasn't until I said it that I knew the truth: I wanted my brother with me. There had been times when I'd resented him, and hated Hannah. Times when I hated *both* of them for leaving our home gutted and hollow in the wake of Momma's death. But he was here now, and so was I. Maybe given enough time we could learn to be a proper family. I wanted a chance to try. "I'm working on something. A plan. Not returning to Earth. Something better."

My brother watched me doubtfully. "Hannah told me you fell in love with a boy there. An alien."

I put my hand on the newel post, touching the frigid metal. "He's not an alien. I am. He was there first."

Ronen watched with disbelief. I winced, turning my gaze away.

"Anyway," I said, speaking to the dark corners of his galley, "this isn't about him. It's about us. Our future. Our people. It's about *tikkun olam.*"

"Healing the world," my brother said bleakly, his voice an echo of our father's.

"Right. Our whole purpose here was to settle that planet. That's how we were supposed to save humanity. It's our *duty*, Ro. More than our jobs and our loyalty to the Council. More than being good husbands or wives or even parents. We're supposed to ensure that the human race lives on, and I don't know about you, but I don't think running back to a dead planet will do it."

A wisp of a smile tugged at my brother's mouth, but he fought it. So I pushed just a little harder.

"C'mon. If we give up, what kind of legacy would that be? For Momma—for Abba, too? He worked his whole life for that. Do you really want it all to have been in vain?"

He held up both palms in front of him like a shield—and let out a string of tired, loose chuckles. "Okay, Terra. Fine! Fine. We'll wait. Only . . ."

"Only what?"

"Only what are we waiting *for*?"

That was the question—the one worth a million gelt. I let out a sigh.

"I'm not sure yet. But I'll let you know as soon as I am."

I walked briskly through the district streets that morning, under ceiling panels that flickered so badly that they were dark as often as they were light. The moments of blackness were terrifying—impenetrable, thanks to the streetlights that had all been knocked out by rocks and sticks and fists. I'd never realized before how tenuous the cycles of our lives were here on the *Asherah*, how artificial and easily disrupted. But now that I'd been on the surface of Zehava, seen Xarki lift through the firmament and then sink down to reveal constellations and moons, it had become abundantly clear to me that solar lights were not the same thing as the sun, that glass was not interchangeable with sky.

The streets were still empty except for a few crows and scrambling alley cats. Since the riots, apparently the people had taken to sleeping in. I suppose they were allowed that luxury; for the first time in their lives, they were no longer beholden to the constant cycle of work and school, of duty and *tikkun olam*. But not me. If anything I stomped up that concrete stoop with a new purpose, a clarity that I'd never felt before. Because I was loved, I would find a way out of this. Off this ship, away from the dome, free of the Council at last.

Free.

From the other side of the door came the sounds of burbling laughter and warm conversation. A light was on, just a yellow sliver against the concrete. I watched it blink on and off in perfect timing with the panel lights overhead.

The electrical system is controlled in the bow, I thought, forgetting for only a moment that Vadix was with me as he rose from his bed in his house below, pulling his long body toward the shower.

Are you sure Silvan's to be trusted?

My throat tightened. I had the sudden urge to rush across the dome—through the fields and pastures, past the hospital and school. I would beg Silvan to leave us alone, to let us leave. We'd find a way, Vadix and I . . . But Rebbe Davison had told me to wait. My *teacher.* He'd been a rebel longer than I had. Helping Aleksandra plot and scheme. If I was to take her place, I'd have to learn to be patient.

Yes, I said simply. Then, pushing the thought away, I raised my hand and pounded it against the door.

It swung open. Koen Maxwell stood on the other side, an uncertain smile lighting up his face. He held a redheaded toddler on his hip. It was Corban, Van Hofstadter's son. The shy little boy buried his face in Koen's neck.

"Terra?" Koen said in surprise, the grin still frozen on his mouth. He glanced back over his shoulder toward the warm space inside, where Van stood over the stove frying eggs while his wife, Nina, set the table for all four of them.

"Terra Fineberg's here," he said. The only sound was the sizzle of the pan, the clatter of silverware. Around us the lights winked out again, and then back on.

"Koen!" Nina called out past the threshold at last. "Invite her in."

Koen grabbed my hand, holding my fingers in his cool, calloused fingers. Their touch brought back strange memories—of all those months when I'd fantasized their cold, clammy pressure against my body.

Really? Vadix thought. He wasn't offended, not precisely. More incredulous at the thought of this shy, gawky boy serving as the object of my desires.

There was no one else, I said. *I was desperate.*

I let the door shut behind me. Standing there in the entryway, stomping the feeling back into my cold-numbed feet, I could feel the knife's edge of Van Hofstadter's green eyes slicing into me.

"They told me you were dead," he said. "Crashed on the surface of that planet."

"Here I am," I said helplessly. I wasn't sure whether I should take off my coat or not. I didn't feel particularly welcome in their home. Perhaps better to keep it on. "Not dead."

For the longest time no one said anything. Even little Corban was silent, his thumb stuffed into his mouth. Finally Nina let out a long sigh.

"Well, *I'm* glad you're okay, Terra. We've lost so many in the past few days. The last thing we need is to lose you, too. Come in. Sit down. Van, get her some coffee."

I hesitated only a moment. It was clear who was in charge in this household. Van wore a scowl as he poured me a fresh cup of dandelion coffee and thunked it down on the table before me. I wrapped my fingers around the mug, glad for its warmth.

"Thanks," I said. "I shouldn't stay long." Then I saw the look that shadowed Nina's expression—a heavy eclipse over a bright moon.

"Have many people died?" I asked. She sat down across from me, drinking deep from her own coffee cup.

"The last I've heard, forty-seven."

"More than that. On the shuttle—" I began, then winced, remembering Deklan's expression just before the beast ran him through—that wild flash of fear just before the pain. "We lost some on the shuttle, too. My old neighbor, Mar Schneider. And Deklan Levitt and Laurel Selberlicht. You remember them, Koen? They were in our class."

He stood in the doorway still, clutching Corban to him. His wide mouth fell open.

"I do," he said. "Laurel was—she was my *friend*."

I hadn't known that, hadn't known much about Koen in the years before he became my father's student. But apparently Van knew. All at once the man was beside him, sliding a reassuring arm around Koen's lower back. Funny, how it no longer made me angry to see the two of them together. It felt right; normal. Like they were a family, the four of them. And I guess they were. Nina didn't even blink at the show of affection between the two men, like it was normal—expected.

But when she spoke up, she *did* sound sad. Like she couldn't bear the loss of one more life, much less three.

"Why are you here, Terra?"

Overhead the lights dimmed, then sparked back to full life. I took a long sip of my coffee, steeling myself. It was as dark as mud and twice as bitter.

"Rebbe Davison has asked me to spread the word. We're going to hold a meeting tonight."

Koen stepped forward, breaking away from Van's strong arms.

"A meeting? What for?"

"We're reconvening the Children of Abel. I need you to spread the word. We have to discuss our next actions now that Aleksandra—" I cut my words short. Van glowered.

"Now that Aleksandra *what?*"

"Died," I said, forcing my gaze down to the crackle glaze that coated the mug. "She died. On the surface. She led an attack on the aliens, and they caught her, and—"

"Oh, no."

Now it was Van's turn to stand, weak-kneed, pressing the back of his hand to his teeth. He stifled a cry. Beside him Koen shook his head over and over again.

"Aleksandra? Gone? But she was supposed to lead us!"

"I know," I whispered. Part of me wanted to point out to them that Aleksandra had fled the ship at the first chance she'd gotten, as though the people left behind were worthless, meaningless. But it seemed like an insult to whatever memory of her that they still held dear. I flashed a pair of fingers to my heart.

"What will we do now?" Koen asked.

"Well," I said, speaking slowly. My gaze went to Van, who watched me with wounded eyes. We'd never gotten along, not when we'd competed for Koen's affections, not when I'd been desperate to prove my loyalty to the rebels. And now Rebbe Davison needed me to take him under my wing, to make him follow me. It seemed impossible.

"Mordecai Davison wants me to lead the rebels."

Van let out a snort. "You?"

"Yes, me!" I squared my jaw, leveling my gaze at him. "I've been working with one of the aliens. A translator by the name of Vadix. He's petitioning the Zehavan senate on our behalf."

"I really don't think you're fit to lead—"

"And the Council didn't think you were fit to love each other!" Leaving my coffee steaming on the table, I rose to my feet. "I thought the whole point of this rebellion was that we got to choose our own futures. Well, I'm working toward *tikkun olam* now. Harder than Aleksandra ever did, if you ask me. You don't want to follow me? Fine, then follow the Council. I'm sure they'd be happy to have you."

I started toward the front door again, shouldering between Koen and Van. Neither of them called out to stop me. But Nina did, her voice firm and clear.

"Terra, wait!"

I stopped, turned back. Van's wife was hardly any older than he was. Her black curls were thick and lustrous, her eyes bright with a keen intelligence. I'd never thought of her as a rebel before—only collateral damage in the love between Koen and Van. But now, for whatever reason, she was willing to join us. To join me.

"Of course we'll come to the meeting tonight. The library?"

My gaze flickered toward Van, then back again. "No. The school. Nineteen o'clock."

"Thank you, Terra," she said. She reached over and picked up the mug of coffee she'd poured, letting the heat steam her face. Then she glanced up again.

"Koen," she commanded sharply, "go with her. The districts aren't safe to walk alone. Not anymore."

The air was so thick, you could slice it like meat from a bone. Koen dropped Corban into his father's arms while Van pushed his lower lip out in a sulk. He watched as Koen wound his scarf around his neck and buttoned his coat tight.

"Thanks, Nina," I said, turning back to nod at her before we slipped out through the door. She smiled up over the steam, saluting me so briefly, I wasn't really sure it had happened at all.

"Go in health," she said. And, with that, we did.

We hustled through the districts together, our hands stuffed down into our pockets to keep them from the biting cold. Just like in the old days, before we were to be wed, our words stuck and froze before they could burst through our lips. The first lights of dawn made the panels overhead glow a feeble blue. In their illumination the angles of his face were as sharp as the edge of a shard of ice.

In the old days, when we made our plans for marriage, it always seemed like he was holding something back. A joke. A secret. A hidden pain. His long spine had often been slumped—his shoulders hunched up from nerves. He walked differently now, taking wide, confident steps. Even as he glanced around him, mindful of the sound of footsteps in the distance, of the children who roamed the alleyways, liberated from the chains of formal schooling, he walked proudly. It was as if he'd somehow grown into his own skin.

I wanted to tell him that I was happy for him. He'd found his place in Van's home, even if it wasn't the normal, perfect life the Council had once planned for us. But it didn't feel right, not quite. Koen clearly didn't need my approval.

But that didn't stop him from beaming at me.

"You've changed," was what he said.

"Changed?" I asked carefully. With Rachel I'd been quick to agree. But Koen and I had never had the same kind of friendship that Rachel and I had enjoyed. And even Rachel hadn't taken my news well. What if he drew back in disgust at my love and the way it had transformed me?

He blew hot air into the cup of his palms, letting out a burst of laughter. "It's true. You have. You can't hide it from *me*, Terra!"

I stopped beneath the flickering illumination of a streetlamp. "I—" I began, groping for words.

But I didn't need to stammer and mumble. I didn't even need to explain. Koen's chestnut-colored eyes were filled with a warm amber light.

"You've fallen in love, haven't you? I'm so happy for you!" And just like that, I was buried in a hug—warm and full and wonderfully real, so different from the strange, stiff embraces we'd shared when we were going to be married and our lives were full of lies.

He still smelled the same, though. Cedar boards and dust. I breathed it in, laughing too. "You are?"

"Of course I am." He rocked me in his arms. The words seemed to echo inside his chest, right through his corduroy jacket. "I always wanted you to be happy. I'm sorry I couldn't love you like you needed."

"Oh, Koen, no," I said, pulling away from his embrace. "Don't apologize. You were doing your best."

"It wasn't good enough—"

"For who? My father? The Council?" I held his cool fingers in my fingers. He gave my hands a weak squeeze.

"Well, yeah!" he exclaimed. I shook my head.

"Maybe our mistake was trying to live by their rules," I began, holding his fingers firm. "The Council gave us rules to live, but they couldn't see the light of your love. There were no words in their vocabulary for it. You tried to live a good life, but how could you?

Your very nature fractures their world. That doesn't mean that you're wrong, Koen. That means they are."

Koen let out a loose titter of laughter as he pulled away, running those long fingers through his hair. "I'm glad you're not angry with me."

"I couldn't stay mad. Not now."

He arched an eyebrow, examining me for a long time in the growing rosy light. "Terra, who is it that you've fallen for?"

The cold was back again, ruddying my knuckles. I drew in an icy breath of air. "He's . . . different, Koen. Really different. If I have my way, we'll be back on that planet soon. And you'll get to meet him—to see for yourself."

Now both eyebrows lifted. Not in dismay—Koen wasn't Rachel, and despite the place he had stolen in my heart, he never would be. But he was surprised. His mouth formed an O.

But before he could respond, something happened. Something terrible. Something that had never happened before, not in all my years on the ship.

The lights went out. The world around us was black, pitch black. In the distance, in the dome, I could see a thin line of purple illumination. But otherwise the universe was blackness, shadows, and the distant barking of someone's dog. The creature yelped over and over again, assuring us that he was just as afraid as we were.

Koen's icy fingers found mine. I heard my breath, my heart. I was just about to say something, to remind myself that I was still here, still alive, in all this darkness, when there was a great whir. The lights came on again, one at a time, revealing Koen and how his brow wrinkled in worry.

"It's been happening for days," he said. I watched the light flicker against the planes of his face. "The ship's just falling apart. And all we can do is wait and watch while it does."

I shook my head. Someone had to do something—find us a place on the planet and restore peace to our people before our whole world crumbled before our eyes.

That someone was me. But as the lights blinked out again, then winked back to life, I had no idea how I would do it. The problem was so much bigger than me, than Koen, than all of us.

"We'd better go," I said, still clutching his hand in mine, holding on more tightly than I'd ever held on to anything else in my whole life, as I gave his arm a tug and dragged him toward the safety of my brother's home.

24

unch, then supper, with my brother and his wife and daughter. We listened to the steady *thump thump thump* of rocks against his front door, watched the lights overhead flicker on then off then on. And we talked about none of it, pretending that this was normal. I guess after a lifetime of ducking the flat of my father's hand, my brother and I could ignore almost anything. Not Hannah, though. Every time another stone rattled the windows, she jumped, clapping her hands over her daughter's ears.

"Not again!" she cried, rising to her feet after a particularly raucous *crack*. She lifted the curtain back, glimpsing with a scowl the long fissure that ran from one end of the window frame to the other. "Why doesn't anyone *do* something about them? Get those children under control!"

Ronen gazed at me, his eyebrows lifting mildly. "That's a good question," he said.

I pushed my chair away from the table and hustled up toward the guest room, ignoring the heat behind his gaze.

Stiffly I lay down in my bed. There was nothing to do but wait now—wait for our meeting in the school that night; wait for Vadix to make any headway with the senate. The lamp by my bedside table flickered so wildly that I would have never been able to even draw. So I folded my hands across my belly, closed my eyes, and let my mind stretch and stretch. Somewhere below, Vadix waited for me.

Where are you? I asked. His mental voice came swiftly back.

Home, of course. There was laughter in it, like it was some kind of joke. But I wasn't laughing. I turned toward the gray wall, watching my silhouette appear, then disappear, then appear again as the light went on and off and on.

When I'm here, I began, *it feels like you don't even exist. Like you're something I only dreamed up to keep from feeling lonely. Like I'll be stuck up here forever, alone and in the dark.*

A pause. Long, too long. In the city below, Vadix stared at his reflection in his bathroom mirror. He wore no shirt. His torso was bared to the open air. So many scars, small and white. Like a thousand comets, streaking their way through blue space mottled red by solar flares.

You don't really feel that way?

Now it was my turn to fall silent. *No. No, I don't,* I said finally. *I'm only afraid.*

Of what?

I closed my mind, thinking of the long road ahead. If I couldn't convince the rebels to follow me, it was all lost. If Vadix couldn't convince the senate, it was all lost. If I couldn't convince Silvan . . .

I'm afraid of failing.

In a house in a copper city on a planet far above me, Vadix gave the spigot a tug. He splashed water over his shoulders, his face, drinking it in through his pores. Then he sat down on the cold tile floor. He could still see his own reflection refracted in the dozens of tiny, opalescent tiles. It seemed broken, strange, as alien as I felt.

I've been thinking about what you said last night, he said. *About life beyond the one you've always known. It was unusual, hearing those words in someone else's mind.*

Pepper came snuffling along my bedsheets. I reached out to him, pulling his soft body against mine. And held him close.

What do you mean?

I used to say the same thing. All the time. To Velsa. Vausi xodsak zhie-selakh, xedsi zhieserak. *"We must hope for a tomorrow better than the one that we know now."*

My cat purred, kneading his claws into the blanket. I buried my face in his fur. *She had doubts about your plan? But I thought it was something that you dreamed together.*

It was. He paused, leaning his shoulders back against the tiled wall. I could feel the cool bite against his skin. *Eventually. I—I think sometimes I may have talked her into it. I said it was all for her, to build her a city big and beautiful and new, a place where our seedlings could spread long after our lives were over.*

But?

But sometimes I fear I lied to myself. Lied to her. Perhaps it wasn't about Velsa at all. Perhaps it was about me. My boredom here in Raza Ait. My line has roots here that stretch down deep, thousands of years walking these same streets, paired and safe. My ancestors stopped dreaming about the lands beyond the walls of the twelve cities generations ago. But from the moment I sprouted, I imagined new cities, sprawling in directions I cannot predict. A cupola new and shining, not cobwebbed by ancient cracks. I picture new Guardians, humming new tunes to themselves—tunes I haven't yet translated but that my very soul understands.

I thought of the craggy, wild shape of the continents I'd once sketched in the margins of my notebook. I thought of my own des-

"Probably because the clock keeper is waiting with him. Van Hofstadter, too. Where are you going, Terra?"

I gazed at him. My eyes had adjusted by then. I could see him press the edge of his cheek against the doorjamb. He looked nervous—hesitant. But I couldn't shield him from the Children of Abel. Not anymore.

"There's a meeting. We're gathering to discuss our plans for facing the Council."

My brother watched as I stuffed my feet down into my boots and laced them. But he was silent.

"What is it, Ronen?" I asked, pulling the laces into bows.

"I'd like to come with you."

I only let out a soft laugh at that, groping through the dim light for my old winter coat. My brother—Council husband, the contract-abiding man that my father always wished he himself could have been. But he cleared his throat, squaring his shoulders in the yellow hallway light.

"I mean it."

I flashed up my gaze. Ronen's eyes were hazel, just like my eyes. But when I gazed in the mirror, I saw that my own stare had hardened—gone flinty and sharp. My brother's had a softness, a sadness. He might have been the older one, but I worried about him.

"You shouldn't. It's dangerous. If something happens to you, what will happen to Hannah and Alya?"

peration to leave this ship, this dome, this life that had been pla

for me, where nothing was ever new or fresh or surprising. I tho

of my father, all those times he told me to be dutiful, to be *good*,

inside, my temper burbled and roared. It wasn't just that I'd

angry. It was that I knew there was more for me—somewhere, s

how. But so long as I was imprisoned by these walls, this glass, th

be nothing more than a shadow of an ordinary girl.

I used to think my only hope for a new and different life was one f

the land where I was sprouted, Vadix went on. *But now I realize: y*

new. You disrupt the balance of our city, yes. But you will transform th

ahead with your very presence. Once, I would have had no future a

would have been a lousk, a walking specter. Dead already, if not in fle

in spirit. Now . . .

Now?

Now I might have a future, too.

I bit my lip, holding the smile in. I wanted to ask him if this

he was staying—staying with me, staying alive. But before I

respond, the door angled open. A clear bolt of light was cast

over my face, jagged and bright. I shielded my eyes with my w

"Terra," came my brother's voice, low and urgent. "There's

one here to see you."

"Rebbe Davison?" I asked, sitting up straight. It must hav

nearly nineteen o'clock. "I didn't hear the bells."

His lips parted. He glanced down the hall. But then he gave his head a shake, setting his jaw determinedly.

"I talked to Hannah. We've both agreed. We've changed our minds. There's no use in hiding like her parents. What good is safety without freedom? A voice? The Council doesn't care what we have to say. Silvan Rafferty won't listen." He paused, taking the time to cross his arms over his chest. "But you will, Terra. I know you will."

I sighed as I buttoned up my coat. "Fine," I said at last. As I walked down the stairs toward the galley, I spoke over my shoulder at him. "But you know that Abba's gotta be turning in his grave right now."

Ronen clomped down the stairs after me, laughing a little with every step.

"Good," he said. "Let him."

The old oak doors of the ship's school were unpolished, and yet they shone in the evening light from the thousands of hands that had touched them on the way to class each day. Back then we'd been proud of our place here—buzzing from classroom to classroom like worker bees, happy to pollinate the world with the Council's lies. Now we flocked to the school under the cover of uneasy night. Though the planet was radiant in the glass overhead, sparkling with the electricity of the twelve cities that sprawled out across the northern continent, our steps were heavy, fearful. Tonight, here, in the place where we'd all been inculcated into life on our ship, we would finally decide how to leave it behind.

We walked through the old hallways—me and Ronen, Van and Nina and Koen, and Rebbe Davison at the front of the pack. As a child I'd often fantasized about what our familiar school building would look like after it closed for the evening. But I'd never seen it. Now in the darkness the hallways seemed longer than I remembered—and yet the ceiling seemed to have dropped down low over my head. If I reached up, I could touch the lights, flickering in their fixtures. Had I really grown that much in the last year? Or had this world gotten smaller as the universe outside stretched out and out beyond the dome, encompassing the wilds of Zehava, Raza Ait, Xarki. Now I had Aur Evez, an entire planet—and it seemed so much more *real* than the graffitied cubbyholes that watched our arrival like rows upon rows of eyes.

We passed through the swinging doors and into the old auditorium, but I hesitated at the sight of all who had gathered there. Our meetings in the library had been small, just twenty or thirty bodies—a tiny cell of a larger movement. Now my gaze swept over the hundreds of people gathered underneath the high rafters. Had the Children of Abel always been such an army? Or had everyone become a rebel—like my brother now was—in the days since the Council fell?

Some of the people stood up at our arrival, touching their fingers to their chests. I looked to my old teacher; he walked with his head held high, commanding the room in a way that I'd never seen before. Even when we were young and naughty, he'd only ever chuckled and given his head a shake. Now he gritted his teeth. Without Aleksandra at his side, I suppose he had to be a stone pillar—resolute.

In the front row sat a boy and a girl whose dark curls neatly matched Rebbe Davison's. Beside them was an olive-skinned woman who eyes swelled with pride at the sight of him. His family. It must have been. I'd never even thought about them before—my focus had been so narrowed upon our journey across the planet, and then conditions on the ship. But he had an entire life beyond that, one that he'd nearly sacrificed to follow me to Zehava.

He walked to the podium near the front of the room. The crowd quieted as he stepped forward, their murmurs turning to whispers and then nothing more than a few awkward coughs. His children sat forward in their seats, gazing expectantly at their father. He faced them sternly, gripping the podium with either hand. I wondered how he did it. Looking out at all those faces, all those starving, expectant eyes, I found myself almost dizzy. I sought out a shadow of any familiar face—Ettie and her grandmother, Jachin, Mara, old friends from school. But unlike Rebbe Davison, I found no family in the crowd. I'd never had many friends beside Rachel, and the features of every rebel seemed to run into the next. Rebbe Davison lifted his broad fingers up, then touched two to his heart.

"Liberty on Earth," he said.

A whole auditorium of voices came echoing back: "Liberty on Zehava."

"I'm not one for speeches," he began, his eye holding in a wink. "I could deliver a lecture on the history of rebellion on this ship, but it would likely fail to stir your passions. You all know the truth: the situation here is untenable. Every day that passes is one where we lose more citizens to the Council's rule, where we're more at the mercy of the ship and her crumbling machinery."

The lights dimmed, then flashed up to full brightness. There was a dismayed murmur from the crowd.

Rebbe Davison went on: "But I'm not here to tell you what you already know. I'm here to offer assurances: we are working with the Zehavan natives to negotiate an accord. There's no need to run back to the Council, or flee for Earth. Though we've lost many friends in the days that have passed—though we have even lost our own leader, may she rest in peace—we *will* see our promised future come to fruition. Isn't that right, Terra?"

He looked at me. They all did, hundreds of pairs of expectant eyes. And then it only got worse; Rebbe Davison stepped to the side, one hand held out, offering me the podium. The people shifted in their seats expectantly, coughing, murmuring.

But I didn't budge. Couldn't. The fear was thick in my throat.

I'd never been one for a crowd. Oy, I didn't even like *talking* to people under the best of circumstances. Rebbe Davison knew that. He had to—all those years when I'd muttered my school reports, palming the back of my neck and squirming. Or those years that came later, when I drew trees when I should have been jotting down history notes, just to avoid looking him in the eye. I knew that didn't matter, not anymore, knew I needed to step up to the podium, be a woman, be a leader. But I couldn't. Didn't.

What's wrong? came Vadix's gentle voice. He must have felt it, from all the way up here—how my pulse sped and my mouth suddenly went as dry as sand.

I'm scared, was all I managed to say. I could feel him assessing the situation, pausing where he stood in his kitchen to join me in our old rickety auditorium. But before he could respond, Rebbe Davison leaned forward and lowered his voice to a whisper.

"Are you all right, Terra? They're waiting to hear from you."

I glanced at the gathered Asherati. To my surprise I found Mara Stone near the front, sitting forward in her seat. Her pruney mouth was pursed; she was disapproving.

"Rebbe Davison," I began, "I—"

His big, calloused hand cut through the air. "No more of that, Terra. You'll call me Mordecai from now on."

"Mordecai."

And just like that, he was no longer my teacher but my equal. A rebel, a father, a husband, and a young man, too. Or maybe it wasn't that *he* was young. Maybe I was old now. Not a child, and no longer a strange, sad girl stuck somewhere in between. I was an adult, and it was time I acted like one.

"Mordecai," I said again. Then I gave a shaky nod and stepped up to the podium.

So many eyes. And restless mouths, barely able to hold in their whispers. I drew in a steadying breath and glanced at Mara again. She'd sat back in her seat, and now she waited expectantly for me to say something, anything. To offer her even a sliver of hope.

I didn't know how to talk to the rest of them, but I knew how to talk to Mara. What was the worst she could do, tease me? I cleared my throat and began.

"I've found an ally among the Zehavan people. His name is Vadix, and he's well connected within the Grand Senate of Aur Evez." Some of their mouths turned down at that. I winced—they didn't know what I was talking about, not at all. But it wouldn't do any good to hesitate. All the leaders I'd known—Captain Wolff and her daughter, Van Hofstadter and even Mordecai—were smooth, fearless in the face of a crowd. Even if I didn't *feel* fearless, I needed to act like I was. "He's down there right now petitioning their senate to open up negotiations once again."

"Why should we be at the mercy of these aliens?" an old woman shouted, struggling to her feet. Several biddies around her grumbled their agreement.

"No one will be at anyone's mercy," I said, struggling to keep my voice even. "We'll work together as partners to find an accord that meets all of our needs."

"How do we know we can trust them?"

This came from my brother, standing calmly on the sidelines. I wondered what Hannah had told him of my new love—if he found it as unbelievable as she did.

But that didn't matter. There were myriad reasons to trust the Xollu, and Vadix was only one of them. "Their society is built on consensus—a partnership between two disparate races. And yet they've lived in peace for thousands of years. No war. No violence. Their biggest problem is that they've been so successful at it that their cities have grown overcrowded—"

"Well, then they're not going to have room for us, are they?" a young man demanded. They were all talking now, one voice bubbling over another like water in a stove pot. But Mara Stone only watched me. Finally she gave her head a slow shake. I was losing them, losing it all. If I wanted them to listen, I'd have to be more convincing than this. As I'd seen Mordecai do, I gripped the podium with both hands—as much to stop my hands from shaking as anything else. I drew in a breath, opened my mouth to speak—

And the whole auditorium went pitch black.

How long was it before anyone spoke? It felt like a lifetime during which the only thing I could hear was my pulse in my ears and the shallow, wheezy effort of my lungs. But it couldn't have been more than ten seconds, maybe twenty. At last someone cried out—a child, maybe Ettie? I couldn't see my nose in front of me, much less the people who now jostled and cried in the auditorium seats.

"Everybody stay calm!" Mordecai bellowed. Then I felt the pressure of his hand between my shoulder blades. But it didn't do a thing to calm my fear—or the fears of the crowd. Their voices roared up, louder and louder in the face of the darkness.

What's wrong? Are you all right?

My words stormed back, furious as a blizzard. *This is wrong, it's all wrong! I can't just wait for the ship to fall apart while we stand around and make speeches.*

Vadix hesitated, unsure of how to respond. But I wasn't. I shrugged away Mordecai's hand, turning to him in the darkness.

"I need to go talk to Silvan," I growled.

It was as if my voice had some magical effect on the wall sconces—on Silvan's hand, poised over the controls in the command center. The lights woke to life, greeted by a smattering of applause. My feeble eyes fell on Mara Stone. She shook her head again, rose to her feet, and then rushed out of the double doors at the back of the room.

"Citizens!" called Mordecai, but he was hardly able to fan back their grumbling *now*. "Citizens! That will be all for tonight! Go, be with your families. We'll call on you—"

But most of them had already risen to their feet, yammering to one another as they flooded toward the auditorium door.

Mordecai turned to me, the frown deep on his forehead. "The people need to be reassured, Terra."

I still faced out toward the auditorium, watching as the crowd funneled through the double doors. Both of my hands still gripped the podium. But it couldn't shield me from what came next. Facing Silvan Rafferty, facing my guilt.

"I'm no Captain Wolff," I said, speaking through gritted teeth. "I need to take action—to speak to Silvan and see that we're secure on this ship. I don't need to waste my time making speeches."

"You'll have to face your fears eventually. The people need a strong leader. Someone who can offer comfort. Inspiration."

I swiveled to face my old teacher. His expression was a strange one, a muddle of regret and fear. Not fear for himself, I think—but for what came next. A future that was strange, new. A future led by someone too weak to manage. But he had chosen me, and I was doing my best. I lifted my chin.

"Is this why you chose me, so you could tell me what to do? I'm not Aleksandra either, Mordecai. I'm no figurehead. If you're going to follow me," I said, "then you need to listen to me too."

Mordecai drew in a breath, then let it out. At last he squared his stubble-scattered jaw.

"Very well, Giveret Fineberg," he said. I stood straighter at the name. Even Mordecai knew I'd changed. I was an adult now, not the frightened girl I'd once been. "What do you propose we do?"

By then we were alone—or nearly. Ronen had hung back by the stage, looking as if he wished he were anywhere but here, trapped between our tempers.

"I propose that I go speak to Silvan immediately," I said. Then, when Mordecai turned toward the door, I put a hand on his shoulder. "I propose that you and Ronen escort me to the lift. I still need your help, Teacher. Just not for this."

I indicated the abandoned auditorium with a flash of my hand. Mordecai looked out too, sighing.

"If you're going to lead," he said, "you'll have to learn to face a crowd *someday*."

Overhead the lights flickered. I bit my lip, gave a nod. He was right. I'd have to confront my fears eventually, if I was going to be a leader, if I was going to learn to stand up for my people.

But not today—not yet. I had bigger fish to fry first.

"Silvan's waiting," I said as I started toward the auditorium doors.

25

They walked with me, but only as far as the lift that sat in the pavilion at the center of the ship's bow. It was a short walk, hardly anything more than a stroll down the narrow alleyway that sat between the school and the library, and out, across the broken cobblestones. I knew I'd travel the rest of the way alone. For one thing this wasn't their battle—not my sweet, dopey brother's, and not my old teacher's, either. Mordecai might have taught Silvan for more than a decade, wrestling with his temper, trying to reign his teasing in. But he knew very little of what had passed between the two of us over those tumultuous weeks.

At the lift Mordecai pressed his fingers to his heart. My brother watched him, his expression something between a smile and a perplexed frown. He put a hand on my shoulder.

"Be safe, Sister," he said. "We'll be waiting for you."

I nodded quickly as I stepped into the lift. The glass door shivered shut behind me, sealing the dome out of my reach. I pressed the button, and then leaned back against the rail. Waiting.

Why did he tell you to be safe? Vadix asked. He had a guest. Two, in fact—a partnered Xollu pair of lower-ranking senators who had deigned to hear his case. But he'd slipped away into the kitchen, bright even in moonlight, just so that he could speak to me.

Because Silvan is powerful. And—I paused. I was going to say "dangerous," but that wasn't quite right. He'd never been like his father, plotting and sneering and cruel. Nor even like Aleksandra Wolff—no bloodthirsty streak ran through *him*.

Silvan. Like Koen Maxwell, you cared for him once too? Vadix asked, his approach so delicate as the lift rose up and up that I couldn't help but smile.

In a way. He was a comfort to me after my father died. He cared for me, but it wasn't love. It was . . . something else.

Surely, he wouldn't harm you, then?

Any semblance of a smile fell. The door dinged open. I stared down the long, dark hall that led to the captain's stateroom, thinking of Silvan. I remembered his plush lips, and the way he'd pouted them when his father had denied him something—when his father had treated him like the boy he truly was. Sometimes he'd rage against the man, ranting and throwing up his hands. Other times he'd channeled his anger into his lust as he pressed me down against the rotting leaves. I blushed to think about it, how I'd taken his kisses, his heat, and never even gave it a second thought. Back then I'd hardly had to worry about Silvan's temper. He never seemed particularly angry at *me*.

But back then he hadn't been on a fool's quest to return to Earth. He hadn't had the loyalty of his father's people behind him. And I hadn't been the girl who killed his father.

I suppose we'll see, I told Vadix as I took the first lonely steps down that echoing hallway.

The stateroom was packed full of people. It was a wonder that the room could fit them all—crowded on cots and in corners, whole families gathered on the polished marble floor. They still wore their uniforms, their rank cords. It was clear that they expected the rebellion to be over soon. Zehava herself—shining in the glass overhead—would seem like nothing more than a bad dream. When the *Asherah*

was en route to Earth, they would travel down to the dome, this whole ordeal only a memory, take up their old houses, their old jobs, and continue living in the manner they'd become accustomed to.

I couldn't help but shake my head to see it. All those gold-threaded cords.

But their guards were upon me almost as soon as I arrived. They didn't have guns; those were ours, hidden in our houses, waiting for some opportunity to be used. But they did have knives tucked inside their thick belts, shining blades sharpened to fine edges. I knew the wickedness that a knife like that could bring, and so I held up my palms.

"I have no weapons!" I shouted. The rumble of conversation that had been brewing across the stateroom stuttered to a stop. For the second time that day, all eyes were on me. But despite my upturned hands, the guards still grabbed me by either elbow.

"Do you pledge your allegiance to the Council?" one of them growled. I flashed my gaze down to his dagger, then up again.

Lie! a voice intoned in my head, so urgent that I couldn't be sure if it was Vadix who spoke or if the thought was my own. But I was no good at lying. No good at following my better instincts—or his, either.

"I pledge my allegiance to no one!" I spat, shaking the guards off. But their gloved hands found me again, and fast. "I'm here to speak to

Silvan Rafferty. I come on behalf of the Children of Abel. I have no weapons. Will you strike an unarmed woman down?"

The guards grappled with me, but my words did their work. The Council citizens, who roamed beneath a dark glass sky, all gazed up at me. They saw; they watched. They were disapproving. If anything, our leaders had always been about the *appearance* of propriety. Their murders were buried under lies. Fallen bookshelves. Cancer. Their guards would never kill me with an audience.

I hope you're right, Vadix said, and this time I was sure the words were his. I stiffened my spine, resisting the guards' grip. Finally their hands fell away.

"Take her to Rafferty," one of them grumbled. The guard to my left looped her arm through mine, dragging me across the marble floor.

"Come on!" she shouted, though we stood far too close for shouts. I winced as we headed toward a wide stone staircase near the back of the room—passing dozens of cots, a whole army of Council families.

I was taking staggered steps up the wide steps when I saw them. Solomon and Miriam Meyer, Hannah's parents, rising up together from their cot. They reached out for me even as I was yanked up the stairwell.

"Terra!" Solomon called. "I've heard Hannah is back. Is she all right? When will she come join us?"

I resisted the guards' hands. Mordecai's words echoed in my mind. The people needed a leader, one who could give them strength. Even at times like these.

"She's okay. She says she loves you. She'll see you soon."

One of the guards gave my arm a yank and dragged me up the stairwell.

The last time I'd been in the command center, just a week before, I'd wondered at the blinking dials and ancient machinery—this strange, secret place, hidden from most of the ship's inhabitants. But now that I'd grown used to the idea, the room just seemed dusty and ancient, the computer terminals all edged with rust, the screens feathered with cracks. More surprising were the two figures who stood in front of the wide viewer, staring down at the planet overhead. Silvan and Rachel, shoulder to shoulder, holding hands. Rachel turned first, her eyebrows lifted at my arrival.

"Terra, you're here!" she said, dropping Silvan's hand and rushing toward me. Before I could respond, she'd cocooned me in a hug. But Silvan stayed where he was, his feet fixed to the metal floor as Rachel talked and talked. "Silvan was worried you were still plotting your way back to that planet. But I knew you'd come around. Oh, I'm so glad you're here!"

"I—" I began, and then stopped, pulling away from her embrace. I wasn't here for Rachel—and I certainly wasn't here to join her on her journey. I stared at Silvan. Garbed in white, his muscular arms crossed over his chest. I think he knew the truth, that I hadn't come for her.

"Hello, Silvan," I said.

With that, his mouth softened. Standing there, in the Zehava's vibrant light, he looked so *handsome*. After days among the unwashed shuttle crew on Aur Evez—and then two more with the tired-eyed rebels on the ship—I was struck by how hale he still appeared. Shining black curls graced his shoulders. His skin was deep amber and freshly scrubbed. And his linen shirt was so *clean* that you could practically count the fine threads. He moved past the center console with measured grace, coming close.

"Terra Fineberg," was all he said.

His eyes, edged with dense lashes, were dark enough that they almost appeared black. I tried to read the emotion there. I saw pain, confusion, maybe even a drop of desire. And heaps and heaps of pride. But that couldn't even begin to compare with what I felt, standing there with my former intended, and my old best friend.

"I guess congratulations are in order," I said. "I've heard you've declared your intentions to each other."

Silvan looked surprised. But Rachel reached out, putting her smaller, darker hand on his.

"I know you wanted to be with me when I told her about the engagement, but I just couldn't wait, Sil."

"We're going to be married in the captain's stateroom," he said stiffly. I felt my throat go tight. There had been a time—just one week ago—when Silvan and I were going to be married there. But that had never happened. The riots did instead. And then I ran off.

"Just like you always planned, Rachel."

She glanced down, nodding shyly.

"Mazel tov," I said, and then glanced toward the viewer.

They think I'm going to be there to celebrate with them, I found myself saying to Vadix, as I stared at Zehava's continents, faint blue in her endless night and pinpricked by a thousand artificial stars. He was out there somewhere—if only he could have been here with me. *I don't want to hurt them, Vadix.*

Terra, came Vadix's response. But I don't think he quite knew what to say to calm me, to quiet all my fears and guilt. He only said my name again, soft and sad. *Terra.*

"What's it like?" Silvan asked, the velvet tenor of his voice almost enough to pull me out of my anxious haze. I snapped my head back, staring at him.

"Silvan!" Rachel chided, but her new husband rebuffed her.

"I'm allowed to ask. What's it like there, Terra?"

I thought of the endless ice fields. The craggy mountains that jutted up toward the sky. I thought of her forests, dancing below us in the night like a whole crowd of bodies, and of the ocean that stretched on and on and on. I thought of her beasts. The Ahadizhi. Raza Ait, and the sparkling cupola. All those plants growing and growing through the false summer. I thought of one plant. Vadix. Mine.

"It's wonderful," I said softly. I thought of his three-fingered hands, dark against my hip. And his belly going red in his lust for me. I thought of his lips, of deep kisses, of everything we'd done on that long night. Of everything he'd done for me since. Begging the senate to let us return, working day and night to see me safe. I felt his mind stretch far, up and up and up like a vine, touching mine—and that was only a wavering shadow of his real caress. "It's so much better than we ever imagined."

"Bah," Silvan said, and with that single, gruff syllable, he washed away all those memories. All that hope. "It's no good with people there. It will never be really *ours*."

Silvan leaned forward, the heels of his hands resting against the center console and all his weight resting against his hands. He was gazing down into the terminal embedded there, those smoldering eyes distant with thought. They were beautiful eyes, but I didn't like the emotion behind them. Like he was owed something.

"What's it matter if it's ours? It will be a good home for us—better than this creaky old ship!"

The corner of his mouth twitched.

"This 'creaky old ship' might be *our* home, but that's a sacrifice I'm willing to make if our descendants can one day live to see Earth. Jerusalem. Israel. Zion—it was *ours*, Terra. Her deserts and the springs that pour from the rocks there, as clear as glass. Her mountains, green and dappled, and the sky, blue and endless overhead. The smell of pomegranate on the air in the summertime. All those sacred buildings we lost. Can you imagine?" He had to be quoting Rachel. These pretty words were not his own.

"They're gone," I said through clenched teeth. His gaze had gone hazy, like he was looking into the future and the past all at once. "The asteroid destroyed it all. Destroyed the whole planet, Silvan. Do you think a tiny piece of land would have been spared?"

"We were spared, weren't we?" he asked. "I've asked the Council-loyal scientists what they think. Even had an audience with Mara Stone. The chances are slim, based on their projections. But it's not impossible. There's even a chance the asteroid missed Earth entirely. Our ancestors left before it happened, after all. All this wandering might have been for nothing. Worthless. A waste."

I glanced toward the purple slip of land that floated in the glass. On that planet Vadix waited. His guests had left; he'd sunk into the circular sofa, sliding his eyelids shut. Tired. So tired. But he had work to do, still, and hours to go before he joined me in the dreamforests.

"It *wasn't* for nothing, Silvan! We have a chance to achieve *tikkun olam*. Can't you see?"

He watched me for a long moment, pressing those plush lips thin. "No," he said. "I can't. Why won't you join us, Terra? We'd be happy to have you. Mara Stone will be retiring soon. We'll need a botanist."

"I don't want to be *your* botanist."

He looked wounded at my words, and more than a little puzzled, too. To Silvan there was no greater honor than to serve him, and no greater insult than to turn him down. But after a moment his expression brightened, as if a new thought had just occurred. "Is it because Rachel and I are to be wed? You don't have to be alone. There are boys here among us—unmarried boys."

I massaged my index fingers over my forehead. "I don't *need* an unmarried boy. I'm working with their translator to negotiate—"

"Yes, yes," Silvan said as he began to roll his eyes. "You're going to negotiate an accord. I've heard all about it. It's not happening, Terra. The aliens will never welcome us on their planet, and I'm not going to stick around to wait for them to prove it."

"You don't even know them."

"I don't have to. I know my people. We've survived these five hundred years by sticking together. It's how we'll survive the next five hundred. I've been warning them—" He broke off, setting his fingers down on one of the console switches as if to demonstrate. He flicked it up and down and up again. I thought of the lights flickering in the ship. Off and on and off. The darkness was nothing more than the stupid, thoughtless movements of this *boy*.

"And if they don't listen?"

"They have no choice. I control the engines. The lights. The air. I'd rather they go willingly, but we *belong* together, Terra. It's what my father worked his whole life for."

"Your father." I grimaced at the memory of Mazdin Rafferty, telling me I was worthless, telling me I was no threat to him. Telling me that, in the end, all rebels became obedient Asherati—or died.

But Silvan lifted his chin. His curls tumbled down his shoulders. He was beautiful, but young and proud and foolish, too.

"Abba understood the importance of keeping the people united. How you sometimes have to make hard choices to keep the ship running."

Like killing my mother, I thought. In that moment I wanted to say it. I wanted to fling accusations at Silvan, to tell him the whole truth about what had transpired between his father and me. That night in the Raffertys' quarters, my temper had flared more brightly than it ever had before. I'd thought it was a righteous anger, though as soon as I shoved the wine bottle, full of poison, back on the rack, the doubts began to grow within me.

"Your father," I said again. Silvan peered curiously at me, blinking his dark lashes hard.

Killed him. I killed him, I thought. The words were threatening

to spill past my lips. Perhaps if I told Silvan, the weight of the death would lift from my shoulders. Silvan could absolve me—set me free.

But I saw his fingers, how they caressed the dials. Silvan had a temper too. He could be selfish and spoiled, sullen, temperamental. And though I wished I could say with certainty that he wouldn't do a single thing to harm me, in truth I didn't feel so sure.

Terra, don't, Vadix said at last. But he didn't have to. My mouth was open, and I was already speaking.

"Your father was a great man," was what I said.

Out of the corner of my eye, I saw Rachel let out a breath of relief. On the night before we landed, I'd told her bits and pieces of the truth—that I'd hurt Mazdin, that my hands had wrought shameful things—and she must have figured out the rest in the days since Mazdin's death. And yet she hadn't told Silvan, not one single word. My heart swelled at the sight of her. Rachel, my loyal friend. Holding my secrets in.

"Of course he was a great man," Silvan said peevishly. He gave the controls one last flick, on and off, before standing straight. "No matter what the rebels say."

That's when I knew for certain that Silvan would never absolve me of my guilt. Not that he really could anyway. The only person who could ever forgive me was Mazdin, and he was gone, lost to the foxglove. Just like Momma.

"They don't understand," I said, swallowing hard. It hurt to even breathe, much less speak, as I heaped praise upon Silvan's father. "Your father sacrificed so much for them, and they don't understand at all. And they never will. We're too different. Too much has happened for us to ever live in peace."

His lips fell open. When he looked at me again, it was with sadness. "I wanted you to join us. I don't mean the rebels. I mean you, Terra. I thought we could be friends. Even if—"

"I know." Stepping closer, I reached out, taking his hand in mine. I needed to still it, to keep it away from the controls. "You were always good to me. But you have to let us go. We're no good to you. You have Council men and women, and loyal commoners willing to follow you too. We'll just get in the way of your father's dreams. You can see them to fruition better without us. Take the ship and leave us here, and let us make our own mistakes on the planet."

He hesitated, running his thumb over my knuckles. Such a familiar gesture. But then, as if he'd just remembered Rachel standing beside us, he snatched his hand away.

"The natives will have you?"

It was my own turn to hesitate. I sucked in a breath. "Not yet. But soon I hope."

When Silvan turned toward the viewer, his black curls shone— as if the stars were trapped inside them. His gaze went dark as he

watched the planet. The world spun silently, and he was thoughtful.

"Might go faster if I helped you. It's what Abba would have wanted. Near the end he kept asking where you were, you know."

I didn't know what to say, so I didn't say anything. At last Silvan filled the silence for me.

"He said it was cancer, just like the one that killed your mother. Isn't that strange?"

My stomach clenched. Rebbe Davison had once told me that Aleksandra's mistake was in not dealing with the consequences of her actions. I guess these were my consequences—the heavy burden of my guilt, and Silvan and Rachel, lost to me forever.

"Yes, strange," I said, but my voice came out as nothing more than a whisper.

I streamed out of the lift and straight into the darkness. Someone had broken the pasture fence; a flock of sheep had strayed down to the main path, and they bleated at my arrival. I pushed past their heavy bodies. I'd lose this soggy field soon—the silent clock tower where my father had once worked, and the ground where he rotted now. Would lose it all, the glass overhead, honeycombed, full of Zehava's beautiful continents. Would lose my beautiful best friend, too. No, wouldn't lose them. That wasn't quite right. I'd given them all away, ignoring the fact that there was nothing left for us, nothing assured.

"Terra!" At last I stopped, turned. Mordecai ran toward me; my brother trailed behind. They both looked hopeful as they approached, their mouths stretched with stupid smiles. They'd waited for me— waited in the stuttering dark. "How did it go?"

"It was fine," I croaked out painfully. "But we're not. The ship. I gave him the ship."

Without waiting for their response, I turned and hustled through the field again. It was Ronen who called out, amid a nest of laughter. I stopped again, frowning, to listen.

"What do we need a ship for?" he asked. "We have a whole damned planet!"

I looked back over my shoulder at my brother, my naive, sweet brother. He'd cast both arms upward, gesturing to the world above. I wondered at the shape of her as she slept in the darkness. I thought of all of our troubles ahead—the senate and their mandate, the beasts, the Ahadizhi in the south. But for the first time I gazed not to the sparkling continent up north but to her southern land, steeped in darkness. And I wondered if maybe, just maybe, Ronen might be right.

umans as Guardians? It is an unlikely proposal.

Vadix sat on his doorstep in Raza Ait. He took in the sight of the dark grove. He watched the silhouettes of trees wavering before him. They reached and stretched, up and up and up toward the cupola above. But the stars were out that night, the glass shadowed by snow-heavy clouds. In a way I sat beside him in the doorway, my knee knocking his. But only in my mind. In flesh I was sprawled out in Ronen's pitch-black guest room, Pepper stretched across my belly.

Unlikely, I said. I heard the baby bawling in the distance, the cat yawning on top of me. In Raza Ait I heard the wind blow. I couldn't hear my own heart. *Many things are unlikely. You are unlikely. I am unlikely. We—*

I don't speak from a lack of faith, zeze! In the dark of the night, Vadix laughed at me, but there was fear behind his laughter. *You would face so many dangers. The beasts! You met one, did you not?*

I did. I remembered Deklan's body, gored straight through, the yellow horn dripping blood. I remembered mouths packed full of teeth. Savage, wild eyes.

Then you know the impossibility of this.

I ran my hand over Pepper's knobby back. The cat had teeth, and claws that he loved to sharpen against the leg of my brother's galley table. He was sweet, but sometimes dangerous, too, like when he slipped out an open door and returned dragging a squirrel by the scruff of its neck—its little belly already open and licked clean. I remembered the Ahadizhi vehicle that had swept up through the forest, a stream of color: red and gold, purple and green. And their intoxicating music lacing its refrain around my heart.

Tell me what happens in the winter, I said. *When the Guardians are awake and you walk in the dreamforests.*

Vadix stretched his long legs out, putting his slippered feet against the cold ground. He looked up, as if he could see the storm looming beyond the glass. But he couldn't—the cupola was clouded with condensation, opaque as polished steel.

I have never seen it, he began. *Of course, I have only ever slept through the long season. But I have read the accounts kept by our Guardians. They leave their work in the winter to defend our city—forming parties that hunt twice daily. The old and the young. The feeble and the strong. With their prods and knives and songs, they fell the beasts. So that we may be restored to life in spring and repair the damage done to our cities, so that we may all live in peace.*

And what happens if they don't?

Vadix closed his eyes. In his memory I could see the shadowed spaces where he retreated during the winter. The dank smell of cave was all around. But the mouth of that dim space was open, filled with light.

We are vulnerable. Without them we die. Our partnership dies. Our city dies. We have no industry. No ingenuity. We are just slender vines at the whim of tearing claws. We are impoverished. Defenseless. This is why the Xollu are afraid. We all know it, down to the root. Our essential weakness.

It was true. If I dug deep inside him, uncovering the parts of him he'd worked so hard to hide, I could see his fear. Taste it too. He was little more than a quivering child, flinching at every wind that passed. I shifted in bed, unseating Pepper. He stretched, then sank down again, tucking his black nose between his paws.

Could humans be taught to hunt?

I do not know. You are clever. But you are also prey. The Ahadizhi art raises desires in you. It is hypnotizing to you—tempting. I know. I have felt it in you. That day in the city, when you were almost lost to me.

I cast my head to the side. On my desk sat my sketchbook, scattered with pencils. *I'm an artist too. Maybe I can learn to resist it—to be like them. There might even be others on the ship. People who can dance and sing, or play instruments. There hasn't been much room in our lives for art, but maybe once we settle on the planet, there will be.*

Vadix sounded hopeful—cautious but hopeful. *Perhaps.*

You need to ask them for me. You need to make this happen. Please, Vadix?

He didn't answer, not right away. Instead he only sat back on his steps, turned his gaze up, and watched the snow begin to blanket the cupola.

That night I dreamed alone.

When was the last time that had happened? It must have been ages and ages ago, while the ship was still drifting through open space. Lately I'd become accustomed to meeting him at night. Even if we spoke without speaking, even if our minds were together more and more as the days went on, there were always moments of tumult, of darkness—moments that could only be healed by his touch. When

we walked through the dreamforests together, I knew that I wasn't alone, wrong and strange. I knew that I was understood. Strong. Beautiful. Solid. Real. His lips were a reminder that I was someone worth kissing; his arms an assurance that I was worth holding, too. I looked forward to our nights together. I craved them, like a hungry ghost, insatiable.

So on that night, when I stumbled through the dark corners of my own mind, I couldn't help but feel unsettled. Where *was* he? He was supposed to be here, my support, my scaffolding. Cradling my hand in his hand and saying my name. Reminding me that I was still a living creature, not just some small scrap of memory left behind when my father died.

Abba. He was here in my dream, his voice echoing down the long hallway of the house where I grew up. I took ponderous steps down it; the hall seemed to stretch longer and longer. When I opened his bedroom door, I found him sitting on the bed. It was wrong, all wrong. He was dead, and nothing would ever change that. But then he smiled, and it didn't matter. My Abba's true smile, wide and gummy. It had been years since I'd seen him smile like that.

"I've been packing," he said, turning to a basket full of clothes beside him. I glanced down. There they were, those corduroy uniforms, each shoulder marked by a blue rank cord.

"For what?" I asked. I braced myself for bad news, that Abba, my strange, temperamental father, would take off with Silvan for the Earth again. But he only shook his head, letting out a chuckle that went on just a beat too long.

"That's the question, isn't it?"

"Isn't it?"

My father nodded his bald head. He lifted his index fingers, glancing between them. "It seems to me that there are two options. Zehava or death."

That's when I realized that he didn't *know*. He didn't remember dying up in those rafters—hung from the frayed piece of rope that was still knotted through ancient wood. I studied his features—the feather of hair surrounding his bald head, the single silver eyebrow hair that gnarled up out of the black ones, the pores along the side of his face, all ruddy from shaving. All these details that I had forgotten, the tiny markers that had once proved that he was a living, breathing man.

His eyelashes shivered. I wondered what would happen if I told him the truth, that he was dead, gone already. Would he be upset? Would he vanish, like smoke? In my dream my father had packed for a trip—seven pairs of identical trousers, identically folded, small scraps of paper, a pressed flower that had once been Momma's. He didn't want to die. Tonight he wanted to come with me, to finally achieve *tikkun olam.*

"I guess it's Zehava, then," I said, and pressed a kiss into his forehead. My father leaned into my lips' touch. I got a strong whiff of him. Wine and cedar boards. Dust.

I woke with my body sopped with sweat, the sheets tangled around my torso.

"Vadix!" I called, out loud, until I heard my voice echo against the blackness and clamped a hand over my mouth. Afraid of waking the baby, I spoke silently instead.

Vadix, where are you? A pause, too long, so I added in a panic: *Are you all right?*

I waited a long time for him to answer. I pulled myself upright, feeling my heart pound right through my nightshirt. Touching a hand to my throat, I listened to myself breathe. What if he was gone? I thought of the inviting darkness of the funerary fields, the desire that urged him to join Velsa. But I shook that thought away. He was alive somewhere down there in the city. His compulsion to join Velsa wasn't just a memory but a real, present wish, that indelible part of himself that never would be washed away.

Vadix! I chided, more firmly this time, and I felt his awareness slam into mine, hard. I closed my eyes against the dark, saw the gray fingers of light come dawning in the glass over Raza Ait. The whole city was like a bud, gently unfurling in the spring.

He stood on the senate steps, his shadow dim and long out in front of him. He was tired, so very tired; he hadn't slept a single wink that night. That's why we hadn't roamed together through the forests. He'd never even gone to bed, much less succumbed to dreams.

And yet somehow, inexplicably, he was happy. I felt his mouth stretch from earslit to earslit, the air cold against the dozens of tiny blades that were his teeth. The emotion that filled his chest wasn't heaviness or dread, or even his old, familiar friend solitude. It was something else, some small, giddy sliver of hope.

I have a gift for you, he said. He watched Xarki peek out over the shadows of the tallest buildings at the city's edge. In the morning the skyline looked jagged and full. Even though it was still dark in Ronen's guest bedroom, I found myself squinting, resisting the sun's beams.

A gift?

I sat straighter in bed, kicking the blankets back. There was only one thing I wanted. Well, that wasn't entirely true. I wanted *him,* too, thousands of nights with him, time to grow old, to have our first fight, to sleep beside him as humanity put down roots on Aur Evez. But barring that? The only thing I really wanted was a home. A small patch of land all my own.

They've agreed to let us stay? I asked. But Vadix pulled back, smoothing his lips.

No. They've agreed to let you speak to the senate. A hearing. First thing tomorrow morning.

The senate. I'd only glimpsed it through the antechamber glass—rows upon rows of gold-robed Xollu, hundreds of Ahadizhi all talking at once. Me? Speak to *them*? I'd hardly been able to speak to my own people.

I—I can't!

I will be with you, he said gently. *They have agreed to let me translate for you. After what happened with Aleksandra, they will not hear anyone else. But I vouched for you. I told them of your character.*

I grabbed my blankets in both fists, tugging at the soft fabric. This wasn't what I'd expected, not at all. Vadix didn't even try to hide his disappointment.

I did this for you! Your people! Your future and your safety. You will be the first animal to ever speak in the senate room. The first! I know your words will move them. He paused, feeling the warmth of the sun as it began to crown the sky overhead. *They have done much to move me.*

Even in the cool dark of the empty room, I felt my cheeks heat. *Thank you,* I said. I felt something rumble back in response. A tiny crackle of something—laughter.

Do not thank me yet, zeze. We have much work to do still.

27

hough I would be the only human allowed in the senate room, Vadix suggested I bring a team of advisers with me to Raza Ait. For me the choice was easy. That morning I'd board a shuttle with Mara Stone and with Mordecai. My teachers, who had taught me more in my years on the ship than anyone else. I couldn't imagine departing again without them. We planned to travel alone, the three of us and a shuttle pilot. Vadix assured me that we needed no guards, and besides, they were occupied that morning. With their sonic rifles in hand, they gathered the children who roamed the streets of the ship and herded them toward their homes—accomplishing in a few hours what the Council had failed to do in days.

But we were surprised that morning when we went to board our shuttle and found someone waiting for us. Standing tall in white wool, the rank cord vibrant against his shoulder, was Silvan Rafferty.

"What are you doing here?" Mara demanded, her craggy voice hard. Silvan only put his hands on his hips.

"The peace you're brokering concerns us, too. We need to divide the ship's resources fairly. The Asherati need a say."

It was the first time I realized that, after this, we would no longer be Asherati. We'd be something else—Zehavans. Colonists. Different. New. I put my hand on Mara's shoulder and pulled her gently away.

"He's right," I said. "He's their leader, and they deserve a voice too. He can come."

"Are you sure, Terra?" Rebbe Davison asked. I looked at Silvan, at the proud, firm set of his jaw. And nodded.

"Yes, I'm sure."

On the long journey over we tried to prepare him for what he'd find in Raza Ait. We told him about the copper city, domed against the impending winter. We told him about the beasts that roamed the mountainous wilds. Mara explained how the plants there were different from ours: motile rather than grounded; purple, not green.

Silvan nodded. He seemed to understand. But for some reason he had trouble with the idea of the people there.

"Talking plants," he said, snorting through the glass of his flight suit helmet. "It makes no sense. It has to be a joke. It just has to be."

"It's no joke," Mara said peevishly. "And you'd better not go saying that around our hosts. Until they decide we can stay, we're going to be guests on this planet, you know. We need to act graciously."

Beneath the glass of his helmet I saw Silvan go a shade paler. I don't think he'd ever been called out like that before, not by someone like Mara Stone. After a moment of visible discomfort—eyebrows knitted up, jaw tight—he relaxed and let out a burst of laughter.

"Fine! Though you're one to talk about niceties, Mara Stone. 'As hard as a rock,' that's what Abba always said about you. I can see that he was right. You do your job, and you do it well. We'll be sad to lose a good specialist like yourself. A fine worker. And a fine citizen."

There was a gleam in his eye. And hers. She pursed her lips, but I couldn't say she didn't look at least a little flattered.

"Oh, come off it," she said.

The workers had brought their boats in for the winter. The pier itself was blanketed in gray. If, once, the edge of their cloistered world had seemed open to me—ocean and sky, stretching on forever—that had been lost to the season. The world's curving lip had disappeared behind a thicket of fog. Though it wasn't snowing now, it might as well have been. That's how dense the air seemed as we stepped out of the shuttle.

I couldn't help but think that this was how it should have been from the beginning. Careful. Planned. Not the insane quest of a half-drunk girl, her heart full of fear and her mind running wild. Beneath my flight suit I wore the robes I'd borrowed from Vadix, their downy-soft fabric hugging my body tight. I may not have been dressed like a senator, but I hoped I looked like someone worthy of entering the senate chamber. My hair was combed, my eyes bright, even after eight hours of voyage through the silence of space. I'd put on makeup, returning to the ritual that I'd adopted during the era of my romance with Silvan Rafferty. It had been a comfort to me then; it was one now, too. And I needed everything I could get to calm my nerves that day. After all, I was about to see Vadix.

I knew he was there waiting for me. I could see the world through his gaze—the end of the long pier as he hustled down it through a rolling fog. In the murky distance he spotted a flash of light. Was it faint yellow sunlight against the water, or the gleam of a white hull, long preserved within the belly of our ship? I waved away Silvan's hand, pulling myself out of the shuttle alone.

I'm here, I said. *It's me!*

Vadix headed a pack of lesser senators, each one garbed in a silver shade that seemed to disappear into the cold of the world beyond. But he wore blue, vibrant and bright. It matched his skin, his hands, his lips, which parted at the sight of me.

"Who's *that*?" Silvan asked. Mordecai gazed at him sternly.

"Our ally. Our friend," my old teacher said.

Vadix ran toward me. I knew it hurt, in this cold, to make his limbs move this fast, to push himself closer and closer to me across the length of the foggy pier. I could feel it, splintering the cells in his arms and legs. But Vadix didn't care. I was here, and I brought with me hope—hope for the future he never believed would come to fruition. Hope for a new city on Zehava.

"Terra," he said when he finally reached me, "you have painted your face. You are a clever hunter. "

Before I could answer, he swept me up in his long arms. His body may not have been warm, but it shielded me from the world beyond. I pressed my face to the soft, sweet plane of his neck, leaving a trail of kisses along his earslit. His arms enveloped my lower back, as tight as a vine as he lifted my feet straight off the pier. I thought my heart would burst through my chest. I thought I might cry at the way that his body fit mine, like we had been made for this. I thought I had never felt such joy in my life as seeing him again.

"Her lover," Mara Stone added at last, her tone teasing as Vadix bent me in a kiss. There was no reply at first, only the whistle of the wind and the sound of the waves breaking against the pier. Then, as Vadix's mouth met mine, as I tasted the sweet truth of him, the wild smell faint in the impending winter, came Silvan's grunted answer.

"Oh," he said. "I see."

We gathered in the senate antechamber that afternoon to plan our approach. While the senators milled about below, Vadix sat at the head of the round stone table, explaining our situation:

"Tomorrow morning they are convening on several matters of local import. Terra must come forward to speak to them before their interest begins to wane. Each representative will be eager to have his or her voice heard on problems pertaining to his or her constituency. We must be fast. We must be direct."

"What are these local matters?" Mordecai asked, his hand flat on the stone table. They'd piled it high with food for us—burned beast legs, as thick as tree trunks and sliced into blackened disks. But no one had touched it.

"Zoning," Vadix replied without hesitation. "Water treatment. Funding for new crèches. The usual politics."

Beside me Silvan flinched. My *bashert* turned to him, looking more like a curious bird than a plant. "What is the problem, Mar Rafferty?"

"We have a ship full of waiting citizens," he said as he leaned forward in his seat. "People who traveled five hundred years to reach this planet. And you're telling me that your government is more concerned about issues of water treatment?"

I felt my stomach clench at the anger that underscored his voice. But Vadix was patient. He lifted up his fingers, pointing them toward the sky.

"I tried to dissuade the senate from disregarding your problems so hastily. But to them what remains is only a technicality. They believe they have already dispensed with 'the human problem'—that soon you will be only a memory, consigned to the darkness of space. We must understand that this is just a small disruption of their normal daily lives. And they have little room in them for . . ." He trailed off. His brow furrowed with worry.

"Aliens," he concluded at last.

"Aliens." Silvan's lip curled. "We're not aliens. We're *people*. You can't just throw us away."

Vadix looked at me. His black eyes were calm as he considered. "I agree. I don't intend to throw you away. Tell us what your ship would need, Mar Rafferty, so that if my mate settles here, she can live in peace."

My cheeks warmed under his gaze. Silvan, watching, lifted his lips in a slow smirk.

"We can split the library," he said. "Rachel has plans to curate a collection of religious texts. And as for the hatchery—" He hesitated.

That's when I realized how well the Council's secrets had been kept.

"They don't need it," I said, feeling the blood drain from my cheeks. "Or at least, not all of it. The Council boys haven't been sterilized."

When Mordecai drew in a breath, Silvan only pressed his lips together. Nodded. "Not the last dozen clutches. And those older than that have already had their children. Only those common-born citizens who join us will need the eggs, and even then, not many. If we stop sterilizing our boys, we should be able to survive without the hatchery within a generation. We'll need to be fruitful to have the ship back up to working capacity, but we can do it. Rachel says—"

Before we could find out what Rachel said, Mara Stone threw her hands up into the air. "Of course. Rachel says. I'm sure you boys are fertile enough, eh?"

Silvan didn't blush. He only angled his chin up in proud assuredness.

"Yes," he said. "I'm sure we are."

Mara rolled her eyes, then turned the conversation back to more pressing matters. "We'll need land enough for a small hatchery of our own, then. And space to build a library as well. Labs. A school. Living quarters. Fields for our crops."

Vadix pulled out a long scroll of paper from his robe. It had handles carved in the shapes of wild beasts, each one so real-looking I thought they might walk across the table as he unraveled it. Ahadizhi work, surely. As he pulled them apart, he revealed continents. White-licked seas. Zehava. Or Aur Evez, depending on how you looked at it. He pointed to an area in the south close to the wide central ocean, a long peninsula of dark vegetation and apparently little else. But because I knew Vadix, I knew that there were dangers waiting there for us. The native Ahadizhi. The beasts. The long ravages of winter.

"We call this place Zeddak Alaz. The lost land. I will ask the senate to give you this place," he said, and then his black eyes flitted up at me. Once I would have called them unreadable, but now I knew the passions—the fear, the hope, the intensity—that lurked behind them. "But the decision is up to them."

We plotted well into the evening, long after all the senators had returned to their homes for the night. Vadix explained the intricacies of senate procedure, and detailed, with a flourish, the contentious relationship between the Ahadizhi of the southern continent and their northern counterparts. Though Ahadizhi learned language far faster than any Xollu—a facility I'd seen myself over my days in Raza Ait—those in the south were ascetics. They saw no need for the lavish city dwellings of their northern counterparts and so had no reason to speak to the Xollu, either. And no Xollu had broken the language barrier that stood like a wall between them. For thousands of years they'd been at a stalemate. No new Guardians, and none willing to cross the wild sea, straying far from their sprouted fields. So no new cities, either.

"You will have to recruit northern Ahadizhi," Vadix said. "And have them train you in the role of Guardian before your departure for the southern continent. Perhaps someday the southern Ahadizhi could be persuaded to join the thirteenth city, but this would take time and skill. Diplomacy."

It would be easier if we had you there to translate for us, I thought. Then, when Vadix looked sharply at me, I clamped a hand down over my mouth. Of course, he was the only one who had heard. The others merely gazed at me, puzzled. Mara let out a tired sigh.

"I'm sure we'll manage," she said. Vadix rose to his feet.

"I believe we have planned all we can for this evening. Terra must speak to the senate early tomorrow, and we all need our rest," Vadix said. Did I imagine it, or had his reedy voice gone cold at my rejoinder? But it *was* late. Maybe he was only tired. I definitely was. My neck and back ached against the stone chair.

"Yes," Silvan said, a little too loudly. When the conversation had turned away from the ship's resources, he'd stopped trying to feign the slightest interest. "Show us to our accommodations."

"Very well," Vadix said.

He led us into the hall of the empty, echoing senate building, then down the wide steps to the mosaic-dotted pavilion below. It was strange seeing this space so empty, as if the life had been drained right out of it. The night was cool, as fragrant as spring as we walked out into the city. Peaceful. I was glad we hadn't brought a guard.

"It's emptier than it was a few days ago," Mara said, stepping quickly down the stone staircase. She was right—fewer Xollu pairs now strolled arm in arm, though the Ahadizhi still loitered and lazed outside each residential building. The pungent smell of meat hung heavily in the air. I suspected that would only get worse as winter wore on and the hunt began in earnest.

"Some of the crèches have already gone to the winter caves," Vadix said. "And the elderly as well. As the cold sets in, the urge to sleep overtakes us. Soon all but the most necessary Xollu will sleep. And then we all will."

"Well," Mordecai said, "we appreciate that you've stayed behind for us."

"You have no idea," I murmured, and though they all gazed at me strangely as we headed beneath a curving overpass, I ducked my head and didn't answer.

Maybe I should have taken his hand in my hand, savoring every precious moment we still had together. But as Vadix led us through a cluster of commercial buildings, toward the enclave of round houses at the city's heart, I couldn't help but be aware of how every step we took brought me closer to his ultimate end. Not just winter, not merely sleep, but death. If all went according to plan, our safety would soon be assured. He'd depart for the funerary fields knowing that he'd done his part for me, helping me to establish this home for my people on Aur Evez. He'd rend his flesh, destroy himself, just to be with Velsa—and he would rest well too, knowing he'd helped me, knowing he'd secured my fate, just as promised. In the grove the boughs had all begun to curl up, shielding themselves from the cold. I wished that I could do the same, staving off this future. But I couldn't. If my people's settlement was to be secured, I'd have to risk losing him. I knew it in my gut. There was no use in hiding.

He took us all to his own house. As they saw the walls, which were dark and sparkling in the moonless night, and the delicate, curving shape of the architecture, even Silvan had to draw in a breath.

"Lavatory," Vadix said, pointing to a slender door. "Kitchen. Do not drink from the golden spigot. I'm not certain it's safe. I have placed cooked meat for you there on ice in a small refrigeration unit. You will sleep here." He led us toward the sitting room, where he gathered blankets and small, round pillows from beneath the seats. As the others began to make their beds, I started to trail after Vadix, away from the round room.

"Terra," Silvan called, flopping his body down against the circular sofa, "aren't you going to sleep?"

Vadix stood, halfway to his bedroom, his tired shoulders squared.

"She's to sleep with me," he announced. I hesitated, standing in the door between the two worlds. Then I took one look into Vadix's black, sad eyes and shook my head at Silvan.

"I'll see you all in the morning," I said. I saw Mara arch an eyebrow, heard Mordecai and Silvan share a snicker. But what did that matter? Hastily I closed the door behind me.

"I hear your thoughts," he said as he sat down at the edge of his round bed. The clouds seemed to be bright silver through two layers of glass. Even with the lights off, the thread in his robes caught the light and scattered it.

Do you? I replied. But when I did, he gave a wince. He was so, so sad. I could feel it in every cell. He lifted two fingers and pressed them to his mouth.

"Speak like this," he said.

But I was tired. Sad, too.

Taot? I said.

For a long time he didn't answer. Instead he bent over, taking his cloth slippers off his feet. His long blue toes flexed against the floor. I could feel how they wanted to be rooted there, to make themselves permanent. He set his shoes in a line at the end of his bed, rose, and began to unknot the belt of his robe. But he didn't watch the progress of his own hands as he did. He watched me.

"Because it hurts too much right now," he said as the cloth slipped off his shoulders, revealing his body, as gnarled as an old dome tree that had been marked by the thoughts and wishes of too many long-dead lovers. I wanted to go to him, to slip my arms under his and press my face to the cool surface of his chest. But it didn't seem right.

"I am not angry," he said. "You think I am angry, but I am not angry."

"What, then?" I asked as I edged closer, finally sitting on the edge of the bed myself. I glanced down at my own robe and slippers. They were too big on me, meant for him. He let out a baleful hum.

"Sad. You want me with you. I understand this. But Velsa—"

"I've never asked you not to do it," I cut in. In response, silence stretched on long, too long. He just *looked* at me as he stood there, the darkness spilling over the steep curve of his shoulder. So I added, "I never would. Love isn't something you lock up in chains. But that doesn't mean it doesn't *hurt*. Maybe I'll never miss you like you miss Velsa. But I'll still miss you, Vadix."

After another moment's pause he came and sat down beside me. Both of us sat with our hands on our knees. His were dark as night—mine, white as bone.

"I know," he said. "I know you have never asked. You have been fair. I know I will hurt you. Perhaps if I had done my duty to Velsa, then your life would be easier. With less pain."

"No!" I said. Our eyes locked. His were so wide in his face that he reminded me of a doe. Gentle, delicate. Fragile. "I'm glad I know you. Without you my life would have been just one dark day after another. You know what I told you, about hope? You gave me that. No one's ever loved me before you, not like this. I didn't—I didn't know that I was someone who *could* be loved. I didn't think I was worthy."

I felt his cool fingers slip around mine and squeeze tight.

"Of course you are worthy," he said. His voice had gone husky, coarse with emotion. "You are bright. Brave. Fighting for your people and your people's place on a new world."

"I wasn't always like this." I closed my eyes, remembering, even as I clutched his cool hand. "I was afraid once. Angry, too. I hurt people. Mazdin, but not only him. My friends. People who got in my way. Selfish. I was selfish."

"But you learned to be strong," he said. "The senate will see that. And then you'll have a city all your own."

"Your city," I said, leaning my head against his shoulder. For a moment he stiffened against the contact. But then his body softened, leaning back into mine. "The one you hoped for, all your life. All your training and sacrifice. It was for this dream, Vadix. And you gave it to me."

So much for strong. My throat was tight, aching with tears. He wrapped his arms around me, holding me. But he didn't speak.

I'm grateful, I said in his mind. *I'm so grateful. But that doesn't mean I won't miss you. I'll always miss you. If the senate agrees, this will be a victory. But it will be bittersweet. We're not only talking about hibernation. I know you still want to join her, Vadix. Not in sleep—in death.*

He rocked me in his arms. Xollu children never knew their parents. I wondered how he knew how to do that, whether it was instinct or some buried memory that he'd plucked from my mind.

Come, he said. *Rest beside me. We have much to do tomorrow.*

I angled my face to his. His lips were soft, and gently smiling. I kissed them. But the sad thoughts were too close. I couldn't chase them away.

"Will this be our last night together?" I asked. He pressed his soft, printless thumb against the center of my lip, touching the wetness there.

I will not rest until you and your people are safe.

He drew his hand away. I could still taste his skin, his sap.

Promise?

Of course. Now, zeze, lie with me. The night is long and we are together and that's reason enough for joy.

I kissed him again and let him wrap his arms around me. As we lay back in his bed, we pretended that the world outside was nothing— that we were the only creatures left in the whole wild world.

olden morning. We were up at dawn, before the sky had even
begun to green through the glass over Raza Ait. Vadix lent me his
finest robe, an opalescent length of sea-green cloth embroidered
with purple vines at the hems. I folded the flaps over my chest,
then began to knot the belt—when he stopped me, reached his fingers
around my waist, and began to elaborately interlace the tasseled ends.

"There," he said, standing back. His soft lips parted to show the
sharp edges of his teeth. "Now you look like an *ezzu*."

"'Ezzu'?" I asked, looking down to examine the flat knot that sat against my left hip. It matched the one on his perfectly.

"A thinking creature. Like Xollu or Ahadizhi."

I bit my lip, holding in my smile. "What did you call us before?"

He hesitated.

"What?"

"Okka," he said slowly, drawing away. *"Okka."*

"Taot?" I demanded, then, grinning, added: "What means this?"

He was halfway down the hall when he answered shyly, shamefully. "Beasts, *zeze.* We called you beasts. "

They'd called us beasts because that's what they thought of us. To them we were feral, hopeless creatures, barely capable of conscious thought, much less worth their regard. That's why they'd packed us into that quarantine camp, why they'd experimented on us, and why they'd been so quick to banish us from their land. They thought we were animals, and we'd acted like it too. Striking out against them, tempestuous. Violent.

On that pale morning the wind was high and cold even beneath the glass cupola. The senators streamed into the magnificent senate building as they had every day the senate was in session for thousands of years. They thought our future was already decided; I was determined to change their minds.

We waited outside a side doorway whose surface was carved with leaves edged in shining copper. I sat in a small chair against the wall, my legs shaking. The others gathered around me as we waited for Vadix to appear from behind that door. Mordecai seemed worried; he kept running his hand over the scruff of his jaw. Mara's narrow mouth was set into what appeared to be a permanent frown. Silvan kept pacing back and forth before us, warily eyeing the Ahadizhi senators who couldn't help but lick their lips at the sight of us.

At last the door creaked open. Vadix's blue face appeared behind it, his black eyes searching and searching until they fell on me.

"The time has come," he said. They all stepped back, even Silvan, as I rose from my chair.

"Wish me luck," I said. No one answered. They only stared at me. I couldn't blame them—I'd have felt uneasy too if I'd been them. But there wasn't time for fears or doubts or insecurity. This was my moment, the one I'd been waiting for. I tugged the shimmering robe down straight and passed through the slip of space between the heavy doors.

There were 248 Xollu pairs in the senate, and 326 Ahadizhi beside them. That's what Vadix had told me the night before—two representatives for every six thousand citizens spread between twelve cities. I wasn't sure how many people they represented in all. It was a number so large that I couldn't really fathom it, one that made the population of the *Asherah* look like nothing more than a drop in an enormous ocean. But I understood easily the power and the force of the senators themselves. As Vadix led me into the chamber, I heard the roar of their voices—like waves crashing against cliffs, like the ship's thrusters woken to life. As we walked down a hallway crisscrossed by the jagged shadows that were cast by the rafters high above, alien voices echoed and tumbled. Reedy voices, whistling voices, clicked laughter and raucous shouts. It was the most terrifying sound I'd ever heard, worse than a thousand death rattles.

The ship's tiny auditorium was little more than a faint shadow of this: rows upon rows of seats carved from heavy marble; yet another wide glass ceiling above. Xarki's light, amplified by the rounded glass, lit every senator's robe brightly. But their eyes—hundreds of eyes, as black as holes burned into paper—remained dark as Vadix and I streamed into the room, our long robes rippling after us. I felt scared. Small. But I refused to let it show.

I climbed the narrow steps toward the central platform's apex. There, dangling from two skinny posts, hung curving beast horns, hollowed out and yellow with age. Two long wires ran from their points down to some invisible power source hidden beneath the carpet. Vadix lifted one of the heavy things in his hand, letting its end wrap around his slender forearm. Then he gazed back and smiled.

Though I could hardly hear my own thoughts in the chaos, his cut right through it all, nestling in the forefront of my mind.

Be strong, he told me. I gave a nod.

He put his lips against the bell of the horn. Soon his voice resounded through the entire enormous rotunda.

"Vhahasa zasum!" he shouted, calling for silence, but it wasn't until his words echoed three or four times that the senators finally began to turn their attention forward. *"Vaoso ezzu aum aukri esevhom zezekk tora?"*

I am asking them if this woman will be permitted to speak before this sacred house.

When I turned to face the jumble of rows, I made sure to make my smile proud, to hold my jaw firm despite the fear that I felt. I needed to be brave in the face of them, to look worthy no matter the doubts that lurked inside me. Slowly a roar spread across the senate chamber: *"Zhieseoui tore!"* Yes, they would permit this.

Vadix turned toward me and indicated the horn. I reached forward and took it; like him I let the curled end envelop my arm. It was heavy; I nearly dropped it, and a few clicks of laughter rose up from the crowd. But Vadix helped me to steady myself. I stood straight and spoke into the hollow.

"My name is Terra Fineberg," I said, speaking slowly, as Vadix had instructed. But even so, I couldn't help but wince at the volume of

my voice, bouncing off the glass ceiling and the girders that loomed high overhead. The horn was made for thin *ekku* voices, not a thick human alto like mine. "I come on behalf of the Asherati of Earth. Five hundred years ago our planet was destroyed. Now we are lost, without a home. And we need your help."

Silence. Echoing silence. Vadix gazed at me, then put his own lips to his horn. The translation came out as fast and slick as oil. I kept my eyes on him. I couldn't bear to look at the senators as he spoke. They were too scary, too intimidating. I only lifted the horn up again and went on.

"We are not invaders. We are refugees. We have no land to call our own. There are those among us who would drift into space again in search of a world with room to spare. I say let them go. But the rest of us are at your mercy. Though you owe us nothing—not land, not food, not even kindness—I ask that you might let us settle in your southern lands, upon the slip of earth called Zeddak Alaz."

Vadix pressed his mouth to the horn again and began translating. But the murmurs of dismay began almost before he was done speaking. My throat tightened; my breathing grew shallow. Already so many of them had decided. I told myself that it didn't matter. I *would* be heard.

"Esteemed senators," I said. "I know it is a danger—for my people as well as yours. But your cities are crowded, and I know the Xollu are curious about what lies beyond the great sea. Before winter falls we will train with your Guardians. We will learn to take up prods and knives, learn to fell the wild beasts that would destroy us all. We will utilize Xollu building techniques to make our city strong against the wilds. And we would welcome any pairs who would join beside us as we strike out on this new endeavor."

I tried to read their faces as Vadix spoke. Did those black eyes hold skepticism? Fear? Laughter at our expense? I couldn't tell. Though I'd grown familiar with the boy who stood beside me, holding a carved horn against his mouth to catch his words, the emotions the others felt were strange to me. Foreign.

"My people are accustomed to sacrifice," I said. "For five hundred years we have scrimped and rationed, all for our last, desperate hope: that we might find a world where we can live in peace. And that's all we want here, a home where we can live good lives, rich with friends and love and work. We are not conquerors or tyrants. We are workers. Scientists. Artists. Mothers and fathers. Children, too. And we are at your mercy."

Vadix spoke again, though now his voice was almost entirely swallowed up by theirs. When he was finished, he turned to me and gave his head a doubtful shake. I was about to let my mouth crease into a frown, when a voice cut through all the others. It was a Xollu senator who stood near the back on one of the highest risers. She stood, grabbing the horn that sat in front of her, and spoke into it.

"Etez arri aum auru sheseoa taura seosoi?"

Vadix squinted at her words, then cupped his hand over his horn and turned toward me.

"Senator Zera wishes to know how they can trust your words. How do we know you will not harm us as we sleep, animals that you are?"

I swallowed hard, looking up at the senator. In the filtered light her skin was as bright as rubies. She stood tall above us, that horn in her hand. But she wasn't alone. Sitting beside her was her mate, an especially slender Xollu who watched her with large, pleased eyes. I saw in his expression the same emotions I felt when I looked at Vadix: wonder and joy, fascination and admiration. Not only had I been twinned, but twinned so well—as if my heart had been removed from my chest and doubled. Perfectly reproduced.

When I spoke, my voice was husky, low. We hadn't discussed this, Vadix and I. We'd talked about the peace we'd broker, every aspect of the new law we were asking the senate to approve. But we hadn't talked about *us*. Still, no words would better convince them. My confession was necessary—integral.

"You can trust my words because I would never harm my *zeze*. My *bashert*. My heart's twin. My destiny. Translator Vadix is my mate, and we walk the dreamforests together. I might be a stranger, but surely you can trust in that. I cannot deny it, cannot deny my mate."

The senators' conversations rumbled and echoed all around us. But for the first time Vadix's voice didn't cut over theirs. He lowered his hand, letting the horn drop to beside his knees. He simply stared at me, mouth open, brow furrowed in dismay. We hadn't planned this. He'd never consented to have his love revealed to the leaders of his world.

Tell them! I urged. It was our single best chance, and he knew it. So he lifted up the horn again and began to translate, even as his sad, confused eyes stayed on me.

"Taudiz voslax zhosoua, zozze ahadhazhi. Zeze aum voslax daudez. Dokk thosora, dokk eziz zhosoua. Tatoum taudiz sadl zhiahaolou zhosoua ut eziz Vadix. Taudiz voslax zhosoua, zozze ahadhazhi, aum eziz thosora."

It was as if his words were a spell, some sort of incantation that could magically quiet the senate chamber. Because just like that, their voices died down. The senators who had sat bent over their desks, hiding behind their long hands to speak to one another, all began to turn toward us. Their black eyes were open. They were trying to understand.

"Taot?" one senator demanded. *"Taidaz zhiahaoloa zeze aum vheseoazhi reraz. Taidaz saudsix aum taizzi zhiahaoloa okka taidaz?"*

Vadix shut his eyes. He rested the horn against his bare forehead, steeling himself.

What? I asked. I wanted to reach out, to take his hand in mine. But he was so far away.

Even if you are my zeze, she says, "*What assurance do we have that the rest of them are any better than beasts?*"

"Ettie!" I blurted, speaking into the horn without thinking. Vadix's eyes flew open as my words resounded across the senate chamber. "Esther! Esther Schneider. The little girl. She's walked the dreamforests. Her mate must be here somewhere. Your scientists saw that she was different from the others. We can't be the only ones. Tell them, Vadix!"

Eyes wide, he did.

When he was all done, the room erupted into fractious shouts once again. Senator Zera lowered herself back down into her seat, but several others had risen up in her place, shaking fists toward the glass sky. I watched as Vadix hung his horn back up on the stand. He threw an arm around my shoulder and drew me close.

"I believe the deliberations have begun," he said, his lips gracing my ear as he spoke. My hands were cold as I hung up my horn too, then let Vadix whisk me down the platform and away.

We waited in the antechamber for the senate's decision. After all this time I felt like I had practically memorized the patterns of purple moss that clung to the corners of the walls, the nicks in the stone table, the smudges on the glass that stood between us and the expansive chamber below. These hours upon hours of fighting, scheming, plotting had led to this—all of us gathered round, staring across the expanse of slate, and waiting.

Vadix stood by the window, staring down. I tried to reach out to him, to let my mind envelop his like a pair of arms. But he held me back. I couldn't tell if he was angry at what I'd done, laying our love bare for all to see. Or maybe he was just nervous about the senate's decision. Whatever the case, he didn't want me to read him right now, and so I couldn't. I wondered if someday I would learn how to block him. If only the senate would relent, if only Vadix would stay with me, if only we had the time.

"This will never work," Silvan said, at last breaking the silence that had fallen over us. "We should have sent someone else. Someone qualified."

"Who?" Mara demanded. "You?"

"I've been trained for leadership," he said, sitting back in his seat. He folded his arms over his broad chest. "All the Council-born were. We could be trusted." His gaze lingered on me for a moment, as if he were intent on reminding me that I was common born worthless.

But Mordecai cut in. My old teacher, who had watched me struggle, as awkward as a duckling, all through my childhood. Now his voice was firm.

"We had a Council-born leader. Aleksandra Wolff. The captain's daughter, destined for leadership. She got herself killed."

"Aleksandra," Silvan said, and snorted. I saw Mordecai clench his fist. I knew that I should stop them, step in before their tempers spilled over. But I was worn out—tapped. I couldn't find the words.

Luckily, I didn't have to. As the men argued, Vadix moved away from the window. I felt him settle his cool hand between my shoulder blades, a reassuring weight.

"Regardless of her qualifications," he said, loud enough that they all glanced up, "Terra did exemplary work down in the senate. The most educated Xollu would have flinched and shivered before such a crowd. She was strong. Convincing. I believe—"

But we never got to hear what he believed. The door slid open, and an Ahadizhi page stuck her head into the room.

"*Tatoum sase doza osouezhi zhiososek ut oliz xezlax,*" she said. "*Sase vauri zhiososek, zalse esevhe, aum oliz ahasazhi.*"

Vadix went silent, staring after her long after she withdrew and the door closed behind her. Mordecai rose from his seat. He cracked his knuckles, his anxious gaze falling on my *bashert*.

"What did she say?" he demanded. "What did they decide?"

Vadix's mind was a haze of emotion. But the words were there, floating at the forefront of his mind. So, my eyes welling with tears, I spoke for him.

"They've agreed. They've agreed. We're going to settle Zeddak Alaz."

They broke out into whoops of victory, joyous shouts. Mara Stone threw her arms around Mordecai, letting out ripples of relieved laughter. Even Silvan gave his fist a pump. He'd be able to return to Earth, as he and Rachel wanted, unencumbered by the rebels who had upset their lives.

But I didn't cry out in joy. I didn't even speak. I'd done it—and soon we would all achieve *tikkun olam* as our ancestors once hoped we would. But what was I going to have to sacrifice in return? I gazed up at Vadix, his endless gaze still frozen at the door.

This is a time to celebrate, isn't it? I asked, though I didn't feel certain about it. Not at all. My lover turned to me. For the first time I saw how, behind all that black, his eyes were a swirl of color. He smiled, his mouth full of teeth.

"Yes, *zeze*," he said, enfolding me in his arms. "Of course it is."

29

Two nights later the bells rang out across the pastures, drawing out of their homes the citizens who had cowered through the last several days. That night Koen seemed to throw his whole weight into his task—I'd never heard the bells call out with such clarity or force before, not even when I'd watched my father do his work in the years before he lost himself to the bottle. But on that night I wasn't there to see it. I waited in the ship's bow with Silvan, readying ourselves for the work we were about to do.

The controls twinkled, their light flickering against the brass buttons of his uniform. At Rachel's suggestion he'd abandoned his white wool for the familiar navy uniform of captain. Though his skin didn't look quite so radiant in the dark shade, he remained undeniably handsome. His long curls had been tied back at the nape of his neck with a blue ribbon. He stood tall, proud. Every bit the Council man who had been born to lead.

"Are you ready?" he asked. I gave the sash of my borrowed robe one last tug, squaring the knot just as Vadix had instructed. I wondered if our people would be shocked at the sight—one of their own wrapped up in alien garb. But soon the Xollu wouldn't be aliens anymore. They would be our friends, neighbors. The citizens would have to grow used to the sight of robes and spires, of copper and filigree.

"Yes," I said, smoothing down the fabric. Silvan offered me his arm, but I didn't take it. This wasn't a wedding—and not a funeral, either, I thought as we loaded ourselves into the lift. Tonight the bells rang for something else, something new. Something that hadn't happened before and wouldn't happen after, either. The doors dinged open. We marched into the cool of the dome evening. The scent of frozen earth and frost-tipped grass was all around us. For years after the same smell would remind me of that night. The last night that we were all Asherati. The night we began to say good-bye.

• • •

"Good evening, citizens!" Silvan cried out across the pasture. More than a thousand faces stared up at us. Some sneered at Silvan's words. Others pressed two fingers to their hearts in salute. Already our people were divided. But on this night we'd drive down the final wedge. "We're here to speak to you tonight not as Children of Abel or honored followers of the Council but as Asherati!"

He turned to me, nodded. So I stepped forward. As I spoke, I kept my hands folded in front of me, determined to quell their shaking. You'd think that after the last speech, my fear would be gone. But it wasn't; it was a part of me, just like my past was a part of me. Just like Vadix was a part of me.

"I have met with the senate of Aur Evez," I called, lifting my voice above their murmurs of confusion, "the ruling body of the planet we call 'Zehava.' They have agreed to let us settle on the southern continent, on territory they call Zeddak Alaz."

I saw several of them turn their gazes to the planet in the glass above. Their faces were lit by smiles. But I couldn't allow them such a simple joy. This wasn't the promised land. The lives for which we were about to depart would be ones of hardship, sacrifice. Not so different from the lives we'd known on the ship.

"But it will not be a life of unrestrained liberty," I said. "We must work with the native inhabitants to be certain that all of our safety is assured. We will defend them over the long winter, when the

STARBREAK · 397

city-builders hibernate in underground caves. We must be loyal, be true, and be committed to peace. I ask all of you willing to make these sacrifices to follow me into the open air and wild lands of Aur Evez!"

There were murmurs. Grumbles. Puzzled sounds from the crowd. I watched as the Asherati turned to their neighbors, full of questions and confusion. That's when Silvan Rafferty lifted up his hands. The conversation ebbed back, just like that. In some ways Silvan was right. He *had* been born to lead.

"I know that some of you are unwilling to make these concessions," he said, then loosed dry, self-assured laughter. "As I certainly am. If you would like to continue living in the manner to which you've grown accustomed, then stay with me here on our ship, in the safe belly of our mother *Asherah*. God willing, in five hundred years our descendants will live to set foot on Earth. *Our* planet! We will stop this wandering and return to our home. It will be a long journey, but I have faith in the mettle of our people. Come with me and claim the land that is our birthright."

More conversation. I heard the first spark of disagreement flicker, white hot, over the crowd. Some wanted to join me. Others—their friends, standing right by their sides—wanted to follow Silvan. I glanced at him and then, aping his gesture, lifted both hands up. I hoped that their trembling didn't show.

"This is a choice that every Asherati must make for him- or herself, one that will determine the shape of our future for generations to come. We know that you have much to talk about and a hard decision to make. The *Asherah* will leave Zehava's orbit in two weeks' time. Until then, go in health."

A few stray voices called back to me in turn. I pressed my lips appreciatively together.

"You really *are* becoming a leader," Silvan said, turning to me, grinning.

I shrugged.

"Someone has to," was all I said.

It's done.

That night I sat on the front stoop of my brother's home, watching as the Council-loyal stragglers made their way back to the districts from the safety of the ship's bow, carting their belongings behind them. Soon they'd be able to get to work, righting the chaos of the past few weeks. They'd repair windows, patch up crumbled brick, put their lives back together. Their lives wouldn't be quite as seamless as they once were—we'd all been changed by our sojourn in Zehava's orbit—but their lives would be safe. Familiar. I watched them exchange hopeful smiles. They were so lucky to be together for this, with their families, their children, their spouses. They were lucky not to have to face the future alone.

It took a long, long time for Vadix to answer me. He was there. I knew he was, floating just beyond the reach of my mind. But he'd drawn away from me in the time since our departure from the planet. Except in sleep, when our bodies moved in concert, oblivious to the dark days ahead, I was alone now. Once again a solitary person.

I know, he said at last. *I saw. You did well.*

Thank you.

I smoothed the thin robe down over my knees. The day was chilly, but soon it wouldn't be. Silvan said that the Council had plans to turn the ship back to four seasons. Better for planting. Better to prepare the people for Earth. The Council-loyal citizens would get the summers that we never had.

Will you miss it? he asked.

I sat straight, surprised at the curious tone of his voice in my mind. Lately he didn't allow himself the luxury of conversation, of my companionship. He was shutting down, preparing for the end.

Miss what?

The ship.

I gazed at the cobblestone and the streetlamps, at the cats who dozed on their front stoops, at the ancient curtains that hung, faded, in the window. I wanted to lie to him, to tell him that it all meant nothing to me and that I'd be glad to never see it again. But I couldn't.

For sixteen years she's all I've ever known. This is where I lost Momma,

and Abba, too. This is where I had my first kiss and where I met my best friend. Of course I'll miss it, Vadix. I licked my chapped lips. *But that doesn't mean I'm not excited about Zeddak Alaz. This is where it all started, but I have my whole life ahead of me. Years and years and years. Why do you ask?*

Silence stretched on between us. I couldn't see him, but I knew he was somewhere dark, shadowed. At last he turned, facing a feeble light.

No reason, he said.

I think the weeks that followed went quickly for the rest of them. Those were busy days. The Asherati divided the spoils of our journey, portioning out our supplies and technology between the new colony and those who would remain on the ship. It was hard work—emotional, too. I watched as Hannah and her parents squabbled over a few pots inherited from some long-dead ancestor. As they argued, the pain was clearly etched in my sister-in-law's face. I think she'd never anticipated leaving them, and so she tried to hold on to every single object she could. As if a vase or a rug could fill in the space left by a whole, vital *person.*

"I think," I heard her tell Ronen one night, her voice drifting toward me down the hall, "I'll never shake the feeling that I've forgotten something."

My brother's answer came after a pause. I could have hugged him for it. "They're just *things*, Hannah. What really matters is that we're together."

We began to send shipments planetside, necessities and books and hatchery equipment, medical supplies and genetic samples of crops and animals. Most of the wildlife would stay on the ship; our first year would be one of famine, but only in preparation for the decades ahead. Soon we'd wake animals that hadn't been seen in generations—pollinators and herdbeasts and predators. Horses to ride and birds to fill the skies with song. And plants, too. Mara Stone was beside herself. Though our colony would be small, slightly more than seven kilometers squared, she said that it was plenty of acreage to sow *Triticum mara*, Mara's wheat.

We were visited by senators and researchers from the surface, Xollu and Ahadizhi both. New translators, a clumsy-tongued young Xollu pair who spoke in garbled Asheran, accompanied them. They came to view our half-dissembled labs to gauge our progress—and to examine Ettie. Her mate still hadn't been located in any of the twelve cities. As I sat there in her *bubbe*'s galley, the senators questioning the girl, I found myself filled with apprehension. What if they told her that it was all a dream, a child's delusion, impossible? But they didn't. One of the Xollu scientists said something; the female translator inclined her head.

"*Tatoum*," she said. "There have been changes to our *aita* in the days since departure yours. Unpaired *lousk* surface from the funerary field. Xollu who once must die. Surely Ettie-*zeze* is among these spirits."

I couldn't contain my excitement. Sitting forward in my seat, I let my mind stretch down to the surface.

Vadix! Did you hear? Unpaired children! What if there are more like us? What if we're not alone?

But I'd forgotten. We were no longer an "us." To him our existence wasn't a joy. Now, in the living days before his death, it was a source of pain.

Yes, I heard, was all he said.

That was why those days stretched on for me, one after another, interminable. He was there somewhere on the planet above. But I didn't know for how long. Most days he shielded himself from me entirely. I couldn't blame him. Some day soon—too soon—he'd depart for the funerary fields beneath Raza Ait. Every night I'd tuck myself into the guest bed in my brother's room and stare up at the ceiling, terrified that he wouldn't join me in the dreamforests. I was afraid he'd be gone and I'd be left to ordinary dreams. When I found him there, relief filled my limbs, my gut, my heart. We didn't speak. Our bodies did the speaking for us. The joy of his flesh was singular, except for the joy in mine that matched it.

But every morning I'd wake with guilt weighing down my mind. Not my guilt. His. He'd stayed too long. He was being selfish. He needed to go join her in the funerary fields. He needed . . . As I rose from my bed and dressed, readying myself for the day's preparations, I felt him shutter himself from me. He needed to steel himself if he was finally going to fulfill his purpose and lay himself down beside his first mate.

Busy days, but long days. So very long. Because soon he'd join her in death. And I would be all alone.

Our final night. Everything was packed; the shuttles would be waiting for us in the morning. In total 872 citizens had made the decision to join us. A clear majority. They'd grown used to liberty, I suppose, and to the dream of open skies that had been promised to us. But more than two hundred citizens would remain behind. Council-born mostly, but a few others, too. Their first years would be lean—they'd have to get their population up if they were to support the ship's basic functions. But looking at Silvan, his arm wrapped around Rachel's slender waist as she lit a pair of electric candles and set them on their long table that night, I had faith that they would thrive.

With her hands cupped over her face, she said a prayer. Then she turned to all of us who had gathered there at Silvan's family's oak galley table. It was the finest table in the finest house in all of the districts.

A guard was posted at either side of the door. This was the captain's house now, and none would forget it. Especially not Silvan's mother; she gazed up at him, dark eyes bright with pride. She didn't know what I'd done to her husband either. I suppose it was better for her. Easier.

"Amen," Rachel said. "Now, to begin the festive meal."

She rushed off toward the kitchen. I went to help her. There was a turkey, freshly butchered; emerald vegetables; hard boiled eggs. And a loaf of knotty egg bread. My contribution. The recipe had been Momma's. I'd found it as I packed that morning, tucked at the back of her ancestor's book.

"Thank you," Rachel said as I took the potato kugel from her and set in on the table. There were nearly twenty people gathered—her family, and his, and mine. Hannah and Ronen and Alyana. Mordecai and Mara Stone. Maybe they weren't all my flesh and blood, but they were family nonetheless. Their boisterous voices rose up as Rachel went to carve the turkey in the galley.

I watched her. She wore another long skirt and blouse, but brighter now, reds and yellows. She still looked beautiful as she went to work, slicing the meat away from the breast, but so different from the girl I'd once known. Adult.

"I'll miss you," I said. She flashed her dark eyes up to me.

"I'll miss you, too," she said. Then paused, glancing over her shoulder. "Will you hand me that platter?"

"Sure."

It was a night for good-byes, but it seemed that Rachel had no time for those. She carved the turkey and then carried it to the table. I lingered behind her, watching from the counter as she grabbed her glass and lifted it.

"Before we begin," she said, "I'd like to say a few words over the wine."

Everyone raised their glasses. I reached for the bottle that sat on the counter and raised it, too, sloshing the few centimeters of liquid at the bottom. I watched Rachel, ready to hear her wish us luck on our new home—ready for her to give us a chance to wish *her* luck on her long, long journey back. But instead she bowed her head and intoned, *"Baruch atah Adonai elohaynu melech ha'olam boray pri ha'gafen."*

"Amen," said Silvan, lifting his glass. The others faintly echoed back the word, though Mara seemed particularly confused by the recitation. Letting out a sigh, I lifted the bottle, said "Amen," and drank the wine down. Then I watched Rachel and the way her smile glittered as she sat down at the table.

"Wonderful, wonderful," she said. "Silvan, you say the blessing over the bread."

Silvan looked up at her, his inky eyes sheepish. "I don't remember how," he said.

Her smile was gentle, patient. As if she were looking forward to the future they'd share together, during which he would learn this, and so many other things.

"I'll help. Repeat after me: *Baruch atah Adonai . . .*"

Silvan, pink-cheeked, bowed his head. *"Barach atah Adonai . . ."*

As he spoke, Rachel's eyes caught mine. I lifted my lips, but the smile tasted as bittersweet as the wine. She was right here with me, but she might as well have been thousands of kilometers away. Her heart, after all, was already promised to someone else.

That night, while I was preoccupied with the light and the laughter of Rachel's feast, the boisterous conversation and the lingering fare-well hugs, Vadix went completely silent.

I didn't realize it until I lay down in my brother's guest room bed one final time. The night was seamless black, without stars, without a moon, but that was nothing new. For sixteen years I'd faced those nights. Windowless bedrooms. Impenetrable dark. They were my companions, utterly ordinary. But what was unusual was the silence. Echoing and absolute. It was a quiet that seemed to swallow up my whole world.

Vadix? I asked, but no voice came thundering back inside my mind. My breath was suddenly shallow. Absent. I sat up in bed, tug-ging open the top button of my nightgown in a panic. *Vadix!*

Nothing. Nothing. No flowers turning their faces to the light. No vines to bolster me. When I closed my eyes, the only thing I saw was a dark cave wall streaked with limey water. I smelled metal and packed-down dirt where the perfume of life should have been. I heard silence where there should have been music. Felt pain where there should have been joy.

These were the funerary fields—underground caverns below even the winter caves, pungent with the odor of decay. Purple seedlings curled up from mounds. Some would swell into lavender flowers. Blossoms. Fruit. *People*. But the season was early, the light at the cave's mouth feeble. There was no life there, not now.

He was down there somewhere, deep beneath the city. If I could have, I would have kicked back my covers, raced through Raza Ait with my hair unbound. I would have pulled him back toward the moonlight, to the place where the living still walked and worked, laughed and loved. But I was hours and hours away. There was nothing I could do. He was as good as gone if he wasn't already. Swallowed by a darkness so much deeper than any I'd ever known, even on the ship.

I pulled Pepper against me. He let out a mewl of protest, but I didn't care. I buried my face against his warm body, cried and cried and cried. It was my last night on the *Asherah*. The next day I'd take off for a new planet, a new life.

And I would be alone.

30

In the shuttle bay Hannah cried. She embraced her mother first, then her father, then her mother again, the tears streaming down her face. Even Ronen looked a little choked up as he bid them farewell, watching as they pressed kisses to Alyana's fat baby cheeks. I stood off to the side, holding Pepper in his carrier. He scrambled and yowled, throwing his body against the bars.

I felt nothing.

As we made our way down through the air lock, my fingers were ice cold; my heart, numb. I hardly heard the pair of voices that called out for me. But then they came again, louder, rising over the sound of the departing crowds. Lifting my eyebrows, I turned. Rachel and Silvan rushed down the narrow walkway, elbowing past the gathered crowd.

"Terra! Terra!"

I put the carrier down on the metal grate, raised my arms, and accepted Rachel's embrace. Silvan stood off to the side, watching us. She was weeping already, her face shining with tears.

"I'll miss you. Oh, I'll miss you so much."

I felt my chest squeeze. It was almost too much for me; I had to swallow down the lump in my throat. "I'll miss you, too, Raych. Are you sure you don't want to come?"

She glanced over her shoulder to Silvan. He stood tall, proud. When their gazes locked, he gave a firm nod.

"Of course," he said, answering for her. "This is what we want."

But Rachel stayed frozen for a moment longer, squeezing my ice-cold fingers. "Silvan told me all about the planet," she said. "I can't wait to tell our children about it. About the green-gold skies and purple trees, and how they stole away the heart of my sister."

"Didn't I always tell you you'd be a great mother someday?" I said, my voice creaking coarsely out. She smiled through her tears, let out a bell of laughter.

"Yes," she said. "You did."

The line moved forward. I bent over to pick up Pepper's carrier and shuffle it ahead. Rachel's dark eyes were locked on me. There were words on her lips, but I could see that she didn't know how to speak them.

"What is it, Rachel?"

"Well," she began, picking up the pleat of her dress and worrying the fabric. "I wanted to ask. If your people want to worship, you'll let them, right?"

I stopped, standing straight, and looked at her. The crease between my friend's eyebrows was deep. I was still no believer, though I remembered too well what Jachin had said. In the distant past, before we'd lost our planet, religion had helped humanity thrive. The biologist had already boarded one of the shuttles with his family—probably speaking prayers to the darkness beyond, thanking God for changing his wife's mind, asking God for a safe trip home. He was one of us, but faith was important to him. As it had been to Vadix, once.

"Of course, Rachel," I said, watching as relief flooded her features. "That's what 'liberty' means."

Her smile was wide and bright. I watched as Silvan threw an arm over her shoulder and drew her in close. Though the line moved up again ahead of me, I hesitated beside the pair.

"Be good to your people," I said at last. Silvan frowned, but not

Rachel. She only angled up her chin, listening. "No matter who they love or how they wish to live. Please. Be good to them."

Rachel's hand darted out and grabbed on to mine. She leaned up and pressed a kiss to the corner of my mouth. She smelled like perfume. Springtime. Freshly laundered clothes.

"I will, Terra," she whispered, just before Silvan pulled her away. "I will."

The others all jabbered the hours away on the shuttle ride over, fogging their flight helmets with their breath. Not me, though. I sat with the cat's carrier on my knees, my eyes closed as I tried to reckon everything I'd lost.

Momma. Mar Jacobi. Abba. Captain Wolff. Mar Schneider. Deklan Levitt. Laurel Selberlicht. Aleksandra. A whole ship, and the people inside it. Silvan. And Rachel, my first, best friend.

I could recover from these losses, from the gap they left inside me, bright and raw. I'd done it before, and I'd do it again, just like I'd told Laurel. Day after day I'd put one foot in front of the other and pull myself slowly forward. I'd live so that our colony could live, so that our new city could burst forth with life and laughter. One day it wouldn't hurt so much. I knew this because I'd done it before.

But I didn't know how to reckon missing *him*. I couldn't even wrap my mind around his absence. When I tried to imagine the days ahead, they were gray with loss. I'd saved my people, achieved *tikkun olam*. And yet my heart was heavy.

We'd shared only two nights together, a scattered handful of conversations, a few caresses in the dark. Yet he'd become a part of me. Maybe I would love again. Maybe I would lead my people well. But I would only ever feel like half myself. A shadow. A shade, defined by his absence.

A *lousk*.

The rest of them cried out joyfully upon impact, throwing their arms into the air and laughing to one another. I just silently clutched the armrests. We pulled up to the dock. The door lifted, revealing a white space beyond. The others all shielded their faces from the light, but I unbuckled my harness and stood, removing my helmet, unzipping my suit. While they were still blinking back the brilliant light of day, I had already stepped past the threshold, cat carrier in hand.

The pier was crowded with Asherati. They squinted into the sunlight, pointing toward the white-licked sea and the expanse of sky high above. The weather had grown even more frigid in the weeks since my last visit. I hitched my wool coat tighter around me, my eyes scanning the pier for someone or something familiar.

And that's when I felt it. That steady pull that began somewhere deep in my solar plexus and drew me out and out, past my body and into the world beyond. Here. He was here. I could feel it—*see* it, the whole pier laid out through his eyes.

I hefted the cat carrier high and pushed through the crowd. Families gathered, laughing and jostling, moving in slow waves toward the *ekku* who waited by the city's walls. I shoved through the bodies, trying to let myself see what he saw. But it was all a jumble. People, hundreds of them, with their musty, animalistic smells, making their odd, beastlike noises. If he hadn't known me, he would have thought them savages.

I heard Pepper's cries. I heard someone calling for me. Mordecai. Waving me over. He stood beside his children and wife, all dressed in their flight suits. Their grins were broad, elated at the new world they'd found. They turned their eyes expectantly toward me.

"Come, Terra, give us a speech!"

But I shook my head and pressed forward. This was no time for speeches. He was here. He was *here*! Vadix was here!

That's when I spotted him. That bald blue head, those eyes, as black as onyx. He stood, posture slumped, against the city's outer wall. He was dressed in a robe of fine, pale gold. He smiled when he saw me, those soft lips full of teeth. Once, that mouth scared me a little. But now I found myself wake to life at the sight of it. His mouth. His grin. *Him*.

"You're here!" I said. I wanted to thrust myself into his arms. But I didn't, not at first. Dead. I'd thought he was dead. And yet here he was, eyes wide at the sight of me in the white light of day, resting his hands on his legs to better see the creature mewling in my carrier.

"What is this?" he asked. I set the carrier on the ground. Pepper sniffed at the chilly air.

"My cat," I said. I felt the corners of my mouth lift, but forced them down. It shouldn't have been this easy—for him, for me. He'd disappeared, left me to wander the evening alone. "You were *gone*! What are you doing here?"

Vadix stood straight. He tucked his hands into his robe, regarding me gravely. "I am here for you," he said, and then he tilted his head to the side. "But for me as well. This city. I have dreamed all my life of it. Now I dream of sharing it with you."

"With me," I echoed. My cheeks warmed. I gazed down toward the toes of my boots. "But what about Velsa?"

"For days I deliberated. At last, yesterday evening, I went to the funerary fields. I bid her farewell. It is a sacred space, Terra. Ours. I could not speak to you there." I thought of the dank cave I'd seen the night before. The new bodies, sprouting from the old. I remembered the sensation I'd felt, that he'd disappeared far beneath the planet's edge. He'd been gone, surely. But apparently I hadn't lost him. Not really. Not for good. He went on. "Always I shall miss her. But that does not mean I am not excited about Zeddak Alaz. That does not mean I am not excited about what lies ahead. We have a city. A place. And years and years and years."

Reaching out, he interlaced his fingers in mine. His hand was cool against my hand. His body's scent was fresh and fragrant on the winter air. He leaned in, lowering his voice to a conspiratorial tone.

"Besides, the senate asked me to join them with my *zeze* by my side. We are to be the first representatives for our new city. Over these weeks, I tried to convince myself this duty was one I could shirk. But I could not. In the end I realized this truth: there is no better way to keep you safe, Terra, than to serve at your side."

I felt my heart beat in my mouth. I wanted him to taste it, to feel what I felt—my blood, coursing through my body; every corner of my mind illuminated. Our fingers were still intertwined. I drew him close, pressing his body to my body.

"Not safe," I whispered, angling my face up to his. He brushed my hair back off my forehead, caressing the side of my face. "I never needed you to keep me safe. But strong. You make me feel strong. And strong might be enough."

We kissed. Of course we did. Not a long kiss—just lips meeting lips for a few precious seconds. But we had a lifetime ahead of us for kissing. A world. A city of our very own. A future.

Early Spring, 1 Year and 2 Months After Landing

You know what happened after that. You were there, of course, through the grueling weeks of training, when I woke each day with muscles so stiff, I thought they might have been caked with rust. But we needed to work hard to prepare for the southern winter, when we would be alone for the first time in the face of the beasts and the cold. So we hunted, all of us, even the children, as the Xollu who would join us gathered supplies to break new ground. By the time we set sail for the south, we were both new creatures: me, as well-muscled as a field-worker; and you, your flesh as dark as blood. Fertile. No longer even a shadow of the lousk you once were.

By then it was truly winter in Raza Ait. Each night I felt desire rack your body. Not for me but for your long winter's sleep. I felt how the cold seared your flesh, made it ache. But you were brave. You fought it off. It wasn't until we reached the south, cool summer in full swing, that I saw you restored to life, energy. Which made me glad; we had so much work to do.

That first season we sowed the fields full of Mara's wheat, and built a wall around them. A cupola, too, and the first enclave of houses. Nautilus houses, their white walls stuck full of shards of glass. A sentimental choice, maybe. But we're a sentimental people.

Like the name of our city. Zarakk Ait. The golden city. We've taken the dreams of our ancestors for a just-right home and found them here, on this stormy peninsula, thick with forests and full of beasts.

Of course, no one calls the planet "Zehava" anymore. We've adopted the local word for it. *Aur Evez.* Hannah once told me that it meant "the crowded land." It wasn't until weeks after landing that you told me that there are other translations for the phrase. Pronounce it a little differently, the words mean "promised home." How could we resist that?

But you know all of that. So I suppose I should tell you what you've missed since winter set in and you went into the caves to sleep. Those Ahadizhi that you contacted this fall? They've joined us, Vadix! Not all of them. Only twenty-five young sprouts, intent on rejecting the lives of their parents. Rising up. Rebelling. As new generations do. They want to see how city dwelling suits them. So we've made room, gladly. They serve by our side during the hunt, help us make art and dance and music. The dream you once shared with Velsa has made our lives so much brighter. I can't wait until you wake up to see it, until I can thank you for what you've done.

Otherwise life is good. Busy. On some days I help Mara in her lab. On others I hunt or paint. On still others I take command. It's a different sort of life from the one my mother lived, working one job day after day after day until her hands were stiff, arthritic. I fear it's not what she dreamed for me when she spoke to Ben Jacobi about "liberty."

I imagine she wanted a life of leisure. But my life is a good life. My days pass quickly and are full of new joys.

Why, just two weeks ago, in the dead of winter, a boat arrived from Aisak Ait. In it was a young Xollu, half dead from the cold. A child, blue-skinned and alone. A lousk. I knew on sight who he must be, and I sent a messenger to fetch Esther from her grandmother's house. She came at once, her hair a dark net around her face, and immediately threw her arms over his shoulders.

"Help me!" she cried out. "Help me bring him to the winter caves!"

And so we did, all of us carrying his cold-heavy body, loosing the roots that tried to plant themselves in the frozen dirt as we dragged him along. I see her sometimes when I come to visit you. She sits by his side and speaks to him, just like I speak to you. Telling him her story, her dreams. She's only a child—just turned eleven last week. She doesn't even know his name. But she tells him that she loves him, that he's her best friend. I don't doubt it. Not for a second.

He's not the only new arrival. Koen has made a child for himself in the hatchery, a brother for Corban. He told me he plans on naming him Arran after my father. I told him he could do better—a misstep. My old friend so wanted me to be pleased by this news. But maybe this new Arran will have a better chance at this life. He'll start it with a loving family, after all. Two fathers and a mother to teach him the meaning of hard work, affection, kindness. That's twice the family that my father ever had. *Ronen and Hannah are also expecting. A son, Solomon. And Alyana will be walking before we know it. This spring will be a fruitful one, I hope, full of new joys.*

As for me, I don't know if I'll ever have children of my own. I'm only seventeen, and lately I feel younger than I ever have. I laugh more easily than I ever did before. I joke and swagger. I even sing sometimes. I'm not the same girl I once was, strange and serious, old before my time. I have time, I think, to be young yet.

But I know that you'll grow old before me. I remember the night you told me, just before the winter's frost set in. A Xollu lives until only sixty or so, you said, and you're older than me already. Sure, it made me sad to think of it. Someday I'll be an old woman, my hair streaked silver, and you'll be gone. What then?

Well, I think I know. We'll never be able to have biological children, you and I. Our bodies are too different for that. But I know that Velsa still waits for you in the funerary fields of Raza Ait. Someday, when my eyes are feeble, when my hands are knotted from years of work, I'll take your lifeless body to the city where you were sprouted. Your skin will be as red as a pomegranate, as red as wine, as red as human blood. I'll scatter your body, and then I'll wait.

A season later, when your children are born, I'll tell them about you. I'll tell them of all the things we sacrificed for each other: you, your first love; me, an entire ship, my best friend, the life among the

stars that I once knew. Then I'll tell them about all the things that we accomplished. The city we built. The peace we brokered. I'll tell them of my pride for you, Thosora Vadix Esh, the father they'll never know.

Then I'll kiss them, take their three-fingered hands in my hand, and carry them home, across the sea.

ACKNOWLEDGMENTS

It takes a village to launch a spaceship. Infinite gratitude and thanks to the following individuals:

The bloggers, reviewers, librarians, booksellers, and readers of *Starglass*. Thank you for letting me put planets inside your head. Your enthusiasm made all the hard work worth it.

James Dashner, Jodi Meadows, and Lenore Appelhans, for lending their kind words of praise to my first book. I hope you enjoy this one, too. SPAAAACE!

The Bruisers—Douglas Beagley, Nicole Feldl, and Fran Wilde—for reading early chapters and drafts of *Starbreak*, and especially to Wayne Helge, for pointing out precisely where Terra needed to be when the book began. An extra high five to Kelly Lagor, for assuring me that psychic plant people are, in fact, possible.

The women of YA Highway, Kirsten Hubbard, Stephanie Kuehn, Kody Keplinger, Kaitlin Ward, Kristin Halbrook, Kristin Otts, Amy Lukavics, Sumayyah Daud, Sarah Enni, Leila Austin, Kate Hart, and Lee Bross, for sharing snippets and support. You will always be my favorite community of writers.

My dear writer friends: Veronica Roth, for her beta letters and her sanity. Jennifer Castle, for coffee and kvetching. Sean Wills, for stories and snark. Rachel Hartman, for her empathy. I'd be lost without you.

Michelle Andelman, the best agent a nerd could hope for, who has supported Terra and her journey from the time it was nothing more than a snippet on some blog. For your killer eye and your even deadlier pen, *Nocki Vot*! (That's "Thank you" in Tenctonese.)

My team at Simon & Schuster: Lucy Ruth Cummins, Anna McKean, Ellen Grafton, Bara MacNeill and Angela Zurlo. Thank you for all of your work getting the *Asherah* off the ground!

And especially Navah Wolfe. When I was thirteen years old, I used to stay up late watching reruns of *Star Trek*. I once dreamed of leaving the solar system; you've helped me do the next best thing—to invent an entire universe. I am so, so proud of what we've created in these pages.

My family: Phyllis Fineberg, Emily North, Elayne Rudbart, Frank Etzel, Barbara Etzel, and Jason Etzel. And my friends, who are as good as family: Nicole Talucci, Andrew Wirick, Tarah Dunn, Patrick Artazu, Eric Zuarino, John Zuarino, John Penola, and Jeffrey Krachun.

And finally, Jordan and Sammy Katz. My home, my loves. Without you, there would be no books.